KENSINGTON GARDENS

Rodrigo Fresán is the author of seven novels. *Kensington Gardens* is the first to be translated into English. He was born in Buenos Aires and now lives in Barcelona.

RODRIGO FRESÁN

Kensington Gardens

Translated by Natasha Wimmer

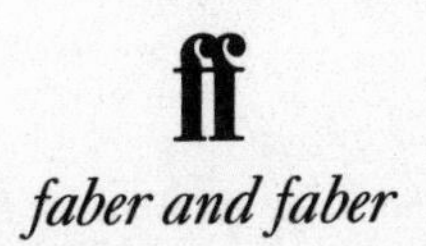

faber and faber

First published in 2005
by Faber and Faber Limited
3 Queen Square London WC1N 3AU
This paperback edition published in 2006

Typeset by Faber and Faber
Printed in England by Mackays of Chatham plc, Chatham, Kent

A CIP record for this book
is available from the British Library
ISBN 978-0-571-22281-0
ISBN 0-571-22281-1

2 4 6 8 10 9 7 5 3 1

To Ana:
Here, There and Everywhere

It was in Kensington Gardens that J. M. Barrie, who used to walk his dog there everyday, met Llewelyn Davies.

The Peter Pan statue was created in the studio and installed only when complete, as Barrie wanted children to believe it had appeared as if by magic.

Ed Glinert

A Literary Guide to London

Best of everything is being a child.
Second best is writing about being a child.

May God blast anyone who writes
a biography of me.

J. M. Barrie
Notebooks

The Condemned

It begins with a boy who was never a man and ends with a man who was never a boy.

Something like that.

Or better: it begins with a man's suicide and a boy's death, and ends with a boy's death and a man's suicide.

Or with various deaths and various suicides at varying ages.

I'm not sure. It doesn't matter.

Everybody knows – it's understandable, excusable – that numbers, names and faces are the first to be jettisoned or to throw themselves from the platform during the shipwreck of memory, which always lies there ready for annihilation on the rails of the past.

One thing at any rate is clear. At the end of the beginning – at the beginning of the end – Peter Pan dies.

Peter Pan kills himself and here comes the train. The scream of steel hurtling through the guts of London like a curse, like the happiest of lost souls.

Peter Pan jumps onto the tracks at just the right moment. Peter Pan is one of those two people a week who – statistics say – throw themselves onto the rails with British punctuality just before the train's triumphal entrance.

A woman screams when she sees him jump. A woman screams when she sees a woman screaming. All at once – screams are more contagious than laughter, and there are so many screams in this story – it's the same scream that leaps from woman to woman, from mouth to mouth. The same scream makes the cars brake, and the brakes scream too at the unexpected and futile effort of having to stop all those wheels and all the steel riding on those wheels. Yes, without warning the whole world is one single scream.

It's 5 April 1960, the hypothetical day of my increasingly hypothetical birth (the scream of my hypothetical mother who spreads her legs to push me and my hypothetical first scream out), and it's the day of the death and suicide of the respected publisher Peter Llewelyn Davies, founder of Peter Davies, Ltd, considered an 'artist among editors'.

'Peter Pan Becomes a Publisher', ran the headline reporting the professional birth of the man who now emerges at dusk from the Royal Court Hotel and crosses Sloane Square, thinking that he became an editor in an attempt to vanquish the horror of having been a character for so many years, too many years. And I like to think – because it's so fitting at the start of a book, and because certain gestures tell us so much about a protagonist – that Peter Llewelyn Davies is accosted by an anachronistic pack of Chelsea beggar boys; I hesitate when it comes to deciding whether he passes out a handful of coins. What I am sure of is that Peter Llewelyn Davies goes down the stairs to the underground station and waits a few minutes on the platform until he sees the light at the end of the tunnel, a light that grows steadily stronger and closer. Peter Llewelyn Davies jumps and doesn't scream. Let everybody else scream, thinks Peter Llewelyn Davies, in the enormous second it takes his body to autumn to the rails, then comes a blue spark, and a smell of electricity, and the wheels, and the scream, and the screams.

To believe – if karma's concentric spirals and the zigzagging laws of reincarnation don't deem it impossible – that the immortal spirit of Peter Llewelyn Davies abandons his ruined body and floats far away, and then enters my brand new self at almost the instant I am born, is immensely tempting. If that's how it was and always had been, my story would be so clear, so easy to understand, that it would no longer be necessary to leave all the windows open or closed each night, waiting for some act of redemption or punishment to justify the course of my life.

But sorry – nothing is that simple. Certain explanations are pertinent, inevitable.

Certain explanations take time.

Others are quicker: Peter Llewelyn Davies is the real name of Peter Pan, or Peter Pan is the real name of Peter Llewelyn Davies. It doesn't matter who's the shadow of whom, or whose shadow is sewn to the other's heels. What matters now are the cars full of people on their way home; the screams and the scream bouncing off the tile of the underground walls; the oxygen breathed too many times down there in the eternal concave dusk of train stations.

There was a time, thinks Peter Llewelyn Davies, when we came down into these depths not to die but to keep from dying. The long, tribal, brightly lit nights of the Second World War, of the War Even Greater than the Great War. The word *war* brings Peter Llewelyn Davies bad memories, takes him back to *his* war, to the trenches of the Somme.

So Peter Llewelyn Davies makes an effort and remembers the other war, the war that came after his. The war he didn't fight in, but that reached him anyway because wars always manage to find you wherever you are. Everybody together down here in the underground stations turned into shelters, singing Vera Lynn's 'We'll Meet Again' at the top of their lungs to drown out the sound of the sirens and the shudders of the Blitz. Everybody together reading magazines by torch, magazines with some cartoonist's sketch of Hitler as Captain Hook, his hook raised. Everybody drinking tea, nearly transparent and hardly tasting of tea, like members of a secret society, like the first Christians, like prehistoric shamans telling stories and painting them on the walls. Everybody together experiencing the queer contradiction of burying themselves in order to be closer to God, to heaven. Yes, for once heaven was underground and hell was the skies where the Luftwaffe flew, and beyond – much higher and farther, second star to the right and straight on till morning – was Neverland.

Peter Llewelyn Davies looks up and looks down and grips his furled umbrella and light briefcase so as not to go flying off, swept away by the wind of his past towards that faraway island inhabited by pirates and crocodiles and the terrible promise of eternal irresponsible childhood. That's how Peter Llewelyn Davies feels: light, like a ghost of himself; like a reversed X-ray, bones on the outside; as if he's gone back in time and is running in Kensington Gardens again; like a story worn out after having been told too many times and whose only salvation is this unexpected ending – real, undeniably true.

Peter Llewelyn Davies is sixty-three when he jumps, kills himself, dies. Peter Pan is some years younger; but age and the imprecise precision of dates matter little where Peter Pan or Peter Llewelyn Davies are concerned; Davies, who, according to the coroner's verdict eight days later, 'took his life while the balance of his mind was disturbed'.

As I say, Peter Llewelyn Davies jumps, and it's only logical – normal, proper, appropriate – to imagine him taking a small step forward to where there is no platform, the end of the flat earth on the maps of the ancients; to watch him fall into the jaws of monsters and leviathans. But I don't think that's quite right. It occurs to me that there's only a second in the brief life of the person who kills himself. Those who commit suicide live as fleetingly as some butterflies: a lightning trip, a held breath, a snap of the fingers, the blink of an eye, the *now you see it now you don't* it takes to get from A to B. So that second must be tremendous, an instant of pure understanding, of knowing everything; because is anything more important than knowing which way you're going and how long it'll take to get there?

I'm imagining what Peter Llewelyn Davies is thinking.

Peter Llewelyn Davies is thinking of James Matthew Barrie, who – in the dedication 'To the Five' that prefaces the book version of the play in which Barrie immortalized them all – says to Peter and his brothers:

I made Peter Pan by rubbing you all together at once. My dear boys: I rubbed you against one another just as savages with two sticks produce a flame. Peter Pan is nothing but the spark I stole from you.

Peter Llewelyn Davies is thinking of James Matthew Barrie, who, weeks before his death, wrote in his notebook:

> Death. *He who dies is simply one who finds himself a short way ahead in the procession of millions all headed to the same place; the person we lose sight of for a few seconds because we fall behind a little upon stopping to tie our shoelaces, and, when we look up, he isn't there any more.*

Peter Llewelyn Davies bends down to tie his shoelaces. It would hardly be elegant to trip just now, at the head of the procession. Beside him on the platform, a boy watches him with new, animal eyes, eyes ready to devour everything. A boy at the age when going to sleep is a terrible form of injustice. Children aren't afraid of what might be found in the dark. What they can't stand is the fear that all night long there will be *nothing* to see, and that their eyelids will close like shutters. A boy very like the boy who, half a century later, I'll watch collapse on the same platform of the same station, his eyes rolled up in his head, foaming bluishly at the mouth through clenched teeth, and howling *Jimyang-Jimyang-Jimyang*, for reasons that are my fault and no one else's.

Peter Llewelyn Davies is thinking of his family.

If the story of a family can be the story of the world, then the story of his family sometimes weighs on him as if it weren't just the story of the world but of the whole universe. Peter Llewelyn Davies began to compile it in 1945, in enormous notebooks in which he himself is barely mentioned, and where he has arranged photographs and documents punctuated by his notes, illuminating and cryptic by turns. A kind of reconstruction and chronicle and commentary on the past. An explanation. Now there are six volumes – it never occurred to him to publish them; he considers them simply a kind of memory-hobby – that he tends to refer to, rather acidly, as 'The Family Mausoleum' or 'The Morgue'.

Peter Llewelyn Davies began to put all this material in order some time ago, and the task proved unhealthy, so much so that a few nights ago he was obliged to burn in his fireplace many family mementoes and thousands of letters that he and his brothers had written to Barrie. Peter Llewelyn Davies is depressed; he has nightmares; his dead brothers appear to him at the most unexpected times and places. The past is a dangerous game.

Peter Llewelyn Davies is thinking of his four brothers, and he's thinking of the last entry he made in his *Morgue*, in memory of his dead brother George.

Peter Llewelyn Davies is thinking of George ('Peter Pan Dies On Battlefront'), and he's thinking about the time he visited his grave in 1946, in the cemetery for British troops at Voormezeele; he thinks of George's tombstone, with the bas-relief of a cross and a medal, and of himself standing there, 'thinking vaguely of the dust and skeletons and the conqueror worm, and older days that were happier, and I'm not ashamed to admit that I piped an eye'.

Peter Llewelyn Davies is thinking of Michael, who of them all was most Peter Pan ('Peter Pan Drowns With Best Friend in Sandford Pool: Suicide Pact Suspected'), and he remembers going to Oxford to search for his brother's lost body, travelling from London on a long, dark night when he too felt that he was submerged in water and that there was no air to breathe.

Peter Llewelyn Davies is thinking of Nico ('Peter Pan Marries'), who these days only goes out to visit rare book dealers in search of first editions of ghost stories.

Peter Llewelyn Davies is thinking of Jack, who died a year ago and about whom he can't remember any headlines, maybe because Jack never entirely trusted Barrie, and because Jack was always the least Peter Pan of them all.

Peter Llewelyn Davies is thinking of his parents, though he can't remember them very well.

Arthur and Sylvia.

Two names that always seemed – whether he said them aloud or not, it was enough just to think them – like the names of heroes of ancient legend or the landscapes and faces discovered beneath a painting's surface, landscapes and faces the artist decided to cover up, having changed his mind or been disappointed. *Pentimento* is what that's called, he thinks now, his mind still firmly made up as the time comes to jump.

Peter Llewelyn Davies is thinking of all the times he was asked what it felt like to be the inspiration for Peter Pan. Peter Llewelyn Davies is thinking about how Peter Llewelyn Davies always referred to *Peter Pan* as 'that terrible masterpiece', and he is thinking – he sees it all at once, as if someone had struck him – that none of the following day's newspapers will resist the temptation to title his obituary 'Peter Pan Dies in London Underground Station', 'Peter Pan's Death Leap', 'The Tragedy of Peter Pan', 'Peter Pan Commits Suicide'.

Peter Llewelyn Davies is thinking that none of this matters to him now – although his editor's instincts would have caused him to react in disgust at the error the next morning in the *Daily Express*, which will give his age as sixty-eight instead of sixty-three – or at least that it doesn't matter as much.

Peter Llewelyn Davies is thinking – as I am thinking now – of the wretched statue of Peter Pan in wretched Kensington Gardens in the wretched city of London. A bronze boy with a flute at his lips, appearing between the trees. A bronze boy that – like all statues – won't ever grow old. He never liked the statue. Barrie didn't like it either ('It captures nothing at all of the little devil in Peter,' its creator said to its sculptor). I don't like it then – as night falls on the night Peter Llewelyn Davies falls forever – or now, all these years later, beside this open window, telling you the story that begins with a boy who was never a man and ends with a man who was never a boy.

Something like that.

Or better: it begins with a boy's death and ends with a man's suicide.

Or with various deaths and various suicides.

I'm not sure.

It doesn't matter.

One thing is clear: at the end of the beginning, Peter Pan dies.

Peter Pan kills himself.

Peter Pan is thinking – he's thinking again – that dying will be an awfully big adventure, and he jumps and thinks of Peter Llewelyn Davies, and Peter Llewelyn Davies is thinking that he's so *tired* of thinking.

Peter Llewelyn Davies is thinking that it's 5 April 1960, that there's no time left, that now is the time (what time is it?), that the train is coming into Sloane Square station, on time as always, that he hopes he'll be forgiven, I'm sorry to have to go so abruptly, so rudely, good night, God save the Queen and God have mercy on my soul and forgive me, forgive me, forgive me, forgive me.

Lately, Keiko Kai – 'I read the news today, oh boy' – I've been remembering too much too.

The Brother

That old-fashioned boy, that sepia-tinted boy, sitting under the walnut table where they've set his brother's coffin, is called James Matthew Barrie, and he's six years old, and he's pretending to hide from a terrible pirate. They won't find him here, he's sure of it, hidden by the skirt of the tablecloth, protected in the ship's hold by the dead new body of David Barrie: the family's great hope, the chosen one, the electrifying light in a home lit by candles.

David Barrie: athletic and handsome and good at school and sure to become a minister, to bask in heavenly and academic glory as an admired Doctor of Divinity; and who will read all those books of philosophy and theology now, who?

'Why him? Why did it have to be him?' weep the women who've come to weep. And the sound of their tears makes James Matthew Barrie think of the treacherous singing of mermaids, of shipwrecked adventurers, of distant shores. James Matthew Barrie isn't very good at games: short, his head too big for his too-small body. James Matthew Barrie is the constant worry of his teachers, because James Matthew Barrie, tiny James Matthew Barrie, always seems to be somewhere else, somewhere far away. So unlike David they might belong to two different races.

David was, is, and always will be the favourite of his mother, Margaret Ogilvy, who's kept her maiden name according to old tradition and has now retired to her rooms and closed the windows and drawn the curtains so she won't hear anything or anyone. The constant noise of the looms coming out of all the houses and up the street makes James Matthew Barrie imagine – under the table, playing with his little sister Maggie under David's coffin – that he's hearing the clash of the many blades of many gentlemen fighting simultaneous duels for the heart of a single, unattainable princess. James Matthew Barrie has the rare ability to travel without going anywhere.

Margaret Ogilvy won't rise from her bed, not even to deposit a last kiss on the ever bluer lips of her favourite prince. David, the best of her ten children. David, dead in a skating accident just as he was about to turn fourteen, on an icy lake as cold as a mirror, in the Grampian Hills outside of Kirriemuir, in the county of Angus once known as Forfarshire, five miles northeast of Forfar, in Scotland, in the terrible and unforgettable winter of 1867.

James Matthew Barrie will immortalize this place in several of his books, calling it the Thrums, the name the inhabitants of Kirriemuir – a town of spinners and looms – have given to the skeins spinning on wooden frames.

And here he is now.

Spinning on his own axis.

James Matthew Barrie (Barrie, from now on) was born on 9 May 1860, and was baptized in the church of South Free the following Sunday, the ninth child of David Barrie and Margaret Ogilvy, who were married at twenty-seven and twenty-one and had seven daughters and three sons. Alexander, the oldest boy, was born in 1841; Mary Edward, the oldest girl, in 1854; Jane Ann Adamson in 1847, David in 1853, Sara in 1854, Isabella in 1857. Elizabeth and Agnew died very early, in their cradles. A good yield for the age: just two lives lost out of ten, though perhaps I'm overlooking some death. Mark a cross beside their names in the register, lay them in little pine boxes, cover the boxes with earth, and life goes on; there wasn't even time for them to learn to say their own names. And, thinks Margaret Ogilvy, you don't miss, or don't miss much, someone you haven't even come to understand.

Margaret Ogilvy doesn't really understand Barrie, the youngest of her sons, very well either. There's something incomplete about him, about the way he looks in the few pictures taken of him; because why bother to photograph a boy who doesn't even seem interesting enough to impress his image forcefully on paper? In his childhood photographs, Barrie always looks imprecise. More like a sketch than a portrait. More like the oils of an apprentice than the brand-new and almost automatic miracle of photography's developing fluids. Barrie, always dressed in little suits that try to impart some distinction to his small body with its short arms and big feet and enormous head. His moon face crowds as many features into as small a space as possible. It's as if his eyes and nose and mouth seek the exact centre of that pale circle, which always seems to have just emerged from the eclipse of a long and dull and exhausting illness.

In her photographs, on the other hand, Margaret Ogilvy looks strong and determined: a gentle despot, a professional mother, head of the tribe. Her husband occupies himself with affairs outside the house. Her husband is one of the most respected men in the community, and he's known and admired for his business skills. Her husband would never let her children be devoured by the mills, always ravenous for wool; her husband has better plans for those who bear his name. Margaret Ogilvy steers the house like a ship, not letting go of the wheel for a second, her eyes always fixed on the horizon, looking ahead, searching for land. It's hard for me to imagine either of these two – Margaret Ogilvy or David Barrie – telling their children stories. It's hard for me to believe they know any stories.

What a change between this photograph of Margaret Ogilvy before young David's death and that one, taken several years after he was brought to her on a sled, dead and almost unmarked, his neck broken and bones jumbled nonetheless as if by one of those whirlwinds of dead leaves that come rushing down the Highland rocks, kilt blown up and sex exposed, shrunken by the cold and the rain. David's eyes are open. I always wondered what it meant, that final choice: dying with eyes open or shut. When a person's eyes are open does it mean that what they saw in the final second of life was too beautiful; or, conversely, when their eyes are shut, does it mean that what they glimpsed on the other side was so terrible that the darkness behind the curtain of their eyelids was preferable?

Open your eyes.

Let me show you, Keiko Kai.

In the first of the photographs, Margaret Ogilvy is the perfect incarnation of matriarchal power and self-satisfaction. A woman with a mission, her modest but dignified bonnet tied with a bow under her chin. Margaret Ogilvy smiles the smile of someone who feels invulnerable, the winner of wars that no one should ever have bothered to declare against her. What was the point, why fight in retreat without ever having joined battle? The photograph is out of focus, not because the photographer made a mistake but because it was impossible to keep Margaret Ogilvy still in those days of long exposures. A minute was too much time to waste staring at a wooden box with a glass eye, with its foul-smelling flash of magnesium, thought Margaret Ogilvy.

The second of the photographs, from 1871, is a typical studio portrait that shows her with her gaze lost and her skin nearly translucent; she is dressed with great elegance, but Margaret Ogilvy is now a weaker and more fearful woman. A motionless woman. A woman who's had one of the most important chapters ripped from her life story. In this photograph, one hand is raised to her face but doesn't quite touch it, perhaps for fear of not finding it, or even worse, of passing through it as if it were water or air. It's the photograph of a living ghost, of a woman who – beginning January 1867, after 'My son is dead! My son will never die!', and until her own death twenty-nine years later – has been living on another planet for too many years. The planet David, in the Nebula of the Oldest Son, near the constellation of the Dead Skater, far from earth.

*

Barrie will say one day that 'nothing that happens to us after we are twelve matters very much', disguising with this clever exaggeration the lucky shock of the most important thing: the thing that will mark the rest of his days, that happened to him when he was only six years old and had an older brother who'd just died.

Barrie remembers that two telegrams arrived from the office at Forfar. The first brought news of the accident (David hadn't even been skating; a friend was pushing him from behind and David fell and hit his head on the ice); the second told of the tragic outcome.

David is brought on a sled as night falls. He's brought on a sled by tinted men, men recently come from the mills, covered in the red, green, gold and blue of the enormous barrels of dye. It looks, thinks Barrie, like the funeral of a king of the elves. It's trolls that bring David slowly along Brechin Road, in a solemn procession, to the house at Lilybanks in the Tenements, Kirriemuir. A house the same as all the rest: a pitched roof, chimney, windows, a front and a back door, and it's not easy to say which of the two doors is the front door, which is the front of the house.

Barrie's sisters – who aren't sure either – divide into two groups and come out the two doors and begin to howl so neighbours and family won't mistake the path to grief. Barrie hears them from the little washhouse on the other side of the street, across from his house, where he spends most of the day thinking up plays. Barrie comes out of the little house and encounters the body of his brother, who now seems like a puppet whose strings have been stolen, and yet still wears a smile of surprise that not even the priest will be able to smooth away when he prepares the body for the funeral.

Barrie stands on a chair and looks into David's coffin, on the table. Barrie smiles back at David, and doesn't quite understand what's happening. The grown-ups tell him to get down from there, and Barrie crawls under the table so he won't have to see his mother shouting. If there's anything more terrible than shouting, it's seeing where the shouting comes from: shouting always transforms those who shout, turns them into something new and terrible; and Barrie doesn't recognize his mother any more, struck as she is by the lightning bolt of her own shouting. The window panes tremble, outside a dog barks, and someone else shouts too; because stray shouts always find a shout to join.

Barrie's father orders his daughters to take their mother to her room. The daughters – smaller shouts paying obeisance to the big shout – obey immediately and little Barrie hears them going up the stairs. A shout for each step from oldest to youngest in turn, then back to the beginning. A door opens and a door closes and for the next few days the house seems to hang in the air, as if frozen in time, as if Margaret Ogilvy's shout has forever altered the mechanisms governing time and motion.

Nothing important ever happened in Kirriemuir, but after David's death the only thing that happens in the house on Brechin Road is his death. Over and over again. Settled at the head of the family table, at church, everywhere. Barrie evades this non-event of living death. Barrie escapes by losing himself in books. Barrie opens books like windows, opens books to let the light of a story into his gloomy life. Barrie reads to leave his surroundings behind, and the books become part of him. Barrie and *Robinson Crusoe* and *Treasure Island* and *The Arabian Nights* in a deluxe children's edition, without scandalous illustrations. Barrie reads stories about lone travellers and lost travellers. Barrie imagines his mother as a queen taken prisoner. Barrie enters his mother's bedroom, which is always dark, as if he's venturing into a treasure cave or a storm at sea. He enters books and closes them, and Barrie asks himself what happens when a book closes, when the story it tells is interrupted. Barrie asks himself what the book's speed is: is it the author's speed as he was writing, or is it the speed readers reach as they read? And also: does a book stop when it's set aside or are books perpetual motion machines that work with no need of readers? Books are like magic engines that never stop driving their heroes and villains towards new shores and palaces, and that's why it isn't a good idea to interrupt your reading of them, thinks Barrie: you miss so many things when you close a book. There are nights Barrie could swear he hears the books talking among themselves, mingling, recounting their lives and works, recalling their plots, their best moments. Barrie thinks that reading is the making of memories and that writing is also the making of memories. The memories of the person who writes – the only thing writers do is *remember* something they happened to think of, something that happened to them or never happened to them, but that's happening *now* as they write – are incorporated into the memories of the person who reads until it's impossible to say where the memories of one end and the other begin. The writer as intermediary, as spirit guide, as elucidator of how books are the ghosts of living writers, and dead writers are the ghosts of books. And maybe *this* is immortality, never getting old, Barrie says to himself. Ink as the elixir of eternal life, drunk through the eyes, and Barrie thinks that if there's anything better than being a writer, it's being a character.

Barrie thinks about all these things.

I know it seems unlikely that a six-year old would think like that back then; but I swear to you, Keiko Kai, I thought that way a century later, when I was the same age as Barrie. And like Barrie, I thought all those things, and these things, as useful defence mechanisms: there's nothing better than contemplating the way fiction works when you're trying to flee reality.

Barrie wonders about the meaning of certain illustrations in certain books. Barrie thinks about the happiness we feel when we reach a certain paragraph and understand at last why a chapter's called what it's called.

Barrie thinks about the subtle vibration of everything around us the first time we read a sentence we'll never forget.

Barrie thinks about all of this so he won't have to think that now it's time to go up and see how his mother is. Barrie doesn't like to go into that room where the air scarcely moves, where everything drags itself on its knees begging for explanations from a merciless God, God's fury barely disguised by his pious cloak of prayers and rogations.

Margaret Ogilvy is the daughter of a fanatically religious bricklayer, and she was brought up in one of the most puritanical Protestant sects, known as the Auld Lichts, or Old Lights. Her task in the sect was to care for the motherless children, the littlest ones. When she got married, she moved to another kirk, her husband's parish, as specified in the marriage laws: the Free Church, which split from the Established Church of Scotland in 1843. This splinter branch had no backing and depended on the generosity of its members, who were more liberal, and supporters of new lights. Even so, Margaret Ogilvy always remained attached, body and soul, to the unswerving faith of her elders, among whom it was preached, 'If a man who denies the Holy Spirit, then that man could not have been created by Him.'

Margaret Ogilvy – destroyed by grief and the shock of her grief – never renounces God, but she does renounce her youngest son. James Matthew is so insignificant compared to David. Even under the ground, David seems more real and present than James Matthew.

And this is what happens to Barrie when he's six years old, the instant that marks his whole life, and, so many years later, will end up sparking the legend of a boy frozen in time. This is the day Barrie receives and conceives his ten commandments.

'Everything is pure supposition until the age of six,' Barrie will write much later; but he'll always remember this moment perfectly, as if seeing it at the theatre or in a book: the date of his real, second birth. Barrie ascends to the summit where Margaret Ogilvy lies, and descends with the tablets of his law, on which a single command may be read. An unchanging voice of stone and its echo that only knows how to count to ten, which is more than enough:

Never grow up.
Never grow up.
Never grow up.
Never grow up.
Never grow up.
Never grow up.
Never grow up.
Never grow up.
Never grow up.
Never grow up.

Barrie climbs the stairs. His older sister Jane Ann has told him that it isn't right the way his mother's forgotten him. 'The living must be at least as important as the dead,' reasons Jane Ann. Barrie thinks about the story of a night in *The Arabian Nights* that he's only half-finished. He wants – needs, yearns – to return to that perilous adventure as fast as he can, so it's best to face this other perilous adventure as fast as he can, he tells himself.

Barrie recalls the episode years later in *Margaret Ogilvy*, his successful memoir about his mother published by Hodder & Stoughton in 1896. The book that has more to do with him than with his mother, since all the while it analyses the woman who gave birth to him, it evokes his despair at having lost his way back to the Land of Childhood.

Here's my copy. A first edition.

What would you prefer, Keiko Kai: that I read it to you or tell you the story? Well, let me reread it myself for a few minutes, so I remember it. And then I'll tell it to you.

Ready.

Listen, look; here it is:

Barrie climbs the stairs. First he stops in his bedroom – until recently 'David's bedroom' – and opens a wardrobe, taking out one of his older brother's suits and putting it on.

The Sunday suit. It's very big on him, but, oddly, it fits him better than his own Sunday suit. His suit seems the product of an operation by an incompetent surgeon, with scars in the strangest and most unlikely places, he thinks.

Barrie knocks at his mother's door. There's no answer. He opens the door. He goes in. He hears nothing from the bed, but that doesn't matter: he can't see the bed in the dark, the kind of darkness that existed in the world before electricity reached everywhere – a *dark* darkness. The light of the sun and the moon and even firelight were different back then, too.

Barrie remembers the way to the bed and goes towards it. Barrie breathes deeply, and maybe he's crying without realizing it. Barrie makes a noise. He starts to whistle. It's taken him hours, whole days, to perfectly imitate the way David whistled. The cheerful tunes that were always on David's lips as he buried his hands in the pockets of his trousers and strode around the sitting room digging the heels of his boots into the scuffed wooden floor: 'Three Legged Paddy', 'Pour Me One Last Pint for the Road, Kathleen', 'All the Men Were Really Boys', 'Lovely Rita Bedroom Maid' and 'Another Day In the Life' . . .

This is how Barrie moves now: hopping in the dark, dancing badly like bad dancers, who, as they dance badly, think constantly 'I'm dancing . . . I'm dancing . . .' This is how Barrie dances and this is how Barrie whistles and Barrie closes his eyes because he can't see anything anyway.

Then he hears a voice and a question. 'Is that you?' asks his mother. Barrie understands – with the terrible logic of children, logic that's lost as the years go by – that Margaret Ogilvy has confused him with his dead brother. Barrie doesn't answer right away. First he says 'Yes.' After all, she's asking him if he's *him*, and, yes, Barrie *is* Barrie. He hasn't lied, he hasn't sinned. Barrie hears a surprised intake of breath and – this is what scares him most – the beginning of a laugh. It's been a long time since Margaret Ogilvy laughed, and what comes from her throat sounds to Barrie more like the cawing of a crow that's been lost for years and finally returns to its nest. There's something mad in that laugh. It's the laugh of someone who's sure the dead don't die but instead are trapped in an instant, forever unscathed and free from the dictates of the body and the passage of time. It's the laugh of someone who believes in ghosts that never grow old and in dead bodies that don't rot. Barrie can't help feeling proud, for the first time in his life, that he's an indispensable part of something important and extraordinary. Suddenly, the darkness seems a strange form of light.

'Yes, it's me,' says Barrie happily, and his mother reaches out and finds him and hugs him. What Barrie feels first is the force of love in the arms that clasp him, and then immediately a powerful disillusion as they let go of him and push him away. Margaret Ogilvy lets out a long, sad moan, like the wind that blows on winter afternoons over the crests of Grampian Hills, and buries her face in the pillow.

'No, no, I'm not him; it's only me,' says Barrie, and he leaves the room and shuts the door, and the pain lasts the exact time it takes him to run down the stairs and open a book to see the footprint left in the sand of a deserted beach, or the wake of a flying carpet in the golden skies of Baghdad, or the gleam of gold in a chest. He doesn't care. He isn't sure. For once, the letters are only letters. Black symbols on white paper that seem to have lost their ability to combine and make stories. Sinbad and Man Friday are no more than creatures of black, leaden blood, men of dry ink. Nothing like what he's just discovered he can become: a cannibal aristocrat. One of those hybrid Eastern beasts the sultans fight. A corsair of make-believe. A writer and a character living inside the same name. Yes: Barrie has learned not to call up ghosts but to be a ghost himself. He has learned the crucial lesson that those who are loved best are those who never grow old, who never grow up.

Ghosts, the dead.

The dead who in time become ideals rewritten by the living. The dead are – always – masterpieces of literature.

Phantasmagoric fictions, true; but fictions of the kind that manage to survive and surpass any fleshly reality. The dead never grow older but they do expand: like a gas, a poison, a perfume.

'I won't grow up,' swears Barrie.

And he closes the book.

And opens all the windows in the house.

When the window of a book closes, the window of a life opens.

Mine.

My first memory is of a ghost; for what is childhood but the ghost that haunts our later years: that refuses to abandon us in death but materializes at the end of a corridor when we least expect it, rattling its chains.

My first childhood memory – if I try to see myself from a distance, as if looking from outside into an open window – is of me and a book. In my room, in the room that was also Baco's room but that in the end would be only mine. Up there, at the top of the house. Reading.

I remember it – I remember myself reading – because it was then I realized that it was something I never wanted to forget, and I felt the delicate but unmistakable gears of my memory turning cogs even smaller than a clock's, a device capable of preserving the instant as if it were a sculpture on display in one of the most exclusive wings in the museum of my life.

A book and me and the particular, distinctive silence that fills a room when there's someone reading in it. A different kind of silence; because the complex silence of reading has nothing to do with the simple silence of just being quiet. The silence that emanates from books and envelops us is a silence full of sounds, a silence that changes the coordinates of eternity, which means that you can spend hours reading in the bathroom without noticing it, trousers around your ankles, hypnotized by the secret scent of the letters and the intimate fragrance of your own bowels. Books are a point of escape, a place to let go, to let yourself fall and run into the forest with surprising ease and swiftness. It isn't a coincidence, I think, that books are made from the flesh of trees, and that libraries ultimately turn into petrified forests, into branches and roots that burrow into us and flower in our imagination.

'It's only during childhood that books have a profound influence on our lives,' wrote Graham Greene, and I agree. Keiko Kai: if there were any sense in giving you advice that you'll never have the chance to follow now, I'd tell you to read as much as you can while you're young. That's when stories help us learn to struggle against forgetting, to formulate our realities, and, yes, disguise them and make them better than they really are; so that when we've grown up we won't remember our life but the lives in the books we read back then. Edmond Danté's escaping his unjust imprisonment and Heathcliff embracing the dead body of his beloved become key moments in our other existences, skins inseparable from our bones. We attach ourselves to those stories like flies stuck to strips of sticky paper, and when the moment of our death arrives, we die happy, I guess: our life story ends up having as many heads as books we've read, because we've lived so many lives through reading . . .

That, Keiko Kai, is how our first books – the books that work their way inside of us the way zinc works its way into bone – reveal to us not only the stories of others but the possibility that we might structure and write the plots of our own existences according to the style and genre we like best. Fortunate are those who read as children because theirs may never be the kingdom of heaven, but they'll be granted access to other people's heavens, and there they'll learn the many ways of escaping their own hells with the non-fictitious strategies of fictional characters.

Keiko Kai: I look into the heavens of my hell as if I'm looking into a book, through the open window of a book.

I look in and of course there exists – how could there not – the temptation to equate or superimpose in a single landscape the reclining figure of Margaret Ogilvy in the winter of 1867 and the dancing figure of my mother, Lady Alexandra Swinton-Menzies. My mother, one hundred years later, spinning in a lysergic spiral, hand in hand with Marianne Faithfull, Nico, Patti Boyd, Edie, Jane Birkin, Anita Pallenberg, Twiggy, Jan de Souza, Britt Ekland, Catherine Deneuve, Jean and Chrissie Shrimpton, Rita Tushingham, Patti D'Arbanville, Vanessa and Lynn Redgrave, Verushka . . . Is it possible that I saw them all together, on a single day? Or is it my memory that links them forever? Who cares; what difference does it make. There they all are: mad priestesses in that winter and summer of 1967. I recite their names like difficult ingredients in a miracle brew: mane of a chaste unicorn, eye of a misanthropic cyclops, poem of an insomniac minstrel.

Bob Dylan wanders the top floor of our house, comes into my room and makes a scene. 'A scene' is what my parents rename the thing my grandparents would call 'a shameful scene'. The loss of the adjective – of that *shameful* – is what separates the two generations: an abyss where what seems improper from one side is experienced from the other as something that barely happened.

What happens is this: Bob Dylan comes into my room. The room that until recently was our room. My room and Baco's. Bob Dylan comes in thinking that it's the bathroom. Bob Dylan is pale and green and dressed in a black suit and a black shirt with white polka dots and he has dark glasses on and he vomits on my neatly arrayed collection of lead soldiers and he apologizes and I can't understand a word of what he's saying. 'Don't worry, darling, I don't either . . . No one understands what he says; that's why he's so successful,' my mother will explain to me later as she insists that my filthy, smelly soldiers are much more valuable now than they were when they were clean and only smelled like metal.

Margaret Ogilvy and Lady Alexandra Swinton-Menzies have just lost sons – the former her oldest and the latter her younger – and the two are plagued by surviving, guilt-ridden sons. Barrie's guilt is imaginary, and in the end it helps him construct his aesthetic credo. Mine is real, and it's been useful to me too.

Not long ago, I read an article in an airline magazine that explained that the death of a child increases the likelihood that his parents will die young. You know, Keiko Kai: one of those reports based on surveys that *The Lancet* publishes every so often, in which figures pile up and percentages are boiled down and it's revealed that for as long as three years after the death of a child, parents live in a state of extreme vulnerability in which anything – any bad thing – can happen to them; and that their chances of disappearing are 60 per cent greater than those of parents who haven't suffered a similar loss. I suppose my parents fit this profile, although the article says nothing about the bereaved parents, before they died, going gracefully mad.

Here, a long time ago. Downstairs in the basement recording studio of Neverland, the family cottage at Sad Songs. The real name of my family's house isn't Neverland, of course; but I've called it that for almost as long as I can remember, and please don't confuse it with that pathetic, one-note, plastic ranch belonging to one-note, plastic Michael Jackson.

Here, in those days – in the 60s, in what were once the secret chambers where a decadent nobility cosied up with their housemaids – my father Sebastian 'Darjeeling' Compton-Lowe and his band the Beaten a.k.a. the Beaten Victorians a.k.a. the Victorians, keep recording songs and filming everything that moves and everything that's never moved or ever will move. They haven't slept for many days and nights. All but for my father have nostrils dusted with Colombian snow. It's cold and it's hot and there are moments when it's nothing at all, as if it were outer space here in the depths of Neverland.

Over and over again, my father and his colleagues record and film what they presume will be their masterpiece: the never-released quadruple album titled *Lost Boy Baco's Broken Hearted Requiem & Lysergic Funeral Parlor Inc.* Peter Blake and Andy Warhol go so far as to design the cover: a mirror in the shape of a tombstone in which you see yourself. The idea was Andy Warhol's, and it was also Warhol who directed part of the shoot. When you open the cover, it unfolds – like a certain kind of children's book – to reveal a crowd of famous figures from the British Empire, among them James Matthew Barrie, paying their respects beside an open grave. Peter Blake's idea. At the bottom of the tomb lies Baco's old teddy bear – I think its name was Murphy – which with the years and the erosive forces of love had become something that might have been a cat or a dog or a rat. Warhol doesn't like the interior collage much. It strikes him as very 'highbrow'. Peter Blake isn't sure whether he didn't use the same idea for the cover of *Sgt. Pepper's Lonely Hearts Club Band*. Peter Blake isn't even sure of his name. Peter Blake has just signed a contract that stipulates he'll receive only a single payment of two hundred pounds from the Beatles' label for services rendered. In time he'll go to court, realizing that his *Sgt. Pepper* cover is almost as important as the music inside. But what's signed is signed, believe me, Keiko Kai.

So my brother Baco's grave suddenly becomes a pop shrine. More than once, I've seen T-shirts with the photograph of my mother holding Baco and my father's arms around them both. I'm not in the picture, but I *am* in the picture: I'm the taker of the picture, I'm the click and the flash; I asked them to smile, to smile at me.

Baco's the real son. I'm the not-so-real son. I'm the real lost boy. It doesn't matter; it doesn't matter to them; it matters to me. For my parents these are times of absolute truth, and, paradoxically, of instant mythicization. Countercultural amnesia causes Baco's face, Baco's blue eyes, Baco's golden curls, the fleeting memory of him, to be rapidly assimilated as the only memento of his parents: renegade aristocrats, shaming their parents, noble members of the nobility who can't understand how their children could change so much in so little time. Baco and the memory of Baco are the surface of a lake set rippling by songs like stones, by the rocking of long, drawn-out songs, and hey! if our son's died, better to make something of it, turn it into something new and creative: 'Here comes the son,' ha ha ha. An acid-opera in memory of Baco, my dead little brother. The recording sessions began with star-studded enthusiasm, but the party wound down like a fire burning through the darkest of nights. The *de luxe* guests left one by one. Some went without saying goodbye, waiting until my father was momentarily distracted; he kept them almost like hostages, working, forbidding them to go out in the daylight. At last, my father is left alone with his guitar. He isn't in the best of shape: he's lost weight, an ear infection has made him nearly deaf, his scalp and his hands are covered in psoriasis, and his retinas are damaged from staring unprotected at an eclipse. Yes, my father's the last man on a deck approaching the vertical, the captain who's decided not to abandon his sinking ship. The ship is him.

Not long ago they called me from the reissue label, Rhino. They offered to launch *Lost Boy Baco's Broken Hearted Requiem & Lysergic Funeral Parlor Inc.* for the first time, with all the requisite pomp and circumstance, in a mirrored case with two silver compact discs as well as a DVD of film clips and a little book written by me, of course: the universally celebrated creator of Jim Yang, hero of children everywhere.

They asked me whether I had the tapes. I lied and said no, that they had gone down in the never fully explained shipwreck of the transatlantic liner *S.S. Regina Victoria*. I told them they were lost with my psychedelic progenitors (my mother was found, but it can hardly be said she survived the disaster) and their crew of flower-bedecked dandies on their way to the ashram of Rishikesh where the Maharishi Mahesh Yogi was waiting for them and where my father – I discovered years later in a diary in which he explained his plan – intended to humiliate the Indian holy man, or 'if possible kill him', in order to later 'propose or establish, whichever is easiest', a neo-Victorian pop Raj, or something like that.

'We'll get there before the bloody Beatles! Our *S.S. Regina Victoria* is better than their idiotic yellow submarine,' my father told me, hugging me on the dock and demonstrating yet again that his competitiveness with John, Paul, George and Ringo had by now reached pathological levels. More about this later; I'll tell you soon . . . Oh, since we're on the subject: do you like the Beatles, Keiko Kai?

'Take care of that great big little brother of yours,' added my father. I thought it inappropriate to remind him that my 'great big little brother' had been dead for almost a year. My mother didn't say anything. For months she'd been living behind a perpetual smile and discovering that what worked so well for centuries for the Mona Lisa could work for her too. My mother offered me a daisy as solemnly as she might have handed me a jewel, full of the childish gravity with which flowers were offered in those days.

I waited until the ship had disappeared on the horizon and threw the flower into the water. Dermott – I ask myself whether certain British surnames make it inevitable that a butler will germinate where once there was a man; I ask myself what secret shears prune the first names of butlers so that only their surnames grow – took me home. Dermott brought me to Neverland, where a few days later we heard news of the shipwreck, and I thought Dickensianly, 'an orphan at last', and went out into the garden to make two snowmen. A man and a woman: my parents. I needed to see them melt, I thought; and the invisible man on the BBC signed off with the mantra 'This is the end of the world news,' which still disturbs me today with its promise of an unjust final judgment, with its insinuation of an end without return.

So I said goodbye to the record company executives. One of them asked me, with hungry pride, whether I knew that in the recently discovered discarded footage of *A Hard Day's Night* there was a brief scene in which I appear, practically still a baby, beside Phil Collins. Then I felt the horror of realizing that for some people my childhood was part of a new archaeological adventure, or an ancient curse on anyone who defiled the grave. I told him I had no memory of such a thing, then hung up with the excuse of an appointment or a call on the other line, and went down into the cellars of Neverland to look for the tapes of *Lost Boy Baco's Broken Hearted Requiem & Lysergic Funeral Parlor Inc.* I'd never heard them. I was sure they'd be sad somehow. Excruciating and vulgar and facile as only the revolutionary gestures of those years can and could be: substituting white for black and up for down and war for peace and Chanel for patchouli. I imagined them like one of the messes my father was so fond of organizing. Everything and everyone in a single song. What do Jane Austen and Oz's Emerald City have in common? Or Winston Churchill and the courtesan who ruined an idiot politician and later had her picture taken nude, leaning against the back of a designer chair?

It took me a while to locate their whereabouts: the tapes were stored in an empty orgone box and again, after I'd found them, I didn't want to listen to them. I also considered it best not to expose myself to the dozens of canisters of celluloid. Highly toxic radioactive material. There's something terrible about the ability to compare the memories of a childhood with the incontestable evidence of what happened then. I ask myself whether there isn't something terrible about the careful way videotape preserves the present and future lives of all those who're filmed from the very moment of their birth, all those who'll be able to see themselves now and forever – years after the contractions and parted legs – covered in blood and placenta, howling as if they've just been expelled from an amniotic paradise and been confronted with an excited idiot holding a Made In Japan camera. Yes, I suppose it happened to you, Keiko Kai. And yes, the idea that everything is recorded scares me: one's own life as a documentary that can be consulted at will, thus assuring the death of the absolute mystery of our past by professing to elevate a banal sixth birthday party to the historical and documentary level of that home movie shot in Dallas in '63 and yet . . .

That's why I choose to remember rather than to see.

I prefer to see with my eyes shut.

I remember everything, everything, everything I've decided to remember.

It's not as if I've forgotten the rest, I've just chosen not to remember. The same thing happens with certain songs: we know them perfectly well, but we can't recall their titles or the name of the person who sings them. That's why I preferred to decide for myself in advance what was forgettable and what wasn't, before giving in to chance or the ageing of my neurons. Whole continents have been swallowed up by the waves of my memory.

I remember little or nothing, for example, of my school days. A private school, the other students all like those alien children in *Village of the Damned*, I completely unlike them. The certainty that I would never be good at maths, because by the time I was faced with dreaded decimals, I had no understanding of that kind of thing: I couldn't help reading equations by pausing at the periods as if the numbers were part of a sentence, not a sum.

But I *do* remember when I was just an egg inside my mother. And I remember my dead mother's open eyes. And the eyelids of so many other dead people; eyelids, I'm told, are the first things to disappear as the body begins the slow process of shedding skin and flesh and personality. Bodies dancing that striptease of the perishable and incidental until they're left bare, naked to the bone, and – cloaked in death – so shamefully identical to all other skeletons.

I remember everything I want to remember because almost from the beginning – from the day I discovered the thing called *memory* that would allow me to recover almost intact what had happened the day before – I told myself I wouldn't forget anything I considered unforgettable.

The method is simple and almost obvious: spend two or three hours a day going over what's happened, *making* memory; because yes, memory's constructed in the same way that buildings are constructed. It's obvious that it's an undertaking doomed to failure; no matter how little there is, it's impossible to remember everything. Sooner or later windows disappear, whole rooms are lost, greenhouses are abandoned, passageways lead to locked doors, and gardens are ravaged by sunstorms and hail. It doesn't matter. What's interesting is what remains, what's left intact. The immortal stuff that won't pass through the holes in the mesh of the sieve and that ends up forming our identity. The things we decide to remember forever. What's tangled and can't be unknotted. The strings of the past that move the marionette of our present.

This is how I remember my little brother Baco's funeral. Nothing like David Barrie's. This is how his swift passage through our slow life was honoured: with a party of suns and moons and amped-up light, my mother dressed – unlike Margaret Ogilvy, in her rigorous mourning – in coloured fabrics, her eyes made up, a third open eye painted on her forehead. A fake but plausible Eastern princess, the daughter of the rajah of Carnaby Street in the kingdom of the Swinging Sixties, vibrating, as David Bailey – who has just married Catherine Deneuve – orbits counterclockwise around her and her priestesses: pointy high-heeled boots, studied Cockney accent, his 35 mm Rolleiflex like an artificial satellite taking pictures. They dance. The new and ephemeral gods who've come to upset the centuries-long generational equilibrium dance as the ancient gods once danced.

And all of this happened so fast. A vertiginous canonization. In a few months – or maybe it happened after a single secret day with hundreds of nightfalls – the city seems to have changed completely. London reincarnated as another London. New colours, different sounds, and an army of young people taking over the theatre of operations, the battlefront, the command post. The adults fought their retreat choking in a cloud of scandal and shame: the Argyll divorce, the Profumo case . . . Now, in the new London, after so many decades of paralysis, to be forty is to be old, to be finished, to be part of what's over and will never come again. Now, my parents and their friends enjoy their new youth without ever thinking that time moves faster than they do, that time is already winning the race; not realizing that many of them won't live to tell the tale. My mother dances with her best friends. They're all slim and elegant. The postwar babies of the rationing era grew up undernourished, and, as a result, they're very different from their robust progenitors: thin, perfect women with the ability to eat anything in intimidating quantities without gaining an ounce. Lovely, elegant women. Eyes darkened with kohl and eyelashes stiff and long as the sensitive pistils and stamens of carnivorous plants. Women who do strange things with their arms and hands and feet and legs. Women who shake themselves as if they've been bitten by a spider, who share cigarettes and glasses full of strange colours, who flow and oscillate.

And now that I think about it: we never dance the way we think we dance and we realize it when we see ourselves dancing in a movie someone took at a party. Oh, we can't possibly move like *that*. The same thing happens when we hear our voice recorded for the first time: it sounds almost nothing like the voice that comes from inside our body and circles back to our ears. The same kind of thing is true of most of the relationships we're involved in over the course of our lives: they don't dance the way we think they dance, they don't sound the way we think they sound, but we'd rather not know it, and we keep ouselves and our loves as far as possible from microphones and movie cameras.

My mother hardly knows her best friends, but it doesn't matter because they're all alike. And they all dance alike and all their voices sound the same. And they've all been reborn under the sign of Aquarius. And they all buy their clothes at Biba or Bazaar, or any other boutique that opened a week ago and will close in fifteen days. And their hair's been shaped in the clean, geometric Bauhaus style by the small, frenetic scissors of Vidal Sassoon, aesthetic enemy of David Bailey, in his salon at 171 Bond Street, Mayfair.

The haircut all her friends have is originally called the Bob, but its name keeps changing according to the celebrity daring enough to try it: the Quant, after Mary Quant, and the Kwan, after Nancy Kwan. My mother is the only one who wears her hair long, almost down to her waist; and when she brushes it hard on staticky summer nights, coloured sparks light up my dark room.

And I'm not sure whether my mother and her friends are fairies or witches. Some – like my mother – died at the precise instant required by their wavering legends and continue to be as beautiful as ever in their metallic dresses and their prisons of shaky Super-8 and on the pages of fashion magazines, where they're photographed looking more angular than curvy. They didn't want to grow up, and they didn't grow up.

The survivors haven't aged well; they've grown old gracelessly. Their wrinkles seem more like knife slashes than life lines. Every once in a while I see them on television, saying cruel and politically incorrect things; presenting albums of 'autobiographical songs' (one song always features the wheezing gasps of a Dolby orgasm) on which they're accompanied by musicians who could be their grandchildren and who look at them with a strange mixture of disgust and fascination. There they are, spun-out, rambling divas, remembering the old days as if they were much longer ago, as if they're referring to ruined castles and kings toppled by the wind – winds with names like *amarcord, almásy, cafard, faey'rihtel* – whistling in the black wind of black history, quadraphonic, round, spinning, scratched, and with a little hole in the middle.

Tell me, Keiko Kai, are you bored by all this? Do you miss your parents? Would you like to see more pictures of the young Barrie? Did I make the ropes and gag and blindfold too tight? Do you need me to give you a kiss good night? Do you want me to tell you another story before bed? You're not tired, are you? You want to know what happens next, don't you? Don't you want to hear the same old story again?

The Friend

> The horror of my boyhood was that I knew a time would come when I must give up games (this agony still returns to me in dreams, in which I find myself playing and being watched disapprovingly by the adults); so it was also then I understood that I had to keep playing, but in secret,

wrote Barrie many years later, when he had stopped being a child, never to become an adult.

To compare Barrie's Victorian childhood with my lysergic childhood would be unfair, not to say absurd. But I won't deny that I envy Barrie's childhood – Barrie's childish years – when I compare it to the constant turbulence of my flying youth, in which the Fasten Seat Belts sign was never turned off, and all that could be seen out the window of the plane was a terrible sky lashed by long, dazzling streaks of lightning.

Jim Yang was invented and born, yes, out of a perfect mix of Victorian elements: his story is the saga of a boy who is 'old-fashioned and démodé compared to his modern parents' and possessed of intellectual powers far superior to those of an ordinary six-year old. A kind of young Sherlock Holmes with 'the intelligence of a boy of eighteen or a man of forty or a sage of three hundred – not necessarily in that order!!!'

In the first of his adventures, Jim Yang discovers the time machine in the attic, buried under old furniture; it looks like a bicycle, and it was built by Maximilian Max – Max Max – a generous, mysterious uncle no one has seen in years. On this bicycle, Jim Yang flies through the centuries in search of his mother, Raven, and his little sister, Lucy, who have been kid-napped by an evil genius: Professor Cagliostro Nostradamus Smith, Max Max's dastardly former partner, driven out of his mind by the horror of having such a common last name, and in love to the point of madness with Alice Liddell, the little girl who was the inspiration for Lewis Carroll's Alice.

It's no surprise that Alice – see *Jim Yang and the Wonderland–Neverland–Pepperland Express* – soon falls in love with Jim Yang, who, in that book, takes her with him on his travels out of time, for he knows that, with Alice by his side, Cagliostro Nostradamus Smith and his mother, Raven, and little sister, Lucy, won't be far away. At the end of *Jim Yang and the Wonderland–Neverland–Pepperland Express*, Alice dies: cornered by Cagliostro Nostradamus Smith, she throws herself into a well and breaks her neck, thinking she's found the passageway to another dimension. It's just a well; a very deep well, but an ordinary one.

And yes, there is a problem, a dark side, something that torments Jim Yang more and more in each book. Time travelling becomes an addiction, and it has an odd and terrible side effect, too: time travelling makes Jim Yang stop growing, and numbs his feelings, while at the same time drastically increasing his intelligence. Thus, on one of his last adventures, after so much coming and going, Jim Yang reflects with almost metafictional bitterness:

'Now I'm like one of those characters in children's stories, too . . . Those books that grown-ups concoct for young readers, books that're ultimately all about what the grown-ups believe children must or should be like. Now I'm someone who watches in desperation as his readers grow up, someone who resigns himself to starting over again as new and younger readers appear. Someone who realizes he's been trapped forever in a space–time crack, in an eternal, golden, terrible instant, for centuries upon centuries, twenty-four hours a day, three hundred and sixty-five days a year – or three hundred and sixty six, because I was also unlucky enough to be born on 29 February. So, as if everything else weren't enough, I only get to blow out the candles on a birthday cake once every four winters . . .'

My editors at Bedtime Story Press read this and asked me whether it wouldn't be better to lighten up Jim Yang's reflections a little, because it seemed to them he'd become 'rather dark and bitter for children's tastes'. I told them no, that they didn't understand anything, that there are no darker beings than children, that we're so bad when we're children that when we grow up, we choose to forget it. Adult amnesia about childhood is a fascinating phenomenon, and one of the least studied by the scientific community, which, in my opinion, is always more interested in prolonging old age than restoring youth.

And I'm sure Jim Yang thinks so too.

Jim Yang, yes, is a typical child of the Swinging Sixties, shuttling back and forth and back again as he fights Cagliostro Nostradamus Smith, who takes on the different guises and mannerisms of the monstrous villains of each era. A serial killer, one of Genghis Khan's deputies, a Latin American dictator, a Caesar whose hobby is crucifying everything within reach.

Someone pointed out that the Jim Yang books are so colossally successful with children because they're 'novels with special effects, independent of film'. Maybe. Or maybe not. Because if a movie of the first instalment of Jim Yang's adventures hadn't been planned, with a budget big enough to feed all the bloated-bellied children of some African country for several years, I would never have met you, Keiko Kai.

And you wouldn't be here, listening to what I have to tell you.

But I think the most important factors in the equation, and the almost subliminal secret of Jim Yang's success, lie in the clash and contrast of British discipline at the end of the nineteenth and the beginning of the twentieth century with the Aquarian revolution of the 1960s. The perfect cocktail in book form, now bought by the well-off children of ex-hippies and neoconservatives for their own offspring so that in some way they'll understand what their parents' upside-down youth was like: where they were, what they saw, the visions that blinded them forever. Or maybe the books are read by men who, like Barrie, decided never to have children so they could take their youth with them to the grave and not feel obliged to be like their parents.

I like to think of Jim Yang as a forerunner of what might be called New Victorianism, a kind of renaissance or updating of certain positive habits in the interaction of children and adults. A return to childhood as a source of regeneration, and not a cesspool of degeneracy.

I like to think about Jim Yang because it's an elegant and subliminal way of thinking about my parents as if they were characters in a Jim Yang book.

My mother – once she was rescued, floating on a raft, almost a month after the never fully explained shipwreck of the *S.S. Regina Victoria* – was almost black from the sun. Nothing like the elegant, bronzed sunlamp tan with which Lady Alexandra Swinton-Menzies had prepared herself weeks before, in another life, to welcome the frantic London summer of love. My mother wouldn't stop talking in the strange language of those who've lost themselves forever, suffering from what nineteenth century novels – before the invention of Freud and his inventions – called 'soul sickness'.

In her few lucid moments, before she was confined to a convalescent home where I visited her at the weekends, she asked me about my father, and repeated over and over again that I had had a 'privileged childhood', not realizing that I was still a child. Afterward, she showed me abstract paintings she had done in the garden. She thought they were figurative; but she wondered whether that turquoise splotch – which, she assured me, was Baco – had come out right, whether it looked like the original, and 'Why doesn't Baco ever come home?' she asked again. 'This elephant I painted next to your little brother isn't, isn't, isn't . . . It isn't the Indian god Ganesh: it's Dumbo,' my mother explained to me. I nodded without really listening – the magnitude of her pain was so overwhelming that I tried to think about anything else – and stared at the painting as the nurse requested silence with a finger to her lips. An artificial and terrible silence. The bottled-up silence of hospitals that tries to make patients forget the healthy, bustling racket of the outside world.

Once the brief programme during which my mother's antenna seemed capable of emitting and receiving signals that were more or less comprehensible but hard to credit came to an end, she would return to the usual static. To the white noise of a madness in which she smiled goodbye with the sweetest of smiles, and settled into a deep conversation with the ghost of Baco, my little brother, who had finally 'come home'.

All right: so Bob Dylan vomited on my lead soldiers. A great story to tell years later as I rather half-heartedly tried to seduce the derailed daughter of some oil tycoon; but I wouldn't call that a 'privileged childhood', just as I would never consider Barrie's childhood a paradise; though even so . . .

One night, maybe in search of my dead father, whose body was never found, my mother fled her elegant room in the celebrated clinic and – how, no one could say – managed to walk naked to Neverland and throw herself into our pool. Who knows, maybe her intention was to reclaim the fate of a failed drowning victim. All this happened the day of the moon landing, and we didn't hear my mother arrive because we were all watching television trying to figure out the trick of the thing, the truth behind the biggest lie in history. All of a sudden, that bone-coloured ball orbiting the earth was a Neverland within reach of our hands and the foot that took a small step or a giant leap. At some point, one of the maids – who said she was 'too scared to watch . . . something will go wrong and the moon will fall on us' – looked out the window and saw that the water in the pool was choppy, as if it were boiling. A pool full to the edges, a pool sealed with water, suddenly alive.

Together Dermott and I pulled my mother out (the blue at the bottom of the pool was like the blue of space and I floated there, as light as air, happy to have learned to swim not long before), and we laid her down on the grass and watched her die like a jellyfish as we listened to the chirping of the crickets and the ambulance's siren, ever nearer, ever more futile, and the maid kept saying over and over again 'I told you so, I told you so.'

I thought then that it wouldn't be so bad if everything ended that night: if Neil Armstrong killed his fellow astronauts, seized by a fit of madness; if the pattern of the tides changed because of the extra weight of the men up there; if a symphony of universal cataclysm were the counterpoint to my chamber tragedy.

My mother was saying something in a low voice, and I put my ear to her mouth and she said it to me and I heard it. My mother was saying over and over again 'You're not mine . . . You're not mine.' My mother was singing her one relatively successful song. The song she'd recorded years ago, and that some biographies say was a gift from Bob Dylan in return for a night of love, or something like that.

My mother was singing in a cold, dispassionate voice, and it seemed to me that her body gave off the scent of violets that saints are supposed to give off at the moment of their departure from this world. The voice of my dying mother – Saint Alexandra of the Pools – was more techno than pop. Then – I want to believe it was her first and last death spasm, and not an eruption of secret hatred – my mother bit off half my left ear. I fainted from the pain. I fainted, thinking Dickensianly again, 'A real orphan at last'. I fainted at precisely the final second, as my mother exhaled her last breath. I thought I saw her soul leave her mouth: a slender column of coloured fog, sinuous as an odalisque in a trance, light as a rising ribbon of silk, or definitive as the smoke trickling from a revolver that's just been fired. I lost consciousness and fell into a dream of a world where I didn't exist. A better world. A normal world like any normal child's.

When I woke up, I was sure it had all been a terrible nightmare. The illusion didn't last long: in front of the mirror I saw what remained of my left ear, and I realized that from then on I would be asymmetrical, different, solitary, marked.

Like Jim Yang.

And – as Jim Yang also thought – there are two ways of accepting the disappearance of your parents and acknowledging that suddenly you're an orphan as well as a son: you can feel like a circus freak or you can feel unique.

Like Jim Yang, I decided to feel unique.

In *Jim Yang and the Imaginary Friend*, Jim Yang travels in his time machine to the year 1867.

Jim Yang's time machine – as you know, as I've already said – is a kind of bicycle. A chronocycle on which Jim Yang pedals furiously forward or backward. The idea came to me when I saw that scene from *The Wizard of Oz* again, in which the evil Miss Gulch rides her bicycle in the middle of a black-and-white tornado.

In *Jim Yang and the Imaginary Friend*, Jim Yang comes – on the trail of Cagliostro Nostradamus Smith – to Lilybank, Scotland. There, Jim Yang meets little Barrie. Barrie's brother David has just died; his mother, Margaret Ogilvy, spends much of the day shut up in her room; and Barrie discovers in Jim Yang the perfect adventure companion.

At first, Jim Yang doesn't tell Barrie anything about his life, about what he's doing there or where he's come from. Barrie doesn't ask much, either, because the important thing is having found a friend, someone like him, and he doesn't want to risk losing him.

Jim Yang's fans have no doubt that this is the strangest book in the series: a kind of parenthesis within parentheses in which reflection outweighs action. The critics called it the 'most disturbing' or the 'worst of all'; and my editors usually refer to it as the most 'problematic' of the books I've written. They published it anyway, of course, because at the time it came out, the name Jim Yang could sell a pitcher without a handle, or a pen without ink. Who would dare challenge the man who'd saved Bedtime Story Press and turned it into a multimillion dollar company; the visionary creator of NTV; the man adored by parents and children worldwide?

Someone once told me that if I ran for prime minister, I'd clearly be impossible to beat. I preferred not to comment, just as each time rumours arise that I'll inevitably be knighted in recognition of my services to England, I send Buckingham Palace signals of my unease to make them reconsider.

That's how things are. Things that will never be the same as they once were.

Jim Yang and the Imaginary Friend – which only reached number three on the bestseller list and stayed there for two months; a triumphant failure – is my favourite of the Jim Yang books, of course. It's the one I like best because it's a book about childhood as a territory to be explored; as an era that Jim Yang – frozen in time – refers to as 'Eternity'; as a place where everything happens over and over again, with slight variations, as if in slow motion or gathering strength to endure the horrors of the rest of life.

Compared to the frenetic pace of *Jim Yang and the Pyramid of the Cyborgs* or *Jim Yang and the Children's Crusade* or *Jim Yang and the Brotherhood of Midnight* – for example – little or nothing happens in *Jim Yang and the Imaginary Friend*.

But in fact, things do happen. Various things, lots of things; but always at the gentle pace usually set in pastoral novels. Yes, I admit it: *Jim Yang and the Imaginary Friend* is closer to George Eliot than Indiana Jones.

Marcus Merlin (I'll never be able to call him Marcus or Uncle Merlin or M. M.) liked it, although, as is his habit, he couldn't help pointing out that the title lent itself to confusion.

Said Marcus Merlin: 'In the book, Jim Yang becomes little Barrie's imaginary friend . . . Or at least that's what everyone thinks, since no one in Barrie's family ever sees Jim Yang. But the novel is called *Jim Yang and the Imaginary Friend*; so what you probably meant to say is that Barrie becomes Jim Yang's imaginary friend, yes? But how can that be when Barrie *exists*, when Barrie *existed*?'

But Marcus Merlin is mistaken: Barrie's imaginary friend – and Jim Yang's, too – is none other than the shadow of Peter Pan sewn to Barrie's heels, the character they gradually create together over the course of their long conversations as they walk the moors of Kirriemuir, outside of Lilybanks in the Tenements, beside the lake where the luminous David Barrie died.

In *Jim Yang and the Imaginary Friend*, Jim Yang and Barrie theorize about the nature of childhood. Jim Yang *can't* grow up and Barrie doesn't *want* to grow up. They're complementary opposites. Barrie envies his brother because now that he's dead, he'll never become an adult and he'll always have his mother's love. Jim Yang – wise beyond his years – reflects on the strange fact that every great historical moment seems to have a corresponding age:

'Youth was the legacy of eighteenth-century books, childhood that of nineteenth-century books, adolescence that of twentieth-century books . . . What will the twenty-first century's "age" be? I venture to predict that it'll be old age: a century brimming with healthy, despairing old people . . . In this nineteenth century where I'm stopping now, writers seem particularly attracted to childhood. So many towering little characters: Oliver Twist, Alice, Jane Eyre as a girl, young Cathy and Heathcliff, Mary Lenox and Dickon and Colin, Little Lord Fauntleroy, Little Nell . . . some manage to grow up, but they never forget that their stories began long ago. Some die along the way. Others give in to the temptation of the fantastic, and, like Dorian Grey, are unable to bear the hideous sight of a portrait or a mirror. The Victorians pay homage to childhood with a mixture of sacred love and pagan passion that leads to the spreading of a novel sentiment: the discovery of children as a species, kindness to the young as a sort of hobby. Kindness that translates into the writing of laws that put more humane limits on child labour, into greater and easier access to education and shrinking family size, which leads to closer relationships between parents and children and also fosters the corresponding neuroses, until then unknown. This is how, in the Victorian age, with the booming growth of the enlightened middle class supported by Victoria herself (unlike the ambitious, extravagant exploiters of the House of Hanover who preceded her, and who preferred a world of aristocrats maintained by the humble toil of an abysmally lower, uneducated class), a true industrial revolution is produced in the realm of toys. Lowther Arcade opens in London – a full-scale shopping centre where the Empire's principal toy stores are clustered – and the first children's books read and enjoyed by adults appear too, books to be read aloud by parents to their children. This sentiment will shift again when the figure on the throne changes, and a looser moral and aesthetic code is adopted, inspired by the immature and short-lived Edward VII, Prince of Wales, the perfect company when what's desired is an irresponsible good time, it's said. A king who dies after ruling for just nine years is a king who dies while still a boy: it isn't his biological age that matters, but his *real* age. I'll meet him one day; and, of course, the First World War sets things straight.

'That's why, in my travels back and forth through the past and the future, I always come back here. To these golden years. To the last of the old days to restore my strength and spirits, to contemplate all of this. Still distant from the time when Lolita Haze and Holden Caulfield – adolescence will be our new Promised Land, and instead of simply enduring the adult world, the young will question it – take over and assume the curse of being protagonists perpetually lost in a crazy world of adults who behave like children. A world that'll soon become a place where children are connected to consoling consoles and commanding computers and no longer know where they end and the machine begins. A video game starts and game over is announced and the next thing you know you're buried up to your neck in the lost cemetery of Tamagotchis with the ghost of electricity howling in the bones of your face.'

Why does Jim Yang talk like this? What's happened to him? What's happened to me? Naturally, my editors at Bedtime Story Press were concerned at the new turn things had taken – by this dark, discursive and almost motionless Jim Yang – in the same way that they'd been worried about publishing the first instalment, the manuscript rejected by thirty publishing houses because of Jim Yang's slightly risqué origins as the product of a single night of passion between his mother (a middle-class London girl) and an illegal immigrant (a teacher of martial arts and Buddhism) born alongside the Great Wall of China.

I calmed them when, just six months later, I sent them the swashbuckling, suspenseful and – they liked this – gently sensual *Jim Yang and the Mermaids of Urkh-24*, in which Jim Yang, a little tired of the hormonal hallucinations of an almost adolescent Alice, succumbs to the charms of a beautiful extraterrestrial princess who at first is very bad and in the end is very good, though this doesn't mean she gives up certain vampish attitudes.

Twenty-four months at number one, and the paperback edition was postponed for half a year so as not to disrupt a very pleasant situation for Bedtime Story Press, a family business for several generations which until then had survived on the tiny sales of forgotten eighteenth- and nineteenth-century children's classics which were in the public domain, didn't require the payment of royalties, and, most important, didn't expose them to dealings with individuals of 'artistic temperament'. That wasn't and isn't me. I don't have an artistic temperament, unless being artistic means having a double self, a secret face.

What do you think, Keiko Kai? What's your opinion? Don't you have any thoughts on the subject? Are you one of those who believe that Batman is a psychopath? And what about Jim Yang? And me? And Barrie?

I insist: *Jim Yang and the Imaginary Friend* is my best book, not only because it reveals the shadowy side of Jim Yang as an 'old child, neither one thing or the other', but also because – first in the Victorian dawn of Empire, and then, over the course of the novel, returning regularly to that splendid, mutant England populated by lights and shadows – it exposes and proves for itself what we all suspect: that we're never born into the era that suits us best. All of us are lost, in one way or another. Our brief life – the construction of our biography, our personality – is nothing but a futile attempt to accommodate our true temporal sign, much more important than the sign of the zodiac for orienting ourselves in the chaos of the era that we're allotted to suffer by the wheel of time. Leonardo da Vinci, I'm sure, must've suffered very much. There are exceptions, of course: the Beatles (as much as my father hated them), Johann Gutenberg, Pablo Picasso, Bill Gates. The right men for the right time.

Jim Yang only feels comfortable among the Victorians, and that's how Jim Yang meets Barrie. Jim Yang comes to Scotland in search of Barrie because he senses in him the more or less certain possibility of a twin, a comrade, the other half he requires despite their unbridgeable differences. Jim Yang is strong and agile and Barrie is sickly and very small. Jim Yang is grown up and Barrie is exaggeratedly childish. Jim Yang is rational and Barrie spends all his time dreaming . . . It doesn't matter; they need each other, so that by reading each other, they can finish writing themselves.

In *Jim Yang and the Imaginary Friend*, Jim Yang and Barrie don't go off on any 'great adventure'. Cagliostro Nostradamus Smith is nowhere to be found, and for the first time, Jim Yang has no interest in pursuing him.

Nor does he think much about his mother, sweet Raven.

Or his naughty little sister, Lucy. Lucy is really his half-sister; the product – depending on his mother's mood – of a single night of passion with Mick Jagger; or with a high-ranking member of the conservative party (married, of course); or with an Italian playboy.

Or about the many dangers and adventures that await him the minute he starts pedaling his chronocycle again. None of that interests him. Jim Yang isn't thinking about any of it.

In *Jim Yang and the Imaginary Friend*, Jim Yang and Barrie only use the time machine to go back a few days into the past to try to prevent the death of David Barrie on the frozen lake. They succeed, but David dies a few hours later after being trampled by a runaway horse. They prevent that death, and David dies again by falling into the jaws of a loom. Ten attempts later – Barrie's older brother has died over and over again in the most horrible and ridiculous ways, the last time in a fit of laughter brought on by a dirty joke – David comes to Barrie and Jim Yang and asks them, please, to let him die in peace once and for all; he explains to them that it isn't being dead that's so terrible but the precise instant of dying. And that, despite their good intentions, they've turned him into a 'kind of immortal corpse . . . And it hurts, it hurts so much'.

Jim Yang and Barrie understand then that David will always die, in all the infinite forms death can take; that death can't be thwarted; that the dead are dead; and that it isn't the place of the living to alter their fate and will and wish.

So David, Jim Yang and Barrie walk back to the frozen lake, David puts on his skates, waves to them, and glides swiftly away, disappearing into the fog, his hands clasped behind his back, smiling, dying of happiness.

The rest of the book – the incident with David is the closest thing to an adventure in *Jim Yang and the Imaginary Friend* – is pure description and reflection, and almost nothing happens. Margaret Ogilvy appears as a fairly important character through the stories Barrie tells Jim Yang about his mother. Jim Yang decides not to say anything to Barrie about his own mother, so as not to frighten him; instead he tells Barrie some of the things that've happened to him in his personal history and in History. Also, when Barrie swears that he'll never forget him, Jim Yang explains what he's explained to dozens of characters and people over the course of the novels:

'I'm made of time, Barrie; and time is made of dreams. I shouldn't be here. I'm a crooked stitch in the fabric of the years . . . An error that will be corrected as soon as I leave your era: you'll begin to forget me the very next day, and after a week at most, you'll think of me as someone you might have imagined but never known.'

That's almost all.

In *Jim Yang and the Imaginary Friend*, Jim Yang hides his chronocycle. He unscrews its pedals, so no one can use it if it's found. Jim Yang lives in a granary on the edge of town. Every day Barrie comes to visit him and brings him food; they talk, they exchange penny dreadfuls (those bastard predecessors of comic books full of pirates, killers and desert islands) and they read them, as Barrie later writes,

Standing in the store where they were sold, very quickly so as not to have to pay for them; the most exquisite way of reading.

It's in those days – in Barrie's real life, beyond *Jim Yang and the Imaginary Friend* – that the Scottish boy decides to be a writer. So in a sense *Jim Yang and the Imaginary Friend* also ends up being an adventure novel, but a novel about a different kind of adventure: the adventure of an artistic calling.

In the book's final pages, Jim Yang and Barrie part after a long embrace, but – in a brief coda – we see how Jim Yang pedals back into Barrie's life on various occasions over the years, and, hidden, observes what's become of his friend. On one of these return visits, Jim Yang watches him leave for Dumfries Academy. There Barrie adopts the bold alias of Sixteen String Jack, in the same way I took the name Peter Hook to write about Jim Yang. I think that writers should always find themselves new names, because when you write – just as when you read – you become another person. I'm thinking about the secret names the ancient Egyptians gave themselves: names that were truly their own. They didn't reveal them to anyone and they only said them alone, in front of a mirror, as if speaking to the most trustworthy of friends.

At Dumfries Academy, Barrie will be happy playing cricket and soccer, participating in the debating club, and writing his first play, a success. Barrie usually takes the roles of 'young lady' or 'younger daughter', and his Opus 1, written especially for an end-of-term programme, is called *Bandelero the Bandit*. The work will be denounced by a clergyman in the town paper as 'vulgar and immoral', and the story will reach the London papers and make Barrie a minor but respected celebrity among the students. His classmates, the girls, award him the prize for the 'school's sweetest smile', and Barrie, horrified, decides 'never to smile again'.

Jim Yang – disguised as the son of the gardener at Dumfries Academy – discovers that something strange is happening to Barrie: he isn't growing. Or rather, he's getting older but not bigger; the machinery of his bones has shut down completely.

– Ashamed to be so short that I can still pay half-fare on the bus,

writes Barrie in his notebook, and at seventeen, he's barely five feet tall and doesn't know what it is to shave. Barrie – ignored by his classmates – begins to play with students from the lower forms. Jim Yang watches from the distance knowing he can't help him or show himself again, and Jim Yang explains to his readers:

'As you already know, it isn't advisable to visit the same person all through his life. It can cause imbalances, especially in adulthood. I'll never forgive myself for what I did to little Mozart and little Rimbaud, wonderful playmates.'

And Jim Yang pedals away.

*

In 1878, at the age of eighteen, Barrie leaves Dumfries Academy and returns to Kirriemuir intending to become a professional writer. He'll start as a journalist. Being a journalist back then is much like being a writer, because the stories require the same kind of effort as a novel: reality must be conjured up for readers who will never know the wider world, who will never see famous monuments or great men, who will scarcely leave the towns where they were born. There are no photographs in the newspapers; the drawings of national leaders on the front page are like those of the heroes in dime novels; the type is small and uneven; and a news story might easily be confused with a tall tale.

His mother, however, has a different plan: Barrie must take David's place and attend university. Barrie obeys, enrolling at Edinburgh University and heading there with Jim Yang following close behind, in a variety of disguises and masks.

At the university, Barrie is unhappy as he never was at school. He has no friends. He walks alone. He decides to keep a diary, a disciplined record of his days and nights. Until now, he's been noting random thoughts in the margins of his schoolbooks. Barrie buys several notebooks. I imagine them small and light brown, the colour of certain fast, dangerous cats. He fills them quickly. They aren't dutiful diaries; they don't follow the fixed and precise course of datebooks. They're stranger specimens, of irregular and synthetic habits, and, occasionally, wickedly obscene. Sometimes Barrie rereads them with fascinated horror. He asks himself what would happen if they fell into the hands of strangers, or, worse, of people who know him. His notebooks are the keyhole through which Barrie spies on others. If anyone else read them, Barrie thinks, the equation would be inverted and he would be the one observed. Writers' diaries are spears that can turn into boomerangs, or, like the genies in Arabian tales, turn against their master at the slightest slip or misstep.

Barrie decides to guard against the risk with a trick, a childish trick but one that, paradoxically, makes him even more vulnerable and transparent and cruel to himself. Barrie adopts a habit that he'll retain until his death: writing about himself in the third person, a third person that sometimes rebels and becomes the most desperate and elemental of confessions:

> *Men can't get together without talking filth . . . He is very young looking – trial of his life that he is always thought a boy . . . There are finer things than romancing a girl . . . Great horror – dream I am married – wake up shrieking . . . Sudden and strong impulse to go into a toy store and buy myself something, but I don't dare.*

Jim Yang realizes that in Edinburgh, Barrie is lost among men. Women pay no attention to him. Only children seem to understand him. His brother Alexander married in 1877, and now Barrie has two nieces he visits as often as he can. He contemplates them as if they're works of art, studying them, analyzing them; it intrigues him that he's happy with them, that in their company all his worries and sorrows melt away like clouds spent after a storm.

Barrie returns to Kirriemuir for the holidays without having forgotten his literary calling; but he can't discuss it with a mother who lives to see him become the Doctor of Divinity that David could never be. To console him, his sister Jane Ann shows him a notice in *The Scotsman* seeking a columnist for the regional newspaper *The Nottingham Journal*: light prose and the considerable pay of three pounds a week.

Barrie replies and is hired and writes about things like umbrellas and flowers, and sunsets, without signing his name to his pieces. He writes with a mixture of cynicism and sentiment. Barrie writes constantly. Barrie is ambidextrous and claims that there are two different writers inside him, one for each hand: the left-hand writer is usually gloomier than the right-hand one, and 'there are things that come from the left arm that could never come from the right'. The handwriting of the two sides is more or less the same: script with an almost Eastern look; the left-hand writing is more crabbed than the right-hand writing.

'Pretty Boys' – right? left? – is one of his most discussed articles, and it goes like this:

> *Pretty boys are pretty in all circumstances, and this one would look as exquisitely delightful playing on the floor as when genteelly standing, in his nice little velvet suit with his sweet back to the fire-place, but think of the horror and indignation of his proud and loving mother . . . When you leave the house the pretty boy goes with you to the door and holds up his pretty mouth for a kiss. It's at that moment when you realize that if you wish to continue on good terms with his mother you must do everything he wishes; if you are determined to remain a man whatever be the consequences, you slap his pretty cheek very hard while the mother gazes aghast and the father looks another way, admiring your pluck and wishing he had the courage to go and do likewise. It would, on the whole, be a mistake to kill the child outright, because, for one thing, he may grow out of his velvet suit in time and insist on having his hair cut, and, again, the blame does not attach to him nearly so much as to his mother.*

Barrie's particular brand of humour provokes a certain unease in readers, so he decides to write on less 'polemical' matters. Barrie questions his mother about her past, and turns her into his first great character. He begins to publish a series of stories about the Auld Licht sect and Margaret Ogilvy's childhood, and he sends them to the *St James's Gazette*. Frederick Greenwood, the editor, likes their 'Scottish flavour' and asks for more; he pays him better and lets Barrie write in his own name.

Barrie decides that the moment has come for him to make his assault on London and become, definitively and forever, the writer he's always wanted to be. No one requires a writer to have a beard (with great effort, Barrie has managed to grow a moustache), or to be tall, or handsome.

Barrie studies a number of maps with a strategic eye and comes to the conclusion that the best place to live is in Bloomsbury, near the reading room at the British Museum.

Before he leaves for the big city, Barrie sends another piece to the *St James's Gazette*. Jim Yang, hidden behind his open paper, reads it sitting in the same carriage on the night train to London, 28 March 1885, the train that's taking Barrie to the Empire's great capital. The article is titled 'The Rooks Begin to Build'.

> *Let us survey our hero as he sits awake in a corner of his railway compartment . . . He is gauche and inarticulate, and as thin as a pencil but not so long . . . Expression, an uncomfortable blank . . . Manners, full of nails like his boots. Ladies have decided he is of no account, and he already knows this and has private anguish thereanent. Hates sentiment as a slave may hate his master. Only asset, except a pecuniary one, is a certain grimness about not being beaten . . . Our hero reaches London and has one of those great, never to be repeated, moments in the life of all heroes: he buys a copy of the* St James's Gazette *and begins to read a story written by him less than a week before. Our hero has just reached London and he's already made two guineas! It's a piece called 'The Rooks Begin to Build' and it begins: 'Let us survey our hero . . .'*

The hero Barrie – and Jim Yang the hero – get off the train at St Pancras. I like to think that Barrie recites – like a prayer – all the names London had before it became London, invoking its mysterious origin with the echo of all the possible letters in its name at the time its foundation stone was buried, the name of a city that began to grow at the end of the Neolithic period: Kaerlud, Kaerlundein, Llyn-don, Laindon, Lunnd, Caer Luud, Lundunes, Lindonion, Londinium, Lundene, Lundone, Ludenberk, Longidinium, Babylondon . . . The biggest city in the world. The nucleus of the Empire. The indestructible metropolis capable of enduring colossal invasions, great fires and massive plagues. *Megalopolis Regina Excelso Gloria*: London is a planet in and of itself, indifferent to the passage of the centuries, containing all the most formidable treasures of history (here and now Charles Darwin is rewriting the past and Karl Marx is sketching the future) and shuffling them at its pleasure and whim, as if to say 'Everything that has happened so far has happened solely so that you could come to me; welcome and fare thee well.'

The first thing Barrie buys upon arriving in London is a big bottle of black ink. The second is a hat; to favourably impress his editor at the *St James's Gazette,* he thinks. Later, Barrie pays for a room on Guilford Street and – followed by the shadow of Jim Yang – walks until he loses his sense of direction and finally throws his maps away. Barrie has decided that he's a Londoner now, that he doesn't need maps, that it doesn't matter being lost in London if you've found yourself in London.

The centre of the universe. The colours of London, the noise, the rain. The almost solid air of London that fills your lungs and makes you feel as if you could breathe underwater, or as if you're drowning on dry land. The constant noise of London – the shriek of everyone arriving in London at once, to conquer it or be defeated – as if someone were shouting at you in a foreign language, but all of a sudden you realize you know the language, and begin to understand it word by word. It soothes Barrie not to understand it all yet. It doesn't matter what anyone says or what it seems: Barrie knows he's a man and a boy of twenty-six. The best of both worlds. And he's also a Scot, and he thinks then, and later writes: 'There are few more impressive sights on the face of the earth than that of a Scotsman determined to succeed.'

Barrie reads stone markers that proclaim *Ex Hoc Momento Pendet Aeternitas* and *Vestiglia Nulla Retrorsum*: 'Eternity rests on this moment' and 'There's no turning back', more or less; and he translates them as if they were telegrams composed by superior beings and sent to earth solely to be read and deciphered by him. Bulletins that announce a definitive love. Barrie has fallen in love with London at first sight. Little Barrie's little heart is pierced by immense London: a sharp-shooting

Amazon whose only breast is the cupola of St Paul's Cathedral. And yes, my lyricism does sometimes border on preciousness and even go beyond it; but maybe I slip into these excesses because Marcus Merlin was always irritated by my very British tendency to freight certain small moments with the pomp and circumstance of historic events. I do it to annoy him; and now, seeking his approval, I'll continue in the panoramic and cinemascopic style he liked so much.

Take 1: It's the time of night when the prostitutes of Whitechapel come to the banks of the Thames to throw their dead foetuses or their newborn babies or themselves into the river while the high priests of Oriental sects go down into the sewers in search of the true, secret source of the Nile and John 'The Elephant Man' Merrick returns to his room at London Hospital after a night at the theatre. The distant throb of the factories can be heard merging with the silvery voice of Nicholas Hawksmoor's cathedrals and Christopher Wren's clocks, pulsing in a secret tongue for the glory of the triangular eye of God, the Great Gothic Architect of the Universe, who lives here and nowhere else. Criminals emerge from the sewers and aristocrats enter their private clubs, or maybe it's the other way around – it makes no difference. The resurrectionists wait for nightfall to harvest fresh cadavers so they can sell them to medical students eager to discover what happens inside the jigsaw of the human body. Thousands of extras and supporting players – oh, look at all the lonely people, where do they all come from, where do they all belong – and yet each and every one of them is the unchallenged protagonist of his own novel. And even the rats are proud to be citizens of the most powerful Empire in the universe. And someone has turned on the fog machine and everything seems to tremble, as if it were built on the armour-plated back of one of those sea monsters that inhabit the atlas-edges of a world that's scarcely been explored, a world no bigger than a great city. And someone will turn on the fog machine tomorrow morning. There are so many machines in this new machine age.

Machines are invented each day in this ever more mechanized metropolis, where men give birth to devices and devices swallow up men. London, London, London . . .

Barrie explores a city that isn't mine yet, but will be. The names are the same. The names will always be the same, no matter how much the substance and mood of what's inside the container of the names changes flavour and scent. Londonian names of London: King's Road, Chelsea, Bond Street, East Ham High Street, Primrose Hill and Carnaby Street . . .

And here, here again, is another of those collisions between my life and Barrie's. A temporal misalignment in which yesterday's and today's maps are superimposed, and swept away by a gust of information. Information that I've gathered for years, information that only serves to distract me from other facts that don't appear in any history book except the secret guide to my life. Information in which the public realm intersects with the private.

An example: Carnaby Street, which in the seventeenth century was called Karnaby House (there is no record of what or who Karnaby was); and which later was part of Abingdon convent, and, after that, property of the Crown (which used it as a morgue during the twin catastrophes of the Great Plague and the Great Fire); and then a riding field; and soon afterward a neighbourhood inhabited by fleeing French Huguenots: and then, one twentieth-century morning in the middle of the 1950s, John Stephen, son of a Glasgow shopkeeper, opens the doors of Vince Man's Shop – nearby, around the corner, on Newberg St – one of the first London haberdasherieswhere it's possible to buy clothes in colours that aren't grey or blue or black; and one afternoon there's a short circuit, and everything burns; and Stephen is offered an empty storefront on Carnaby Street; and by 1962, Stephen has four boutiques on the street.

All of this just to be able to match up my Carnaby Street – the Carnaby Street of my childhood – with Barrie's Carnaby Street. And who knows whether all those places, all those hallucinogenic boutiques drenched in Oriental incense smoke, aren't already there when he arrives: in place, though invisible, with their phantom roots already vibrating under the pavement like the tremors of the earthquake that's to come.

Barrie comes and I go, and Barrie rounds a corner that I'll turn many times many years later, and Barrie discovers a park. Hyde Park. A man shouts that the end of the world is coming and that God doesn't exist; another man shouts that the Messiah has returned to punish all those who say that man is descended from the apes instead of ascending to the Creator. Both are perched on platforms and both jab at the same point in the same sky. Barrie walks along the edge of the park, down the stretch that borders Knightsbridge, and crosses a small street – Exhibition Road – and it's as if he's crossed the border of one country and entered another.

Kensington Gardens, he reads on a metal plaque on a gate. Barrie enters the park and sits on a bench. He smiles. Suddenly, Barrie feels he is being watched; he turns rapidly, and leaps over the back of the bench and catches a boy who is hiding in a bush. He peers at him, half-closing his eyes, as if looking for something lost a long time ago. For an instant he thinks he's found it; but the memory slips away, along with the boy, who goes running and crosses a green bridge over a blue stream and disappears from his sight forever.

Barrie loses a memory but in its place he finds an idea, a good one. It's not entirely clear to him yet; but there will be time to polish it like a diamond held up to the light, next to a window that opens onto the thousand colours of the London sky.

Jim Yang escapes Barrie and keeps running, and doesn't stop running until he reaches his chronocycle. He mounts it and pedals as hard as he can. Jim Yang pedals forward and the figure of Barrie sitting on a bench in Kensington Gardens begins to dissolve like a painting in the rain, like those pictures drawn in coloured chalk on the grey pavement in that film, the one Jim Yang saw with his mother when he was still a boy like any other boy. Before Cagliostro Nostradamus Smith and the hurricane of millennia became part of his life forever; before the eye of the hurricane fixed its unblinking gaze on him, spinning and spinning and still spinning.

That's how *Jim Yang and the Imaginary Friend* ends.

My favourite of the books I've written.

The longest of all my books.

Five hundred pages in which – as in most lives – almost nothing happens so that everything can happen.

The Hero

I'm not a hero.

I've never felt like a hero.

What's more: I never wanted to be a heroic children's writer (I would've been perfectly happy just being a reader, but . . .); I never liked children; and, by the time I was fourteen, I was six feet tall and I'd experienced a remarkable concentration of tragedies more befitting an adult than an adolescent.

I'm telling you this, Keiko Kai, to erase any notion that I'm interested in or obsessed with drawing a parallel between my life and Barrie's, in being a pale shadow of him, a fake double, a cheap imitation. Nothing of the kind.

The only thing Barrie and I have in common is having created a child hero and gotten rich as a result. But Jim Yang isn't much like Peter Pan either.

True, Jim Yang never grows up, but the reasons he doesn't are very different from Peter Pan's; Jim Yang can't grow up. And whereas Peter Pan is addicted to the amphetamines of eternal childhood, Jim Yang is a junkie who shoots up over and over again with a syringe full of the liquid of millennia, someone hooked on the naive illusion that time *must* have a positive effect on reality; that if everything past is better, then the future *must* be better yet, and can be manipulated to one's convenience and satisfaction.

The eternal problem is always the present.

It's also true that Barrie and I have a dead brother in common – older or younger – and slightly unbalanced mothers in our pasts.

But I – unlike Barrie – don't write in order to be someone. I write to be someone else. And that someone else is none of the many *Is* circulating out there. Barrie wrote to be recognized as the famous author of his famous creations; I write to be able to disappear behind them, so that Jim Yang is more real than me, so that the character trumps the person.

Not that this prevents my invisibility from creating false impressions, urban legends, fairy tales; it's impossible to avoid.

I'm *not* the tycoon hermit of children's literature, though it's true I refuse to participate in book fairs and sit at rectangular round tables alongside my colleagues. I'm sure they hate me, that they consider me an interloper, simply because I don't make public pronouncements on the significance and profundity of children's literature and its purlieus. Similarly, sorry to say – I'm not sorry at all – I'll never be found signing books elbow to elbow with S (creator of the Great Catsby, melancholy millionaire cat), R (creator of Lucypretty and Tonyugly), Y (proprietor of Frogman Capote, the gay frog, hero of children with homosexual leanings), A (inventor of Tick-Tock, the imprecise little clock), or M (lord and master of Frank and Drac, the cowardly monsters). Nor will I be seen in front of hordes of children and flocks of parents, much less contributing to anthologies for the benefit of sick children suffering from one of those terrible syndromes with hyphenated names that are so difficult to pronounce and so easy to get.

I'm *not* the evil playboy with a taste for supermodels.

I'm *not* the saint with miraculous powers who brought Merceditas, the daughter of Mexican narc Milicio Mantra (boss of the Nostalgic Rancheras Cartel) out of a deep coma when her favourite book – *Jim Yang and the Revenge of Moctezuma* – was read aloud to her in a Houston hospital.

But it's always possible to spot the pattern of the threads of truth on the loom of myth, Keiko Kai. And here are some raveled notes for an unauthorized autobiography I'll never write:

I like to be alone; solitude is full of people.

Despite having eliminated all sexual impulses from my being, I had a casual, unexpected affair with the Argentinian supermodel Piva. Nothing serious: every night she begged me to tell her a story to ward off the nightmares of bulimia and anorexia.

As I was walking through Trafalgar Square, I was kidnapped by a small mariachi commando group. They put me on a plane and took me to a house in a place called Tapalpa, in the mountains of Mexico, where an active volcano throbbed. From up high you could see horrible enormous black birds, like men dressed as birds – turkey vultures – crossing the sky on the horizon. And you could also see how storms took shape, picturesque storms, storms that could only be appreciated from the prow of a nineteenth-century ship or from David Lean's folding director's chair, I suppose. And I could *understand* them better than in any of those computer graphics on the Weather Channel. Suddenly, right there, everything was like one of those Weather Channel pictures, except that it was real and natural, no artificial colours or flavours. And we had to close the doors and windows to keep the clouds out of the house. Clouds you could see coming from far away, and suddenly they were right there, engulfing the house in something that wasn't fog. It was cloud. And it was such a lovely sight, Keiko Kai, that it gave you the urgent desire to be struck by lightning so that you could stay in that cloud landscape forever, a random and electric suicide. I didn't know what I was doing there. My captors never spoke to me, except in heavily accented English monosyllables, which emerged from the depths of their broad, hairless chests, tattooed with virgins rising up to heaven. There was, I think, a private zoo. One day I went up to a zebra and discovered that it was just a white horse painted with black stripes. It seemed best not to go near the supposed giraffe and rhinoceros. I spent all my time watching the fire in an immense fireplace: I added wood, small logs, building complex structures that were devoured by the flames; and the hours flew by. Watching the fire is never boring. Like water, it's an inexplicable mystery, and, along with the waves, it's our first narrative form, the initiatory book read by new-fledged human beings. One night, it's true, they did bring me to the dying Merceditas, and she looked almost like one of those angelic folk-art dead girls who're photographed for the Day of the Dead, and her father ordered me to cure her, and I must have said something or done something, I don't remember, I don't know. I danced, possessed by the peyote juice I'd consumed in memory of my father, and when I returned from the place you go when you eat sacred mushrooms, Merceditas Mantra was laughing, her fever gone, health restored, and I was quickly removed and tied to a seat on a rented Concorde, ultra first class, all expenses paid courtesy of the Tijuana Cartel. I think that's how it was. I don't remember any of it very well. Yes, suddenly I was walking in Trafalgar Square again, in that almost invisible, constant rain that's so much like oxygen, as if nothing had happened.

I'm almost none of those people and almost no one else except who I am: and no one could imagine the person I am except Marcus Merlin, who, I hasten to add, wasn't a hero either, but who could launch into almost epic tirades when he was in the mood, or simply with the help of an opium pipe – 'The effect is almost immediate for a veteran like myself in these affairs,' he would say – the smoke narrowing his eyes.

Said Marcus Merlin: 'I'd never want to be the hero or the protagonist of anything. It's a nuisance. Too much work and responsibility. I like, even prefer, being a supporting character, but one who's key to understanding the story. You know: someone important, but who influences the story from the margins. A small but unforgettable part. The kind of role that, in film credits, after all the names of the cast have scrolled by, requires that "and" . . . all by itself and in last place. But indispensable. For example: . . . *and Christopher Walken*. Though no, Christopher Walken is always so extreme. Instead . . . I know: . . . *and Donald Sutherland*. Or even better, he's one of ours: . . . *and Michael Caine*. The kind of actor who always seems to be playing himself, but at the same time can play anyone. Robert Redford has that talent too. The ability to do anything and still be himself. Reporter, fireman, horse trainer, hired killer: he's always convincing. And he doesn't have to resort to stupid tricks like gaining weight or wearing a prosthesis or researching some degenerative disease or changing his accent until he's unrecognizable. God, if there's anything I hate it's actors who *act* . . . You, on the other hand . . . You're . . . You'd be more along the lines of Bill Murray. Or William Hurt. Thin lips and sad eyes, the look of a silent film actor taken aback to find himself in a movie where everyone talks too much . . . Oh, and thank Jesus for movie stars: they give us such a useful, easy way to define ourselves. They're much better than the characters in books. And you don't know how happy I am that you've finally given up those stupid old-fashioned scruples and restrictions now that the golden opportunity's arrived for a film version of the adventures of our beloved Jim Yang . . . And that you've quit your stupid fantasizing about a Jim Yang play . . . Do you know why God invented the theatre? So ugly actors would have a place to work, ha ha ha. Ugh: those plays, those *classics*, that in the end are nothing but boring versions of the unjustly scorned gladiator movie . . . Seriously now: children's books and film have much more in common than you realize. I think it was the producer Irving Thalberg – he died young – who used to shut himself up in a dark screening room, until, he said, he'd "gotten inside the head of a twelve-year-old boy: that's the intellectual coefficient of the average American." Yes, my dear, movies are made for man-boys . . . And books for boy-men? I don't know . . . Anyway, spectators aren't the same as readers. Readers are the book's producers, in a certain sense; they're workers . . . Spectators aren't.

Spectators are naive, lazy people, ready to be taken in by any magic trick . . . After all, the miracle of corn turning into popcorn is as respectable as the transformation of your ideas into books. And it's a much gentler miracle, too: there's no need for whole forests to die for a movie to be filmed, wouldn't you agree . . . ? And I think I already know what I'll wear on opening night, which I'll have to attend in your place . . . I can see it coming,' smiled Marcus Merlin, his pupils clouded by the green opium smoke, looking up unseeingly at a ceiling as high as the sky.

All right: I read as much as Barrie during my childhood, and I escaped into books too. But I also watched television. Lots of it. Television that began broadcasting around noon and ended after midnight, and newscasts that had the feel of the nearly fictitious or the instantly historical, with none of today's options for when you need to interrupt the uninterruptible. And as I think this and say it, I ask myself whether all the kingdom's plasma TVs aren't being bombarded by breaking news bulletins reporting what Jim Yang's adored creator has done.

Better not to think about that.

Better to think about other television sets, yes?

Sets with electrical insect antennae that had to be angled with skill and patience to find the perfect position and that occasionally gave you an electric kiss that raised the hair on your arms and made you give a sharp little cry. Sets with switches that no longer exist and functions that've disappeared from remote controls like useless appendages, like the hairy coat shrugged off by evolution, like the lower jaw that used to jut forward and now slants back. Buttons for the vertical and the horizontal and to wipe out that ghostly image hovering like an aura over Professor Quatermass or Professor Rudolph Popkiss. A viciously sticky dial, a knob for changing channels that at first was hard to turn, and then, as the months passed, became smooth and loose, and you ended up spinning it with a precise flick of the wrist, as if the television had become one of those old safes that only opens if you give it the kid-glove treatment. Sets that, back then, were like a piece of science fiction pulsing in our living rooms: turned on, they took a while to warm up and show a picture; turned off, they sighed a slow farewell, the insomniac zombie eye of a white point in the centre of the screen refusing to close and remaining there sometimes for as long as an hour. Sets like mechanical dogs, like robot best friends. Sets that didn't yet have the power and potency of today's sets, those machines with the ability to turn you into a modern-day child of the Middle Ages, bombarding you with so much age-inappropriate information that your childhood is used up and you're thrust into a premature adulthood. Sets in their infancy, with just a few channels and only the strictly necessary programmes at set times, once a week. Sets that sometimes worked and sometimes didn't.

And amid all that, the 60s television my father hated. I was always sorry he wasn't here to enjoy those retro-series especially designed to celebrate the eras of Victoria the First-and-Only and Edward VII and even George V, as the horror of the 70s was already beginning to settle over everything. I drank in that 60s television, which no one had yet accused of being harmful – though there was room to suspect that *something* must not be quite right, because if photographs stole your soul, then what would the effects of that small and imperceptibly flickering screen be? If photography stole your soul, then it made sense to think television crushed it, killed it.

I watched *Voyage to the Bottom of the Sea* (and pretended to be tossed from port to starboard, from one side of the room to the other, as if some monster of the deep had the *Seaview* trapped in its tentacles; my favourite character was the psychotic sailor Kowalski, perpetually seized by oceanic frenzies and furies); I watched *Star Trek* (and pretended to be tossed forward and backward, sitting at the controls of the *Enterprise* as it was attacked by extraterrestrial rays; my favourite character was any of them, all perpetually seized by galactic frenzies and furies); I watched *The Forsyte Saga* (twenty-six episodes in the Victorian life of a Victorian family perpetually tossed by internal earthquakes); I watched *Dr Who* (battling those Daleks that looked like washing machines); I watched *The Prisoner* (and accompanied the spooked Number Six trapped in the disturbing landscape of a village/jail); I watched *Top of the Pops* (my father and mother appearing just once, singing and dancing spasmodically, always facing the wrong camera); I watched *The Avengers* (no, I wasn't in love with lithe, elegant Emma Peel; I was in love with Emma Peel's black leather cat suit, and, especially, the S&M version of Emma Peel who appeared in the unforgettable episode 'A Touch of Brimstone'); and I still remember my surprise and dismay when, soon after I turned twenty, someone explained to me that Hanna-Barbera wasn't an incredible woman cartoonist but the last names of two men.

I saw all these series and cartoons in black and white, not colour. I read in colour. We were the first mixed-breed animals (learning to *read* and to *watch* at the same time), and the last to grow up believing that television was something fake. We were sure that movie special effects were nowhere near as good as the ones we imagined in our heads; it was impossible to turn all those dazzling stories from books into images. They bored into our eyes through our pupils as we daydreamed in an infinite range of shades, and they established themselves in the underwater planet of our brains.

Television today is the exact opposite. The need to escape reality has gradually been replaced by the temptation to imitate reality. The other day I read an interview with one of those angry blond teenage singers with an onomatopoeic name, who said that he couldn't remember his childhood if he didn't break it down first into twenty-five minute segments with a laugh track: 'Like one of those infinite reruns. When we're kids we're our own TV sets, and our favourite show inside of them . . . Even now, when I wake up, I can't help feeling my scalp to find the place I'm sure my antenna is. Where's my antenna? Who pulled off my antenna? Did they take it out with my appendix? It's my parents' fault, I'm sure. I talk about that in "Zrapping", the *Rap You* single that will be on sale next . . .' said the boy, his eyes full of static and his arms waving. In the picture in an airline magazine, his arms look out of focus, his body hunched like an albino monkey's, his fingers transmitting almost Masonic signals. I didn't understand what he was talking about, but I thought I understood what he was referring to. It's from this, from an upbringing like this, from having been overexposed to too many hours of radiation, I suppose, that we come to need all those strange competitions in which 'real people' – not actors – are held captive and made to live under extreme conditions and participate in sadistic experiments in exchange for the prize of celebrity. We're living and watching the Warhol Channel; and what interests the spectator is seeing how mortals have invaded the old television of the immortals to banish the gods and become like them, and ultimately endure the same slow but irreversible retreat of spotlights and cameras.

I haven't *watched* television again – when I say watched, I mean in the sense that I think of myself as *watching* it – since the television of my childhood. Although sometimes, when a world catastrophe or private tragedy makes its regular surprise appearance, I tune into the news channels to see a fairy princess's carriage smashed into a cement pillar. Or to watch death shown live in the form of twin aeroplanes hurling themselves against twin towers. Or to listen to the slow voice, its desperation hardly disguised, of an intellectual speaking to no one, in the lowest-ratings time slot, late in the dark night of the soul. A man with a generous face, a foreigner who – in correct and passionate English – says, and says to me alone, and, if he's lucky, to a handful of insomniacs who're trying to be hypnotized back to sleep:

'The gods are elusive guests of literature. They criss-cross it with the wake of their names. But they often abandon it, too.

Each time the writer sets down a word, he has to reconquer them. Mercurialness, a sign of the gods, is also an indication of their ephemerality. But it wasn't always this way. Things were different when there was a common script: a template of gestures and words, a controlled aura of destruction, an exclusive use of certain materials. All this pleased the gods, so long as men wanted to address them. Then all that remained, like banners waving over an abandoned camp, were the stories of the gods implied in every gesture. Uprooted from their territory and exposed to the crude light of the word, the gods could come to seem shameless and vain. And that was the end of everything in the history of literature.'

Why is it that anything exciting is even more exciting when it's told to us in our own language by someone who comes from far away and who's taken the trouble to visit us and learn our language? Who knows; but the truth is that his words inspired one of my most subversive ideas – and most epic too, probably. So if anyone wants to ascribe some heroic gesture to me, some magnificent deed, I suppose the most admirable thing I've ever done, in my opinion – and the most demented, in everyone else's opinion – was to create NTV: a television station that rejects the idea of television. *No Television.* Clicking to NTV with the remote control, dancing the channel-surfing waltz, meant finding a blank screen across which the most beloved stories and novels in the history of literature marched: letter by letter, word by word, sentence by sentence, from beginning to end. Yes, the idea was to watch television and read, to watch as if praying – by scrolling through classic pages – for the reconstruction of our lost communication with the gods. That was all. No sound or colour or special effects. Just a suddenly electrified book. It didn't last long, of course, but it was worth it.

I'm told that lots of people watched NTV while taking drugs or making love or just doing nothing and enjoying the rare privilege of feeling that they were doing *something*. All those people whose parents accused them – each time they saw them with a book in their hands – of 'wasting time', and made them go outside and move around, maybe worrying that the act of reading would diminish the flow of blood to the simple heart and increase it to the problematic brain.

And it's always the same, Keiko Kai: the people who talk most about television are the ones who say over and over again that they aren't interested in television, while those who watch most are the ones who talk about it least. For the former and the latter, for all of them: NTV.

And it didn't take long for the paranoid prophets to appear, swearing they'd detected subliminal pulses, hidden signals, and satanic messages between the lines. None of it was true, of course; but how to fight the seekers of new world order conspiracies, who – during the special marathon broadcast of *À la recherche du temps perdu*, at the point in *Le temps retrouvé* when Saint-Loup describes an air attack on Paris with 'aviators like Valkyries' who 'form a constellation' and 'make apocalypse' in the skies – believed they detected a subliminal, coded call from an Islamic group for the imminent bombardment of Buckingham Palace, or something like that.

These were, of course, the early days of the new millennium, when everything explodable exploded, and, due to the arrogance of the calendar, we started over again, became children again, and – as in Barrie's time, but for very different reasons – there was an explosive new boom in children's literature.

The targets to bomb were the proud possessors of happy childhood memories. They were so easy to spot: people who nothing bad had happened to back then, and who therefore remained partly stuck in those early years. People whose voices grow suddenly and naughtily high, who laugh like lunatics at any little thing, who can't resist the momentary urge to play an annoying practical joke, or who fall abruptly into a wilful and absurd silence. People who – surprise – found out on the news about a new advance in genetics intended to double our age, to fold it up in sections like chromosome origami. Nothing was definite yet, but they were already enjoying an unexpected boon that allowed them to kill time and slay impatience: the consumption, as adults, of phenomena intended for children. The loudly whispered secret, the subliminal message of every classic of children's literature, is nothing but the recuperation of the past as reward, whether it be in the skin of a beggar girl remembering her days as a princess, or in the armour of an old king on his last battlefield pining for his first nights as a naked prince.

These men and women – 'grown-ups' – wanted a return to childhood by any means possible. And they bought the 'adult' editions of Jim Yang by the thousands: black-and-white photographs on the jackets instead of colour illustrations; a pound and a half more expensive. Holes where they could bury their heads and their fears in the adventures of a time-travelling boy, and thus banish not the dread of night but the dread of the everyday.

Barrie was afraid of the dark, the dark that lived in his mother's bedroom, the dark that had swallowed up David and was surely after him now. Barrie writes in defiance of that dark, unceasingly, and at first with little success. Barrie buys more bottles of black ink but keeps wearing the same hat. Barrie thinks a hat is indispensable for favourably impressing his editor. His strategy doesn't work: the editor rejects his first fourteen articles and accepts the fifteenth, which is titled 'Better Dead' and begins with this sentence:

> *No one who has devoted a few minutes to the question can escape the conclusion and the conviction that there are a good number of our contemporaries about whom Something must be done.*

And Barrie goes on to list different types of people who deserve to pass on to a better life. Frederick Greenwood laughs when he reads it: he thinks the mix of sophisticated spite and immature fury is perfect for the pages of his *St James's Gazette*.

Barrie moves to a cheaper room on Greenville Street. 'No

bigger than a piano box,' he writes in his notebook as he lunches and dines 'more than satisfactorily' on four half-penny rolls that he spreads with the marmalade his mother sends him from Kirriemuir. For special occasions – when an article is accepted – Barrie allows himself the luxury of a baked potato bought at a street stand. At dusk, he often falls into a deep state of depression: he stands by the window for hours, counting the leaves of a tree – is David that small green ghost making faces at him from the highest branch? – until he reaches that perfect moment in which he forgets about himself, about 'my personality difficulties', and then only work, writing, and escape remain.

My most precious possession is the pleasure I experience upon sitting at my desk. I'm not sure when it was that I realized it. It wasn't early in my life; because the truth is that I was lazy at school and I read all the books that I wasn't supposed to read during high school. But I fell in love with the idea of hard work one perfect May morning . . . I found it waiting for me at a London train station and it accompanied me all the way back to Bloomsbury . . . Hard work, more than any woman in the world, is the best thing for a man,

Barrie would recall in a speech at the Author's Club of London, shortly before dying.

And I agree with him. I can't help but agree.

So Barrie writes to forget.

I do too, but I can't; it doesn't work: each page I write – in my first notebooks, the ones I'm burning now to keep us warm through the long night, Keiko Kai – only etches more deeply the thing I tried to deny for so many years and that now I'm trying to make disappear like a tattoo someone etched inside my head. Each of the places I never wanted to see again suddenly acquires the untouchable celebrity of a historic spot: the woods of Sad Songs; Neverland; the pool where my mother drowned; my father's recording studio; the open window of my room, Baco's room and mine, that becomes my room again when Baco dies . . . Everything reappears.

No one told me that memories could be so perfect, so clear. It isn't fair. Curse those who complain about their poor memory; they don't know how lucky they are.

Barrie, on the other hand, writes new memories, invented memories. Barrie writes so he doesn't have to live his life, writing himself a new life. Barrie writes without stopping. In 1891 he's already a regular contributor under his own name – the pen names Anon or Gavin Ogilvy are left behind forever – at the Empire's most prestigious publications, including W. E. Henley's influential *National Observer*, where his name appears beside those of Thomas Hardy, Rudyard Kipling, H. G. Wells and W. B. Yeats.

Barrie pays for the printing of a first novel. *Better Dead* takes its title and subject matter from one of his most famous articles: the satirical founding of a club devoted to the benevolent assassination of unpleasant famous people for the improvement of society. Barrie loses twenty-five pounds in the undertaking. Barrie runs to the publishing house and asks to be given the first copy as it comes hot off the presses. He touches it and smells it and strokes it like a small animal. And he puts it in his coat pocket and carries it with him for days, and every once in a while he takes it out and opens it, each time thinking that maybe the pages will be blank, that all trace of ink will have vanished as if by art of magic, as if by love of art. The novel isn't bad, but it's thought to be too sophisticated for the average reader, who's much more interested in the crimes of Jack the Ripper – in his bestial language, his recipes for the best preparation of prostitutes' livers and kidneys – than in Barrie's clever macabre tale.

One critic goes so far as to say that Barrie is obviously the pseudonym under which Bernard Shaw and Oscar Wilde have composed a joke à deux. Barrie is amused by this unintended compliment, but he also obeys its underlying imperative: Barrie decides that his next book will be written from the heart and not the head – there are already too many clever Englishmen in bookstores and libraries – and he decides to look back, retreat: literature as a time machine, and the Thrums of his childhood as his territory.

Never grow up, never grow up, never grow up ten times over.

Auld Licht Idylls (1888), *A Window in Thrums* (1889) and *The Little Minister* (1891) – books in which for the first time his irony and spite are fused with a deep sentimentalism – turn Barrie into a very successful writer and Kirriemuir into one of the first literary tourist destinations. People go and look and buy postcards signed by Barrie. The local residents aren't happy with the way Barrie portrays them and sometimes pokes fun at them, but soon they succumb to their new and unexpected fame: better to be famous for anything at all than to be nobody. And nobody is as famous as Barrie, who wastes no time publishing *When A Man's Single*, a semi-autobiographical short novel about the life of a journalist, in which the narrator exclaims: 'My God! . . . I would write an article, I think, on my mother's coffin.' Barrie isn't a man who writes: Barrie's a writing machine.

Soon afterwards, *The Little Minister* – about a short man tormented by his height – is dubbed 'a work of genius' on the first page of the *National Observer*, and in the United States four different publishers bring out pirate editions, making it an international bestseller. Robert Louis Stevenson reads *The Little Minister* in Samoa and writes to Henry James recommending that he read it ('You, Kipling, and now Barrie are my three muses') and to Barrie to congratulate him and offer him advice: 'The author shouldn't be like his books; he should be his books.' Barrie obeys, but it's an order he's already given himself long ago, an order he follows better and better until it becomes an automatic reflex, something as simple and unconscious as breathing deeply or dipping a pen into the inkwell.

Barrie is now a writer with writer friends. Barrie begins to correspond with Stevenson, and dines with Thomas Hardy and George Meredith. 'The most satisfactory thing in my little literary history is being able to say that the people I most admired as writers I can now also call my best friends,' he writes.

Barrie recruits Arthur Conan Doyle (who created Sherlock Holmes, the sceptic *in extremis*, as a perfect cover for his belief in fairies and spirits and messages from the Beyond and just about anything) and Jerome K. Jerome (the Victorian satirist of *Three Men in a Boat* and *Three Men on the Bummel*) for his own bizarre cricket team: the Allahakbarries, a playful corruption of the Arabic Allahakbar or 'Allah is great!' Barrie is the ideologist and the captain, and happy as he's never been. The best of both worlds: cricket among literary people dressed in white with straw hats, who smoke, laugh, shout and play like children on a lawn so green it's dazzling. Literary people who bring their children to the matches; and, oh, the pleasure of playing with other people's children, as an equal, without the distance that fatherhood and duty impose. Little Barrie, larger than life, runs with the children, who consider him one of them. Little Margaret Henley – who will die soon after she turns six from one of those grown-up childhood illnesses of the day – baptizes Barrie as 'My Friendy'; but Margaret can't pronounce the letter R (Barrie will be fascinated ever after by women with difficulties pronouncing it) and it comes out at first as 'My Fwendy' and then 'My Wendy,' and thus little Margaret invents a name that didn't yet exist: Wendy. A name that some years later – through the young heroine of *Peter Pan*, Wendy Moira Angela Darling – would become one of the most popular names for girls over and across and up and down England.

Little Barrie and little Margaret laugh until it hurts.

Little Barrie and little Margaret and Allah are great. I like the idea – it makes me happy – that Barrie becomes famous and then almost immediately he's able to have the childhood he never had, a childhood in which he's surrounded by lost boys: by adults who, at least for a few hours, are willing to play along with him in his efforts not to grow up.

I like to think, too, that my father, Sebastian 'Darjeeling' Compton-Lowe, and his band the Beaten a.k.a the Beaten Victorians a.k.a the Victorians were also lost boys, suspended in time and space.

Sixties rock as an isolation tank and a vehicle for travelling to other planets. The rockers as astronauts – and yes, several of them did die during takeoff, or drifting in perpetual orbit, or at the combustible moment of their return home, sinking into the ocean with their suits and capsules and visions.

The faces of the four musicians of the Beaten a.k.a the Beaten Victorians a.k.a the Victorians – despite the several years during which they occupied the comfortable place of pseudo-uncles in my life – have blurred for me, merging into a single person: long hair, pointy-collared shirts, electric suits (embroidered with little twinkling lights activated by a battery hidden in a pocket), Nehru jackets, glasses with coloured lenses.

The drill I imposed on myself with Prussian rigor soon after they all sank forever beneath the waters of their last trip did me little good, if any: remembering each feature, each gesture, in order to fix them in my absorbent young memory. At first it seemed to work, but within a year, the irreversible process of disappearance had already begun. Faces and bodies are made of water, and water evaporates quickly under the fierce, swift sun of time. Even my father's and mother's faces: yes, I remember them better, but they are always motionless, as if smiling from an album cover or out of the sound that rises from the album's circular grooves.

Not long ago I saw them again, unexpectedly, as I was flipping through a magazine at a Victoria Station newsstand. A rock magazine. Every once in a while I buy rock magazines. I like to read them; I like to find that I don't recognize anyone except the people I knew during my childhood. I like to see the wrinkled pictures of Bob 'Forever Young' Dylan and Paul 'When I'm Sixty-Four' McCartney and Pete 'My Generation' Townshend and Mick 'Time Is On My Side' Jagger; pictures of old people more or less surprised to be old and clinging to their electric guitars like canes. I like to see that I don't know anything; it amuses me to think that all those profound theories about something so superficial are important and worthwhile to someone; it comforts me to think that fashions change but that people are still young in the same way. All those strange styles and onomatopoeic names. All those high-flown and elaborate declarations in the mouths of such well-educated idiots. All those analyses of what happened in the 60s as if it were the foundation stone of the present. All those mixed ethnicities and all those blood feuds and the paradox that revolutionary rock is one of the most racist domains in the universe. All those discographies and links and rankings and all that reflexive and automatic need to generate surveys so that young people can vote on their own very recent past, and in which the winner in the category of all-time best album is always a record that's at most five years old. The whole big business resting on the idea that anything new is better than anything less new, and that the classic will always be more modern than any of-the-moment avant-garde. All those new Beatles and new Dylans. Nowhere does one age faster or achieve immortality sooner than in rock.

This month's *Mojo* was dedicated to the 'Cult Heroes' of rock and pop. An elegant euphemism for paying tribute to formerly beautiful losers who now, thanks to the revisionist snobbery of addicts of all forms of consumerism, have been rescued by a new generation inclined to hate their contemporaries and love those who died before they were born. Ghosts they're resuscitating now, digitally and in new editions, with the addition of bonus tracks and demos and booklets.

And what would my father, such a conservative and pop-centric citizen, say about the compact disc format, about the sudden sprawling laser summation of his life and work?

Now that I think about it, my father never would have liked those little disks of metallicized plastic. He always defended the dual psychotic order of Side A and Side B, and besides, he loved to calculate the exact points on a spinning record where one song began and another ended. He'd blindfold himself with a fuchsia or paisley handkerchief, and taking aim at the brief seconds of faintly crackling silence – between 'Pledging My Time' and 'Visions of Johanna,' between 'End of the Season' and 'Waterloo Sunset' – he let the needle fall like a knife thrower who needs a steady pulse and perfect aim to hit his moving target. Neither end nor beginning – the careless noise that made you grit your teeth because of a shaky or unsure hand – but the exact spot; limbo, the nothing that follows and precedes everything. My father would have hated those songs strung one after the other on the last stretch of *Abbey Road* and all the sounds of alarm clocks and telephones and conversations linking Pink Floyd tracks. Once, I think, my father told me it wouldn't be a bad idea to make an album that switched the order of the components: thin seconds of music between thick bands of silence and vinyl. My father, the cult hero . . .

The main pieces in this edition of *Mojo* were dedicated to the Velvet Underground (on the cover), the La's, Big Star, Fred Neil, and someone called Jonathan Richman, who for some reason was labelled a 'pop Peter Pan'. All through *Mojo*, many other cult heroes appeared, synthesized and in the guise of a failed chorus line: the Action, the Pastels, the Short Stories, the Fugs, the Only Ones, the Godz, the Saints, the Replacements, the Pop Group, the Poets, the Soft Boys, the Creations, the Left Banke, the United States of America, the Los Evitas, the Danzig Oskars, the Rampant Barons, the Sea Monkeys, the Blind Cartographers, and, yes, the Beaten a.k.a the Beaten Victorians a.k.a the Victorians. A handful of lines for each and no fighting: there's room for everyone.

I felt a strange mixture of pity and shame: culthood is only interesting and noble when one doesn't have a personal relationship to it. Culthood, up close, is just another of the many ways to say *failure.*

My father wasn't a hero; and if there's anything more terrible than not being a hero, it's wanting to be a hero and not succeeding. Although maybe my father's heroism – and, by resigned extension, my mother's – has less to do with what they wanted to achieve than with what they ended up being. He and She as their own most perfect and accomplished creations: an epic of failure doomed from the start by the dictums and slogans of a decade that required absolutely everything to change (even the things that were fine) in order for anyone to be truly revolutionary, only for them to discover in the end that they'd become nothing but confused children with unrecognizable pieces of supposedly immortal toys. Yes, yes, yes: *Cult Heroes.*

In the magazine, each of the encyclopedia-style entries was itself subdivided into three parts headed *The Band, The Music, Where They Are Now* and *Trivia.*

I bought the magazine and got on the first train to anywhere (I often do that, get on a train as it's pulling out without looking to see where it's going, letting it take me wherever it wants) and I sat down to read what it said under a photograph (one I had never seen before) of my father and his friends dressed as bobbies patrolling fog-shrouded streets.

I read:

> *The Band*: the Beaten a.k.a the Beaten Victorians a.k.a the Victorians was formed in 1962 by the aristocrat Sebastian 'Darjeeling' Compton-Lowe (rhythm guitar and voice) with several classmates at the prestigious public school Charterhouse, where he was sent by his father, Lord Cecil Compton-Lowe, to 'build character'. The other members of the band – signed by the record label Decca after one of its executives, Dick Rowe, missed the chance to sign the Beatles – were the American Tex 'Tax' Dudley-Smith (lead guitar), the French Charles-Charles Mantreaux Chevieux

(bass) and the Italian Dino Di Nodi (drums), with fleeting, never entirely confirmed appearances – according to the acknowledgments of *Armaggedon Tea Time* (1965) – of Bob Dylan 'on harmonica and puking'. Sometimes Alexandra Swinton-Menzies joined the line-up. Well-known in certain social and aristocratic circles, she was also considered one of the most brilliant students ever to attend RADA and the Royal College of Art, but she dropped everything to become Compton-Lowe's wife and to sing back-up on the choruses of some songs. Alexandra Swinton-Menzies had some success with her recording of the single 'You're Not Mine (I'm Not Yours)', with 'Brigadoon Girl' on its Side B. The first of these songs – supposedly written by Bob Dylan, though it was never confirmed – is an off-beat, mischievous response to Sonny and Cher's 'I've Got You'. 'You're Not Mine (I'm Not Yours)' became unexpectedly popular a few years ago when it was rescued to be used in a commercial for a famous brand of running shoes.

The Music: Hard to pinpoint, since their style mutated as the band changed names and Compton-Lowe changed . . . moods. Many call the international hit 'You Really Hate Me' the foundational riff of heavy rock, and a good part of the Beaten's first album – *Royal Noise* (1964) – is constructed around variations on this simple but unforgettable song, which was so often imitated. By 1965, the Beaten were calling themselves the Beaten Victorians and releasing what's considered their 'transition' album: *Streets and Forests*, also known as *Armaggedon Tea Time*, a title that was rejected by the studio at the time but recovered for the 1987 Rhino rerelease. One side of the album is electric and urban (*Streets*), and the other is acoustic and rural (*Forests*), with the band singing alternately about the decadent pleasures of Swinging London ('Why Don't We Do It in the Tube?') and the melancholy pleasures of a walk along the Thames on the edge of the great city ('Up in Trees, Down by the

Water, Here With You Naked, If You Like It, Please'), and it ends with a kind of retro existential battle hymn telling the story of a psychotic devoted follower of the fashions of the times ('Dr Mono and Mr Quadraphonic'). It's around this time – supposedly as the result of a long, rocky LSD trip – that Compton-Lowe metamorphoses his band once again, which now calls itself simply the Victorians, and embraces themes and styles intended to denounce all attempts at 'Beatle hypnosis' while at the same time rescuing, in various unforgettable songs, 'the many time-honoured values we've come to cherish: like cucumber sandwiches at teatime, punctuality and preserving the hymens of the girls of the British Empire until their wedding night'. Compton-Lowe also undergoes a radical personality change, refusing to play live again until he can perform a 'show with fireworks and lit-up fountains' at Buckingham Palace, especially conceived for the Queen's name day. The singles from this era – later posthumously collected in *Small Victories and Big Defeats Enjoyed and Suffered by The Victorians* (1969), like 'Me and the Queen', 'Tate Gallery Raga', 'Bloomsbury In Bloom', 'Acoustic, Not Electric', 'King and Country Revisited', 'Blood, Sweat, Tears and Some More Sweat', 'We'll Meet Again (But I Lost the Address)', 'Who Needs You, Buddha?' and the unintentionally hilarious 'Imperial Forever', a fervent homage to the Canadians who rejected the New World's drive for independence and decided to remain swaddled in the protection and love of the English Crown. The conservatism of the songs sparked a certain critical curiosity, but alienated the larger public, which in those days waited for each new Beatles song as if it was the word of God, or the gods, and which, as a result, preferred experimentation to the defence of traditional values. Compton-Lowe then took his nearly demented – but very funny – hatred of the Beatles even further (the novelty songs 'Beating the Beetle' and, on the B side of the same single, 'Reading the Real News Today' were launched as 'battle hymns', according to Compton-Lowe). The next development is surprising, or not so surprising: the Victorians, convinced that the only way to defeat their 'archenemy' is to do it on their own turf, become a kind of Beatles Part Two, intent on anticipating the Liverpool quartet's every move. This creates some tension in the band, which is already on edge because of Compton-Lowe's increasingly arbitrary outbursts. (Dino Di Nodi leaves and is replaced by the encyclopedic Indian percussionist Battiatavasa 'Bombay' Siciliajun), and the Victorians shut themselves up at the end of 1967 in marathon sessions at the family estate, Sad Songs, where – inspired by the recent death of his youngest son – Lowe devotes himself to the creation of what many believed would be his unsurpassable magnum opus: *Lost Boy Baco's Broken Hearted Requiem & Lysergic Funeral Parlor, Inc.* For its 'construction', Compton-Lowe gathers an impressive number of talents and bon vivants (one of many accounts of the unfinished recording of the album can be read in *Ten Parties That Shook the World*, by Max Glass), among whom were Andy Warhol, Diana Rigg, Jimmy Page, Julie Christie, a very young David Bowie, Stanley Kubrick, Hugh Hefner, Princess Margaret and Truman Capote. Nothing recorded there has ever come to light, but rumours and legends abound as to the dozens of hours of tapes which – according to Greil Marcus – 'could forever change the way we've heard the 60s up until now'.

Where They Are Now: At the bottom of the sea.

Trivia: Sebastian 'Darjeeling' Compton-Lowe ordered his label to eliminate the voices and record just the music on ten copies of *Streets and Forests*, creating a purely instrumental version. The idea was that the ten fans who bought these albums – without realizing that their copies were 'different' – would get in touch with the Victorians by calling a telephone number that appeared on the inside sleeve and be awarded the 'prize', which would consist of the Victorians going to their houses to sing them the whole record karaoke-style. Nothing was heard, nor has anything ever been heard, about anyone claiming the reward, which surely depressed the author of 'Wrong Number, Again'. Sebastian 'Darjeeling' Compton-Lowe and Alexandra Swinton-Menzies were the parents of the popular author and creator of children's hero Jim Yang who publishes his books under the pseudonym Peter Hook (not to be confused with the band member of the same name, member of Joy Division, New Order, Revenge and Monaco) and . . .

I closed the magazine and closed my eyes – nothing interests me less than myself – and got off at the next station and returned to London, continuing on to Sad Songs and Neverland. I went down to my father's old recording studio with a bottle of whisky. A few glasses of single malt make you incredibly brave. I chose some boxes of tapes I'd never heard and – this time I really did it – I put them on the old player. I heard my father's voice saying something incomprehensible, and then I heard a child's voice. I was terrified thinking it might be my little brother Baco's voice, that he had suddenly materialized to play a part in that pop bacchanalia. But it wasn't: it was my voice. My little voice announcing that I was going to sing a song I had written called 'Sewing Your Shadow (Peter Pan's Blues)'. My voice singing it was the clear and terrible voice of childhood, the voice that at some point dies and is lost forever.

It wasn't a bad song, Keiko Kai, if I do say so myself. If you want I'll go down to the basement and find it, and I'll let you listen to it and you can tell me what you think. The funny thing is that I don't remember writing it at all, much less singing it in front of a microphone.

I must have been under the influence of drugs.

*

My childhood was a strange childhood, too, like Barrie's. As I've already said: nineteenth-century novels and Emma Peel's black-leather-clad body. But stranger visions, too: trips, moves, midnight Hammer Film movies with muscular-chested vampire women, the embalming of my first pets (somewhere I read that this is one of the clearest early signs of future serial killers), a sudden interest in my chemistry set and in explosions, visits to galleries like the Arts Laboratory, where a friend of my parents was showing an atrocious array of wrecked cars.

It's an excellent era to die in a car accident, and suddenly every young Briton seems to have learned to drive following the Marcello method from *La Dolce Vita*, which leads to a brutal Romanization of London traffic, until then so very different, so phlegmatic and polite.

On a stormy night on the way to Nice, Françoise Dorléac – sister of Catherine Deneuve – goes off the road; her car crashes and burns and its driver is killed instantly. Tara Browne – son of Lord Aranmore and Browne and the beer heiress Oonagh Guinness; permanent resident of the Ritz; boyfriend of the model Suki Poitier – is killed in his Lotus Elan when he hits a vehicle parked in Redcliffe Gardens, Chelsea, and is instantly immortalized by the Beatles in 'A Day in the Life': 'He blew his mind out in a car, he didn't notice that the lights had changed. A crowd of people stood and stared; they'd seen his face before; nobody was really sure if he was from the House of Lords . . .'

Keiko Kai: one night I dreamed I was Tara Browne's blue Lotus Elan, and yes, it seemed as good a way as any of observing Swinging London in the 60s and fixing it in my mind: a crowd – middle and lower class, smelling of fish and chips – watching an accident, squinting, mouths open; a car with rigor mortis, its colour that unique and indefinable colour cars turn when they crash, no matter what colour they were before. A crowd asking itself where it's seen that face or those legs before, and where that orange suit must be from, or that tie with the design and colours of the English flag, equally patriotic and disrespectful.

Life and death in Swinging London in the 60s as two complementary and adjacent exhibitions you get into for the price of one, and where you're bombarded non-stop with the flashing lights of cameras and discotheques and parties, to which one always arrives in a small, fast car – with literally autodestructive intentions, of course. Cars that were made to be crashed. Name-brand cars – Triumph Spitfire, Alfa Romeo, Mark II Zodiac, Mini, Roller, Rolls, Jaguar E-Type, Chitty-Chitty Bang-Bang and 007 Martin-Aston Martin – which, after their collisions with anything, with whatever's put in front of them, don't leave many marks on their dead drivers, offering them up with hardly a scratch, ready for display. The twisted metal and Marcus Merlin's metal mouthwork (Marcus Merlin, who always manages to emerge mysteriously unscathed from the bowels of cars that even their makers wouldn't recognize) and the metal of the metallic miniskirts of the drugged girls who hug the tires with eyes closed, the red points of their tongues between apple green lips. The 60s were a metallic age, a steel age following the iron and bronze ages.

Sometimes my grandparents – my mother's parents – imposed some normality on my life back then; but it was a strange kind of normality, a Madame Tussaud wax imitation. I remember them as museum pieces, their past unfolding in a kind of constant and unchanging present.

There they are:

My grandparents see me as a pet, albeit a dangerous pet. My grandparents – although they were perfectly aware of their daughter and son-in-law's deaths – kept forgetting that Baco had died and never stopped reminding me to watch out for my little brother, telling me I should learn from him because 'you never hear a peep out of him, he's quite the little gentleman'. Sometimes they think I'm Baco and they ask me about myself, and I prefer to play along with them: 'I'm sure he's doing something he shouldn't be,' I reply. It's beginning to annoy me that a symptom of both my grandparents' senility and my mother's dementia is a Baco returned from the dead.

In the middle of my grandparents' land there's a pond and a little island and I hide there – like Peter Pan on his Marooners' Rock – and make powerful explosives and promise never to return to solid ground, and it rains as if it'll never stop raining.

At dusk, Dermott comes out to find me with an umbrella and towels. My perfect portable butler, the best inheritance from my parents: a cancer is rapidly eating away at him and soon the moment will come when he leaves for the lost cemetery of butlers. Dermott knows it, but he hasn't said anything. He doesn't want me to feel sorry for him, because the secret work of butlers is to feel sorry for their masters and say 'How very interesting' each time they come up with one of their incredibly idiotic notions.

And I'm the perfect testing ground, the ideal opportunity for Dermott to become the secret king of butlers. I inspire – I demand – more pity than anyone; I'm a powerful factory of the interesting. I smile in the flashes of lightning and watch the formidable explosion of my first bomb from the bank, like Oppenheimer, like Shiva the Destroyer of Worlds.

The island seems to quiver and seriously consider sinking; back then, I'm sure, Barrie would have loved to know me. At the time I was the perfect incarnation of what a boy should be, according to Barrie: free of scruples, ungrateful, a liar, intelligent and destructive. Someone 'gay and innocent and heartless', as he wrote in the last line of *Peter and Wendy*. A little monster. An amoral hero.

Like Barrie.

Like Peter Pan.

Like me.

My grandparents come to the window to watch the island burn, with champagne glasses trembling in their hands. I'm sure they think it's another bombing by the Luftwaffe. The war hasn't ended; wars never end for those who live through them. Dermott calls the firemen and I tell my grandfather I can't find Baco, I'm afraid he's been killed in the bombing of the little island. It's a joke; a bad joke, but a joke. My grandmother faints when a convoy of tanker trucks arrives and crushes several beds of her prize-winning roses. My grandfather calls his lawyer and Marcus Merlin and asks them to bring the papers to settle the matter of my guardianship as soon as possible. It will be several months before Marcus Merlin comes of age, but there's a judge who owes Marcus Merlin a favour. I hear from behind a door that Marcus Merlin was always my parents' first choice 'if anything should happen to us', but that my grandparents had refused to accept it and filed an appeal because they considered Marcus Merlin an 'unhealthy presence'. Now they've given up, and they realize it's really me who's the unhealthy presence for them: so the will of Lady Alexandra Swinton-Menzies & Sebastian 'Darjeeling' Compton-Lowe is done.

Marcus Merlin comes to get me one fall morning. It hasn't begun to be cold yet, but the air is golden like the gold of old photographs. Marcus Merlin puts a hand on my shoulder. It isn't the first time I've seen him, of course. I've known him for two or three years – almost a lifetime on a child's calendar – but it's as if I'm seeing him for the first time, separate, alone, out of the motley context of parties and funerals. It was Marcus Merlin who came for me when I ran away to Brighton by the Sea, and Marcus Merlin was there at Baco's burial, and at the service for my parents' missing bodies, and later at the funeral for my mother; but now it's different. Now Marcus Merlin is my guardian. Or maybe I've become Marcus Merlin's guardian. We're a new race of two.

Marcus Merlin looks steadily at me and doesn't say anything. 'My father and my mother and my little brother are dead', I tell him. I don't know why I say this. Marcus Merlin is perfectly aware of the disappearance of my father, mother and little brother; but the words rise to my lips as if I'm spitting them out after feeling them stuck in some part of my throat for too long, as if they're one of those balls of feathers and hairs that every so often even the most phlegmatic of cats cough up.

Says Marcus Merlin: 'Of course.'

And what he says is even stranger than what I say; but there's something rare and precious in that 'Of course.' There's more comfort and affection in his assent than in the hundreds of kisses and hugs I've been getting since the beginning of the end of my family.

Marcus Merlin carries my suitcase to his new Jaguar, explaining to me that later a moving truck will come to get the rest of my things, and we waste no time returning to Neverland, like lords and masters setting out for the reconquest of our ancestral home.

The house has been closed for months. We enter almost like thieves, or savages. We run down empty passageways, uncover furniture shrouded in sheets, open the windows and – Marcus Merlin considers it appropriate – throw a big party.

Says Marcus Merlin: 'Like the good old times last year.' And he smiles.

Weeks later, my maternal grandparents die almost unawares, in their sleep, together, symmetrical, and happy, I suppose, not to realize that their long sleep is simply what follows the brief yawn of dying.

My other grandparents – my paternal grandparents, who never really became grandparents and were hardly even parents – had died many years before, in the Blitz. A pair of V-2 bombs fell on a horse show they refused to leave, disregarding the alarm bells warning of the arrival of flying squadrons over their house on the Thames, just outside of London. I suppose my proto-grandparents wouldn't have been out of place on any of the pages of Edith Sitwell's *English Eccentrics*. Their portraits, painted in the manner of John Singer Sargent by one of his disciples and hanging in a corridor of Neverland at Sad Songs show them to be a couple with fierce, amused expressions. My father was very small when they died and he used to refer to them as 'the ones who went on holiday and luckily forgot to bring me along'. And maybe having lost them as a child unbalanced my father's existential metabolism forever, since afterwards, in the 60s, he was unable to rebel against his elders, and decided to battle his dissolute contemporaries and die – as idiotically as his progenitors – in the name of the establishment of a neo-Victorianism in which the cricket of immaculate uniforms would ultimately be imposed on the muddy vulgarity of football and rugby.

I suppose my mother's parents feared a similar end. Past a certain point, all grandparents merge into a single and indivisible grandparent; it's in old age that all superstitions are finally proved true, fearsome, efficient; and my crazy dynamiter stage ultimately threw them off balance and destroyed their already fragile health.

'Time to go back to Neverland,' I say then to Dermott. And Dermott obeys and the sky fills with new stars, fireworks, real diamonds.

Dear Keiko Kai: those were the first seconds of 1 January 1970; the Beatles had already climbed up on the roof of Apple Corps looking for shelter and desperately singing 'Get Back'; the Blue Meanies were running down mountainsides to ravage Pepperland; and I – still a brand-new orphan, innocent, gay and heartless – watched my first end of the world. The end of the world my dead father had proclaimed so many times, an end of the world that didn't turn out to be the clangorous nightfall of the kind of apocalypse that appears in books about wizards and princes with unpronounceable names, who draw swords and brandish magic staffs to save kingdoms with even more unpronounceable names.

My father had wished for a shadow approaching from the horizon and annihilating everything in its path. A grand finale. That much at least, please.

Now, however, there was nothing but the elegant subtlety

of a snake pausing, changing skins and immediately slithering on. The old skin, once glossy, was shed like a grey, ashy husk, like old, out-dated clothes, and suddenly, down below, the new decade appeared naked and damp, a decade of wide lapels and open-necked shirts and bell-bottomed trousers and hideous music, and with it, as I've already said, the first end of the world in my short but too-long life.

The Walker

Will I ever walk in Kensington Gardens again?

Who knows. I don't think so. I don't care.

Keiko Kai: I don't need to go back to Kensington Gardens to *go back* to Kensington Gardens. I know the place by heart, though I don't know it like the back of my hand. I never understood that phrase: is there anyone who really *knows* the back of his hand?

I know Kensington Gardens, yes, as the spot to which my feet so often took me. The Serpentine, the Baby's Palace, the Round Pond, Bunting's Thumb, St Govor's Well, the Dog's Cemetery, Queen Mab's Palace, the Baby's Walk, the Fairies' Basin, the Big Penny, Chewlett's Street, the Figs: names of places – some of them made up by Barrie – inside a real place.

The scene of the crime, the scene of my life's work, the map of the desert island where my Oriental treasure lies. Back and forth through history, pedalling like Jim Yang, coming and going and returning again to a place that changes not at all with the passage of the years or – maybe more important – the ages.

I'm thinking about Time, that ultimate abstraction. Time as the paradox of a cruel God invented by men, in whose divinity men nevertheless believe from the beginning to the end of their days. A God who strikes men down without even believing in them, simply obeying the rules he must follow. A God whose disregard of Kensington Gardens has preserved it almost intact. Scorn the new refreshment stands and the Memorial Playground commemorating the unbearable martyr Lady Di a.k.a Princess of Hearts a.k.a Diana of Wales a.k.a *Cinderella Part 2: The Unhappy Ending*. Enjoy, instead, its green and leafy molecular structure simply for the pleasure of feeling how the children who play there grow up, get old, come back a last time to say goodbye. Time passes but Kensington Gardens remains, Keiko Kai.

So Barrie, my father, and I stroll the same place, linked forever in a continuum where Victorians, rockers and millenarians can commune under the same sun, reciting 'It was the best of times, it was the worst of times, it was the age of wisdom, it was the age of foolishness, it was the epoch of belief, it was the epoch of incredulity, it was the season of Light, it was the season of Darkness, it was the spring of hope, it was the winter of despair, we had everything before us, we had nothing before us, we were all going direct to Heaven, we were all going direct the other way . . .'

Whatever the moment, then, we're all lost boys now and forever; boys who can only find themselves on the winding paths of Kensington Gardens.

Let's go.

My father pulls me by the hand through Knightsbridge, and we pass the Albert Hall. 'Now they know how many bloody holes it takes to bloody fill the bloody Albert Hall,' mutters my father, grimacing; and he adds: 'You'll never hear me say *fuckin'* like all those idiot depatriated musicians who were born in Chelsea or Fitzrovia and now pretend they're black and sing the blues. Disgusting.' And we enter Kensington Gardens, and I'm seven or eight years old, and I've never been one of those typical park and playground children. I'd rather stay home, reading. Baco liked fresh air and jumping and rolling in the grass, but I don't. And now there's no more Baco. Baco's been adopted as a kind of post mortem pop mascot by the Victorians – or whatever my father's band is called this week – and he's used like a kind of antenna for receiving messages from other dimensions. And my father and I walk aimlessly in circles, and I'm fascinated by the idea that we've gotten lost in the middle of London and suddenly my father tells me to bare my head – though I'm not wearing a hat or cap – in front of the statue of Queen Victoria next to Kensington Palace, and at last we come to the banks of a lake that's called the Serpentine and separates Kensington Gardens from Hyde Park, next to a monument, a kind of outcropping, crowned by a kind of boy playing a kind of flute.

'Don't move until I come back. Or until Cat comes to get you,' my father says.

Cat doesn't come.

Cat's real name is Steven Demetri Georgiou and he's the son of the owner of a popular West End restaurant, the Moulin Rouge. His father is a Cypriot Greek and his mother is Swedish and Cat's young and he likes music and my father has adopted him as a kind of protegé. Cat likes to write songs. He has one about his crazy love for his dog and another about his desperate need to buy a gun. They're good songs, but Steven Demetri Georgiou is a bad name and my father says, commands, renames him: 'From now on you'll be Cat Stevens.' My father gives him that name because Steven Demetri Georgiou has a Mickey Mouse face and if there's anything my father likes it's contradictions. And that's more or less all, I guess. Cat – soon after my father dies – starts to be famous, much more famous than my father ever was. Cat Stevens records 'Matthew and Son' and 'Here Comes My Baby' and when they ask him where he got his name, he answers without hesitating that he came up with it himself, thus stealing a few lines from *Mojo*'s entry about my father, the cult hero. And maybe poetic justice or a curse from above has something to do with the fact that soon Cat Stevens gets tuberculosis (a few times I saw him cough up blood, but since I was used to Bob Dylan's vomiting, it didn't seem particularly disturbing) and he vanishes for a while and comes back as an international star followed by moonshadows and riding peace trains with fathers and sons through wild worlds. Then Cat changes his name again and disappears after almost drowning in Malibu and says he's been saved by the divine will of Allah; now Cat is Yusuf Islam and he hates Salman

Rushdie, and, just as before, he has no time to waste going to look for his mentor's son in Kensington Gardens.

Now and then, I'm alone in Kensington Gardens.

Suddenly it's dark by the statue, which so many years later I'll approach on my knees, leaving my heartfelt and fragile offering – my small, sparkling dead – at its feet. Or maybe this is all the product of my imagination, or the imagination of the product of having written so many made-up things for so many years. Maybe the stories I made up aren't the memories of Jim Yang, but of Cagliostro Nostradamus Smith.

Maybe – unlike Barrie – I didn't return over and over again to Kensington Gardens.

The night of 30 April 1912, Barrie erects the statue of Peter Pan beside which, in 1968, I await my father's dubious return. Barrie's idea was that the statue would be a surprise for the children of London, and it was a strange idea from the start. The controversy reached the House of Commons, where it was asked whether there wasn't 'something improper' about an author using public pathways to advertise his work, barely concealing his intent beneath the subterfuge of a supposedly noble donation to the city's supposedly artistic heritage.

Barrie doesn't really like the statue – the work of Sir George Frampton – but it's done, and that's that. The House of Commons comes to the same conclusion, and somehow it's admitted that Kensington Gardens – although it existed long before Barrie's arrival; it opened to the public in 1841 – now owes much of its fame to the books of the tiny Scotsman, who's made it his favourite place to walk ever since he came to London.

And I remember – when the first Jim Yang book, *Jim Yang and the Extremely Formidable Bicycle*, was such a success – that someone decided it would be a good idea to photograph me next to the statue of Peter Pan and thus link the past and the present of British children's literature, and . . .

I said yes, and I regretted it as soon as I arrived: nausea, dizziness, and again the feeling that night was dropping over me like a heavy veil, though everything was happening at noon on a fiercely bright day. I could swear the statue moved, but who has any interest in hearing me swear to something like that? I said I was sorry and hurried away. Days later a photograph was published in which you see me from behind, fleeing. And that, I suppose, was the beginning of the legend of the elusive, mysterious creator of Jim Yang. And I didn't even turn to see whether the yellow ghost of Baco was still hopping nearby, or smiling, just at me, from the exact spot where Peter Pan smiles at all the children who smile at his feet.

Barrie's legend hasn't yet been established at the time Barrie discovers Kensington Gardens. Barrie remains an unknown, an author of some renown, but still far from becoming a living classic, a proper noun and a name everyone knows, an exceedingly recognizable registered trademark. There's no statue of Peter Pan beside the Serpentine yet, because there is no *Peter Pan*; there aren't any tour guides telling how to get here and where to get off the underground, or that require a whole chapter to outline the points of interest in Barrie's London and locate them on the map.

Barrie doesn't have what he needs either.

Barrie needs to be a few inches taller. There are nights when he dreams he's five and a half feet tall – there are even better nights when he dreams he's six feet tall – and he's walking through a new London in which his gaze sweeps above hats and sunshades and his shoes seem incredibly far below, lost in the kind of fog that drifts at the bottom of ravines.

How to overcome it? What to do? Many years later, Barrie writes a letter to a friend's wife:

Six feet three inches . . . If I had really grown to this it would have made a great difference in my life. I would not have bothered turning out reels of printed matter. My one aim would have been to become a favourite of the ladies which between you and me has always been my sorrowful ambition. The things I could have said to them if my legs had been longer. I read this with a bitter sigh . . .

The ladies whose favourite Barrie wants to be are, for the most part, actresses. Barrie spends all the free time he has at the theatre. Barrie goes to the theatre to see actresses. Thus, his life swings like a pendulum between the fantasies he writes and the fantasies he watches from his seat. Why this fascination with the theatre? Why is Barrie the last to get up and leave the hall? I suspect the answer is as simple as it is strange: in your seat, sitting in the dark, no one can tell whether you're tall or short. And there, in the theatre, reality seems suspended, as it is in a doll's house or a haunted house. The theatre's the closest thing to playing that adults find acceptable; and, maybe most important, the actresses are like girls pretending to be women by putting on fancy dresses that aren't theirs.

Barrie falls in love with actresses, and his form of courtship is based on the cleverest of lovers' games: Barrie writes them plays. Plays are much better than flowers (though he also sends bouquets as lush as jungles), and they're the only strategy he has for feeling powerful beyond the coordinates of his body, over and above taller men.

The first theatre piece Barrie writes is called *Caught Napping,* in honour of Minnie Palmer, to whom he's too nervous to speak a word when they're introduced in her dressing room. The actress rejects the work and its author.

In 1891, Barrie collaborates with Marriot Watson on *Richard Savage* because he's fascinated by the ingénue Phyllis Broughton.

With *Ibsen's Ghost*, a parody of *Hedda Gabler* – Toole's Theatre, 30 May 1891 – Barrie achieves his first critical success, the grateful coquetry of Irene Vanbrugh, and little else.

Again in the third person, as if describing a character, Barrie writes in his notebook upon returning from the opening night:

Perhaps the curse of his life that he never 'had a woman'.

Walker, London – Toole's Theatre, 30 May 1892, as *The Professor's Love Story* opens in New York – is a new bouquet for Irene Vanbrugh, but for this farce about an impostor who passes himself off as a rich man, the script demands the services of a second actress.

The director-actor J. L. Toole offers the role to a member of the company. Barrie isn't convinced, and asks his friend Jerome K. Jerome if he knows any 'pretty young girl who likes to flirt, and is, if possible, a great talent'. Jerome introduces him to the beautiful and headstrong Mary Ansell.

I have a picture of her here, Keiko Kai: a classic face framed by a fur collar; and why is it that all the women in these old photographs seem to have disappeared, why aren't there faces like this any more, faces so obviously of another age. Mary Ansell manages her own acting company and she's free between two productions. Barrie, carried away by enthusiasm and without consulting Toole, offers her the role and a salary higher than the leading actress's, although – a small hitch, Barrie's forgiving – Mary Ansell is very far from being a great talent. Toole and Vanbrugh are angry, but Barrie is adamant. Mary Ansell is smaller and shorter than he is: Mary Ansell may not be brilliant, but she's perfect.

Walker, London is a success. The critics take no notice of Mary Ansell, but they do point to Barrie as an odd, admirable specimen: a writer able to succeed in the theatre as well as in journalism. On opening night, the public applauds until their hands sting, calling for the author. Barrie won't take a bow. He doesn't like to appear on stage at the end of his plays. He didn't like doing it after *Richard Savage*, his play written in collaboration with H. B. Marriott Watson. His admirers propose theories: is he shy, or, like some gods, does Barrie prefer not to show himself so as to be everywhere at once? The explanation has the elegant simplicity of the best mysteries: Marriott Watson was twice as tall as Barrie, and Barrie didn't relish bowing beside his imposing friend.

So he isn't seen, but his presence is felt. The residents of London read Barrie in the paper, where he muses on the character of children in articles like 'Peterkin: A Marvel of Nature' (inspired by his little nephew, Charlie Barrie, a first and distant incarnation of Peter Pan); they attend plays like *The Professor's Love Story*; they buy novels like *My Lady Nicotine* (which extols the pleasures of smoking in Kensington Gardens); and at night they go looking for laughs at light, giddy comedies that reveal, perhaps unconsciously, the nature of the century about to come: unpredictable women, tormented men, the frightening fleetness of sentiments, the ever sharper curves of the road winding along the edge of a cliff where blue and green waves as tall as mountains roar in an immense ocean like a desert.

Barrie begins taking notes for a novel tentatively titled *The Sentimentalist*, a book that will end up being two bizarre crypto-autobiographies scarcely disguised by the mask of fiction and intended to 'contain what ordinary biographies omit'.

I know writers who don't like to read writers' memoirs. It's anyone's guess why not, a mystery. I love it that they write them. And I love to read them. One I remember reading was that other strange crypto-autobiography, by Jack London – the polar opposite of Barrie as a writer and a man – called *Martin Eden*. I remember the strange, unfamiliar happiness it produced in me, a book that even – in a meta-fictional sense, in a meta-realistic sense – risked foretelling the death of the author by having his character and hero commit suicide. But what moved me most and still moves me about *Martin Eden* was and is the idea that a man of adventure could and can also be a writer, the certainty that a writer can and could also be a man of adventure. There were those dazzling paragraphs on the discovery of reading and writing; those pages in which a noble savage discovers new worlds within the new world of books; and I wonder whether there's anything more exciting than a book telling the story of the moment when its author first tells a story.

Sentimental Tommy (1896) and *Tommy and Grizel* (1900) have as their hero a writer, Tommy Sandys, 'who travels between dreams and reality as if through tissue paper', who 'possesses the ability to put himself in others' shoes and wear them until they're his', and who is, of course, 'someone short of stature'. For Tommy, the idea and the practice of sentimentalism signifies a form of constant escape from the responsibilities and demands of the adult world. Sentimentalism as the perfect alibi. Tommy decides not to grow up. Grizel, his friend from childhood, becomes a woman, though. Their relationship is destined to collapse and leave only emotional ruins, doors that lead to rooms without walls and the devouring mouth of a dark forest. Once again, Barrie finds a kind of disturbing consolation in writing about himself – and about his relationship with Mary Ansell – as if he were someone else, a man very like himself, but who turns into someone more bearable, comprehensible, and heroic in the third person singular.

Notes:

– The girl when won't do what he tells her to do (knowing it wrong – he treating her like child) lies on floor with head on chair, twisting about in woe . . . She makes him say he is her slave – then impulsively cries it is she who is his – she wants him to say he is because she knows he isn't. 'I shd hate you really to be my slave – oh, say again that you are!'

– The sentimentalist wants the girl to love him, yet doesn't want to marry her.

Mary Ansell does want to marry Barrie.

Barrie is an excellent match for an ordinary actress. Barrie is an amusing man, and soon the society columns begin to speak of an imminent engagement. Barrie has no comment, but he writes an article for the *Edinburgh Evening Dispatch* in which – under the ominous title 'My Ghastly Dream' – he recognizes the nature of his innermost fears about marriage:

> *My ghastly nightmare is always the same: I see myself married and then I wake up with the scream of a lost soul, clammy and shivering . . .*
>
> *My ghastly dream always begins in the same way. I seem to know that I have gone to bed, and then I see myself slowly wakening up in a misty world. The mist dissolves; and the heavy, shapeless mass that weighed upon me all through my childhood suddenly assumes the form of a woman, beautiful and cruel, with a bridal veil over her face . . .*

Which doesn't prevent Barrie from proposing to Mary Ansell, Mary Ansell from accepting, or Barrie from later writing in his notebook:

> *Morning after engagement, a startling thing to waken up & remember you're tied for life.*

Barrie flees London and returns to Kirriemuir to give his mother the news. Once he arrives and finds himself back at his first home, Barrie becomes a boy again: Barrie is ill. Pneumonia and pleurisy. The papers report his almost inevitable end with a gravity usually reserved for matters of state, and Mary Ansell leaves the production of *Walker, London* and comes to tend to her beloved. Margaret Ogilvy, at first made uneasy by the idea that her son is marrying an actress, can't help but be moved by the care the young woman lavishes on her fiancé.

Barrie and Mary Ansell marry quickly – the groom is thirty-four, the bride thirty-two – and they do it according to Scottish tradition: a simple ceremony in the family home. Barrie is better now and they leave for Switzerland on their honeymoon. In Lucerne, Barrie gives Mary Ansell a wedding present: a little dog that soon grows to be giant-sized, a Saint

Bernard they baptize Porthos, the name of the dog in a novel they both liked very much.

Vicious rumours abound, spiteful barks: Mary Ansell never wanted to marry Barrie, but she accepted thinking he would die soon and that it wouldn't be so bad to be the young widow of a famous, successful man. Or maybe Barrie never asked her to be his wife, but Margaret Ogilvy . . .

Who knows. It doesn't matter. One thing is clear: two days after the wedding, Barrie writes four terrible sentences in one of his notebooks, sentences that once again sum up the sheer agony of a man who doesn't want to be a man, let alone a husband:

– *Our love has brought me nothing but misery.*
– *Boy all nerves.* 'You are very ignorant.'
– *Scene for a play. Wife:* 'Have you given me up? Have nothing to do with me?'
– *How? Must I instruct you in the mysteries of love-making?*

In an interview for *Sketch*, Barrie jokes with bittersweet humour, the kind of Barrie-esque humour that's made his name: 'I only got married because my wife's hairpins are so useful for cleaning my pipe.'

Then Barrie says goodbye to the press, plays for a while with Porthos on the rug, and shuts himself up to write.

With Porthos.

Yesterday I dreamed that I was Porthos, Barrie's dog. A huge and hugely happy Saint Bernard. If dogs are man's best friend, then Barrie is my best friend. And there's also Mary Ansell, my other best friend, who will be inspired by me to write several motherly books on dogs and the love of dogs, since she has no human children of her own. Porthos – that's me – is the son Barrie and Mary Ansell don't have and never will have. A son who barks and doesn't bite, and who in time will become that man in a dog costume in the first stage adaptations of *Peter Pan*, long before animals were forced to be actors by order of the terrible kingdom of Hollywood.

And yes, I know, Keiko Kai – few things are more annoying than a dream that works its way into a story. 'Tell a dream and lose a reader,' I think Henry James once warned; but the adventures of Jim Yang, especially the later ones, are overflowing with dreams and readers still clamour for them. I'm sorry, Henry: it's clear that your dreams weren't as good as mine, that they were the typical *waking* dream that some writers use as a device to explain things that happen when the eyes are open; the bad literature of even worse psychoanalysis. That's not the case with me. My dreams are worthy of being dreams.

So in this dream I'm Barrie's dog and I'm running in Kensington Gardens. The indescribable pleasure of having four legs. What humans know as running isn't running: at best, it's very fast walking, and almost always walking in a ridiculous and ineffective way; all it does is make us miss the hunched, simian way we ran when our arms were long and fast. My voice is deep and furry, and four or five sounds are more than enough for me to interrogate the planet, and for the planet to respond. I don't need or ask for more than that: the boundless happiness of animals that will never know the punishment of evolving into melancholy city beasts expelled long ago from their forest paradise.

Yesterday I dreamed that I was Porthos and that I was lying at Barrie's feet as he wrote; and the sound of the pen on the paper and the sound of the paper beneath the ink made me dream in perfect penmanship, with no spelling errors. Dogs, they say, can only see in black and white; which would make it fair and right that I – Porthos the Magnificent – should dream in colour. My canine dreams are nothing less than the animal, four-legged translation of Barrie's dreams. Our dogs and cats and fish and turtles and hamsters and parrots – we don't know this, but we sense it – are nothing but the secret antennae or hidden lightning rods of our most private desires. That's what our animals feed on, and their addiction to us is what we often confuse with love and loyalty. Our pets smoke us like tobacco and drink us like wine. Our pets bite us. And they bark and miaow, happy, as they inject the rich, heavy liquid of our dreams into their veins. That's why their eyes are always moist and half-shut, with a happiness incomprehensible to human beings. The ball or the stick that we throw far for them to fetch makes us feel powerful. They chase after it and return, smiling, amused by the knowledge that it's really us they're carrying in their jaws. We need these creatures to pluck out the demon of our darkest thoughts and deepest sorrows. And our pets are the first to show us the meaning of death. Our pets die before us with their short little lives because they're preparing us for the end of more formidable lives – of family, of friends – though the death of a pet is no less painful. Our pets are the instructive and refractive Mr Hyde facet of us that lets us be better and utterly fake Dr Jekylls.

I'm carrying an envelope for my master in my mouth. Stevenson has written to Barrie, a long, sinuous letter in the form of an almost hallucinatory diary. The paper Stevenson writes on smells of exotic spices and hurricanes. Stevenson is very ill. One disease after another dances through his body, which is weary of telling stories. Stevenson asks Barrie to visit him. 'Sail for San Francisco, and my island is the second to the right,' he jokes. Barrie won't forget these instructions when the time comes to situate Neverland in the skies of his work, and Stevenson dies almost without realizing it: the fever is everything, and it's a fever that erases the difference between being alive and being dead in the same way that we can never tell a sunset from a sunrise in photographs. Barrie receives the bad news as if it's the dress rehearsal for the final act in a last work: now he'll never meet his most admired fellow player of literary games, now he'll never climb the turquoise peaks of the mountains of Vailima or find treasure there, so far off the predictable route of the tours organized by Thomas

Cook, that cursed, new-fangled domesticator of adventures.

Deaths – as usually happens once the door opens to the first of them – never come singly, and Jane Ann falls first: Barrie's older sister and his eternal accomplice, struck down by cancer, which she never told anyone about. Jane never complained of any pains at all; she always seemed happy. Jane Ann was one of those women especially created to make second and third parties feel that all's well, that nothing can go wrong. Barrie and Mary Ansell, in Switzerland again to celebrate their first wedding anniversary, receive a letter of congratulations from Jane Ann, and then, in the next post, the telegram informing them of her death. The couple cut short their holiday and start on the slow return trip. I bark the way dogs bark when they sense that a new ghost has appeared to bid farewell to her loved ones, or to tell them that they'll have to endure her for the rest of their lives.

Barrie, grief stricken, takes three days to reach Kirriemuir, where he finds two coffins instead of one: his mother has died too. No one expected that either. Margaret Ogilvy seemed strong and healthy, and her new habit of talking to herself wasn't particularly worrisome: old people don't talk to themselves, they just realize they don't have much time left and they're hurrying to say everything they know they won't be able to say from the other side. So Jane Ann Adamson, forty-nine, and Margaret Ogilvy, seventy-six, are buried together, one on top of the other, in the same grave as David – the perfect son, the ideal brother, the invincible ghost – on the hill where the cemetery of Kirriemuir rises.

Margaret Ogilvy's last words – Barrie's told – were the first she spoke after her first death, the night they brought her favourite son home on a sled with his neck broken. 'Is that you, David?' Margaret Ogilvy sighed. And she closed her eyes, smiling.

I, Porthos, when no one is watching, go up to the stone covered in letters and dates and lift one of my back paws, blessing it in my fashion with a jet of hot, steamy urine, and then I give a long, spiralling howl that everyone interprets as a sign of grief, but which is really something very different: I *so* miss running in Kensington Gardens.

When the time comes to propose a possible heart of the universe – that point of pure energy from which everything emerged and to which everything will return – allow me to unfold a map of the sacred metropolis of London before your eyes, Keiko Kai, and show you the exact place where the emerald happiness of Kensington Gardens blooms.

An old map from the end of the nineteenth century, with ingenious, detailed illustrations in the margins intended to disguise the lack of precision in its draughtsmanship. Kensington Gardens, nevertheless, appears as it should, as it is: it's impossible to mistake it or fail to recognize it. At the time, it was the biggest open space in the middle of London, and yes, Barrie likes to imagine that on clear, endless nights when the moon is full, Kensington Gardens is visible to the moon dwellers as a seductive green dot perfectly situated on the blue face of the earth.

When Barrie and Mary Ansell return from their eclipsed honeymoon in Switzerland, they settle nearby, at 133 Gloucester Road, South Kensington, in a house representing one of the most shameful examples of hideous Victorian architecture.

There, Barrie shuts himself up to write *Margaret Ogilvy*, 'by her son, J. M. Barrie', as it reads on the plain jacket. After opening the book, past the title page, there's a portrait of the protagonist: she appears wrapped in a heavy fur cape, with a bonnet tied under her chin, her head bent and her eyes closed. The impression is of a cadaver that hasn't realized it's dead.

Margaret Ogilvy is a brief memoir and a heartfelt requiem for Barrie's dead mother, while at the same time a kind of exorcism and apologia of spiritual possession. *Margaret Ogilvy* is also one of the most exquisitely pathological books ever written. A strange book. Shorter than fifty thousand words, half the length it was thought novels should be back then.

A psychotic book: an overwrought tribute? A biography that becomes autobiography by osmosis? A study of an imaginary past?

In it, Barrie tells everything and reinvents everything, and writers and readers succumb to this disturbing form of literary exhibitionism, excruciatingly intimate and painful. The critics are divided between those who say it's 'the kind of thing which it is almost sacreligious to criticise, since it has to do with an idyll of the divinest of human feelings: a mother's love'; or those who condemn it as a 'shameful way of commercializing the private; its supposed truths seem more than debatable, and it ends up offering the reader something very like an exercise in refined sadism'.

Margaret Ogilvy, of course, ultimately reveals more about Barrie than about his mother, and it may have been the first specimen of the many familiar non-fiction *rêveries* that since then have continuously assaulted bookstores and the best-seller lists, compulsively readable because they're compulsively written. Suddenly off everyone goes, reading *Margaret Ogilvy* to compare their own mothers to Barrie's. This is the secret element, this is what biographies and autobiographies are for: we consume them to find out whether other peoples' lives are at least a little like ours.

I wrote a book like that too, Keiko Kai. I signed it with my real name. My real name back then was already a kind of pseudonym of my famous alias. The title of the book is *A POPcidental Childhood: Growing Up in the Psychedelic Sixties and All That Rock*. I wrote it far from my computer; very far, farther: I wrote it on a manual typewriter. My first typewriter. The one my parents gave me: a portable red Olivetti in a modern design that, now, supplanted by computer technology, has become a timeless museum piece, an instant antique. I wrote my memoir on it to help me remember better, to remember what it was like to write on a typewriter.

A review said – whether cruelly or cleverly, I'm not sure – that it was an 'ideal book for those with an interest in others' sadness and depression, unaware that it's they who're sad and depressed'. The book sold quite well; nowhere near as well as any of the Jim Yang instalments, of course. The readers of children's literature – children – aren't interested in the author of their favourite books, let alone in knowing that he was once like them and that they *won't* be like him; that the future awaits them full of infinite variations that have little or nothing to do with the almost communist uniformity of the first years of our lives, or the set trajectories of stories about witches defeated with a magic wand and wolves riddled with silver bullets from a golden rifle.

Only in our memory, from a distance, does childhood seem something singular and inimitable and beyond all questions of verisimilitude or truth.

Only in memory does our childhood seem to us like a good children's book.

Barrie doesn't care about reviews. Barrie never stops writing. Shutting himself up to work in his studio is the perfect alibi and 'I'm writing' is the most practical of mantras, the most effective and best-planned escape, letting him feel more like a boy than a husband when he's alone. Who's authorized to say what's real or not in his life, or in any writer's life – thinks Barrie – if so much of life, the most important part, occurs in writers' minds, in the luxuriant gardens of their imagination?

And when Barrie must leave his den, luckily there's Kensington Gardens, so close to 133 Gloucester Road that you can almost reach out and touch it: a small, barely tamed jungle with an artificial round lake, the Round Pond, where a small armada of wooden boats sail; and another, natural lake, the Serpentine, that separates Kensington Park from Hyde Park and can be crossed to reach a small bird sanctuary in its centre, Bird's Island. On one bank is the Dog's Cemetery; on the other, the exact spot where Peter Pan will one day alight, and that years later will become famous for a statue that, as I've already said, Barrie never liked because he didn't think it was much like the real Peter Pan.

Barrie and Mary Ansell and Porthos wander here and there. Sometimes, they linger on the main path, the Broad Walk, where all the passers-by go who want to see and be seen. Each day between two and four in the afternoon, the Broad Walk's obligatory tributary, the Baby Walk, becomes the realm of maidservants who push elaborate carriages, palaces on wheels, in which they display the little princes and princesses of the London aristocracy.

Kensington Gardens in those days, Keiko Kai, had little or nothing to do with the Kensington Gardens you know. Here's a picture taken then. Children, fathers, mothers, governesses watching a model sailboat regatta. The open parasols, the water and the trees, all in black and white, as if everything were made of the same mercurial substance. A juxtaposition of postcards – one from then, one from now – would achieve, I suppose, the same odd discomfort produced by identical twins with opposite and incompatible personalities.

Which of the two Kensington Gardens do I like best, Keiko Kai? The old literary one, of course. Barrie's Kensington Gardens; because you always end up preferring what you don't have, what you can't have, what never existed or doesn't exist any more.

I won't say anything here about a hypothetical third Kensington Gardens. *My* Kensington Gardens. A Kensington Gardens on the other side of the mirror, in another world inside this one. The dark, criminal Kensington Gardens that I helped or will help (I think I did, I'm not sure: maybe it's my wild imagination, maybe it's only something that happens sooner or later to all writers, except that none of them, none of us, dares to confess it) to sow with the wrecked bodies of so many lost boys in another of my many possible lives yet to be written. The life my life would become if I didn't stop it. The

Kensington Gardens of the man variously called 'Peter Punk' or 'The Hook' or 'The Lost Man' or 'The Neverland Monster' or 'The Lost Shadow' on the sensationalistic front pages of the newspapers.

In these days, my Kensington Gardens is almost deserted. Mothers don't bring their children here anymore, fearing uncomfortable propositions, and even those addicted to Eastern exercises have moved to other parks, far from the statue of Peter Pan, which is always surrounded by yellow tape ('Simpson-coloured yellow,' Keiko Kai says, his eyes the many colours of the pills I keep making him swallow) printed with 'CRIME SCENE/ DO NOT TRESPASS' in big black letters. Yes, maybe all of this has yet to happen. Maybe it's no more than a breath of my grim future, blown along on what I like to call the Black Wind. I'll tell you about the Black Wind soon, Keiko Kai. It doesn't matter now. There, wherever, I pay no attention: I ignore the command of the yellow tape and cross over and sit down to smoke a cigarette, and I remember myself, growing up beside this same statue that never grows old.

How old was I when my father brought me here and, accidentally or not, gave me a dose of LSD and left me here hallucinating with a toy plane in my hand? Unlike Marcus Merlin, I didn't want to be the pilot of a plane; I wanted to be a *plane*. A passenger plane or a combat plane: first emptying my belly of bombs over Westminster and then flying away as far as I could. At the time, my father was going through one of his increasingly frequent periods of aesthetic psychosis: it was hard for Sebastian 'Darjeeling' Lowe to maintain his Victorian pose and miss the psychotropic party where all his friends were floating happily in the air while he made himself memorize Charles Dickens's *Bleak House* with a possible rock operetta in mind, or something like that. So that occasionally, with the extreme passion of converts or heretics, my father gave up and abandoned himself to drug-addicted bacchanals that could last a week or two. Sessions that he justified as 'ways of trying to connect sensorially with Baco, my poor little Baco, wherever he is.' Occasions that only led to visions like 'I swear I felt I was one of the stones in Virginia Woolf's coat pockets!!!' – as I remember he woke me up one night to tell me, in a state of excitement – or to strange songs populated by crabs and men with lamps for heads, beaches with whale carcasses and glass hotels, trains that went nowhere, favourite buildings knocked down and replaced by hated buildings, sweet ghosts of light and transparent lovers, and the Queen of the Eyes and the Madonna of the Wasps.

Things like that.

Then, autumn 1967, my father took me on walks in Kensington Gardens, where – under the clumsy guise of deep conversations between father and son – what he really did was recite desperate generational monologues. It's strange: I can't remember anything he told me, but I *could* write it down, as if I were possessed by the ventriloquy of his sadness – not the logical sadness of dead flowers but the incomprehensible sadness of medals and military decorations at pawn shops – and it made me speak in his voice, distorted by a shrill distress. A kind of selection of his most frequently recurring and well-worn thoughts arranging and disarranging themselves – the same thing happens to me when it comes to remembering and forgetting decades and parties – like the pieces of an equation that doesn't yield a definite answer. Now, Keiko Kai, I'll be the doll my father uses to speak, the doll with a voice that isn't his, and therefore dares to say what no one dares to tell themselves.

The author of my life's LP, Sebastian 'Darjeeling' Compton-Lowe, leader of the Beaten a.k.a the Beaten Victorians a.k.a the Victorians, said things like this, according to me:

> 'What am I trying to do? What will I never be able to do? Who knows? One thing is clear: we've failed. We're supposed to be the Sons of Revolution and the Daughters of Aquarius. We're supposed to be the chosen ones, changing the world as we've known it until now . . . Lies. True, we

revived a city that was in a coma, we made it the centre of everything for a few years. New York, Rome, Paris and Los Angeles looked to London to see us . . . But we've fallen into the trap: we thought we knew more than everyone, and we ended up knowing less than anyone. The establishment tempted us with the apple of being different and we bit into it with no concern for the worms nestled at its heart. We dressed in bright colours, sang new songs, distilled the juice of artificial paradises, created our own universe at the cost of leaving the established universe. Just what our elders wanted. Those who pretend to be alarmed and dismayed when they speak of our anarchistic tendencies and drug use are really more than happy for it to be this way: addled brains are harmless brains. What a paradox: our idle youth has simply served to prolong their youth – their active life in power. We stood aside, thinking we were rebelling. We isolated ourselves intentionally, instead of putting up a fight and taking their places. The smart thing, the really effective thing, would've been to fight them from inside, infiltrating their establishments . . . But now it's as if we've run away to the park to play until night comes, which is when we discover, surprise, that we don't have the slightest idea which way is home. We burned our bridges before we finished crossing them. We renounced the past without bothering to consider the future. We believed this dazzling present was enough, but what we thought was an epic cataclysm is only a brief, showy meteorological phenomenon. A summer storm. And so we've become a generation of pariahs who enjoy our game of long hair and Indian music and hedonistic commune-dwelling as long as playtime lasts. And playtime is short. Like childhood. We've designed something that could only work *in aeternum*, and only if we possessed a small, crucial attribute: the ability never to grow up. But it's hopeless. Today we're happy lost boys and outsiders, but tomorrow we'll be zombies fried on LSD Made in the USA, radioactive freaks, Lucifer's fallen angels . . . Or worse: hippies. Bloody hippies. I'm told George Harrison went to San Francisco to see what the Summer of Love was all about and that he came back disgusted: people who never bathe, and who dance naked in the mud, too. Nothing to do with us, with our English style. We who in the beginning were unique, chosen, sophisticated . . . Our utopia was a utopia built on the basis of individuals, not tribes. An aristocratic meritocracy where noble names didn't hesitate to dance with the plebeian names of a new caste fed by talent. Now the nobility are returning to their cottages and they've begun to give their butlers the same old instructions: 'I'm not in the mood for that sort; the party's over, Jasper. If anyone calls for me, tell them I'm not here; that I'll never be back.' Never again will the countess open her bedroom doors and her legs to the director of avant-garde films. Never again will gay wild things be invited to Lady Victoria Ormsby-Gore's sixteenth birthday . . . I've said it before: now my generation entertains itself by dressing in Californian rags, by imitating the Americans, and when winter comes you'll see how bad things will be, ha. There's no future. There's no future for mutations. There's no future for my London, which committed the error of spilling its seed in Tokyo, in Berlin, in Prague any day now, and oh, in New York again, always New York. And who's guilty? Again, it's always the same culprits, the banalizers of our Empire: those four disgraces who had to be born in Liverpool, of course . . . Cave dwellers from the Cavern, worshippers of an illiterate farmboy from Memphis who called himself the King. And they invited them to play in the Royal Variety Show. And they even knighted them. And those other five . . . the Rolling Stones, cheap imitators of black singers. We're lost. Morning will never come for those who are simultaneously Dr Frankenstein and the monster, the *Titanic* and the iceberg . . . We'll sink, my son, we'll be shipwrecked between eternal ice and eternal fire.

And with time we'll become just another of those historical nostalgias that people return to once in a while, watching a television series, at a costume party, in some retro compulsion . . . Like the Victorians. Outmoded fossils with an expiration date. We invented something, but what we invented is terrible, too: the premature death of the original, the headlong pace of fashion, the ephemerality of trends, the culture of lightning speed and pop acceleration. Will I be the only one who realizes all this? Must I pay a terrible price for being the repository of such revelations? Who cares? No one would listen to me and now it's too late to do anything. Oh, it's cold already, the golden year of 1960 is farther and farther away, and it's a little closer to 31 December 1969, a little closer to the end of the world . . .'

What was my father really talking about when he fell into these prophetic trances? Was he genuinely worried about what would happen to rock music? Could he glimpse a future ravaged by shorter and shorter-lived cliques, by fashions like smoke? Was he equipped to hear – there and then, so long ago – symphonic pop, violent punk, thick-skulled satanism, the disco spasm, the new-wave joke, techno machinations, the weird new hairstyles of dark and new romantic, grunge nihilism, the squatter rooms of house, ecstatic electronica, the beatification of beat, the canonization of the DJ, the dialectic of rap? Or maybe he already intuited the dissonances of '68, when young people gave up being dandies to go out into the streets and burn their own schools on cinema screens? Could my father have been a clumsy Nostradamus of pop music or an ideologue who – as is often the case – had more vision than real talent?

Maybe not.

Or maybe I prefer to remember him that way now.

Maybe it's good for me to think of him as a visionary martyr and not as a short-sighted leader. The relief of remembering him, with the help of my selective memory, as the statue of a defeated general punished by the inclemency of time and the contempt of pigeons.

Maybe so.

There's always an instant of blazing omniscience in the autumn, the consolation prize for those who understand they won't make the finish line. Maybe my father guessed that all that strange clothing would soon be exchanged for Yves Saint-Laurent and Pierre Cardin suits, and that the new mode of transgression would move on to other areas: protests, wars, assassinations, revolts, revolutions. London had none of that. London couldn't compete. London was a contented city. The only thing London had left was drugs and a handful of films that dated too quickly. There was nothing to fight against now, and all those who'd held out hopes of dying before they got old were still alive and living abroad so they wouldn't have to pay such high taxes.

Maybe the presence of a counterculturist disillusioned by his own counterculture is a cliché as common today – Marcus Merlin, of course, pointed this out to me – as the inevitable SS officer who loves art and saves the life of a talented Jew to ease his guilt and atone for his participation in the Holocaust. And at times I ask myself, noting the shameless frequency of its appearance in books and films, whether there didn't really exist a whole secret German unit of artistic elites in the Nazi party: Helmuts and Günthers and Siegfrieds with a nostalgic look in their eye and perfect uniforms, especially likely to be moved by a painting or a piano, to remember the good times in vanished Dresden, and immediately, with a snap of the fingers, to sanction the survival of long-suffering but hardy Hebrew artists.

Maybe I too am a worn-out cliché: the shipwrecked son of a pair of parents drowned during the electric revolution, saved from the vortex of the 60s because of my ability – like Barrie's – to paper the rooms of real children (always other people's children) with stories.

It doesn't matter. What good can it do to reconstruct

harangues delivered by a desperate father to his son who, even then, listened to him and studied him, calibrating his potential as an imaginary character? Parents, as we know, are the invention of their children. It's the children who turn them into parents, and therefore become their creators. Maybe there's some sort of score-settling and automatic reflex involved. Children begin as footnotes to their parents, and parents end up being footnotes to their children. That's life; and yes, we live in a cruel world. A world that exhibits and maintains constants of behaviour only when the constants are the terrible kind. That's why there are so few books by parents about children, I suppose, and so many books by children about parents – and no, no, no: I'll never have children, children who'd write my life story.

I decided it around the time I had my first wet dream, and reaffirmed my decision with a deluxe vasectomy at a private clinic where they took care of my private parts, which in one fell swoop were deprived of all reproductive capacity. I don't want to have children. Like Barrie. Better – more comfortable and safer – to be the father of other parents' children. To be the Great Father of an infinite number of children who – since they don't know you – are left with the consolation of adoring you through your books. An invincible Great Father; because nothing but your own blood has the power to destroy you. Now that I'm older than they were when they died, my parents have in some sense become my children. My ghost children.

And it's then, Keiko Kai, that I imagine my father's true end, with the attractive hypothesis that it was he, mischievous and mortal, who set fire to the deck or knocked holes in the hold of the *S.S. Regina Victoria* as everyone was sleeping, thus granting himself an epic, Arthurian death, the death of a monarch who has no interest at all in surviving in a promised land that will never be ceded to him.

I go even further and imagine him swimming to an island that doesn't appear on any map, where he'll reign as a new messiah, a neo-Victorian Kurtz, adored by the natives who've been waiting for him for centuries so he can teach them the sacred rite of 5 o'clock tea, as their sacred songs proclaim.

Childish, my father's desire: to suddenly disappear rather than vanish little by little. To refuse to grow old, believing eternal youth is a blessing, without realizing that in the oldest and most respectable legends, the gods usually punish men with the curse of eternal youth.

You won't read any of this in the light, inoffensive, anecdotal, pleasant and previously mentioned A *POPcidental Childhood: Growing Up in the Psychedelic Sixties and All That Rock*, of course. There's nothing in there about my father's despondent visions, or about my triumphant visions as an accidental acid prophet's apprentice. Nothing about what I saw that evening in Kensington Gardens, which I don't even have to remember; because what I saw there transcends memory and all I have to do is fix my gaze on a blank spot on any wall for it all to come back so I can relive it again.

Here I am, there I was, a hero:

I'd finished counting the even-numbered leaves on a tree and was starting to count the odd-numbered leaves (I didn't know what kind of tree it was, but otherwise I knew *everything* about that tree), when Peter Pan stepped off his bronze pedestal and came up to me and said, sure, dying would be an awfully big adventure, but it would be even bigger and more awful to kill, wouldn't it? Peter Pan assured me that a jury would be swayed when they heard I'd ingested psychedelic drugs at such a tender age; it wouldn't justify my actions, but it might get me sent to a better and more exclusive home for psychotic criminals in the country, on the banks of the Thames. The truth is that this was only the beginning of the visions, the first rush of strange chemistry. Pity the child who takes LSD, but don't therefore refuse to appreciate the third and fourth and fifth and thousandth eye that suddenly blinks in the middle of his forehead.

The feeling that the world is opening up as it does in the panoramas and dioramas that stun Barrie when he goes to see them at the Egyptian Hall: the world unrolling before the spectator as a lecturer points out and explains the features of a far-off land that's suddenly been transferred to the centre of London, or better yet, to the space in front of seats fixed to a spinning floor that spins the way I spun then. Orbits within orbits, and what I saw had nothing to do with the facile landscapes of beat surrealism, with diamond skies and ruby Tuesdays.

No, what I *saw* then was something very different. I saw fleets of wrathful glass jumbo jets cradling in their steel bellies cardinals and bishops who preached in the skies over a London that had suddenly become a boundless Gothic airport sinking its spires into the clouds to bring forth holy water and sacred bolts of lightning. I saw all the bishops jumping with wind-parachutes, floating in the airy landscape, bestowing blessings in a new or a very ancient language – *Porpozec ciebie nie prosze dorzanin albo zyolpocz ciwego*, their speaking staffs repeated over and over again, vibrating like tuning forks – as the control towers were toppled by lightning, like the tower in my favourite deck of tarot cards. I saw how all flights were cancelled by divine will, and all suitcases lost. I watched the forced landing of the first, spoiled Jesus Christ, looking so much like my dead little brother; the Jesus Christ who doesn't appear in the Bible but who one senses there, and who I found again later in the best-written pages of the Apocrypha when I wasn't even looking for him. A Jesus using the power of his mind to kill everyone who dares to stand up to him, or – in Thomas's words – turning all his terrorized little friends into goats when they won't play what he wants to play. A Jesus who didn't want to grow up, because growing up was dying, and who knows whether he was interested in the whole resurrection-on-the-third-day thing. Why wait so long to be brought back from the dead, and why do it so modestly and almost secretly? A Jesus too much like Peter Pan, who also says *Suffer the little children to come unto me*. Blessed be he, the Child Messiah we all carry inside of us somewhere, and who sooner or later we're forced to crucify in order to enter adulthood.

I knew then that all of us were no more than the metal spokes in the bicycle wheels of that ruthless little Jesus, of that fifth horseman of the Apocalypse called Faith. Faith and the suicidal impulse to believe in *something* simply because we feel that believing in *something* is better than believing in *nothing*. Faith feeding on our fear of utter nothingness in the end. Faith galloping beside Disease, War, Hunger and Death. And worst of all is that even if we aren't believers, his divine form crops up everywhere, so that the world is full of people who say they're religious but who – by practising the doctrine's cruelty without the myth's poetic grace – only manage to do Evil in the name of Good.

It's not that then, in the centre of the whirlwind, I decided to stop believing in an external God, which or whom I had never believed in, immersed as I was in my parents' high-class paganism. But I did close myself off to any possibility of believing in him in the future, and, obliged to choose a divinity, I opted for an internal God, for Our Lord of the Left Hemisphere.

How could the abstract metaphor of wine turned into blood compete or seduce me when I could experience the private, figurative miracle of ink turned into type? A God who was only mine – is there anything more sensible and intelligent than creating your own religion? – and was ruler of a land where not only did everything occur, but everything occurred to me. A world without a God who was always aloof was much more comfortable and narratively coherent than a world with a silver-pupilled God who'd abandoned us or who we'd betrayed almost unconsciously. Yes, I refused to join the hosts of Pilate and Judas – those millions who wash their hands and quickly and cheaply sell the best part of themselves, the intact, original part of childhood hidden between the folds of DNA – and I pledged myself to a religion in which the totem to be worshipped was the paradise we're expelled from a few scarce years after we reach it: childhood, cursed and incredible, where we feel immortal and powerful and irresponsible, at least for a while. Like Peter Pan. Like Barrie.

And I look again for the headlines in giant red type on the front pages of the *Sun* and the *Daily Mirror*, and they aren't there any more. It's scantily clad girls and the royal family's most recent pseudo-scandal now, and not a single report on the serial killer I supposedly become when shadows deepen. It has its funny side: by day I'm the children's hero, the creator of Jim Yang, and by night I turn into an all-powerful sorceror, the dark prince, the tireless pursuer, the diabolical professor Cagliostro Nostradamus Smith. Or not. Maybe not. Maybe, as I've said already, this is all the product of my delirious mind, of the only part of my body that hasn't changed since my childhood, the right temporal lobe bursting in the skies and on the beaches of the left temporal lobe and laying waste to everything with the fury of its visions. Maybe it's the caprice of a tumour hiding from the X-rays. Or a lysergic flashback, a hallucinogenic echo of my psychedelic pop childhood. Or maybe it's simply a residual effect, an inevitable consequence of the overemployment of the materials of my trade: the constant revisitation of the world of childhood with an organism that's no longer what it used to be and that struggles against the almost complete reshuffling of the body's deck of cells every seven years. Little by little – like machines – we're mutating, recycling worn-out pieces; and it's up to us to find and keep in perfect condition that single screw or last hinge, that irreplaceable replacement on which the motors of children's literature are mounted. The key isn't remembering, then, but the reverse: nourishing the phantom zone where our adulthood is a memory, a forward-looking memory.

The rules of thought must therefore change: when we believe we've come up with something new, most of the time all we're doing is comparing its outline with something old. This is the only way we can recognize anything fresh: by invoking the obsolete.

When I think and write about Jim Yang, I reverse the polarities: I go to live in the sealed room of the past so I can understand the present from there as a kind of spectre of what might or might not come to be.

There's an especially revealing paragraph at the beginning of *Peter and Wendy*, a paragraph I find useful. There Barrie writes:

> *I don't know whether you have ever seen a map of a person's mind. Doctors sometimes draw maps of other parts of you, and your own map can become intensely interesting, but catch them trying to draw a map of a child's mind, which is not only confused, but keeps going round all the time. There are zigzag lines on it, just like your temperature on a card, and these are probably roads in the island, for the Neverland is always more or less an island, with astonishing splashes of colour here and there, and coral reefs and rakish-looking craft in the offing, and savages and lonely lairs, and gnomes who are mostly tailors, and caves through which a river runs, and princes with six elder brothers and a hut fast going to decay, and one very small old lady with a hooked nose. It would be an easy map if that were all, but there is also first day at school, religion, fathers, the round pond, needlework, murders, hangings, verbs that take the dative, chocolate pudding, getting into braces, say ninety-nine, three-pence for pulling out your tooth yourself, and so on, and either these are part of the island or they are another map showing through, and it is all rather confusing, especially as nothing will stand still.*

The map of my mind – a hybrid mind, the map of an adult's mind drawn in a child's hand – must be something like that. A treasure map where the person I am has to be buried to unearth the person I was.

Who am I?

Am I an efficient child-killer or am I a killer child who always suspected the possible existence of the monster lurking in his future?

I don't care.

I'm so tired, Keiko Kai, of being who I am, whatever that might be.

I am – yes – a writer.

And no one is a writer of his own free will, Keiko Kai. No one *becomes* a writer. Being a writer isn't an option, it's a fate. A weak, unhanded fate: writers are never in the hands of fate. Writers escape the generalities of law and luck. To be a writer is to be someone who didn't choose but was chosen by the no-return vocation of the socially acceptable madman. Someone who spends five, nine, twelve hours a day shut up in a room hearing voices that only he can understand, and who consoles himself thinking that once there was a way that would take him back to Kensington Gardens and sleep, little darling, do not cry, and I will sing a lullaby because, boy, you'll be carrying that weight for a long time . . .

The weight of the torment doesn't matter.

I'm ready to accept whatever I've got coming.

Anything to be able to walk in that green, peaceful world again, outside and inside this black, violent world.

Now it's the hour the sirens start to wail, Keiko Kai: the sirens of sleepy police cars, the sirens of insomniac ambulances, the red sirens of London that don't tie you to the masts but toss you overboard and make you swim to the shores of the same park that was once another park. The same park, but different; same but different, like a boy's body into which an adult body could never fit, and yet from inside of which everything came.

Out there, in Kensington Gardens, Barrie and his wife and his dog are a strange, fascinating sight, another of the many attractions of the place.

The tiny man smoking a pipe and almost lost in a hat and coat several sizes too big.

The lady dressed according to the latest and most costly dictates of fashion.

The enormous Saint Bernard that seems to pull both of them

along with the furry force of his four paws, and whose bark is perfect for giving heart attacks to the sheep that graze free on the still-wild lawns of Kensington Gardens like lost woolly babies. Porthos attracts the smallest and bravest children, those who sometimes seem to suffocate in their starched sailor suits and miniature lord costumes, and who seek and find in Porthos's company something of the yearned-for and irresponsible nakedness of the primordial adventure they're already beginning to miss.

Barrie likes this magnetic quality of his dog, which – when he commands it with a loud snap of his fingers – rears up on its hind paws, vertical and monstrous, and boxes with its tiny master, to the glee of those who dream of a dog like this and a father as small and as much like them as Barrie.

Barrie as an amusement park in and of himself. A secret garden inside Kensington Gardens. A man who seems to speak the lost language of childhood perfectly, the wows! and heys! and yippeees! Someone who speaks to children not from the steep crags of maturity but from a gentle hill, the top of which can be reached on a bicycle – a bicycle like any other bicycle, an ordinary bicycle – so that from the top you swoop down again with no risk of being hurt, over and over again, until you've reached the point of happy exhaustion after laughing a thousand and one times, with arms stretched wide and eyes closed and down again, let's do it again, the last time, I promise, once more and we'll go home, because it's getting dark now, it's already dark, because now it's night that's swooping down on us, and night rises high, higher, higher still, above a place called Kensington Gardens.

The Guest

And the next day, fast, running, to Kensington Gardens again. It's a perfect morning and even the air seems to brim with the bright colours of Arthur Rackham's illustrations for those terrible Victorian children's books of fantastic landscapes more real than reality itself. And it doesn't matter; no one dares to accuse the trees with dwarves swaying in their branches of being implausible. I'm referring to the glossy plates that are almost hidden, pressed – like mummy flowers, like colour-blind butterflies, like real letters of false love – between two pages of text, sometimes delicately veiled by a sheet of almost translucent paper, and oh, the surprise of discovering them, always on the right side, as you read further, and the temptation that must be resisted not to skip ahead and find them before having arrived at that point in the story. Seeking them out first. Studying them. Guessing what they're about. Yes, interpreting them as if you were reading the future. These illustrations – trapped in big, heavy volumes it seems no child could lift without an adult's help, and yet sooner or later . . . – are our first experience of rebellion against the unyielding tyranny of our elders. Suddenly we feel so *big* and so happily solitary reading on our own now, without the interference of a mother's or a father's voice. And then the prince in the illustration is no longer anything like the prince we imagine when we start reading for ourselves – no, no, no, nothing at all like him. And yet the forests and parks in ink and oils – the background scenery against which heroes and villains appear – always seem perfect to us, ideal, exactly like the places we explore in our minds.

Which brings me back again to the place I've never left.

Is it possible to become addicted to a place? To feel the need to return over and over again? To count the hours and minutes and seconds until we return to the spot that must be our true home?

Barrie is addicted to Kensington Gardens.

What's more: Kensington Gardens is addicted to Barrie.

They can't live without each other, they're made for each other, till death do them part; together forever, for century upon century.

Upon returning to London, Barrie lets the servants occupy themselves with his suitcases and his wife's suitcases and runs as fast as his little legs will take him down Gloucester Road and finally, like someone racing to plunge into the ocean, lets himself fall into the green park with his eyes open, holding his breath: Barrie will stay down there, underwater, as long as his lungs permit.

Barrie has just come back from his first trip to the United States. He was happy there. Manhattan seemed a magical and almost impossible city to him, its inhabitants members of a different race, a new and strange variety of Englishmen. In Manhattan Barrie felt more British than ever. Nationality is something that's always *activated* abroad, thinks Barrie. Paradoxically, we're more patriotic when we're far from home.

The goal of his expedition to the New World was to meet the formidable Charles Frohman, legendary and always smiling patron saint of the stage. The Beaming Buddha, his friends and even his enemies call him. Charles Frohman is a theatrical and messiah-like producer – no matter that he's short – before whom all the marquees of Broadway bow down.

Barrie and Charles Frohman soon become great friends, soulmates and kindred spirits. The two love the theatre as a space where anything can happen, and does: it's enough to set out to achieve it, to believe in it. The two idolize their mothers and children, all children, even if they aren't theirs.

After three years of marriage, Barrie and Mary Ansell still have no children. Mary Ansell thinks of nothing else, and consoles herself with her increasingly maternal love for dogs.

Barrie, on the other hand, prefers his friends' children. Barrie keeps adding other peoples' children to his list of friends: Cecco and Pia (the children of writer Maurice Hewlett); Pamela (the daughter of actor Cyril Maude); and best of all, his indisputable and overwhelming favourites: three boys always dressed in coats and red tam-o'-shanters, tam-o'-shanters that are never still and look like little flames, the small beginnings of an enormous blaze.

Here they come.

George, five years old, and his brother Jack, four, and their newborn little brother Peter, who can't walk yet and who watches them from the arms of their nanny, Mary Hodgson, who takes them almost every day to Kensington Gardens, where Barrie and Porthos are waiting to play with them.

George grows very fond of Barrie. He likes the way Barrie moves his ears and makes his eyebrows dance. And Barrie can imitate the voices of the strangest animals. George loves the stories Barrie tells. Stories in which there are desert islands and cricket matches and fairies and pirates and murderers and hanged men at lonely crossroads and ghosts that refuse to rest quiet in their graves. Nothing at all like the insipid, dainty stories their mother reads them before bed. George is fascinated by Barrie's shortness, by his sickly air, and – miracle – by his surprising dexterity and strength when he spars with hulking Porthos, more bear than dog.

And Barrie can't take his eyes off George. He seems to Barrie the loveliest and liveliest boy he has ever known. George is like a distillation of the best of childhood. An immense perfume in a tiny, perfect container. An invincible boy full of energy and courage, capable, according to Barrie, of 'striking hundreds of gallant poses in a single day, and when he falls down playing, which happens very often, a second doesn't go by before he jumps up again, like a little Greek god'.

Barrie is so enchanted with George that he doesn't even bother to find out his last name. His first name is more than enough. Last names – the trademark passed on to us by our elders that either ennobles us or dooms us – are, to Barrie, one of the inequivocable signs of adulthood. Thankfully, there's nothing less necessary in childhood than the name that links us to our parents, a chain, a stamp of ownership.

At the park, in Kensington Gardens, parents are forbidden; that's what nannies are for. Sometimes, at the weekend, some of the parents – men and women who're still young but who take pains to assume an air of adult importance – make an appearance at the Round Pond to see whether their children's sailboats speed past the sailboats of the children of their rivals on the Stock Exchange, humiliating them. These are the fathers and mothers with whom Barrie is sometimes obliged to spend long, boring dinners at which – as if drawn by a magnetic force – all the women end up together at the end of the drawing room, while the men swap cigars in libraries where no one reads but everyone discusses the book of the moment: *Dracula*. Barrie has read *Dracula*, and been moved by its power as a fairy tale for adults; he's intrigued by the idea of an evil but heroic character tormented by an eternal thirst, a being who never grows old and feeds on the strength of others. And Barrie's even more impressed when he discovers that *Dracula*'s author, Bram Stoker, refused to learn to walk until he was six, and that he's a member of secret societies, or so it's said; and what must those secret societies be like: could it be that the city leaders secretly gather there to play? Barrie – famous and eccentric – would like to be able to join in some conversation; to weigh in on all of this; to point out that Stoker is also the author of the strange book *Under the Sunset*, a volume of eerie allegorical stories for children; but, like a child among adults, Barrie never knows where to stand on these evenings, and oh, the courses flowing one after the other with the agonizing slowness of a river, and how much longer will it be until he can go home to Porthos and his latest manuscript?

On one of these nights and at one of these dinners – a party at Sir George Lewis's house on Portland Place, in 1907

– Barrie finds himself sitting next to a woman who strikes him as the 'most beautiful creature I've ever seen': Sylvia Llewelyn Davies, wife of Arthur Llewelyn Davies, a promising young attorney.

The young woman has a small and delicious snub nose, grey eyes, black hair, the most mischievous of smiles, and – Barrie smiles at her smile – she's pretending to follow the conversation while she hides sweets in her little silk bag, thinking no one is watching. Sylvia Llewelyn Davies sees that Barrie's seen her. 'They're for Peter,' is the only explanation she gives. Barrie soon learns that before she was married she was called Sylvia Jocelyn de Busson du Maurier and that she's the sister of the actor Gerald du Maurier and daughter of George du Maurier, author of the very successful novels *Trilby* and *Peter Ibbetson*, the latter featuring the Saint Bernard called Porthos after which Barrie named his dog. Barrie says to her, you see, the two of us have so much in common. Sylvia Llewelyn Davies explains to Barrie that her youngest son's name also comes from the novel: he's called Peter, like the protagonist of *Peter Ibbetson*. More and more remarkable coincidences and discoveries: it so happens that Sylvia Llewelyn Davies is the mother of George and Jack and Peter, Barrie's Kensington Gardens playmates. To prove to the young woman that he's the mysterious friend her sons can't stop talking about, Barrie wiggles his eyebrows and ears like mad; because nothing makes a writer happier than coincidences like this, coincidences that seem more appropriate to fiction and intrude into reality without warning, contradicting the laws that determine what's impossible and what isn't and striking them down. Suddenly, sometimes, if proper attention is paid, life seems – life is – a real fairy tale.

Though it's hard for me to believe in certain coincidences, Keiko Kai. Coincidences don't produce themselves. You have to know how to attract them, seduce them, create an ideal atmosphere for their growth and propagation. We writers are experts at creating and fostering coincidences, the things

Chesterton called 'spiritual puns'. Our lives and the lives of our characters depend on them. And I'll go so far as to say that the strength of a literary calling – the desire or the compulsion to be a writer – is firmly based on the number of coincidences we're able to spot and recognize in our first years of life. Once we've discovered the hidden mechanism that makes the world turn, once we've heard the secret music, it's impossible for us to resist the need to add a few beats of our own, an assortment of new gears and pulleys. It's then we realize we've gone over to the other side and there's no return ticket. We accept that we're too emotionally crippled to successfully attempt any 'normal' job. We're terminally ill. There's no cure. The only thing left for us to do is to learn to throw a few bones in the air, analyse the way they fall on the sand, explain them, extract a story from them, and, in telling it, win the respect of more productive, healthier people who've nevertheless been denied our gift: the rare talent of calling forth the same eternal story under the cover of different guises and coincidences, over and over again.

And this is a secret, Keiko Kai: here at Neverland, at Sad Songs, in the too many rooms of my family mansion, everyone who visits from outside – the very few welcome guests and the many inevitable guests who've spent the night here – all dream the same thing over and over again: what's known as a *recurring dream*.

My recurring dream, for as long as I can remember, goes like this: I see myself – because dreams, besides always being in black and white, are also *written* in both the first and the third person, and it's to that simultaneity of dreams that the great unrepeatable moments of History aspire, when everything seems to be happening at once and everywhere – and I see myself running, running without stopping over the roofs of London, Victorian roofs – actually more gothic than Victorian – across which I'm being chased by a furious pack of gentlemen with bowler hats and short silver-handled canes; and maybe the source of this dream of mine has to do with an oneiric warping of the chimney sweep sequence in *Mary Poppins*.

Did Barrie ever have a recurring dream? And if he did, was it a gentle one or an unbearable nightmare? Hard to say just what the night dreams of someone who seems to have lived in daydreams were like. In any case, I don't think Barrie's recurring dream – if he had one – would've been linear, narrative. I suppose I imagine it as something like the dreams of people who've been blind since birth. Sounds and textures and smells. Flashes of a future where men prolong or recapture their childhoods by hooking themselves up to virtual reality machines. A digitized murmur escaping from all those heads imprisoned in headphones and goggles and helmets, and the voice of a hollow, laser-like wind in their ears. Thousands of men tethered with cables and floating like balloons – one next to the other, in orderly rows – inside huge hangars like hollow islands where the only sound to be heard is a sound like the noise fire makes as it runs along the hallways of a burning house. Barrie can't *see* them, but Barrie can feel what they're dreaming, I'm sure.

What's your recurring dream, Keiko Kai?

I suppose the dreams of your generation are a different kind of dream. Sleeping dreams as the synonym of waking ambitions. Realistic dreams. Dreams to be realized. And yours must also have to do with being a movie star, a star of whatever. And don't worry, Keiko Kai: this whole business, this long night, will just help you be an even bigger, more powerful star . . . A legend, with all that entails, and believe me, you'll be immortal when you die.

But as I was saying, what happens to the sleepers of Neverland . . . It's the strangest phenomenon: depending on the bed you occupy in any of the rooms, that single repeated dream, that echo of the subconscious, is varied or amplified, sometimes subtly and sometimes radically. Like when you try to tell someone's life story and by the end it's almost a dream, a fiction, a liquid episode of a television series that's broadcast over and over again at an hour when those who kneel in front of their television sets have lost all hope that their existences will enjoy the greatest possible viewership. To be dead among the living, or living among the dead. It makes no difference: the commercials are the same either way. As is the certainty that our dreams are also our dead.

The dead become the fictions of those of us who survive them; we subject them to the indecency of deletions, additions and revisions in the same way – exactly halfway down the road – that we end up rewriting that other zone: our childhood.

That's why ghosts come back over and over again, Keiko Kai. They don't want to scare anyone; the only thing that bothers them is seeing themselves subjected to the putrefaction of lies that in time will be fossilized into truths. There's something tremendously unfair about the living writing History, because the living aren't necessarily the winners. And sometimes, in our dreams, the ghost of the child we used to be returns and asks us to explain how we could've turned into someone like *this*.

We live, Keiko Kai, between two imaginary countries: that of the children we were and the dead we'll become. And between one and the other – between the children who think of nothing but death and the dead who think of nothing but their childhoods – is all of life, the whole confusing story, which only in a few cases achieves some order, some grace, some moment worthy of being endlessly retold the same way we endlessly tell stories that never come to an end: stories that – for want of a better name – we've decided to call *children's*.

There are contradictory accounts of when and how Barrie met the lovely Sylvia Llewelyn Davies. Years later, the artist H. J. Ford – a friend of Barrie's on the Allahakbarries cricket team – claimed in a letter to one of Sylvia's sons, Peter Llewelyn Davies, that the meeting actually took place in his studio on Edwardes Square: 'It was at one of my tea parties that J. M.

Barrie met your mother; she was wearing a corduroy jacket she had designed herself. Barrie saw her, surrendered, and was won over immediately. That was the beginning of *Peter Pan*, and of everything that came after.'

There are, of course, other possibilities; other places with a thirst for immortality that claim for themselves the honour and privilege of being the exact spot where Barrie kissed Sylvia Llewelyn Davies's hand for the first time. Multiple options leading to a single end; because it's well known that history often sinks its roots into the shifting sands of myth. Therefore, witnesses abound who swear to have been one place or another. All agree and insist that the meeting was coincidental, magical, written in the stars, and not composed in curvy, elaborate Victorian calligraphy by the earthly protocols of English society.

I go even further.

I believe something else.

I have a more disturbing theory that demolishes the charms of happenstance and turns the whole episode into something more interesting and calculated: Barrie knew perfectly well that Sylvia Llewelyn Davies was the mother of his adored Kensington Gardens playmates and as soon as he saw her and realized who she was, he went after her. There's no more effective method for getting what you want, no better way of triumphing, than to declare yourself conquered and thus win over your conqueror.

Just as with the recurring dreams in the beds at Neverland, the day and time and place may change but the result will always, inevitably, be the same. In other words, Barrie *had* to meet Sylvia Llewelyn Davies to make his dream come true. And he did, it did. Barrie knew that Sylvia was the door that led to a perfect world. Sylvia was the Absolute Mother, the Great Procreator, the Fertile Body from which new lives sprang as if by magic or miracle, in a process – as it was believed in the Paleolithic, when females were worshipped as fat, powerful Venuses – that males had nothing to do with; all they did was play at being hunted hunters, at being alive and being dead.

And why is it precisely now that I remember the funeral, the memorial service for my dead parents, my lost parents (my mother wouldn't miraculously reappear until several weeks after the shipwreck of the *S.S. Regina Victoria*); and that it was there, amid scentless flowers and scented candles, that John Lennon appeared. Maybe because he felt as orphaned as me – maybe because no one could be more of an orphan than he was, and he wanted to keep it that way – John Lennon came up to me. He had just been to Brian Epstein's funeral, and with his eyes full of tears, he said to me: 'I'm Christ.' No one was paying much attention to my parents' real-life death – instead everyone was speculating about the rumour ('Paul Is Dead') that was circulating just then – and years later I read in several biographies that Lennon would announce his divinity to anyone he ran into at the time, and that was it for him, that was the end of the poor man.

Lennon needed a gallon of LSD to discover what I'd understood after one or two accidental drops one bright evening in the Kensington Gardens of my childhood, and he still got it wrong. Better read the fine print of the messianic contract before you sign it.

I'm not going to ask you where you were the night John Lennon was shot, Keiko Kai, for the simple reason that you weren't born yet. Where was I? I'd forgotten; but now I remember. Now I can remember my before and my after, like anybody else, like listening to two radio stations at once.

I tune into that night – memories don't come back to you; you go back to them – and there I am. I'd just been to see the statue of Lewis Carroll's Alice in Central Park. I liked it. It's better than the Peter Pan in Kensington Gardens; it's a much more literary statue, I think. Alice goes down into the depths of Wonderland to try to bring order to chaos; Peter Pan goes up into the skies of Neverland to preach chaos. Jim Yang doesn't go up or down; Jim Yang floats, I think. I'm hungry, I think. There I am. At a diner not far from the Dakota Building, in New York, December 1980. I won't lie: I won't say I heard the shots, but I did get the news before almost anybody else from the terse, monosyllabic conversation of two policemen who came in for coffee with their walkie-talkies. 'Beatle,' said one. 'Dead,' said the other. And then the calibre of the gun and the number of bullets that struck the body. In a variation on that same night – yes, I come up with strange things, Keiko Kai; I'm a writer for all the wrong reasons, but I am a writer, after all – I'm assaulted by one of those almost savage-looking juvenile delinquents with a monosyllabic name and I call the police from a pay phone; and a patrol car comes to get me; and they're taking me to file charges at the precinct when an urgent voice crackles from the car radio and one of the policemen says to me 'I'm sorry, buddy, but we have more important business,' and speeding through stoplights we come to a building that looks like a castle in a horror movie; and on the curb there's a young man reading in a quiet voice from a book; and there's a happy warm gun next to him; and inside the building, in what must once have been an entrance for the nouveau riche carriages of the New World, there's a man lying face down with several bullet holes in him; and they turn him over and I'm the first to recognize him because I know him and I tell the officers 'It's John Lennon'; and they look at me first as if I'm crazy and then as if I'm the wisest man in history; and I help them lift Lennon's body into the patrol car; and they turn on the siren and it isn't the siren but the Oriental howls of Yoko Ono; and I'm left there alone thinking 'Christ is dead'; and back at the diner, the policemen are sad. They seem more sad than policemen usually do, and just then the television over the counter at the diner interrupts the baseball or basketball game, and there are live shots of worshippers making a pilgrimage to Central Park as if they're on their way to see the most lunar of eclipses.

Do I need to make it clear here that there was no spontaneous gathering in Hyde Park when my parents' death in the shipwreck of the *S.S. Regina* was reported, and that the stories in the papers spoke not of a great tragedy but rather of the just punishment of the bizarre whims of the privileged classes, in an editorial and almost scolding tone? Anyway, as panoramic shots of people crying, holding candles, and leaving flowers next to the door of a building were shown, the song 'Imagine' began to be played over and over again. A song my father would surely have despised if he'd lived long enough to hear it. A song I find extremely interesting, yes, but for all the wrong reasons. As I see it, in 'Imagine' Lennon was singing and is singing and will always be singing about an inviolable and unspoiled utopia but also – by process of elimination; no more heaven, hell, possessions, borders – about a boring state of mind. A dimension where nothing, or at least no part of what we understand as our life and history, could exist in time or space. 'Imagine' is the universal hymn of pacifists, who – out of laziness – can't imagine the existence of something called *war*. Backed by the melody of an almost somnambulistic piano, 'Imagine' urges us to give up *everything*, and as part of that everything, ourselves. Autistic living, empty and absolute. Living in an unfurnished Neverland. 'Imagine' is a kind of 'Day in the Life' without getting out of bed. The death certificate of the lush 60s heralding the wasteland of my long amnesia, of my other life. The 70s and the 90s and the beginning of the 80s, when the obsessed fan Mark David Chapman came up to Lennon to ask him for an autograph and came back to thank him for it hours later with a bouquet of bullets, unimaginable until that moment. Chapman may be one of the few people who properly interpreted Lennon's message and – as in the Zen parable in which the apprentice must kill the Buddha he meets on the road – Chapman carried out his orders: the only way the world 'will be as one' is if you abandon the world, if you die. *Adieu. Sayonara.* The End. And the headlines in the papers were variations on the morbid idea that now the 60s really *were* over, once and for all. And so, all together now, we entered a new dark age.

I used the assassination of John Lennon in *Jim Yang and the Chance Machine.* Jim saves Lennon from Chapman, but Lennon – like David Barrie in *Jim Yang and the Imaginary Friend* – dies the next day of a broken neck when he slips in the bathtub while he's showering. After that, Jim Yang stops trying. And Jim Yang doesn't like 'Imagine'. Jim Yang thinks it's a 'song about the perfection of nothing', the same nothing Barrie fears. The nothing of the blank page. The nothing of his null marriage. The nothing of approaching the equator of life.

And wouldn't it be fantastic if we could *feel* the exact centre of our own lives? The moment at which death moves into the vacant house of the body and starts to furnish it, unhurriedly but also unceasingly? I'm not talking about isolated and diffuse symptoms. Signs, for example, like asking ourselves for the first time, half horrified and half amused, whether we like *today's youth.* And answering ourselves with ideas meant to be interesting, along the lines of 'younger generations today don't even last long enough to be given a name that distinguishes them from other younger generations' or 'in this millennial border time, youth starts sooner and lasts longer, that's all'. Whatever. Pure static. White noise. I'm referring to something else that has less to do with being any particular age than with being fully conscious of the precise instant life stops being life and begins to be death. The zero-second when you're halfway down the corridor and a door closes behind you and a door opens ahead, and all of a sudden childhood and old age assume the same degree of unreality, of fiction. What was and what will be is written with the same hesitance, with spelling and grammar mistakes. It's then that the waning myth of childhood meets the growing legend of old age and there you are, asking yourself 'what time is it?' and not wanting to look too closely at your watch.

I wrote something about that – about the fantasy of knowing how long it is till the last page in the novel of our lives – in *Jim Yang and the Time Eater*. In that book, my little hero again faces Cagliostro Nostradamus Smith, who – while trying to come up with his own chronocycle – designs a terrible machine. A Time Devourer. A device capable of calculating the exact date that every living being on the surface of the planet will die. The evil professor's plan is monstrous: to incite collective hysteria by sending letters to all the inhabitants of London; black envelopes that, when opened, will reveal the day and hour the recipients will draw their last breath. This, thinks Cagliostro Nostradamus Smith, will topple the pillars of society and halt the proper functioning of institutions, since nobody – conscious of the imminence or remoteness of the end – will care any more about maintaining order in a life almost always ruled by the notion of a surprise death.

Jim Yang decides to ask for the help of a specialist on the subject, and he pedals until he finds the writer H. G. Wells. He tells him his story; he asks for advice. But Wells only seems interested in learning whether any of his scientific prophecies have come true in the future. Jim Yang thinks about it a little and tells him no: the formula for invisibility hasn't been discovered; not only have Martians not tried to conquer earth, but all signs seem to indicate that there are no Martians; Dr Moreau's beasts never rose up to become men; the country of the blind doesn't appear on any map . . . As Wells listens, he's more and more depressed. Jim Yang tries to console him: 'But you shouldn't be sorry, sir: in the end you're the only real writer of fantastic fiction. Your ideas haven't been sullied by reality. They're still powerful, ambitious, unattainable . . . And then there's me and my chronocycle, which I know isn't exactly a time machine, but . . .' Wells loses his temper, calls his secretary, and throws Jim Yang out of the house, shouting: 'Some idiot at the Fabian Society sent you to mock me! Or do you think I believed for one second any of the nonsense you've been telling me!'

Finally, everything ends in a kind of random joke: the deadly letters Cagliostro Nostradamus Smith sends don't reach anyone, because to save a few cents, he doesn't use enough stamps. And on the last page, Jim Yang considers how interesting it would be to know the date of the last day of our lives not when it's too late, but on a day in the exact middle of our lives; and how that knowledge would give us the chance to change so many things, including the moment of our deaths. In general terms, Jim Yang and I almost always agree.

And that's where I suppose I'd be now, Keiko Kai, at the exact point – give or take a year – between ON and OFF, if I hadn't decided to change my plans, move ahead to what comes later, age as fast as possible, push my centre backward, come to a decision about my fast-approaching end. Finish myself off.

And that's where Barrie was when, dazzled by the solar radiance of Sylvia Llewelyn Davies, he felt what an astronomer must feel when his telescope finally finds the stars his passion will orbit until the end of his days. The ecstatic joy of discovery. Barrie sighted the Llewelyn Davies brothers and then their mother, and he's never felt this way before, and his Lennon-style nowhere-man nothing suddenly begins to be occupied by a Neverland full of corners, hiding places, short cuts, secret passageway, and the laughter of children running wild, opening and closing doors. Barrie is thirty-six, I think, or close to that. Almost half as old as he'll ever be. I'm sure that Barrie must've felt *something* then. Again, that's why I ask myself whether it might not be good – whether it might not be *interesting* – to have the ability to be fully conscious of the exact minute you cross the secret line where you begin the inevitable downhill slide. A faint shudder in the air or the clamour of a thousand trumpets, anything. The chance to discover a milestone explaining the signal that tells us precisely where the slow but steady descent from the heights of what we supposed would be our eternity begins. And telling us that from now on time will run faster; it's so much easier to run downhill than uphill. Or maybe all of this does us no good: we know that time is much faster than our ability to fathom its speed. Which leads me to the thought that the world – *this* is what the world is like – is overflowing with forty-year-olds convinced that they're still twenty and who utterly contradict the sentimental notion of the 'inner child'; people who keep their child on the outside, hanging around their necks like one of those deafeningly loud movie chimpanzees that're supposed to be funny. And how funny can a frantic chimpanzee be when it screams and screams and keeps screaming in horror at a story that's increasingly hard to understand because it keeps speeding faster and faster.

Sometimes, however, all falling seems to stop, pausing for an instant of pure, unqualified transcendence. Then, for a moment, we're able to imagine what it must be like to be immortal. We're up there, suspended, our arms spread, looking down, understanding that it's not we who've left the planet but the planet that's leaving us. And that it's right it should be that way.

And then Barrie feels he's flying over Kensington Gardens, over those perfect boys who'll keep asking him now to touch down beside them so they can listen to the stories he has to tell, stories in which they fly too, and visit other worlds.

The discovery of this new planet inhabited by the perfect children of a heavenly fairy, thinks Barrie, gives him the chance to change the established order of life; that immutable law of gravity, the ponderous weight of age that begins to stick to his bones and flesh and suddenly stop time from running – horizontal and continuous, eternal – along the gentlest of sea levels, at the feet of cliffs made of knees.

Barrie's sudden and perfect love for Sylvia Llewelyn Davies is so great that it's beyond jealousy. It's a sublime love that begins and ends in itself, and in its hugeness finds room to include and love everything and everyone loved by Sylvia Llewelyn Davies: her children, the father of her children, her husband, her love.

Have I ever known a love like that, Keiko Kai? I doubt it. I've been with women, but I've been with them in the same way I've visited certain inevitable, predictable tourist spots. And I soon abandoned the women just as I've almost completely given up travelling: because I discovered all too quickly that the inconveniences of the voyage – its back and forths, its emergency landings, its delays and cancellations, its lost luggage, its strange and uncomfortable beds – never lived up in practice to the theoretical pleasures of a stay in a place that was essentially unfamiliar and always foreign. As I've already told you, Keiko Kai, sexual desire is overrated and I gave it up without much difficulty; maybe it's not right for me to talk to you about such things, but I do it more out of resignation than urgency: you're the only one I can talk to and the last person I'll talk to; so . . .

It's easy, I'm sure, to stop making love. That expression – *making love* – always struck me as somewhat inappropriate, elevating a primitive reflex to the category of modern-day work, of *doing* something. It's easier to stop making love than to give up drinking, smoking, gambling, or, of course, reading. This lack of interest – I hasten to make clear – in my case has nothing to do with tragic events or pathological partners, much less with the sexual repression of Victorians who covered the legs of pianos and chairs because they considered them too lascivious to be displayed in public. On the contrary. The women I've been with have always been good and generous to me, and I never succumbed to that Proustian silliness of falling in love with unsuitable women or women who couldn't be *understood* by my immune system. They were all similar enough to each other to be interchangeable, not requiring me to shuffle the files of my heart too much as I approached and apprehended them. They all had the pale, icy air of old-fashioned damsels; they all came with a sigh instead of a shout (I like to think that an orgasmic sigh is like a shout in braille, ha); and at most, in moments of passion, they all closed their eyes and parted their lips to show me two always perfect rows of small crowded teeth, more vegetarian than carnivorous. Each received the news of the end of our affair with knowing, grateful smiles, because in my farewell speech I always made it perfectly clear that the weak-willed failings of my incurable misanthropy had nothing to do with them. The fault was mine, always; and there's no greater happiness than knowing yourself to be innocent and knowing it was the other person who made every conceivable mistake, that you didn't make a single one. So when I left them they were happy to think that they were leaving me. And women, as everyone knows, are better, faster, and more thorough at recovery. They come out of an affair as if emerging from a long bath. Clean. And they dry themselves with fluffy towels. And then – sooner or later – they'd all invite me to their respective weddings. One or two even asked me to be their children's godfather; offers I refused because I didn't 'feel worthy', though I still sent huge, extravagant gifts. And I'd almost never see them again, except in the society columns of the papers and in photographs in the glossiest magazines.

Recently, on the few occasions when I felt possessed by some uncontrollable urge, I chose to resort to the cold, efficient services of professionals: brief, brisk trips with no turbulence or miscommunications of any kind. And yes, I fell in love with them too for a few days or a few hours; once for just a minute. At first I made use of them live and in person. Later I discovered the telephone: the best of both worlds. The hotline is the equivalent of virtual reality when you travel the way I do. I've accumulated many miles and many key touches – I'm a frequent flyer, a frequent dialler – and I always call the same number, the same voice. I've never doubted the unique and unsurpassable beauty of that voice. Hearing it is like admitting what no one dares to admit to themselves: that being part of a couple means never completely knowing the other person; not because the other person is a mystery but for a simple and indisputable reason: you see what you want to see. It's the same thing that happens when you read a novel. Is there anything better than that? I love the way I can hear her saliva sometimes, invisibly. A smack of her lips is like fire when it encounters new wood. When she's good (when I ask her to be good) I call her Wendy; when she's bad (when I ask her to be bad) I call her Tiger Lily.

Maybe – in most people's opinions – I'm not an emotionally or romantically satisfied man. But I'm a man without problems. Really, the great danger doesn't lie in you loving someone but in someone loving you: if someone loves you, you end up becoming the person they love. A doppelgänger of passions, an ideal constructed by someone else that you inevitably end up destroying for the sole pleasure of seeing it collapse, and seeing the collapse in the face of the smitten architect.

Keiko Kai: love is one of those countries perpetually stuck in the third world. A republic subject to dictatorships and financial crack ups and revolutions and droughts and epidemics. A kingdom where sooner or later there's an earthquake, where someone will always come walking out of the blazing ruins unable to understand what's happened – wondering Why me?

My parents' love for each other; what was it like? How will I ever know? Love between parents is the most mysterious love of all. We're an inseparable part of it, and at the same time, it excludes us. Children can never know anything about it, and besides, other people's loves are impossible to gauge; which is a good thing, because nothing could be worse than being able to compare our loves to the loves of acquaintances and strangers with scientific precision. Love as a scientific property and an element we could alchemically distil would be a much more powerful weapon than any splitting of atoms. The mystery of love, revealed and synthesizable, would turn our planet into an even more terrible place than it is, because it would put love on the same level as the brutal, simple, functional logic of hate. The mystery of what ultimately brings a couple together – taking into account the scientific advances closing in on the genome that relegate us to the almost extraterrestrial loneliness of our body in a dead universe, refused an invitation to the big invisible party that everything would seem to indicate we don't deserve – is the only mystery we have left, a mystery that, once solved, will bring us face to face with a reality where literature, film, art, music – and love, of course – will no longer be necessary or make sense. But for now, when we try to *narrate* a couple, all we have are scattered fragments, footprints in the sand that're instantly blurred by the spear point of a wave, by the sound of a voice that approaches and fades away.

Which doesn't prevent us, of course, from venturing to make certain modest assertions, from enumerating some relevant points of contact upon mixing up the couples composed of Sylvia Jocelyn Llewelyn du Maurier & Arthur Llewelyn Davies and Lady Alexandra Swinton-Menzies & Sebastian 'Darjeeling' Compton-Lowe in the same test tube as if they were two different experiments carried out in the same laboratory.

To begin with, the four were shamelessly beautiful. Four perfect children of their time, English through and through, the kind of people it's hard to imagine existing in another era or place, or simply being ugly.

Marcus Merlin once explained to me that there's no more foolproof line to approach someone with – especially someone of the opposite sex – than 'I dreamed about you last night', because it's a password no one can resist, a password that opens all doors and overcomes all resistance. It's hard to refuse to hear more about what the other person dreamed. And everybody knows you can say anything when you're describing a dream, because it's a dream, after all, and dreams can take any shape they want in dreams.

What to say about how my father and my mother met? What were their first words to each other? I know little or nothing about the occasion. My parents never told me much about it. Never – not once did I visit that commonplace of childhood – did I hear or glimpse my parents making love. So I can't claim they felt great passion for each other, either. Once or twice, in conversation, I know they described their mutual courtship as 'pendular': that there was a moment he pursued her and another moment that she pursued him, and that the variables of the chase depended on the weather and the seasons. And that this back-and-forth continued once they were married – a faithful marriage despite the excesses of the era, a bright Victorian marriage with no hidden secrets, I'm sure of it – when they always seemed to be doing different yet subtly complementary things, as in the choreography of a ballet in which the dancers move away from one another while still meshed in a single movement. The only time I saw them doing the same thing at the same time and in the same place – they didn't know I was watching them from the top of the stairs in the dark, they thought I was still asleep under the effect of the sedatives I was given at the hospital – was the night I watched them collapse in front of Neverland's voracious flaming hearth, hand in hand and howling like coyotes at Baco's death.

And of course, from the time they were children, my father and mother were always seeing each other at different gatherings, at the baptisms and weddings and funerals of the grey, boring upper class. Terrain ripe and ready for being revolutionized by the festivities of a new decade primed to change everything. The inspirational fury of round numbers joined with the spiky fever of hormones. Love as a strategy and the urgent need to populate the New World with a fresh litter of children completely different from the children they had been: children who would help them relive their childhoods; different childhoods, improved. This explains the irresistible urge to pair off like rabbits and turn into young parents, little parents, parents with no desire to grow up; and what better way to make that come true than to produce children of their own before it was socially acceptable in those days. Children as experiments that would free them from the influence of their own parents by creating a new dimension of people even younger than them (but not by much) and admit them to a privileged state where their youth would be eternal or at least much longer lasting.

Something like that, I don't know.

Maybe I'm talking nonsense, Keiko Kai.

Maybe all of this is just theories elaborated after the fact, theories worth nothing. The futile ravings of a surviving witness.

One thing I used to be sure of, but, taking into account recent revelations, I'm not sure of any more: my parents were supposedly engaged the night of 31 December 1959, and I was already there, floating.

Yes and no.

It's easy for me to imagine them – because, except for the date marking the legal beginning of their love, they hardly told me anything about the prehistory that parents who aren't parents yet inhabit before their children arrive – with their glasses raised high, almost stowaways at a party of adults headed for extinction. Grandparents and aunts and uncles petrified in the amber of one or two world wars, depressed by the Empire's slow but steady decline, remembering with sadness Edward VIII's speech of amorous abdication that fateful 11 December 1936, when everything finally lay in ruins, asking themselves what had happened; how it could be that 40 per cent of the population of London was now under the age of twenty-five, which surely had to do with the dizzying rise in the crime rate; where had the good times gone; and has anyone heard anything new about Winston's health, eh?

Was it love at first sight for them? Now I know that the fantasy I played with for all those years, the desire and the milestone of having been conceived months before but legitimated that night – in the beat of silence between peal number eleven and peal number twelve – could never have been true. My parents wanted to be revolutionaries, but back then everything had its limits and conventions. And anyway, it was clear that my father's private revolution – a counter-revolution hidden inside a revolution – in reality sought a utopian return to old ways and habits, not the thrill of a fertile, messy orgy.

Keiko Kai: I'm a complete idiot with dates, with calculations involving time. It's numbers, and I've already told you that I can't be counted on with numbers. I don't understand dates. So I'm forced to simply memorize them and repeat them from memory: *this* happened *then*. And that's it. Like praying without believing. Obeying the rules of an abstraction – the idea that time passes, that it goes by, is the only thing that makes time bearable, after all – always seemed to me a vain and difficult task. Time is an aberration beyond the reach of any system, and its only merciful and orderly quality, I repeat, is its perpetual refusal to come to a stop.

Time is above everything, even God. God rules the whole universe except for its vital fluid: time. The Devil is the keeper and caretaker of time – making music out of notes like seconds that add up to millennial symphonies – and that's why most mistakes are made and most soulless pacts are signed in his name. Time is always the foundation on which the complex architecture of sin rises.

At least that's what Marcus Merlin thought.

Said Marcus Merlin: 'You understand it when you spend a little time analyzing religious rites . . . All that standing up and sitting down and kneeling . . . Services of aerobicized faith; you know what I mean. The stuffy air of churches and the idea of burying yourself deep in prayer until you can't breathe and there's no oxygen flowing to the brain and you're ready to believe you believe in anything. It's all just a hopeless attempt to try to take back control of time.'

And Marcus Merlin added that he'd been smart enough to sell his soul to the Devil when he was five years old, during break at his elementary school in Manchester.

Said Marcus Merlin: 'I never understood those people who wait until they grow up to sell it, who take so long to learn to trust the Devil. After all, don't forget that the Devil is Jesus Christ's older brother and that he's always shown more of an interest in understanding human nature, a much more gratifying interest than God's other son, who's always talking in riddles and metaphors and parables. The devil speaks clearly, and as we all know, Evil is the work of craftsmen, while Good is an automatic, mechanized activity. So I never understood those doubts about selling your soul as fast as possible. The sooner you sell it, the better price you'll get. Poor Faust . . . All that wasted time . . . If you sell your soul when you're very young, you don't have to make the obvious choice and ask for youth. As far as I'm concerned, it was an excellent bargain, I can tell you that. I always liked that old Chinese curse: "May you have an interesting life." Though I never understood why they consider it a curse. All right, *interesting* is an ambiguous word when it's applied to lives. And women, ha. But I don't care: I sold my soul to the Devil when I was very young. And in exchange I asked for an interesting life. And believe me: the Devil gave it to me.'

Maybe that's how – of course it is – I came up with the clever concept of my Jim Yang as a hero pedalling over the tyranny of calendars, my young hero as a chrono-illogical anarchist saint.

And it never occurred to me to think that parents might lie. I grew up in an era when children's literature hadn't yet discovered the possibility or narrative device of parents as more or less dangerous monsters. I never imagined that the beginning of my life would contain elements so like those of the books I read by the light of a torch. The obviousness of those commonplaces, their vulgar efficiency – the same thing always happens – is usually clear to everyone except the protagonist. It's hard for us to believe that reality could be so much like a soap opera: arriving in episodes and always postponing the end until it comes all at once and without warning, weary and confused, with so many plot threads still to be untangled, wanting to be over no matter how, simply over. And just as we're dying we realize in horror that the most terrible thing about our death is its scant importance in the novel of which we thought we were heroes, as part of a plot where *everything* keeps happening even though we aren't there. We feel like main characters, but at most we're important supporting players, if we're lucky. We think of ourselves as writers at the controls or in the tallest tower of a castle and we're just barely qualified readers tying ourselves with ropes to the masts and lost among the trees. Our task was simply to propel the ship a little farther or to make someone else's flag flutter. We're the wind in the sails, or the wind in the branches through which I'm fleeing now so as not to face the reefs that capsize you and the axe that fells you.

Not yet, please. Not yet.

All right, I confess.

My parents died young.

My parents never grew up.

I'm alive and now I'm older than my parents ever were. Not old enough to be my parents' father, but certainly an older brother. Or one of those young uncles. The kind of brother or uncle who appears and disappears, now you see him, now you don't, on the farthest fringes of a family reunion. The one who nobody asks about when he doesn't come, and who everyone's surprised to see when he does come. The relative – in fact it's not strictly necessary that he be a *real* relative – who nobody knows exactly what he does and . . .

I'm digressing again, Keiko Kai. And my head hurts. It always happens when the past leaps ahead – a relatively new experience for me, one I was denied for so many years – and mixes itself up with the present, that very brief instant that always seemed completely tedious and superfluous to me. If we lived only in the past and the future, the world would be much more interesting. Not having to think about the present – what's about to be, what is, what's already been – I'm sure would allow us to remember everything and predict everything and . . .

What do I mean? What do I want to believe? Better this blue pill to keep the green pill company and send me floating in the skies of London. Better to fly and choose a window and head towards it.

Anything that comes in through a window and not a door is definitely something that's come to stay.

'There never was a simpler happier family until the coming of Peter Pan,' wrote Barrie.

The courtship of Arthur and Sylvia is perfectly documented in memoirs and social registers of the era, and their marriage is described in the pages of *Peter Pan* – with certain crypto-biographical spite – in the portrayal of the Darlings.

We know that Arthur comes from a family of professional spartans, and Sylvia from a family of frivolous bohemians. We also know that Sylvia, according to a lucky and appreciative witness, 'often displayed the tops of her lovely breasts and her shoulders and neck', and that solemn attorney Arthur at first didn't seem much of a catch to the parents of such a splendid daughter: not much money, though he had a promising future in the world of law. To his credit, they acknowledged, he was an incredibly handsome young man. Together, Arthur and Sylvia produced a dazzling effect, as if two perfect gods had decided to consecrate their love far from Olympus, clumsily disguised as mere mortals here in London.

I have pictures, Keiko Kai. Sylvia has the kind of beauty that wouldn't work so well today. Hers is a face that would better grace a cameo than a magazine cover. Arthur's handsomeness, on the other hand, has weathered the shift in fashions better, and he'd have no reason to envy the looks of a film star or a model of expensive clothing any day. Maybe most important of all: their two beauties are well matched.

Arthur was left three thousand pounds in an uncle's will, and after two years of patient waiting, he married Sylvia on

15 August 1892. When they returned from their honeymoon in Porthgwarra, in Cornwall, the couple moved into a house at 18 Craven Terrace, Paddington.

On 20 July of the following year their first son was born: George.

On 11 September 1894, John arrived, almost immediately known to all as Jack.

On 25 February 1897, Peter was born. Unlike his brothers, he was never baptized in the church, since his parents thought it would be right to let him decide for himself what was best when he was older. And it's true, they're right, they're intelligent, modern parents; because what's the sense of initiating someone into the worship of an invisible, angry god when they're lucky enough to live at a time when the mischievous and omnipresent messiah Peter Pan flies the face of the planet.

And the Craven Terrace house got too small.

The family decided to move to a house belonging to one of Arthur's aunts who'd just died, at 31 Kensington Park Gardens, in Notting Hill, and hire a nanny named Mary Hodgson to help with the little ones and the household chores. Notting Hill was a good neighbourhood springing up around Kensington Palace, birthplace of Queen Victoria. It was a place where writers and artists often moved. Ford Madox Ford described it – ironically but accurately – as 'a Greenwich Village for the upper classes'.

Arthur began to earn money while Sylvia occupied herself designing clothing for Mrs Nettleship's famed costuming shop and for the celebrated actress Ellen Terry. With the scraps and remnants, she made clothes for her sons. One day, Sylvia found in a drawer an old judge's robe that had once belonged to Arthur's grandfather. Heavy red cloth. There would be enough fabric to sew three small coats and three tam-o'-shanters for her boys. The uniform that would make them almost another of Kensington Gardens' attractions. And Sylvia discovers that dressing children, changing their skin, is much better and more fun and more freighted with significance than the almost forgotten game of playing with dolls. To dress children is to reinvent them so that the world exclaims at them and applauds.

Thus Barrie discovered them and loved them, and thus Barrie discovered Sylvia at that dinner at Sir George Lewis's house, and nothing would ever be the same again.

I insist, Keiko Kai: the true mission of coincidences – which are never coincidental and in fact function as a popular and economical and accessible version of miracles – is simply to help us feel part of something we can't resist. In the name of coincidence – which is also nothing but a burst of madness disguised as something of rational significance – we end up doing things we would never have done otherwise. And Barrie isn't the kind of person who needs much help to feel chosen by a superior being, to believe himself someone predestined to play a certain role in a certain play with a plot that only Barrie could have thought up.

The mystery and provenance of the brothers Llewelyn Davies solved, Barrie and Porthos play with them and no one else. Barrie prefers George, and it's George he mentions most often in the notebooks he keeps at the time. And it's George who gives him the idea for the slow gestation, over the course of four years, of *The Little White Bird*. My favourite of Barrie's books, Keiko Kai. The book that'll be published in 1902, and in which Peter Pan will first appear. Barrie writes in his notebook:

– *George admires me as writer.*
– Little White Bird. *Telling George what love is . . . in answer to George's inquiries about how to write a story.*

George is the son Barrie will never have, the son who makes him the father he'll never be: they're an imaginary son and father free of the responsibilities and ties of blood, a father and son whose only and imperative obligation is to play. I like to imagine the two of them in Kensington Gardens, in fast forward or the jerky motion of cartoons. Barrie plays with George in Kensington Gardens and only goes home when it's time to keep writing *The Little White Bird*, the novel based on his games with George.

The Little White Bird is narrated in the first person by a character called Captain W—, 'a gentle, whimsical, lonely old bachelor', and begins with the sentence: 'Sometimes the little boy who calls me father brings me an invitation from his mother: "I shall be so pleased if you will come and see me," and I always reply in some such words as these: "Dear madam, I decline."' Captain W— is a retired soldier who makes a living as a writer and likes taking long walks in Kensington Gardens with his dog, a Saint Bernard that answers to the name Porthos. Captain W—'s greatest wish is to some day love a child of his own who – he has it all thought out, all written down, to the last detail – he'll call Timothy. And so Captain W— comes to know a young couple for whom, under the impish cloak of anonymity, he'll become an infinitely eager and generous benefactor.

At the beginning of *The Little White Bird*, Captain W— meets young William, the husband, walking the deserted streets of London on the night his wife, his lovely wife Mary, is giving birth. They speak for a few minutes. Days later, Captain W— finds out where the couple lives and learns that they've had a son whom they've called David. Captain W— lies and tells them that he too has a son: Timothy. From then on, Captain W— follows David's progress closely, and one day – after finding a distraught Mary trying to pawn some of her dearest possessions because she has no money to buy clothes for David – he tells the young parents that his beloved Timothy has died and that he no longer has any use for his clothes and toys. It isn't long before Mary discovers that Timothy is nothing but the product of Captain W—'s imagination and that it's he who's been the family's mysterious protector all this time. Mary invites Captain W— to visit over and over again, but he refuses, demanding that David come to see him first. Mary accepts – after all, they owe the man so much – and then Captain W— puts into practice a cruel plan to win the boy's affections and make him forget his parents: 'It was a scheme conceived in a flash', 'a sinister project' to 'expose to the boy all his mother's vagaries', it is explained to us.

Mary, of course, is based on Sylvia, and William on Arthur; but Barrie chooses to conduct his relationship with the Llewelyn Davieses in a way that's just as extreme as that of the reclusive and enigmatic Captain W—, though at the opposite end of the spectrum of etiquette: Barrie goes as often as he can to 31 Kensington Park Gardens. Whether he's invited or not. Any reason or excuse to visit Sylvia and the children is good enough. Barrie's finally found what he's been seeking for years: a lovely woman who's the ideal symbol of maternity and a small troop of perfect playmates.

In one of the first biographies of the author, the almost hagiographic *Barrie: The Story of J.M.B.*, by Denis Mackail, who played with Barrie in Kensington Gardens when he was a boy, it says – I have it here, let me read this to you, Keiko Kai, yes, listen – 'What is genius? It's the power of becoming a child whenever you so desire. Barrie adores these little ones and their games, and if sometimes his single-minded concentration on them is really a little excessive and alarming, no one can stop him, because the children rescue him from his darkest depressions, lifting his spirits and making him so happy.'

Yes, Barrie needs the little Llewelyn Davieses the way a sick man needs his medicine.

Barrie is one of the most famous and celebrated of writers: his presence is welcome everywhere; he's just received an honourary degree from St Andrew's University, where he was applauded by all the students; reporters come to every one of the Allahakbarrie cricket matches and allot them the same space required and occupied by historical events. How to close the door on this little Scotsman who all of a sudden seems to have become another member of the family, wonders Arthur Llewelyn Davies.

Arthur's sure the little man presents no danger to his marriage. He's harmless. Sylvia loves Arthur and no one but Arthur; but isn't it a little disturbing that Barrie seems to *love the love* the beautiful young couple feel for each other? Barrie is delighted by them and – Arthur can't help feeling – studies them. And sometimes it isn't very pleasant to come home after an exhausting day at court and – as Mary Hodgson informs him yet again that's she's lost all control over the little ones since Barrie entered their lives – discover that your humble desire to close the door to the world and take refuge with your wife and children not only hasn't been granted, but worse, that your children and your wife seem possessed by the euphoria of that damned pygmy Scotsman who's spinning and spinning like a dervish in the middle of the drawing room.

Yes, Barrie *needs* to see them all the time; he has succumbed to the most delicious and social of obsessions. Barrie visits them and besieges them and accosts them and works on his texts with his usual monstrous concentration, which, when one of his books is opened, at times creates the illusion of watching him write letter by letter as we read word by word.

Charles Frohman, the Buddha of Broadway, has come to London to visit: he tells Barrie that his plays work very well in the United States, but that he wants something else, something that will revolutionize the history of the theatre, that will transform it forever. Barrie tells him that he has an idea, a good idea. It comes to him all at once, fully fledged; there's no doubt whatsoever as to the tone of the first act, the pace of the second, the denouement of the third. It will be called *The Admirable Crichton*, and it's about the shipwreck of a family of English aristocrats on a deserted island with their butler and their life there for two years. On the island – because of his survival instincts and practical sense, by 'natural selection' – the butler, Crichton, takes the lead and the Lasenbys' young daughter, Lady Mary, falls in love with him and . . . When they're rescued, Barrie explains to Charles Frohman with a mischievous little laugh, everything goes back to being the way it was, as if nothing has happened: Crichton returns to his customary duties and his room in the cellar of the big house, the daughter resumes the preparations for her wedding to her old fiancé, and the grown-ups again treat Crichton as an ordinary, capable servant. In a thoughtful moment, feeling guilty, Lady Mary says to Crichton: 'You are the best man among us.' The butler responds: 'On an island, my lady, perhaps; but in England, no.' Lady Mary: 'Then there's something wrong with England.' Crichton: 'My lady, not even from you can I listen to a word against England.'

Charles Frohman smiles and tells Barrie to get to work. Barrie apologizes: it isn't the theatre miracle Charles Frohman was hoping for, he knows; but he'll come up with something.

Barrie works every night, but even so he lets no day go by without making time for a visit to the Llewelyn Davieses. Barrie doesn't announce his visits. Barrie doesn't send ahead one of those cards backed with silver or marbleized paper or printed on papier-mâché. Although taking advantage – writing letters back then is like talking on the telephone, Barrie doesn't take advantage of the city's seven daily mail deliveries, and he doesn't limit his stay to the hours established by the protocol of the era: the best time, the appropriate window, being between three and six in the afternoon. Barrie simply shows up, only leaving in order to give himself the chance to appear again. Barrie disappears for the exact time necessary to buy everything mentioned in his games and conversations with the boys and reappears the next day, accompanied by a valet who helps him carry the huge packages wrapped in shiny coloured paper.

And what does Mary Barrie think about all this? At first she hates Sylvia, but it doesn't take her long to realize that it would be best to win her over. And after all, what's happening to her husband now has happened so many times before with the actresses in his plays: it's a childish, innocent, and surely fleeting voraciousness. Mary and Sylvia have interests in common: clothing design and interior decoration. Although Sylvia can't help being disgusted by Mary's constant rude displays of wealth, and uncomfortable at the way Mary uses Barrie's name over and over again to secure small favours – good tables in restaurants, better seats at fashion shows, and private boxes at Ascot – they soon become friends without understanding very well why or what for. Barrie has brought them together to work on an invisible play.

Dissatisfaction with her marriage gives Mary a boundless hunger, an urgency to 'do things' and 'have projects'. It occurs to her that what she needs is a country house. Something to keep her occupied, and if possible to keep Barrie away from the Llewelyn Davieses and little George; from the boy Barrie can't stop talking about and won't stop talking to.

George has become Barrie's ideal listener, and also a kind of perfect and exalting echo chamber for his imagination and writing. Barrie soon develops a system, a method for assembling his stories (which – in the opinion of the increasingly furious Mary Hodgson – 'have no moral purpose or virtue'): Barrie first tells George a story, then asks George to tell it back to him with all the alterations a child might make to an adult story, then Barrie tells it back again with his own modifications. In this way they toss the story back and forth to each other over and over again, like a ball, until it's hard to say who came up with what.

Barrie is especially interested in George's still-fresh memories of his days in the cradle, asleep and horizontal. Barrie asks questions and George puts his hands to his temples and squeezes his eyes shut and speaks in a deep, serious voice, like someone possessed who is calling up the ghosts of his brief past. At some point a name emerges: Peter, a baby who can fly because his mother forgot to weigh him when he was born. A feather-light baby who abandons his carriage, escaping and building a nest in the trees of Kensington Gardens. Something like that.

According to Barrie – although they may have forgotten it, the trauma of being imprisoned keeps them docile until they achieve the consolation of amnesia – all children were once birds at the beginning of their lives. That's why the windows in their rooms are usually barred: so that when they're assailed by the shadow of that old winged memory they don't succumb to the temptation of waving their arms and trying to fly up into the sky.

Barrie and George – and David and Captain W— in *The Little White Bird* – endlessly talk and offer up theories about Peter. At first, Peter is clearly inspired by George's little brother Peter. But he becomes a more complicated figure and he is given a last name: Pan, in honour of the ancient Greek god, symbol of nature, paganism, and the kind of happy amorality that Mary Hodgson keeps scolding about. If Barrie is a bad influence, then this imaginary and increasingly concrete Peter Pan – who's also easy to associate with the imperfection of certain primitive Christian saints – begins to drive the little Llewelyn Davieses wild with glee, and Barrie too, who soon realizes that this flying child is the perfect embodiment of all his obsessions: childhood as a gravity-free land outside all laws; the firm determination to stop time by refusing to grow up; the verb *to play* in all its possible conjugations.

And so Peter Pan is introduced in the pages of *The Little White Bird* as a kind of subplot, like a surprise within a surprise. Peter Pan establishes his dwelling-place on the island in the middle of the Serpentine, on Bird's Island, ruled by the crow Solomon Caw; he plays with the fairies; sometimes he visits terra firma rowing in a nest he uses like a boat; and every so often he flies to his old home to see his mother crying for her lost son. Sometimes Peter Pan is even a little upset to see her so sad, but the call of Kensington Gardens is much stronger and he returns there 'for ever and always'.

Peter Pan also finds his way into the last-minute revisions of the novel *Tommy and Grizel*, where, in one of the chapters, Tommy asks his wife to kiss the manuscript he's about to send to his editor: 'Wish it luck . . . you were always so fond of babies, and this is my baby.' In the novel we're told that this new book by Tommy Sandys – another of Barrie's alter egos – is *The Wandering Child*: 'I wonder whether any of you read it now. Your fathers and mothers thought a great deal of that slim volume, but it would make little stir in an age in which all the authors are trying who can say Damn loudest. It is but a reverie about a little boy who was lost. His parents find him in a wood singing joyfully to himself because he thinks he can now be a boy for ever; and he fears that if they catch him they will compel him to grow into a man, so he runs farther from them into the wood and is running still, singing to himself because he is always to be a boy. That is really all, but T. Sandys knew how to tell it. The moment he conceived the idea . . . he knew that it was the idea for him.'

At the end of *Tommy and Grizel*, Tommy Sandys kills himself, I think, and Barrie's readers – who were expecting something more like *Sentimental Tommy*, the pleasant first instalment – were taken aback by the novel's bitterness and morbidity and its tragic conclusion, with adorable Grizel destroyed by her husband's childish ways and Tommy hanging himself; or at least it seems to me that he does, but now I'm not sure.

Barrie isn't very bothered by the book's poor critical reception and its relatively low sales for an author of his stature. Barrie abandons Tommy – the end of an era – in order to devote himself fully to *The Little White Bird* and Peter Pan and to go running to the Llewelyn Davieses' house where he tells George and Jack and Peter the new things their hero has done.

Arthur Llewelyn Davies decides to flee, take a break: he goes on holiday with his family to the coast, to Rustington, in Sussex. He needs to spend some time alone with his children and with his wife, who is pregnant again. Arthur dreams of a daughter; but Michael is born, and once again they decide not to christen him or give him a middle name.

The Barries – without sending word, they want it to be a surprise – follow the Llewelyn Davieses just a few days later; they rent a house less than a mile from theirs.

Arthur pours himself a scotch and then immediately another scotch, and goes out to the porch to take deep breaths of the sea air. George and Jack and Peter jump for joy: during the holidays they'll be able to spend *all* day with Barrie, who, as soon as he appears, informs them that he has many things to tell them about Peter Pan, while ceaselessly taking pictures of them with his new toy. Barrie is an excellent photographer and over the years he manages to assemble a sizeable collection of these photographs: Peter and George and Jack running on the beach at Rustington; Sylvia reading under a tree; George and Sylvia; Peter naked from behind; George sleeping on a hillside; and my favourite of all: Sylvia at the edge of the sea as she tries to dry a slippery Peter, naked again, the towel flapping like a flag. The composition of the scene is closer to that of an impressionist painting than anything typical of the static photographs of the time, but it also has the timeless mystery of a perfectly preserved instant, which, like the mute lion roaring behind the glass of a museum display, seems to have been frozen there forever at the precise moment it was about to leap on us and sink its claws and teeth and happiness into us.

I don't have pictures of myself as a child at the seashore. My parents never took me. And I didn't discover the sea until I ran away, after Baco's funeral, pedalling my amphetamine-fuelled bicycle towards the Brighton coast. Maybe it was the distorting effect of the pills, but since then I've been convinced that minors should be forbidden to see the ocean. There's something disturbing about the back and forth of the waves that makes us think about things we shouldn't until we're more intellectually prepared, or maybe less susceptible to the liquid universe we once emerged from, dragging ourselves like shipwrecked survivors of the cataclysm of evolution.

In Rustington, Barrie and the Llewelyn Davies brothers fly kites in the morning and watch meteorites fall at night. The sky is always popular; but in the Victorian era the sky is also the place where the best stories begin. Barrie tells George and Jack and Peter the things that've been happening in Kensington Gardens since they left.

Barrie tells them that Peter Pan rides a goat and that – if you look for it hard and carefully enough – in Kensington Gardens you'll find the only house in the world built for human beings by the fairies. 'But no one has really seen it, except just three or four, and they have not only seen it but slept in it, and unless you sleep in it you never see it. This is because it is not there when you lie down, but it is there when you wake up and step outside.'

Barrie tells them that the stars shoot down because they're tired of dangling in space for so many thousands of years. He tells them that some of them are very strong and hold on easily, until, from the top of the tallest tree in Kensington Gardens, Peter Pan hits them with a stone and makes them fall, and they fall, furious, breathing a last streak of dead light.

Barrie tells them that the children who break their necks when they tumble down their carriages are buried in Kensington Gardens, and that it's Peter Pan who buries them and that those white stones bearing numbers and initials – W. St M. and 13a P.P. 1841; markers indicating the exact point where the parish of Westminster St Mary borders the parish of Paddington – are really small gravestones over the little tombs of Walter Stephen Matthews and Phoebe Phelps.

Barrie tells them that 'Phoebe was thirteen months old and Walter was probably a little younger; but it seems that Peter, as a matter of delicacy, preferred not to put their ages on the stones.'

Barrie tells them that at first there were no fairies in Kensington Gardens because children weren't allowed in Kensington Gardens; but once the prohibition was lifted, Kensington Gardens filled up with children and fairies; and it's the fairies – who're incapable of doing anything useful no matter how busy they always look – who change the notices that say what time the gardens close and thus move forward that moment of farewell. Then, when the gates to the garden are closed and the windows of night have opened, the fairies come out to play and the trees clap for them, slapping their branches together while the fairies dance in the bright, secret, magic air.

Barrie tells them that after all the people out walking have returned to their houses and the gates are closed until the next morning and all the churchbells are ringing, Peter Pan gaily plays his flute and dances on the graves where he sometimes leaves white flowers. Peter Pan searches for little children who've just died so he can bury them, digging in the dirt with his oar, and Peter Pan shouts songs to make those lost children laugh as he leads them to another world, a world of eternal play. Another world that isn't called Neverland yet, but that already exists, a magic place where the terrible bedtime hour never comes.

Jack and Peter fall over laughing: to them, death still seems something that only happens in the stories Barrie tells. Something that doesn't exist, that could never happen in their world and their lives and the lives and worlds of those around them. George listens spellbound. George – Mary Hodgson passes by and can't help putting her hand to her mouth in horror – gets up, puts a hand on his chest, points to the horizon with the other, and exclaims in a deep, heroic voice: 'To die will be an awfully big adventure!'

'To die will be an awfully big adventure!' George exclaims; and Barrie sighs and imagines an eternal, solitary child standing on a rock in the sea, his hair wet and his hands clasped behind his back, contemplating a horizon where icebergs seem to loom and the moon, above a few clouds in the sky, is reflected in the water, and the mermaids sing to the moon before retiring, one by one, to their chambers beneath the waves.

Barrie writes all this down in the notebook he carries everywhere to record the things the Llewelyn Davies brothers say.

He notes them one by one, collecting them like gold coins and holding them up to the light, knowing already that they must be real. Barrie bites them, smiling with the advance satisfaction of someone who knows that he's no longer a guest but has become something much better and stranger and more impressive: Barrie has become an invader.

The Invader

Take notes, Keiko Kai.

Please.

I'll untie your hand so you can write.

Or better not.

Never mind.

Here's a portable tape recorder. The electric animal that's the successor to those acoustic notebooks you can hardly buy anywhere now. A machine that eats voices which – when they're played back, as I've already told you – sound hardly anything like what their owners hear. The person a voice belongs to always hears it blended: the part from inside that he hears with his brain; the part from outside that he hears with his ears. The two parts – as if one's the finger and the other the digital fingerprint the finger makes – say the same thing, but a little differently, skewed; and it sounds slightly false, almost like a good imitation, but an imitation nevertheless.

REC.

1, 2, 3, testing.

Famous places in London that I remember having visited in my childhood:

Abbey Road Studios, Buckingham Palace, Biba, Piccadilly, West End, East Ham High Street, Notting Hill, Mayfair, the offices of the magazines *Queen* and *Vogue*, English Boy Ltd, Madame Tussaud's Wax Museum, the Strand Palace Hotel, the Savoy Hotel, a flat on Ebury Street and another flat on Primrose Hill and another flat on Harley Street, Cavendish Avenue, King's Road, Bond Street in Mayfair, 69 Duke Street, Denmark Street, the BBC, Ennismore Garden Mews, the Establishment Club, the Kentucky Club, the Saddle Room, the Flamingo (also known as the 'Mingo), the Marquee (there are two Marquees), the Piccadilly, the Ealing Club, the Ad Lib, the Scene, the Talk of the Town, the Palladium, the Blue Angel, the Crawdaddy, the Colony Sporting Club, the Pickwick Club, the Playboy Club, the UFO Club on Tottenham Court Road, the Roundhouse UFO Club, the Positano Room, the Speakeasy, Quo Vadis, Regent Street and Oxford Street, Vince, His Clothes, Male West One, Domino Male, WIP's, Blaise's, Quaglino's, Luard's, Esmeralda's Barn, Crockford's, Annabel's, Sibylla's, Osteria San Lorenzo, Trattoria Terrazza, La Poubelle, Le Kilt, Club dell'Arethusa, La Discotheque, Indica Gallery, Tate Gallery, Carnaby Street, Saville Row (where the Beatles, in July 1968, opened the general headquarters of Apple Corps at No. 3 Saville Row, London W1, in a house Lord Nelson once presented to Lady Hamilton; my father – this was just after he was shipwrecked – couldn't have borne it, I think), Sloane Square, World's End, Vidal Sassoon, Chelsea, Bazaar, Granny Takes a Trip, I Was Lord Kitchener's Valet, Hung On You, Skin, Mr Freedom, Mexicana, Hem and Fringe, Just Looking, Forbidden Fruit, Clobber, Blast Off, Through the Looking Glass, Just Men, Mitsukiku, the Fool, Apple, Waterloo Bridge, Hyde Park, and Kensington Gardens.

Famous people I remember having seen during my childhood, at parties. At many parties, which in the telling I'll merge into a single unforgettable party to save time and space. It's better that way, after all: maximum luxury, like in those big-budget history programmes in which a whole period of history is condensed into a single night, and suddenly all kinds of people who never knew each other meet in a big room in the glow from a single fireplace, raising glasses and bumping into each other and signing declarations of war or independence.

Parties – baptisms and weddings and funerals included – usually define an era much better than the careful analysis of everything that was done between one party and the next. And here they are, here they come, the ghosts of my Christmases past, which – because of the way posterity works – have become the ghosts of Christmases present and future. Spirits inhabiting a dimension where it's always Christmas but where the 'most famous birthday in history' isn't celebrated – says Marcus Merlin – and instead we celebrate the possibility of stopping and altering ordinary time with the wild abandon of a neverending party. Ghosts that really exist, because back then they already believed in life after death or – who knows – life after the things they'd done to make themselves famous or infamous.

They aren't guests, Keiko Kai. They're invaders. They're invaders who come early and almost always leave early – early the next morning, or a few days later. They come to Neverland, they alight from brand-new cars, they smile as if aware that a flash might catch them from the bushes, and they step into a painting that's half Hieronymus Bosch and half Wally's World: Wally, that idiot who always has to be looked for, and when we find him, we can never understand why we wanted him so urgently.

Here they come:

Marit Allen (editor of *Vogue*, hunting for new faces and finding too many; never have there been so many new faces in London all at the same time, talking and blinking and kissing and drinking and swallowing: welcome to the safari of the Age of the New Face); Woody Allen (in London filming *Casino Royale*; he makes jokes about Marcuse and Laing that no one understands; someone asks him what band they play in, what gallery they show in, what movies they act in, what restaurant they cook for, what boutique they design clothes for); the Animals (Eric Burdon asks Bob Dylan if Bob Dylan is there yet: 'No, he's not here yet,' Bob Dylan replies); Princess Anne (who I always get mixed up with Princess Margaret); Michelangelo Antonioni (he's passing out an obsessively detailed questionnaire to photographers to help him develop the protagonist of his film *Blow-Up,* with questions like: 'Are fashion photographers asked to highlight the model's sexuality or just the clothes?', 'Are your marriages usually happy?', 'Are you religious?', 'If not, is it because you ignore anything having to do with ethical codes or behaviour or is it a considered and explicable rejection?', 'Do you drink in pubs?', 'Do you have chauffeurs for your Rolls-Royces or do you prefer to drive them yourselves?', 'Do you worry about life and death?'. Then he announces that he plans to paint the grass of Maryon Park, where he'll film part of the movie, a colour 'greener than green'); Jane and Peter Asher (sister and brother); John and Neill Aspinall (brother and brother: being a brother or a sister is in; being a cousin is out); Richard Avedon (he takes a photograph of me when I'm seven in which I look like a kind of miniature Marlon Brando from *The Wild One*; Ringo lent me the cap I'm wearing, the one he had on in those free cinema, *nouvelle vague* sequences from *A Hard Day's Night*); Francis Bacon (in a bad mood); Joan Baez (in a worse mood); David Bailey (he tells everyone he runs into that '*Blow-Up* c'est moi . . . I'm the inspiration for the photographer character in the film, not Brian Duffy or Terence Donovan, got it?'); Chet Baker (who falls down the stairs, a very long flight of stairs, and don't ask me how, ends up on his feet, smiling; one of his teeth is missing); James Graham Ballard (silent and always smiling; he's like a replica of an original Ballard who never existed, strange as it sounds; and all of a sudden, as if charged by an electric current, he starts to talk about the curse of the Porsche Silver Spider that James Dean died in: 'Days before driving it for the first time, Dean had filmed a short spot warning young people about the perils of the highway and speeding . . . What was left of the car fell on a mechanic and broke both his legs; later, while it was being displayed as part of a road education campaign by the Greater Los Angeles Safety Council it fell off the flatbed truck that was transporting it and crushed a teenager's hip; a Beverly Hills doctor who bought the engine and installed it in another car died driving it . . . '); Balthus (he arrives, then leaves almost before he's arrived, after asking us whether we've seen his cat, and, most importantly, whether his son Stash de Rola a.k.a. Prince Stanislas Klossowski de Rola and Baron of Waterville – recently arrested with Brian Jones, his comrade in narcotic adventures, for possession of cocaine, methedrine, and hash – is here); Brigitte Bardot (her English is abysmal; Paul McCartney keeps begging her pardon, in rather poor French, for not having put her on the cover of *Sgt. Pepper's Lonely Hearts Club Band*: 'All four of us think you're the best; I don't know whose idea it was to use Diana Dors'); Syd Barrett (who's not yet with Pink Floyd, and who still hasn't tried lysergic acid; or if he has, it doesn't seem to have altered his behaviour much); Alan Bates (he takes his shirt off at the slightest excuse, for no reason, simply for the pleasure of showing off his chest); the Beatles (who at first remind me of a monster with four heads and then of four decapitated bodies); Cecil Beaton (he looks like a butler who must also be a murderer); Samuel Beckett (he looks like a murderer who must also be a butler); Marisa Berenson (learning to pant); Jane Birkin (teaching people to pant the way she does in 'Je t'aime . . . moi non plus' with Serge Gainsbourg); Jacqueline Bisset (learning to pant); Peter Blake (panting to anyone who comes near how it was that he and he alone came up with the idea for the cover of *Sgt. Pepper's Lonely Hearts Club Band*); Cilla Black (paradigmatic groupie, once coatcheck girl at the Cavern in Liverpool, then glam salesgirl at the boutique Biba, and now chanteuse and protegée of Brian Epstein and the Beatles); Dirk Bogarde (he takes notes in one of those very practical and elegant and proletarian moleskin notebooks; he's dressed up as a servant, very amusing); David Bowie (in mime makeup and serving canapés); Marlon Brando (his English is even worse than Brigitte Bardot's); Tara Browne (a few nights before he died, yet already giving off that odd and unmistakable phosphorescence that bodies that are almost corpses give off); Lenny Bruce (talking to himself, talking fast); William Burroughs (picking up, cutting up and reassembling the pages that someone tore from the books in the library a few nights ago, while perfuming the library with a strange fumigating tank); Michael Caine (constantly trying to avoid Terence Stamp; they have a shared flat and shared ambitions, and they've recently been fighting; things got complicated when the model Jean Shrimpton moved in with them; no, she moved in with Terence, but into the same flat where Michael was also living); Truman Capote (that voice like fingernails on a blackboard singing some song from *The Mikado* over and over again all night – actually just once, but like an infinite shrill sampling); John Cassavetes (with a portable Super-8 camera, but no film); Cher (without Sonny); Julie Christie (who I fell in love with when I was five, for the first time in my life, I think – I'm almost sure; it's so strange to see her up close and in a house when you're used to seeing her immense and gigantic like an Olympian goddess and always in open spaces, on farms and dachas and in meadows and on steppes); Eric Clapton (he keeps stealing glances at Patti Boyd, the future Patti Harrison, his best friend's best girl; he can't stop staring at the future Patti Clapton; best friends are so easy to betray); Cassius Clay (he shouts that he's the KING OF THE WORLD!!!; Clay shouts it in capital letters and with three exclamation points); Sean Connery (unbearable, his hair moves; later I learned that it wasn't his hair; I promised myself there and then that no matter what happened I would never stoop so low as to wear fake hair); Jerry Cornelius (he exists, I saw him); Tom Courtenay (he runs and runs alone through the woods of Sad Songs that surround Neverland); Noël Coward (he tells me that when he was fourteen he was chosen to be Slightly, one of the lost boys, in the 1913-14 revival of *Peter Pan*; I thought it was a lie but it was true; I found a photograph in which Coward appears in costume; here he is: Slightly); Quentin Crisp (learning to pant with the girls); Peter Cushing (he asks whether anyone's seen Christopher Lee); Tony Curtis (I suppose he's here because he's one of the people who appear on the cover of *Sgt. Pepper's Lonely Hearts Club Band*; Peter Blake asked him to be included, I don't know why); Ray Davies ('Raymond is just like me; except he's a genius and . . .' says my father, smiling sadly); Sammy Davis, Jr (Cassius Clay, already Muhammed Ali, accuses Sammy Davis, Jr of being a goddamn black slave at the beck and call of Frank Sinatra, Dean Martin & Co.; then he says that he should be ashamed to be one-eyed, Jewish, and a dwarf; because good Negroes have to be perfect); Catherine Deneuve (imitating Marlene Dietrich); Marlene Dietrich (imitating Catherine Deneuve and then asking Deneuve why she isn't on the cover of *Sgt. Pepper's Lonely Hearts Club Band*; Deneuve pretends not to understand the French of the German who does appear on the cover of *Sgt. Pepper's Lonely Hearts Club Band*); Donovan (I always felt so sorry for him); Françoise Dorleac (a few nights before she died, but already giving off that odd, unmistakable phosphorescence that bodies that are almost corpses give off); Bob Dylan (I've already told you about Bob Dylan, Keiko Kai); Sibylla Edmonstone (I remember her name, but not her face); Magnus Eisengrim (for one of my mother's birthdays, I remember him performing a magic trick in which he cuts off Sibylla Edmonstone's head, and maybe that's why I can't remember Sibylla Edmonstone's face); Brian Epstein (he keeps swallowing sedatives; Carbrital; it's a few nights before he dies, and he's already giving off that odd but unmistakable phosphorescence that bodies that are almost corpses give off); Marianne Faithfull (once I saw her naked); Mia Farrow (who was a horrible television Peter Pan, Hallmark Hall of Fame, NBC, 1976; the kind of woman you have no interest in seeing naked, even when you're very young; if you happen to see her, run, Keiko Kai: she'll try to adopt you); Federico Fellini (he's explaining to Terence Stamp about his next character, Stamp's character, in his next film, Fellini's film, in somewhat Fellini-esque English: 'Terenccino . . . You was party. One orgia. Lotta whisky. Glu-glu-glú. Troppo hashish, marihuana, coca e fucking fucking fucking. Fringüi-frungüi tutta la night. Doppo a Roma. LSD in aeroplàno . . . '); Peter Finch (close to this worldly noise, his hands over his ears, not understanding much, understanding nothing); Albert Finney (shirtless, Alan Bates dared him to take his shirt off, Finney seems slightly embarrassed); Ian Fleming (he came thinking it was my grandparents who were throwing the party, decided to stay, is ignoring Sean Connery, who's filming his first Bond movie; Fleming will die before the premiere, I think); Peter Fonda (he tells John Lennon that he was dead once, that he knows what it's like to be dead, and that 'there's nothing to worry about there'); Robert Fraser (he shows photographs of the works of artists from his gallery and distributes coloured handcuffs; he's wearing a pair himself on his left wrist, as a souvenir commemorating his release from prison, where he was sent on some typical narcotics charge with Mick Jagger); Lucien Freud (he asks, a little desperately, whether we've seen his dog; the answer is no, we're still looking for Balthus's cat); Serge Gainsbourg (he never looks women in the eye, he prefers to stare at their asses; and when they ask him why he won't look them in the eye, he says: 'I'm just so shy all I can look at is your ass'); Judy Garland (she kisses me, she hugs me, she sings to me; I don't understand a word she says); Allen Ginsberg (who even then made me embarrassed for him, and still does); Glenn Gould (gloves and scarf and woollen cap; he says the Beatles 'are a completely secondary phenomenon'; my father, thrilled, hugs him); Graham Greene (who, in one of his several lying autobiographies, *A Sort of Life*, tells how he used to read in Kensington Gardens when he was little; and I wonder whether he ever played with Barrie and Porthos); Hugh Hefner (in pyjamas, like me, who on many of these occasions would come down from my room and stay up like a stowaway through those party nights following upon party days; Hugh Hefner's pyjamas were light blue, mine were a paisley or psychedelic print, always bought at the boutique Granny Takes a Trip or I Was Lord Kitchener's Valet, I'm not sure which); David Hemmings (Michelangelo 'Don't Call Me Signore, Call Me Michelangelo' Antonioni has just informed him that he'll be the star of *Blow-Up*, not Terence Stamp, despite what everyone thinks: 'Keep quiet, top secret,' he warns him); Jimi Hendrix (the most brazenly impossible person to imitate back then when everyone imitated everyone else, because, well, Hendrix was black – he was *hard* to imitate; although Hendrix was easier to imitate than Sammy Davis, Jr, I suppose); Audrey Hepburn (she came with George Cukor, they're discussing the possibility of making a *Peter Pan* together that will never be filmed, Audrey Hepburn in the lead role, her eyes as big as mouths; she might have been the best Peter Pan of all, I thought then and still think now); David Hockney (he asks how nice the weather is in California); Michael Hollingshead (who's come to London with two thousand doses of LSD legally imported from a government laboratory in Prague in a mayonnaise jar, 'Aldous Huxley's favourite elixir; the old man passed on to the other side after one last visit from those visionaries with their holy oils, hallelujah,' he explains); Dennis Hopper (he asks Brian Epstein for pills and tells Lennon that he'll never be dead like that idiot Peter Fonda); Brian Jones (without the Rolling Stones); Danny Kaye (I never thought he was funny; there's nothing less funny than someone desperate to seem funny); the party girl Christine Keeler (and her pal Mandy Rice-Davies, their faces always transfixed by the echo of a past orgasm linked to the sound of the next orgasm; and yet they don't pant, they aren't interested in what Jane Birkin wants to teach them: they know how to pant perfectly well); the Kray brothers (twin gangsters, fashionably dangerous; one night I saw – and, most disturbing of all, *heard* – how they broke the legs of a bon vivant who owed them something: they took him into the bushes at Neverland and then, immediately, there was *that* sound; then they both came out smiling Siamese smiles and adjusting each other's ties); Jiddu Krishnamurti (he gives me a mantra and then, regretting it, demands it back); Stanley Kubrick (the best of all, he comes with a giant monkey which I learn is a man dressed up as an anthropoid, or something like that; Kubrick kneels and smiles at me and asks me whether I believe intelligent life exists on other planets; I ask him which planet he means: the earth or the planet I live on?); Philip Larkin (thinking–saying–writing–reciting his 'Never such innocence again' poem); Peter Lawford (a kind of sleep-walker programmed to say the names Kennedy and Sinatra at least once a minute); Timothy Leary (in orbit, drifting, *mirabile triptu*; he passes out sugar cubes that he blesses with a drop of 'spiritual elixir'); Christopher Lee (he asks whether anyone's seen Peter Cushing); Sonny Liston (after barely two minutes he's KO'd by Clay Ali); David Litvinoff (guru of the Chelsea demi-monde; James Fox asks his advice about his character in *Performance*; 'Oh, come with me to the bath-room, Foxie . . . I have something for you to try,' Litvinoff replies); Joseph Losey (worried about the imminent failure of his *Modesty Blaise*); Magic Alex (born Yannis Alexis Mardas, television repairman and genius in residence at Apple Electronics at the expense of the increasingly chaotic finances of his four bosses; a feverish swindler working on the creation of stereo surround sound wallpaper and the construction of a floating communal house on the Greek island of Leslo so the Beatles could live there with their families; and who knows, maybe that Robinsonian project was abandoned after what happened to my parents at sea); Princess Margaret (who I always get mixed up with Princess Anne); Dean Martin (he looks over at the Rolling Stones and comments, with a smile always propped on a martini: 'It's not that they have long hair; it's that their foreheads are low and their eyebrows are bushy,' and adds: 'Somebody bring me another Dean Martini'); Joe Meek (a music producer whose behaviour has become increasingly bizarre, creator in 1962 of the successful instrumental sci-fi single 'Telstar' – electric guitar and the sound of a toilet – and of *I Hear a New World* – the first conceptual-electronic album – and famous for discovering the amazing acoustics of tiled bathrooms, which are great for recording voice tracks; here he is, a few nights before he dies, already giving off that odd but unmistakable phosphorescence that bodies that are almost corpses give off; he's thinking that it wouldn't be so bad to go home, blow his landlady's head off with a single shot, and then blow his own head off, in the bathroom, if possible, to 'see how it sounds', and so it'll be easier to clean up all the blood; the idea comes to him and then immediately he puts it into practice); Paul Morrisey (Andy Warhol's right arm and left side of the brain; he looks around and scowls and says: 'I can't understand why all of you keep saying 'I'm experimenting with drugs.' What you're experimenting with is illness. Now that scientists have managed to eradicate polio and smallpox and all those childhood diseases, what you're doing is drugging yourselves to see what it's like to be sick'); V. S. Naipaul (what's he doing here? I guess he hasn't been able to shake the habit he picked up when he used to write for the BBC Caribbean news broadcast and they sent him to strange parts of London in search of 'local colour'; if so, he hasn't lost the grimace – part disgust, part pleasure – of the person who slices open a bit of organic matter just before it begins to rot and peers inside to see how the worms generate themselves); Nico (not to be confused with Nico Llewelyn Davies, son of Arthur and Sylvia; it's Christa 'Nico' Paffgen, the chanteuse Warhol foisted on the Velvet Underground; it will be a long time before she dies in a bicycle accident in Spain, and she doesn't yet have that odd but unmistakable phosphorescence that bodies that are almost corpses give off, but you can hardly tell the difference); Rudolf Nureyev (he dances, but the truth is it doesn't impress me as much as what Chet Baker did); Claes Oldenburg (from whom my mother commissioned *something small*); Yoko Ono (from whom my mother didn't commission anything); a handful of young ladies and lords, their last name Ormsby-Gore (aristocrats who enjoy ascending to the hells of the damned, ex-schoolmates of my parents who return to the vaulted bedrooms of their parents' castles when the sun comes out, like vampires who only drink blue blood); Andrew Loog Oldham (Rolling Stones PR man, possessed and prophetic, predicting that in the future 'people will argue about whether the 60s started in '67 or ended long before, when the Beatles left for America'; he uses the fingers of both hands to count how many innocent Soho pedestrians he's hit recently in his new Jag); Joe Orton (a few nights before he died, but already giving off that odd, unmistakable phosphorescence that bodies that are almost corpses give off; he rips pages from books and sticks photographs to them, pages that nights later William Burroughs will find); Peter O'Toole (what, can it be? as usual, he bursts into tears while still smiling, and explains to me why glasses must be tapped when you toast: all the senses are involved in the act of drinking – sight, touch, taste, smell – except hearing, he tells me with a lachrymose smile; and there's got to be that crystalline *drink!* to make everything perfect); Jimmy Page (session man par excellence, not yet with Led Zeppelin, executes complicated magic passes over Hendrix's head; Hendrix has no idea what's happening); Anita Pallenberg (naked, too); Pier Paolo Pasolini (he instructs Terence Stamp about his next character, Terence playing Stamp, in his next film, Pasolini's film, in somewhat Pasolini-esque English: 'He's a boy' and 'Open your legs all the time,' that's all, no more is needed); D. A. Pennebaker (with a portable camera; but, unlike Cassavetes's, it has film in it); Pink Floyd (without Syd Barrett and without David Gilmour; they still call themselves the Abdabs); Alexander Plunket-Greene (husband of Mary Quant, an impeccable suit but no shirt; tie and buttons painted on his bare chest); Roman Polanski (he asks Vidal Sassoon to please fly to New York to cut Mia Farrow's hair for *Rosemary's Baby*); Elvis Presley (I'm not absolutely sure it was Elvis Presley; I don't remember whether it was Thin Elvis or Fat Elvis: either way, it was someone who looked just like one of those two Elvises); Mary Quant (showing just how high she plans to raise the hems of her next generation of miniskirts and laughing when someone says that, according to police records, the rape rate in London has gone up 90 per cent since women started walking around with their thighs exposed); Oliver Reed (shirtless, but drunk); Lynn and Vanessa Redgrave (more sisters); Tom Ripley (he exists, I saw him); Nicolas Roeg (he tells James Fox how to play his next character, James playing Fox, in his first film, Roeg's first, without having to say more than one word: drugs; 'I told you so . . . you weren't paying attention, come on, off to the bathroom,' insists Litvinoff, passing by again); the Rolling Stones (without Brian Jones); Ed Ruscha (one of my favourite painters, one of those painters who seem to paint nothing but the nonrealist moments of reality: letters in place of clouds, the sky as canvas); Ken Russell (one of my least favourite directors); Vidal Sassoon (who tells Roman Polanski okey-dokey, he'll cut Mia Farrow's hair; good publicity for everyone); Telly Savalas (still with some hair); Gerald Scarfe (he drew me, it came out ugly; he explained that no one comes out nice-looking in his pictures, it isn't his style); Peter Sellers (who would've been the perfect Cagliostro Nostradamus Smith, because it was Peter Sellers who was my inspiration for Cagliostro Nostradamus Smith and Uncle Max Max and Jim Yang's ephemeral Buddhist father and almost every other supporting character in the adventures of Jim Yang; and someone comes up to Sellers and asks him to be Hook in a possible new version of *Peter Pan* and Sellers answers in a strange voice, in a voice that is and isn't his, in one of his many voices, *no, thanks*); Jean and Chrissie Shrimpton (more sisters); Frank Sinatra (I'm not completely sure; in any case, someone who looked just like Frank Sinatra and who talked to the person exactly like the large- or extra-large-size Elvis Presley); Lord Snowdon (he takes pictures, drinks champagne, reveals nothing); Terry Southern (all he seems to care about is the fate of the English team in the upcoming World Cup finals of 1966); Phil Spector (with a gun he sometimes shoots into the air: bullet holes in the ceiling, in a suit of armour, in a taxidermied polar bear my grandfather brought back from an expedition); Terence Stamp (who keeps looking at himself in the mirror, the mirror's staring back at him); Cat Stevens (I've already told you about Cat Stevens, Keiko Kai); Sharon Tate (her ghost; or maybe it's a few nights before she died, I'm not sure of the date, though she's already giving off that odd but unmistakable phosphorescence that bodies that are almost corpses give off); Vince Taylor (he's dressed in black leather and has his head shaved and as he burns pound notes he announces to the crowd: 'Money is the root of all evil and I'm Matthew, the new Jesus, the extraterrestrial son of God . . . Rock and roll! I have a plane waiting for us a few miles from here and you're all invited to fly with me to Hollywood'); Ike and Tina Turner (she was hitting him, or at least that's what I saw, I swear); Twiggy (everything makes her laugh); Kenneth Tynan (he laughs at everybody); Roger Vadim (he still hasn't divorced Catherine Deneuve but Catherine Deneuve is already living with Roger Bailey: no problem); Verushka ('I'm in *Blow-Up* too'); Monica Vitti (no one can stand her, especially not Joseph Losey and Terence Stamp); Klaus Voorman (showing off the original of his illustration for the cover of *Revolver*); Andy Warhol (who says 'ah, oh, ah, oh, ah . . . '); Evelyn Waugh (he arrives thinking it's my grandparents who're throwing the party; he decides to stay); the Who (they've just come from playing on *Ready, Steady, Go!*; I saw them on television, Pete broke his guitar and Keith smashed his drums and I, not wanting to be left out, threw my little desk out the window that same night);

. . . and my father and my mother (a few nights before they died, but already giving off that odd, unmistakable phosphorescence that bodies that are almost corpses give off);

. . . and my little brother Baco (a few nights before he died, but already giving off that odd, unmistakable phosphorescence that bodies that are almost corpses give off; but Baco is more phosphorescent than any of them, pure light, one of those deep-sea fish rising to the surface to dazzle the world);

. . . and me (before and during and after Baco, making my way into those parties as if they're lost continents and strange civilizations. An explorer who suddenly feels he's swimming in the dark waters of an almost dried-up aquarium. A sea cemetery where the remnants of a race that refuses to grow up sink to the bottom, a race that would rather die than get old, a race that chooses to let death fossilize it in a golden time and unrepeatable space rather than resign itself to living condemned to remember past glories, perfect instants when London was the centre of the universe, and in the centre of that centre everyone spun on his own axis, special and happy. What's interesting about this, I think, is that none of them seemed conscious of having made such a decision. To vanish early and all that. And therefore the sudden proliferation of dead people made them so uneasy that they could only be soothed by another dead person. Dead people upon dead people. A revolution of the immortal dead, the worshipped dead. Posters of dead people papering walls, and dead people as prayers for meditation and transformation, because the dead don't die: 'They just move on to another level of existence; sorrow at their parting is nothing but an egotistical emotion that disturbs their new karmas; don't mourn, burn incense,' instructs the guru of the moment. A new dead person before the idea of the last dead person has sunk in. Dead people like hit singles, like fleeting songs of the week that lose volume as they slide ponderously down the steep slope of the rankings. Each new dead person as a fresh pain to soothe the pain caused by the previous dead person, so everybody else can keep walking, anesthetized, on the edge of the generational abyss from which their children, on the beach below, watch them fall and shatter, and, like scrambled puzzles, drag themselves to shore, and then the waves and the rocks and the drowning and down to the bottom . . . Or maybe I'm being too dramatic with these memories inside of memories. A mirage – another one – forged out of memory. A useful defence mechanism for when it becomes necessary to try to understand the incomprehensible. Maybe nothing was so ominous and elegiac. Maybe they were all just people who got burned playing with fire or drowned playing with water, not knowing how to use all that water to put out all that fire. Insignificant creatures. Lost children. Maybe – definitely – mythification is the only effective remedy for healing certain wounds and for making certain they never disappear completely, like some scars, the best scars;

. . . and Marcus Merlin, who seems to devour all brightness with the bottomless voracity of a black hole (he lights a match and brings it to a pipe and sucks hard, exhaling a yellow, Oriental smoke, and then he smiles like a dragon, or no, like a man who's just devoured a dragon; Marcus Merlin smiles at me, offers me his pipe, says 'welcome').

Welcome, Barrie.

Barrie everywhere, all the time.

Barrie as an imp, an uncle, an elderly son, an almost intolerable being, thinks Arthur Llewelyn Davies, who clings to that *almost* so as not to say anything, so as to smile, in stiff astonishment, at Barrie's capering outside the realm of decorum; after all, his sons are happy with Barrie and Arthur's happy if his sons are happy.

Distance is no obstacle for Barrie, and he leaves his new country house near Franham, in Surrey, on Tilford Road, near the ruins of Waverley Abbey, to travel with no difficulty at all to Kensington Gardens or Burpham, where the Llewelyn Davieses are spending these holidays.

The house in Surrey is called Black Lake Cottage and

Mary Barrie bought it to console herself for being nobody, doing nothing, having become a decorative appendage of her famous husband. Mary decides to become a decorator appendage: she rallies a small army of builders and gardeners and – to the joy of an at first indifferent and then enthusiastic Barrie – that July of 1900 the merry members of the Allahakbarrie Cricket Team play their first match of the season there. The writer happily discovers that his wife has turned one of the rooms on the top floor into a perfect study: a new sanctuary where he can lock himself away and escape for long hours, far from his wife.

Barrie works harder and harder. On 27 September 1900, *The Wedding Guest* opens at the Garrick Theatre; a work his friend Charles Frohman calls 'too Ibsen-ish'. Which means 'not much happens in it'. Charles Frohman advises Barrie to keep on with *The Admirable Crichton* instead of writing plays like *The Wedding Guest*, a drama set on the day of a wedding at which the groom, an 'artist', confronts an ex-lover and an illegitimate son whose existence he wasn't aware of until then. Most critics – who, since this was a 'Barrie', were expecting another of his light, efficient, uncomplicated comedies – agreed with Charles Frohman but said so less tactfully: 'Unpleasant', 'Painful', 'A defence of promiscuous seduction', and 'Of doubtful morality' are some of the things written about *The Wedding Guest*. Barrie shrugs his shoulders. Barrie believed in *The Wedding Guest* (although years later he would oppose its revival); Barrie smiles and keeps writing *The Little White Bird*, feeding on the commentary of his beloved George (who is seven now), and enjoying newborn Michael. For Barrie it's as if each of Sylvia and Arthur Llewelyn Davies's new sons is a fresh chapter or act in a colossal work in progress: his greatest success, play or novel, it doesn't matter.

The Christmas before, Barrie had taken Jack and George to see the pantomime *The Babes in the Wood* at the Coronet Theatre in Notting Hill Gate. Inspired by the children's excitement, Barrie – competitive, jealous – decides to go one better and write a Christmas pantomime himself to be put on by all of them during the holidays: *The Greedy Dwarf*, subtitled – with a mocking wink to Mary Hodgson's worries about the bad influence of Barrie's stories – 'A Moral Tale'.

The only performance takes place at 133 Gloucester Road on 7 January 1901. The specially printed programme has on its cover a photograph of little Peter Llewelyn Davies, who is identified as *The Author and/or Peter Perkin*. Inside it proclaims: 'The Allahakbarrie Cricket Club has the honour to present for the first and only time on any stage an Entirely Amazing Moral Tale entitled *The Greedy Dwarf*, by Peter Perkin.' Following this there is a cast list: Miss Sylvia as Prince Robin, Mr Barrie as Cowardy Custard, Mr Gerald du Maurier as Allahakbarrie, Mr Porthos as the dog Chang . . . and an enumeration of the different scenes, which take place in a clearing in the woods, at a little schoolhouse, and in 'the horrible home of the greedy dwarf'.

Barrie had kept the role of the cowardly bad boy for himself and – according to the children present at the event – his character was even more terrifying than the dwarf. Barrie's great dramatic moment came when, to delay the start of a fight, he slowly took off vest after vest until counting twelve, each in a different bright colour. Sylvia spent the whole play smiling sweetly and timidly, as if asking forgiveness for this hugely ridiculous thing she'd let herself be talked into by Barrie without knowing quite how. Mary Barrie was fantastic as the Little Good Girl, a dauntless heroine who was clearly more than happy to defeat Sylvia on the territory she knew best. Arthur Llewelyn Davies applauded enthusiastically, or so it seemed.

Once the performance was over – the staging of which had cost Barrie a considerable sum – and while the guests and actors did justice to the cakes and ice cream, Barrie jotted down in his notebook:

– Sea of faces – mouths open.
– I listen to the children talking on the stairs. 'Is my hair mussed?', etc.
– The cat's disdain. The dog's interest
– Children gazed intently – never smiled.
– Their polite congratulations.

Five days after the opening and closing of *The Greedy Dwarf*, on 12 January 1901, the curtain falls for the last time on *The Wedding Guest* after one hundred performances; it hasn't been a failure but no one can say it was a success.

Ten days after the opening and closing of *The Greedy Dwarf*, on 17 January 1901, after seventy-three and a half years of uninterrupted success, Queen Victoria's name comes down from the Buckingham Palace marquee. The longest reign in all of history is over. The Great Queen, the greatest since Elizabeth, is dead. No one believes that such a thing – this ending – is possible. True, people knew she was ill, but Victoria, Victoria Regina, was immortal. Victoria was England. 'I mourn the safe and motherly old middle-class queen, who held the nation warm under the fold of her big, hideous Scotch-plaid shawl,' Henry James wrote at the time.

Did the funeral service take place at Westminster? I suppose it did. Did it snow on that long, terrible day? I don't know. It doesn't matter. I can say that the funeral *was* at Westminster and that the snowflakes were immense and perfect and – for once – all exactly alike, like the snow in those globes you just have to shake to make the whitest, gentlest storm. No one dared yet to say God Save the King – they were practicing it in private, in front of the mirror, like sleepwalkers, the blinds drawn and the lights low, in secret – and all the streets were decorated with purple bows, and all the children were dressed in black, and at last – this is what the grand deaths at the end of great lives are for – the twentieth century had really begun.

*

The fact that my father met Marcus Merlin at the service marking another anniversary of Victoria's death – my father went year after year to honour the memory of the 'only real queen', toying with the idea of writing a song about Victoria's veins, her thick blue royal blood – surely had something to do with the way my father thought about Marcus Merlin. As an almost magical being, ready for anything. The perfect adviser to a king, with his multiple abilities to take charge of almost anything, maybe with the help of the powerful magic of his last name.

I wrote *Jim Yang and the Swinging Gangster* as an obvious homage to Marcus Merlin, in gratitude. Marcus Merlin – as was to be expected – didn't like the book much.

Said Marcus Merlin: 'There isn't enough action or blood to make it a good gangster novel.'

But actually *Jim Yang and the Swinging Gangster* isn't about gangsters, nor is it supposed to be; it's one of those books in which a boy, Jim Yang, is rescued from peril by an ally of uncertain virtue but bullet-proof principles. In *Jim Yang and the Swinging Gangster*, Jim Yang returns to his present, the 1960s, and Little Tony Driscoll, son of Big Tony Driscoll – one of the brutal and criminal brothers Driscoll, masters of the East End gambling dens, obviously inspired by Reggie and Ronnie Kray – steals his chronocycle. Then Memo Monk, head of a rival gang and Jim Yang's unexpected protector, makes his entrance – very much in the spirit of Long John Silver in *Treasure Island* or Abel Magwitch in *Great Expectations* – and helps Jim Yang get his time-travelling bicycle back. Memo Monk is the swinging gangster of the title: addicted to the mystique of Hollywood, famous for his dancing skills, and envied for his success with women, from starlets to duchesses.

Memo Monk is Marcus Merlin; and when was it that Marcus Merlin entered my parents' lives, who invited him, and how is it he went almost instantly from being a visitor to becoming a long-term guest and an invader?

I like to think Marcus Merlin came to Neverland at almost the same time LSD came to London. Dark lightning shooting from a coloured cloud. It works for me as a narrative device, although Marcus Merlin came into my parents' lives – and mine – before that. But I can safely say that beginning in 1966 Marcus Merlin became someone important to me, and therefore – as the narrator of this story, after all – I allow myself to gradually intensify his presence in keeping with my awareness of him. I claim such a right on the basis of the natural properties according to which stories are structured, not only to make them more plausible but also – and most importantly – to make them better.

And if you're sleepy, Keiko Kai, if you're falling asleep, here's a pill that will help you keep your eyes open, help you forget your eyes were ever closed.

Yes, pills have always been my thing, and with the exception of that innocent and accidental trip courtesy of my distracted father, I haven't tried lysergic acid again.

LSD is unfair competition for a writer.

Pills, on the other hand, keep you awake, in an eternal bright noon, your fingers faster and faster on the keyboard of your computer until you reach the speed of the electric brain.

Pills that in the 60s, in the modern and mod 60s, taught you how to dance the new spastic dances (the Shake, the Jam, the Rag, the Writing-Block, the Chit-Chat, the Bang!, the Sheik, the Stutter, the Monkey, the Hitchhiker, the Watusi, the Raj) and to shake those strange new hairdos (the Perry Como, the College Boy, the Nouvelle Vague, the Parka, the French Crew, the Rumble, the Windy, the Broooom!) as you swallowed them dry – or with the help of a Coca-Cola-scotch-vodka-lime-rum-water – all at once, all night, hands full of little helpers. You brought them to your mouth as if you were punching yourself, as if you wanted to hide the hard smile that made your teeth seem to fuse into two single marble walls. Purple Hearts and French Blues (the domestic and imported versions of Dryamil, respectively), Black Bombers and Nigger Minstrels, dexedrine, whatever there was. Pills that fried your brain and genitals. 'I can't remember the last time I could masturbate and I looked *at* a girl, not *through* her,' the Mods told each other proudly. Pills that helped you forget your girlfriend so you could concentrate on what was most important: yourself and your clothes and your hair; the only thing you wanted under you was a scooter with an Italian name. Pills that made your heart beat faster until the throbbing filled your ears and you danced so you wouldn't die, to wear yourself out, so the effects would pass. Pills that made you stammer that you hoped you would die before you were old. Pills that aged you early.

The duel between amphetamines and lysergic acid is the first great chemical battle, the first crack in the once-pristine porcelain: Rockers vs. Mods. The first chance – after so long, after so many wars waged by adults with the flesh of children – for the young to fight their own wars. Before – at the beginning of the 50s – the Teds, or Teddy-Boys, had appeared (gangs with Edwardian roots doing their thing in South London), and beatniks imported from America and mingling with the intellectual Angry Young Men. But back then there was never anything like what there is today: fury unleashed, a war of life or death. It was the first of many battles to be fought until the beginning of the third millennium by successive hordes of successive lost boys trying to impose a new style on a style that was hardly any older. Style as banner. Aesthetic as weapon.

The Mods are a synthesis of the Moderns (who at first only listened to the coolest jazz and feuded with the Trads, who defended dixieland and ragtime and skiffle and blues) and the Modernists (worshippers of Jean-Paul Sartre). Merged, they've now become dandies hailing from the fringes of London – Tottenham, Ilford, Stamford Hill – and they intend to reclaim the city's most exclusive neighbourhoods for themselves after expelling all those brutish, idiotic Rockers. All the Mods care about is dressing well, with class. Dressing alike and wearing their hair the same and looking pale; being Mods twenty-four hours a day and not just when there's some magazine photographer around. Not having fun all the time, suffering a little (flipping through Camus, if they're in the mood) and staying up all night listening to Radio Caroline, the first of the great British pirate stations. By 1964, the Mods have moved to the west and south of the city: West End, Shepherd's Bush, Richmond. The Mods hang out at the Flamingo, the Scene, the Crawdaddy, the Goldhawk Social Club, or the Marquee. For a Mod, there's nothing better than being a Face, the top level of the Mod hierarchy. A Face is a Mod who's more Mod than anyone else; who looks most and best like Terence Stamp; and has the best clothes (the Mods can spend a week's pay on a tie) and the best girl and the best pills and the best scooter; the Mod who's best looking, though he's really more interested in impressing his friends than his girlfriend. And there's nothing more intense for a Mod than fighting alongside his friends – 'we few, we happy few, we band of brothers' – against the Rockers, those cretins who only know how to stroke their leather jackets and go to the theatre over and over again to see *The Wild One* with Marlon Brando until they know it by heart, down to the last still.

The differences are clear: to the Mods the Rockers are brainless lower-class animals; to the Rockers the Mods are effeminate office workers who're only interested in climbing the social ladder and disarranging their hair as little as possible on their way up. The Rockers like Elvis, hard and pure. The Mods memorize the lyrics to songs by the High Numbers (about to become the Who), the Kinks and the Small Faces as if they're gospel, instructions for moving and standing still in the world. The Rockers ride powerful Harley-Davidsons made in the USA; the Mods prefer delicate Italian Vespas and Lambrettas.

The Rockers and the Mods are therefore natural enemies, instant armies, duelling mirror images in search of the best fighting ground. I can't imagine any of this interests you,

Keiko Kai. All these names, like the names of warrior races and vanished civilizations, must sound more like Gandalf than Sgt Pepper to you. Druids and elfs and magic contests for the trove of all-powerful relics. It seems right to me: the greatest legends have humble origins. That's the trick of it, the beauty, the meaning, the mystique that makes you go running out of a trench with your teeth bared, feeling the most courageous fear you ever thought it was possible to feel and enjoy: believe me, Keiko Kai, no one's more *alive* than those who believe they've found the best and most precise reason for dying.

The first big face-offs between Mods and Rockers takes place on a cold weekend in the spring of 1964. It's the coldest it's been at this date for eighty years, it's said. On 26-7 March, a crowd of Mods gather in the rather cockney Clacton-on-Sea in Essex. The town kids don't like the idea that these twits from the capital are making fun of them because they listen to 'Heartbreak Hotel', 'Blue Suede Shoes' and 'Don't Be Cruel'. Some of them decide to start a fight. The incident reaches the papers and soon the whole thing becomes a popular pastime. Weekend getaways: take a stroll along the coast through the crumbling seaside resorts, almost like ghost towns, and along the way, break Mod bones, rocking them and rolling them. Both sides are children fighting over the same invisible toy. Both sides have such a good time they promise to do it again next year, and so the beaches burn: Weston-super-Mare, Great Yarmouth, Brighton.

One of these fights – the last of the great battles back then – is described in *Jim Yang and the Swinging Gangster*, with Stendhalian authority. It was a brutal clash of forces. I was there. I remember, Keiko Kai, that once I read a letter by Stendhal to his sister Pauline. Don't ask me to explain who Stendhal was. I don't have the time, and I'm not in the mood. And there's no reason why I should: Stendhal slips in and out of my story almost without leaving a trace. I'll just tell you that Stendhal – like Peter Hook – is also an alias and that I, like him, approach fiction writing with ambivalence, and frequently, with little enthusiasm.

Stendhal's letter, which I learned by heart from reading it so often – it's a very short letter – was written on 1 April 1814 in Paris, and it goes like this:

> *I am very well. Two days ago there was an enjoyable battle at Pantin and Montmartre. I was witness to the capture of the hill.*
>
> *Everyone behaved properly, there was no disorder. The marshals performed marvels. I'd be most grateful to have news of you, and of your household and M. de Saint-Vallier's. The family is well. I am living at home.*

And the letter is signed by a certain General Terré, another of the aliases that Stendhal – pardon me, Henri Marie Beyle – was so fond of, I suppose.

This letter always intrigued me. Was it a joke? Could it be true that the citizens of Paris carried their folding chairs and parasols to the edge of the city to watch battles as if they were plays? What planet was this where – with little eagerness and even less success – a plodding consul could become the greatest novelist of his age? What was I thinking when, after my little brother Baco's funeral, I filled my mouth with coloured pills and got on my Schwinn bicycle and pedalled south without stopping, much faster and more amphetaminoid than the five-fifteen train, and got to Brighton? What did the seagulls talk about among themselves (suddenly I discovered that inside my head there lived four clearly distinct people: the person I was before Baco's death; the one I had become at Brighton; the one I would be many years later; the one I'll be when this long, historic night with you is over, Keiko Kai) and what did I talk to myself about? Would I some day be able to stop running along that long pier with a strange palace at the end? Is there a more terrible and daunting invention than the sea, the landless sea, that at moments seems like something laid out to dry? The sea – the sea that turns away no river – was it me? Do you become part of the sea by simply taking to the road and hurling yourself with your bicycle from the top of a cliff into the water, the water from which we all came and to which we'll all return? Who rescued me? Who caught me without net or hook? Was it a Mod or was it a Rocker, and what are all those people doing fighting on the beach, what are all those dark, heavy motorcycles doing crashing into all those light scooters with too many rear-view mirrors? How is it – I realize all of a sudden – that there are so many different reds in blood? What are those girls and boys doing in the alleys, why are they leaning on each other and spreading their legs and why do they seem to dance and moan as the police scatter the young warriors? What will happen if I mix this pill with that pill? Why is the moon so big and how can it be that the ocean listens to the moon when the moon orders: 'Now forward, now back, now forward again'?

Please: will someone explain all this to me, and the many other things I didn't understand, that I still don't understand.

Keiko Kai: I lived under the piles of the great pier at Brighton for seven days and seven nights. When they found me I was almost wild. I drank rain, and ate fish and Black Bombers. Step up and see the Wild Boy of Brighton.

Yes, I was shipwrecked before my parents were. Someone must have called them from the police station where I was left; but it was Marcus Merlin who came to get me.

Marcus Merlin smiled at me sadly and proudly.

Said Marcus Merlin: 'My little lost boy . . . I think I'll call you Man Friday.'

Marcus Merlin brought me back to London in the back seat of his Jaguar, with the top down. I was raving, shouting, and hurling myself back and forth. Marcus Merlin tied my feet and hands with his belt and tie, 'my best tie', he told me. It was nighttime and I remember I decided to count all the stars. Or maybe just the bright stars, until I found 'the second star to the right and then straight on till morning': the exact location of Neverland, according to Peter Pan. It wasn't easy, of course. Constellations are never well mannered enough to look like what their names say they are. This is a crab, the hunter, a big dipper, they tell us, they claim, pointing up into the sky. And we don't see anything there, except little lights embroidered on the immense darkness. The names and ingredients of pills – those angular and metallic and dangerous names – never lie to you or deceive you: they're always what they say they are and what they're said to be in that chemical language so like the Latin of the solemnest Catholic masses. I was – amen – more of a believer than an addict. I'd learned to fly extremely well so that later I could learn to crash even better.

They kept me for almost a month at the Great Ormond Street Hospital. The first children's hospital in the United Kingdom. The hospital to which, in 1929, Barrie deeded the rights to the play *Peter Pan* as well as the licensing and control of the character. When the deed expired – in 1987, when *Peter Pan* and its spin-offs passed into the public domain – a special decree by the House of Lords restored to the hospital its share of the income, but revoked its cast-iron right to authorize or veto 'interpretations' of the play and book *Peter Pan* and the character Peter Pan.

I had a private room there. I can't say whether they attached wires to my head, or put a piece of cork in my mouth for me to bite down on. I do remember the honeyed and cloying voice that comes from inside doctors whenever they have to talk to a child. I remember the fever; my hands as big as balls; the overwhelming thirst; being convinced that if I were a train I'd be a train that always arrives late; the sight of a ship with steaming funnels on the ceiling's horizon; the sound of bicycles in motion, at once retro and futuristic; and the unmistakable sense of having spotted something important pulsing just outside my field of vision, something that wasn't there any more when I turned my head, and would never be there again.

Every day books and flowers were delivered to my room. The scent was terrible and powerful and made me dream of whales that smelled like roses. I tried to read but – I'm left-handed, it's a problem we left-handers have – I turned the pages of books from back to front. As a residual effect of the pills, I guess, my eyes always drifted to the last line, and it was as if those last words let me unfailingly intuit everything that had happened in the preceding pages. There was no mystery in those books, and I can't even break them down into pages. It was as if everything they had to tell me was a single, extremely long sentence, horizontal, stretching on and dragging itself out for miles. And I was very tired. So I resigned myself to endings, to the place to be gotten to. And the strangest thing of all – it seems pertinent to mention it, Keiko Kai – is that these were the endings of books that hadn't been written yet. Endings I memorized then and that I've just come across again many years later. And I ask myself whether in childhood – when there's so little for us to remember, when there's so much free space in the chambers of memory – we're allowed to glimpse some episodes from our future in the delirium of our vast childhood illnesses, the fever working like a crystal ball.

I read: '. . . I had never known, never even imagined for a heartbeat, that there might be a place for people like us'; I read 'and continued day after day in a life I believe to be utterly remarkable.' And what sense was there in continuing to read. What was the fun of starting from the beginning just to wind up at endings like these, I wondered.

So I asked the doctors to give the books to the other children at the hospital (their pain and their nightmares, the sound of their moaning, helped me sleep at night) and I gave the flowers to the nurses, who thanked me by pinching my cheek and winking at me with exaggerated coquetry.

One morning, my parents come to pick me up at the Great Ormond Street Hospital in my grandfather's Rolls-Royce. They seem uncomfortable around me. They avoid looking at me and at each other. My father orders Dermott to turn on the radio. A broadcaster announces that the BBC has prohibited 'A Day in the Life', by the Beatles, 'because it considers that the song expresses a permissive attitude towards drugs, seeming to encourage their consumption'.

'Well done,' says my father.

It was the only thing he said all the way back to Neverland.

The Character

The character is Barrie.

Barrie working. Barrie revises and makes final corrections to *The Admirable Crichton*. Barrie sends Charles Frohman the script of *Quality Street*, his new play for the actress Maude Adams: its original title is *Phoebe's Garden*; it takes place during the Napoleonic wars, and it'll open at the Vaudeville Theatre on 17 September 1902. Barrie keeps adding new chapters to *The Little White Bird*. And when Barrie feels his head is about to explode and his hand can no longer bear to dip the pen in the inkwell again, he walks five minutes along a tree-lined path from Black Lake Cottage to Tilford, where the Llewelyn Davieses have rented a house for the summer.

The brothers can almost feel him approaching: a slight but definite change in the quality of the air, and all of a sudden the little man and his immense dog are throwing themselves on the ground beside them.

After *The Greedy Dwarf* none of them are content to simply *hear* stories any more: now they want to see them, act in them, make them come true. Barrie invents characters, makes papier-mâché masks. One with a fierce tiger face for Porthos and one of a pirate for him: the mask of sinister Captain Swarthy, his dancing eyebrows invested with the power to hypnotize little Michael and make Peter walk the gangplank and fall into a lake 'infested with sharks and crocodiles', where the ship they solemnly baptized the *Anna Pink* has sunk. Sometimes the whole thing threatens to become a little dangerous, and Sylvia and Arthur Llewelyn Davies have forbidden the use of arrows and the sharp real knives that Barrie brings from home. Barrie and his friends disappear for hours and only return at teatime, chased by the rain and laughing uproariously, dry under the euphoric umbrella of those who know themselves to be members of a secret society. I like to imagine them playing and laughing and shouting in electric storms; the lightning always hits them, but instead of striking them down it charges them with a new, monstrous, alkaline energy.

Barrie's brought his camera and he's always taking pictures of the brothers; sometimes I shudder to think what Barrie might have done if he'd had a video camera back then, Keiko Kai. Barrie develops his own photographs. They're good ones. Today, only 2 per cent of the pictures we take are out of focus. Out-of-focus photography is an extinct species, a disease almost completely eradicated by the immunity of automatic cameras vaccinated at birth. Back then, 80 per cent of photographs must have come out looking as if they were obscured by a veil, wavering between faithfully reflecting reality and inventing something new and misty. Barrie, however, is very skilled, and – so far as child photography is concerned – in the vanguard. His pictures are nothing like Lewis Carroll's stiff portraits of children. Here, George and Jack and Peter and Michael are always in motion in photographs that never come out blurry: fighting with a tiger, hanging the Captain Swarthy doll, swimming, raising their oars high and triumphant on the deck of the *Anna Pink*. Barrie decides to assemble the photographs and write captions for them, and he pays the publishing house of Constable to put out an edition of two copies, one for the Llewelyn Davies brothers and one for himself.

Marcus Merlin got me one of those two copies.

Said Marcus Merlin: 'Please don't ask me how I did it. I don't think you want to know,' warning me before I could ask; so all I said was 'Thank you.'

The little book was called *The Boy Castaways of Black Lake Island* and I have it here, Keiko Kai. I'll turn the pages so you can see it.

On the cover there's a drawing of the three brothers (back then Michael spent the whole day sleeping; he was still practically a baby, and, according to Barrie, 'an honourary member of the troop') proudly brandishing swords and rifles.

On the first page it reads:

The Boy
Castaways
of Black Lake Island

being a record of the terrible adventures
of the brothers Davies in the summer of 1901,
faithfully set forth by

Peter Llewelyn Davies

London
Published by J.M. BARRIE
In the Gloucester Road
1901

The book is dedicated to 'Our Mother, in Cordial Recognition of her Efforts to Elevate Us Above the Brutes', and it has a preface attributed to Peter, but written by Barrie, of course. Peter is four years old then; he's the youngest of the starring trio and he's deserving of such an honour – according to Barrie – 'for being the one who's most often dragged away from our adventures by a nanny telling him it's time for his nap.' There we're informed: 'The date of our shipwreck was 1 August 1901. I have still . . . a vivid recollection of that strange and terrible summer, when we suffered experiences such as have probably never before been experienced by three brothers.'

In the long dedication 'To the Five' – almost an essay, in fact, that Barrie would write a quarter of a century later for the book version of the play *Peter Pan* – its author recalls the genesis of his most famous character and signals *The Boy Castaways of Black Lake Island* as the opening shot, calling it 'a melancholy volume, the literary record of that summer, and the best and the rarest of this author's works.'

There are sixteen chapters. The last is titled 'Conclusions. Advice to Parents About the Education of Their Children', and, looking for it in the book, we find a blank page. The brief passages of text are set under thirty-five photographs for which 'part of the story had to be made up later, because you always started doing something else just as I pushed the button on my camera,' remembered Barrie. And he added: 'Captain Swarthy wasn't yet called Captain James 'Jas' Hook, Porthos wasn't called Nana, Tinker Bell didn't exist; but I remember that one afternoon, as we went into the woods carrying Michael – it was almost twilight – the boy was fascinated by the twinkle of our lanterns and that's how Tink was born.'

Barrie kept his copy like a treasure, as if it were the Holy Grail or the Holy Shroud or a splinter or a nail of the Holy Cross: the humble seed from which a luxuriant religion grew. The other copy – Barrie noted – 'as befits any object related to Peter Pan, managed to lose itself forever in a railway carriage'.

Actually, Arthur Llewelyn Davies lost it, and – as Peter Llewelyn Davies writes in his *Morgue* – the children's father never felt particularly sorry for having lost it, or rather, for having helped it to be lost.

The copy that disappeared on a train was never found, until Marcus Merlin made it reappear – like so many other lost objects – as if it were the long-delayed finale of a magic trick.

The character is Marcus Merlin.

Naturally, Marcus Merlin thinks *character* can only be a synonym of *protagonist*.

Says Marcus Merlin: 'Why settle for being a bad person when you can be an excellent character?'

As Marcus Merlin sees it, a 'bad person' isn't someone 'bad' but someone completely uninteresting. And an 'excellent person,' for example, might be a 'bad person' from an ethical or a moral point of view, but nevertheless still be an 'excellent character.'

And yes, that's the kind of question Marcus Merlin asks. The kind of question that would be an excellent character, if it were a character. The kind of question that – it's understood – has no interest in the proximity of any response. The kind of question that answers itself, its question marks hooks that you swallow almost without realizing it, hooks that snag you forever. And you don't care. You even like it. The feeling that nothing depends entirely on you any more. Certain people have that rare power. Ruthless fishermen. I suppose Jesus was a little like that, for those who believe in him. I'm sure Barrie and Marcus Merlin were like that – I believe in them.

Says Marcus Merlin: 'Don't ask me certain questions because you'll make me answer you with half-truths; and a half-truth is much more dangerous than a lie.'

Says Marcus Merlin: 'An excellent character is the most invincible person imaginable – good or bad – but also filmed to look his best. An excellent character doesn't need an eyebrow hair smoothed or a petal of the flower on his lapel adjusted.'

Says Marcus Merlin: 'Let me give you some advice: the key to a great life is to invent yourself first, and then invent everybody else; to be the director and star and writer of your own film. Most people do the opposite. They think they have to understand the world first, and they waste their time on that. They die having been just visitors at a museum when they could've chosen to be works of art.'

Says Marcus Merlin: 'My grandfather, also known as the King of Fitzrovia, killed himself. My father killed himself. My uncles killed themselves. My brother killed himself . . . I, however, will be murdered. I'm sure of it. What I don't know for certain is whether that will mean the evolution or deterioration of my family history's double helix. One thing is clear: they won't get me without a fight.'

And Marcus Merlin smiles. Marcus Merlin's smile is like

the smile of those giant statues that loom unexpectedly in the Tasmanian jungle, except that it's a smile with teeth. Metal teeth, teeth Marcus Merlin has attired in metal jackets. A dangerous smile. A Cheshire cat smile.

Marcus Merlin is the son of an Englishman and a Jamaican woman. His father was the perfect, consummate spiv: he made good money on the black market during the war; he stole silk intended for parachutes from the warehouses of the RAF and brought it to his wife so she could make women's stockings that they later sold at exorbitant prices. Marcus Merlin shows me a photograph of his parents. Martin Merlin is almost a twin of the young Trevor Howard (maybe that's how Marcus Merlin got the habit of almost automatically translating the faces of strangers into the faces of famous actors) in his impeccable striped suit with wide lapels, unmistakeably spiv, and that incredibly spiv pencil moustache that seems tailor-made to pull taut a subtle, ironic, constant smile. Bertha Spencer, his mother, is a dark beauty with long legs and a scorching gaze that gives the frightening impression that each of her eyes has several pupils.

Said Marcus Merlin: 'My mother worked in the costume department at Ealing Studios. She hid her pregnancy until the last minute. She was afraid she would lose her job. So it was there I came into the world, a different world, surrounded by the scenery of sophisticated English comedies, comedies that always featured some elegant crook . . . Maybe that's why I'm so mad about celluloid. Anyway, my mother was never the same after my first scream ruined one of Alec Guiness's scenes. In *The Man in the White Suit*, I think. My mother never forgave herself. I, on the other hand, considered it an honour. An unmistakable signal, an indisputable sign that I was someone different: I was someone who refused to be born in a place as obvious as the hospital; I would be someone who refused to do vulgar things or be a part of them; I would be unique, different.'

Said Marcus Merlin: 'My father threw himself from Big

Ben. A question of debt. My mother is mad. You and I were born to be orphans, my friend . . . Dead fathers, mad mothers,' he concluded. And that was the last time he brought up anything having to do with his family.

Marcus Merlin is another Englishman of mixed blood. A white negro. Another product of the mixing of different ways to be English. Like Jim Yang, who in Marcus Merlin always criticized for being comfortably Oriental.

Said Marcus Merlin: 'You should've made him Pakistani and you'd sell even more books.'

Yes, Marcus Merlin is part of that broth seasoned with fiery colonial spices – the Caribbean, Africa, India, China, New Zealand, Australia – that began to simmer hot and furiously in postwar London. Marcus Merlin was born in 1950; he's ten years older than me, but it's as if he belongs to another period of history, as if he's on the other side of one of those massive slices of time that separate the dinosaurs from man and the Spartans from the Crusades.

It's 1965 when I meet Marcus Merlin – or rather, when I begin to remember Marcus Merlin. I'm five years old then, and Marcus Merlin is fifteen, and to me, Marcus Merlin is as grown-up as my parents. He's much closer to them than to me, and even now, I've never quite been able to catch up with him. Now Marcus Merlin is still closer to my parents: he's older than me but somehow as young as them. Marcus Merlin doesn't have an age: he has an era. I know perfectly well how old he is, but the number of years doesn't seem to correspond to the timeless air with which he's moved through life since the beginning.

Marcus Merlin was always a youthful adult. I, on the other hand, was an old child. It isn't unusual for the telephone to ring, and, when I answer, for the voice of some silly new girl to ask whether I've seen my little brother recently: 'Darlin' Marcus.' The difference between forty and fifty – compared to the abyss between five and fifteen – is like the distance from one side of the street to the other; but it's a street with too much traffic going too fast, the unpredictable traffic light changing when you're halfway across.

So Marcus Merlin flies higher than me to the very end, Keiko Kai. Marcus Merlin likes to fly. He likes planes. I don't. Sometimes we fly together and it's on the plane, after his armoured smile has made the airport metal detectors go off, that Marcus Merlin is happiest.

Said Marcus Merlin: 'You wouldn't understand it. But I had one of those terrible childhoods. Really terrible. Like in those bloody old novels you like so much, with the children who starve to death. I never would've believed it was possible I could go up in a plane. Planes for me were something you saw in the sky. Very far away. Almost invisible. More noise than substance. That's why I skipped school and went to the airport: to watch the planes, to see them take off and land. Could anything be more beautiful? That moment of absolute, magical power when the planes leave the runway, when they break free of the pull of the earth . . . I watched them go up and I said to myself: "Yes, someday I'll be in one of those. In first class." When it became more or less clear how hard it would be to get the money to buy one of those expensive tickets anytime soon, I wanted to study so I could sit even farther forward than the rich passengers. That's what I wanted to be: a pilot. Or at least an air steward. But there wasn't any money at home. So I made up for it by forming a gang that stole merchandise and luggage from Heathrow, ha. Let's say that we were a kind of Lost and Found office. Or a Lost and Lost office.'

Once I told Marcus Merlin that I had come up with an idea for a novel: the story of a boy who's marooned at Heathrow. A boy whose parents lose him while they're checking in. A boy who's never found and who grows up there, moving from one terminal to the next like a cross between Tarzan and Robinson Crusoe, becoming a kind of urban legend. Marcus Merlin gave me a strange look – I didn't understand it then, but I understand it now – and suggested it would be better for me to 'stick with Jim Yang and not mix yourself up in weird stuff'.

Weird stuff. Marcus Merlin and his weird stuff. Is there anything weirder than Marcus Merlin? Where did Marcus Merlin come from? Or was he always there? Every once in a while, over the years, he reveals bits of his legend to me, tossing them to me like pieces of an infinite puzzle or like crumbs for the pigeons at Trafalgar Square. He tells me he spent 'educational holidays' in the prisons of Bristol, Winchester, Exeter and Dartmouth.

He tells me he 'spent a long weekend' at Long Grove Mental Hospital because 'they let me choose between that and something much worse'.

He tells me he had a 'business' in Gibraltar.

He tells me he learned the art of hypnosis from a German magician. He explains that it's true, you can't make anybody do anything they don't want to do, no matter how deep a trance they're in. He also explains the secret clause, the small print between hypnotizer and victim: most times no one really knows what they want, so . . .

He tells me he worked for the legendary record producer Joe Meek; that he 'went out to hunt sounds' with a tape recorder for Joe Meek's strange creations: sonic collages about trips to the moon and robots and ghosts. That's the official version. The unofficial, off-the-record version – the track hidden in the last concentric grooves – is that the young Marcus Merlin is ordered to go from record store to record store buying singles by the artists produced by Meek so that they'll rise up the charts. That's at first. Almost immediately Marcus Merlin discovers that it's 'easier, cheaper and more fun' to bully the record store owner and keep the money for himself: he advises them that it's in their best interest to put the artists produced by Joe Meek on their bestseller lists. Then Joe Meek starts to go crazy. He leaves on his sunglasses while he sleeps; he doesn't even flirt with Marcus Merlin. Joe Meek almost never sleeps. Joe Meek hires mediums to put him in touch with his hero, Buddy Holly. Joe Meek hears voices inside his head. Joe Meek claims he's being spied on by British intelligence or by the KGB, whichever. Joe Meek spends his time recording and sending and receiving 'messages' in his flat. Joe Meek almost never goes outside. Joe Meek talks to his gun: he calls it 'my one and only'. One day, his gun replies, returning all his love at close range.

Marcus Merlin decides the moment's come to seek a new boss, an easier-going mentor. I suppose that's when my father makes his entrance. Marcus Merlin starts coming to the house all the time. The first thing he does is help my father build his studio in the cellars of Neverland. Marcus Merlin knows how to do these things.

Said Marcus Merlin: 'I was initiated into the mysteries of the world of electronics when I discovered what a car battery directly connected to the nipples of a not-so-nice guy could do.'

Marcus Merlin works for my father but he also works for the Kray brothers, London's most glamorous gangsters.

Marcus Merlin has free run of the city's clubs. He knows them like his own home, better than his own home; Marcus Merlin isn't home very often: the 100 Club, Marquee (Oxford St), Beat City, Roaring 20s, Top Ten Club, Marquee (Wardour St), Ronnie Scott's, Jack of Clubs, Round House Pub, the Scene, Piccadilly Jazz Club, the Flamingo, Studio 51, the Ad Lib, Notre Dame Hall.

I was at some of them. I think I was at some of them. Or not. There's a moment when all clubs seem alike, or they're simply shuffled like cards in a deck and fall back into place as the reincarnation of other clubs. Some clubs disappear abruptly. Others die without warning. Or they burst into flames in the middle of a party. 'Or someone helps them burst into flames,' says Marcus Merlin.

At the beginning of the 60s, Marcus Merlin is the new star of a large and long-established family of criminals. Marcus Merlin is a gangster with swing. Marcus Merlin snaps his fingers and smiles and wears the wildest colours well. His mother's tropical blood lends no colour at all to his pale moon face, but it makes it shine with a new light, like stolen sunlight. No, Marcus Merlin will never kill himself.

The first time I see Marcus Merlin – the first time I remember seeing Marcus Merlin – is at a party at Neverland. One of my birthday parties. Marcus Merlin comes up to me.

Says Marcus Merlin: 'Kid, I'm going now. I have to go feed some trees.' I tell him trees don't eat. I tell him trees *drink*.

Says Marcus Merlin: 'No, no, no. Trees also eat: you dig a hole a few feet deep and a few feet long and a foot or two wide. You throw the meat in there. You don't need to strip it or cook it first. You cover it up well. And you go whistling home.'

The last time I saw Marcus Merlin, Keiko Kai, was a day or two ago. I don't remember it very well. The pills, you know. I went to visit him at the hospital. I went straight from the airport, from the airplane that brought me from Hollywood. The intensive care ward. Marcus Merlin had lost lots of weight and was full of tubes. Ten years older than me, but now an eternity separated us and not only did he seem to have caught up with me, he'd gotten so far ahead he was almost lost on the horizon. Marcus Merlin was older than me at last. His skin was hanging from his bones, making him look like someone who's dressed too fast after leaping out of bed to open the door to someone who won't stop knocking, who's banging as hard as he can with his fist.

Said Marcus Merlin: 'My boy, this is it . . . I told you I wouldn't kill myself; I promised myself years ago. That's why I'm going to ask a last favour of you. I want you to kill me. The best of both worlds, I know, and the question must be asked whether inviting someone to murder me isn't just a lesser form of suicide. I hope not. One thing's for sure: it can't be very complicated. Press a button or two. An air bubble in a vein. Or the old pillow method. I leave it up to you, you've always been the best at coming up with good endings. I was better at beginnings . . . I don't think the doctors will realize. I know: maybe if you pull out some of these tubes . . . And then put them in my hand. They'll think I did it. I don't care what they think. What I care about is not being the cause of my own death . . . Don't look at me like that. I know it won't be an easy thing for you to do, I know you think you can't do it; but if there's anything men are perfectly equipped for it's killing. It's in our blood. All you have to do is pull the right lever. So I'm going to help you. I'm going to help you hate me. I'm going to stop being an excellent character and just become a bad person. Let's see . . . How to begin? Ah, I know: what was the last thing your mother said before she died . . .? Perfect . . . I think that's the best place to start, the magic words to turn you into my assassin . . . Now I'm going to tell you a story . . . A children's story . . .'

The character is childhood.

Childhood was invented by adults. Childhood can only be appreciated from adulthood, so all children's books are nothing but more or less desperate exercises in nostalgia and revenge. And oh how nice it would be if there were a series of children's books written entirely by children, children's classics produced by children between the ages of five and six. Real stories, not invented; stories that would relate, in just the right amount of time and space, the precise texture of weekends, the epiphany of birthdays, the fear of losing teeth or wetting the bed or the dark, the irreconcilable difference between winter and summer, those two completely separate dimensions.

There were always children, of course, but when is childhood invented? Jim Yang says – because I make him say it – that the idea of childhood is conceived in Victorian England. Previously, all through the eighteenth century, children were thought to be simply miniature adults, impish beasts, nearly wild; empty vessels to be filled with the fluid and substance of basic knowledge so they'd grow up fast and occupy their proper place in society, or the place luck had bestowed on them.

The arrival of the romantics begins to alter these expectations, and suddenly childhood isn't a blank page but a weighty volume written in code, full of strange ideas and portentous thoughts waiting to be deciphered by adults who haven't fully grown up. Or who've grown up different. Adults who're usually unmarried or have no children; adults who write monumental little books. Childhood is deciphered in children's books by Victorian authors who feel a strange and unprecedented kinship with children: Lewis Carroll, Charles Kingsley, Edward Lear, Frances Hodgson Burnett, Kenneth Grahame, A. A. Milne. Looking glasses to pass through, the wind blowing in the willows, little bears and moles, little lords and little princesses, and, most important of all: secret gardens. All these books have something in common: hidden places a person can only reach if he or she has it, transparent conceptions of Eden regained. Parents may have been expelled for their sins; but children can set out to find Eden, find the road home, return. What's important is having enough time to be told the story. Suddenly, what's important is to hardly grow at all, to be small enough to go through all the little magic doors.

And to believe.

I believe in Peter Pan because one morning – I can't be more than five, I'm still reading letter by letter, word by word, sentence by sentence – I go out walking in the gardens of Neverland. It's dawn, or the dying moment of one of my parents' long parties, and the air is full of goodbyes, of engines revving up, of people coming slowly down the stairs, shielding their eyes so the sunlight doesn't make that crazy migraine any worse.

The need to get away from the house. Maybe forever. I remember feeling that. And thinking that maybe I'd climb a tree in the forest of Sad Songs and never come down. I walk with my hands in my pockets and I come to the summer house, where the Victorians sometimes rehearse, and I go in, and – mystery of mysteries – on the floor there's a book, and the book is called *Peter Pan*.

I open it.

I enter it.

I read:

All children, except one, grow up.

And all books, except one, grow up. *Peter Pan* – unlike all the other books we read in childhood and reread as adults; like the author of *Peter Pan*, like the reader of *Peter Pan* – doesn't grow up, will never grow up. *Peter Pan* is like Peter Pan.

I enter *Peter Pan*, never to emerge from it again.

The character is the writer.

The writer of children's literature.

The writer of children's literature becomes what he is as the result of a childish decision, made, of course, in childhood. Only in childhood can we face the oceanic vastness of words; the adventure of reading them and writing them, of acquiring all those tools of knowledge in such a short time. If you think about it a little, logically we should learn to read and write when we're older and rational and thoughtful, and not in that almost savage state. But of course, if it worked that way, no one would dare to be a writer. Because if you think about it a little thought, there's no more childish decision than to become a writer: a decision that – with very few exceptions – is always made when you're a child, because only then are you crazy enough to face a challenge and a calling like that. It's a decision as unreal as choosing to be an astronaut or a hero of the Foreign Legion (I ask myself whether any profession could be at once nearer and more alien to that of the writer than that of the legionnaire or astronaut, always in orbit and off base and suspecting it won't be easy to come home), and it's always made at a moment of exquisite and extreme and fictive irrationalism. Keiko Kai: we decide to become writers when we realize we won't be able to be anything else; when we finish reading the children's book that will influence us at every stage of our life to come; when – yes, all writers of all literature always emerge in the shadow of a children's writer of children's literature – we discover that we're mutants beyond help or cure. We're little readers then, and we tell ourselves that we want to be big writers, and we tell our parents and our parents look at us with a kind of horror, asking themselves what went wrong and where we've come from. The formation of a writer carries implicit within it the deformation of so many other professions, and thus we find ourselves orphans of a first impulse sparked in childhood, that freak age of all ages, that short and long time when each day and night we change a little for the sole satisfaction of knowing that we're unique and chosen and doomed, understanding that we'll never grow up now, and that because we're writers we'll be children and childish until the end of our lives. All vocations change and grow, except one. Writing will be an awfully big adventure.

A mutation, yes, but aren't mutations the irrefutable evidence of the artistic nature of the evolutionary process? Of those rare moments when regimented evolution experiments, changing style and frequency, just to see what'll happen?

Writers of children's literature are strange animals, beings delicately removed from the profession's battles. All of them are writing very far from the front and the reflexive need to make it onto the *Granta* or *New Yorker* lists where young writers – of adult literature? – want to appear at all costs so they can set sail as soon as possible, knowing that time keeps moving faster and faster and that literature, like everything else, has achieved pop speed and authors don't last as long as they used to, seeming increasingly like short-lived, disposable rock stars: here comes another one, a new one, a newer one.

The process of children's literature is different. It isn't a game in the slick casino of immediate fame but something much more complex and paradoxical, a long-term effort.

Children's literature doesn't seek posterity for the author; instead, it finds immortality in its characters. The name on the cover is what's least important in the end. Of greatest value is the title, and the name of the hero. These are books to be read by the most primitive readers, and also possibly the most passionate; readers who care nothing about the writer's life or his style; pure readers, though not necessarily innocent.

Children's literature is enjoying a golden age, invested with the same grandeur and sense of the epic as certain classic texts of the ancient world. These are specimens with no expiration date, and perpetual inhabitants of a planet at the exact point of maximum perfection. My father – always lost in the thickets of his frustration; only he could've come up with the idea of an imperial rocker – would've understood: there are few trades more authentically Victorian and victorious than that of children's writer. And maybe I've simply made his first and only and last wish come true: that I be a perfect, complete gentleman.

Maybe.

The truth is that children's fiction is almost an impossibility: something concocted by adults for the consumption of children. That's where its difficulties and dangers lie. It's a voyage begun by many, with only a privileged few ever reaching the end. Most die – or grow up, or lie too much – along the way. It isn't easy. It never will be. It's stories made up by people who must understand children while being perfectly clear who they themselves are as adults, remembering where they've come from and where they're going. That's the Faustian pact and the rule in effect for most of the creators of children's books.

And every so often there's a mutation within a mutation: a children's writer who isn't necessarily grown up.

Barrie's case.

My case.

If adult literature is generally the product of hidden childhood trauma, then children's literature is the product of plainly visible childhood trauma, the worst kind: the kind about which everything is known; the kind that's always there, waving to us from a corner of the room; the kind that never ages, but seems to grow larger and more powerful with each passing minute.

Peter Pan's case.

The character is Peter Pan.

Peter Pan, or The Boy Who Would Not Grow Up. A play by J. M. Barrie performed for the first time at the Duke of York's Theatre, London, 1904; and ever since anointed as a Christmas tradition, a classic production with a succession of famous actresses or would-be famous actresses in the leading role.

Peter Pan occupies an uncertain place between drama and pantomime, although it began as purely a children's entertainment whose renown and appeal had more to do with its stage incarnation than with its later adaptation to the medium of literature. Does Peter Pan spring from Apollo's wise forehead or Dionysius' wild laugh? Does it matter? Why choose one or the other? Why can't Peter Pan be a symbol of sanity and madness at the same time? Why can't I be?

The play begins at the Darling family house in Bloomsbury, with the arrival there of Peter Pan, a boy who fled his home on the day of his birth after listening in horror as his parents made plans for his future and talked about what their son might be when he grew up and became an adult.

That's why Peter Pan distrusts parents; he especially hates mothers, ever since the time he tried to go home and found the window closed and his mother with her arms around a new boy. 'Mothers are satisfied so long as they have someone,' thinks Peter Pan bitterly.

But all that happened a long time ago. Now Peter Pan slips into the Darling house and is discovered by Nana, the dog. Nana frightens Peter Pan, who flies away and leaves his shadow in the children's room. Mr and Mrs Darling's children are called Wendy Moira Angela Darling, John Napoleon Darling and Michael Nicholas Darling. Mr Darling is jealous of his children's love for Nana – Mr Darling is a man of simple and petty sentiments – so that one night, when he goes out to dinner with his wife, he chains the dog in the garden. Which allows Peter Pan to return in search of his lost shadow. The three little Darlings find him in their room, and after Wendy sews his shadow to his heels, Peter Pan explains, in gratitude:

> *I ran away to Kensington Gardens and lived a long long time among the fairies . . . Most of them are dead. You see, Wendy, when the first baby laughed for the first time, its laugh broke into a thousand pieces, and they all went skipping about, and that was the beginning of fairies . . . When a new baby laughs for the first time a new fairy is born, and as there are always new babies there are always new fairies . . . You see children know such a lot now, they soon don't believe in fairies, and every time a child says 'I don't believe in fairies,' there is a fairy somewhere that falls down dead.*

Right away, with the help of his magic fairy dust, Peter Pan teaches his new friends to fly so they'll accompany him to the island of Neverland and join him in great adventures. In Neverland, Peter Pan lives with the fairy Tinker Bell and his lost boys, who're always in search of a mother: Tootles, Nibs, Slightly, Curly and the twins. Six boys who never get any older, and who are some of the 'children who fall out of their perambulators when the nurse is looking the other way. If they are not claimed in seven days they are sent far away to the Neverland to defray expenses,' explains Peter Pan. And he adds that it's said that girls are too clever to fall out of their carriages. The rest of the population of Neverland is composed of mermaids who like to play cricket with the bubbles of rain water they make by slapping their tails; a swarm of mauve and white fairies (and another swarm of silly fairies, blue in colour); a tribe of Indians whose chief is Great Big Little Panther, father of the beautiful Tiger Lily; and the villains of the land, Captain Hook and his crew of pirates: Smee, Gentleman

Starkey, Cookson, Cecco, Mullins, Jukes and Noodler. Truth be told, Hook is only a relative villain. His presence fills the need for the establishment of a little order and discipline on an island overrun by the anarchy of those who refuse to grow up. In any case, Hook and his men defeat the tribe of Great Big Little Panther while Peter Pan is away, and Wendy, who has become the mother of the lost boys, is captured by the pirates with all of her 'family'. Peter Pan returns just in time to prevent Captain Hook from causing 'a holocaust of children' by making them 'walk the plank' on the starboard side of his galleon, the *Jolly Roger*, and – according to Wendy – 'die like English gentlemen'. Peter Pan beats his rival in a duel and throws him overboard to be eaten by a crocodile that's been pursuing him for years, ever since it devoured his hand – which Peter Pan cut off – and swallowed his watch – the only watch in Neverland – thus becoming the master of time; this is the only sign that time passes and must pass.

With all problems solved and Neverland at peace again, Peter Pan brings the little Darlings home, where he rejects Mrs Darling's offer to adopt him; so that he won't be sorry to part from his dear Wendy, Mrs Darling promises him that Wendy will be allowed to return to Neverland each spring, to help with the spring cleaning. What isn't entirely clear to me – unlike the unambiguous conclusions of other children's classics – is whether the ending of *Peter Pan* is happy or not. With Hook dead, what happens to that childish continuum of childhood, in which all days are more or less the same and the battle is constant and neverending and keeps starting and being interrupted and starting over again? And I ask myself whether Peter Pan – dying of boredom – wouldn't slice open the crocodile in the end and rescue his enemy so he could keep fighting, as if time hadn't passed, weren't moving, were unchanging.

And Barrie builds Peter Pan the same way Victor Frankenstein builds his creature: with the assorted pieces of different bodies.

One Christmas, Barrie takes Jack, George and Peter to a vaudeville performance. The show, Seymour Hicks's *Bluebell in Fairyland* describes itself in the programme as a 'musical fantasy.' It's the triumph of the season. The children of London come to see it over and over again. And the adults, Barrie notices, don't seem too bothered to have to accompany them each Friday.

Barrie starts taking notes:

– Fairy Play. *The characters fly through the air in sheets carried by birds in their beaks.*

And at last Barrie finishes *The Little White Bird*. It's the summer of 1902. The book's chapter about Peter Pan, one of the stories Captain W— tells David, into most of the rest of the novel.

Barrie turns the manuscript in to his publisher, and to celebrate, he moves even closer to – right across from – Kensington Gardens and the Llewelyn Davieses. Barrie leaves 133 Gloucester Road and settles into a little Regency-era house on Bayswater Road – Mary calls it Leinster Corner – on the north edge of the gardens. When Arthur Llewelyn Davies finds out, he shudders in private and publicly smiles.

At his new house, Barrie receives the news of his father's death: David Barrie – who scarcely appears in Barrie's autobiographical writings, and plays almost no part in his childhood memories – has died at the age of eighty-seven, run down by a carriage on Kirriemuir's High Street. A little later, another of his sisters, Mary, dies.

Barrie is depressed, recovers, and on 4 November 1902, at the Duke of York's Theatre, *The Admirable Crichton* – his play about a butler who becomes the leader of a family of shipwrecked aristocrats – opens and is a great success. Barrie oversees everything down to the last detail, and makes surprise appearances at the theatre every so often to ensure that the actors aren't improvising or altering their lines: Barrie hates it when that happens. It's with *The Admirable Crichton*, too, that Barrie experiments for the first time with his need for things never to end. He changes the ending of the script, several times. Each performance is a surprise, and Barrie decides that plays can also be like children's stories, to which improvements are made each time they're told at the request of children who never seem to tire of hearing the same story. Thus, there are nights when the butler Crichton remains in England; nights when he returns to the island and sends a letter to be read by an actor before the audience after the curtain has fallen; there are nights when he marries the young noblewoman and nights when he rejects her. It isn't that Barrie isn't satisfied with the first ending, but that Barrie isn't satisfied with the concept of endings. The end of a play – the moment when everything finishes, when reality comes back to claim the territory fiction has snatched from it – is for Barrie the equivalent of being ordered to bed early by the grown-ups. And Barrie wants to keep playing. So he invents excuses – new endings – to put off as long as possible the moment of going up the stairs, getting under the covers, turning off the light.

The Little White Bird – a novel for adults about childhood – takes the same tack. It's a serious story about the need for the fun never to end, fun being the only thing that must keep growing.

Barrie keeps taking notes:

– *Play.* The Happy Boy: *Boy who can't grow up – he flees pain and death – when he's caught he's become a savage (Ending: he escapes).*

The Barries invite Sylvia to Paris in return for acting as inspiration for *The Little White Bird*. Arthur stays in London working and taking care of the children. 'Sylvia is in Paris with her friends the Barries,' he writes in a letter. *Her* friends, not his.

Barrie returns to London and to his strolls in Kensington Gardens, and he receives a great honour: the Viscountess Esher – a habituée of the theatre and a fervent admirer of his work – feels Barrie has written 'so charmingly' about Kensington Gardens in *The Little White Bird* that he deserves a fitting reward. She speaks to Lord Esher, who holds the position of Secretary to His Majesty's Office, and asks him to intercede with the Duke of Cambridge – also the Ranger of the Gardens – so that Barrie is given a key to Kensington Gardens for his personal use. Barrie thanks them for the honour: he has no interest in walking in the gardens at night, when they're closed; but he's fascinated by the idea of having been chosen as the guardian of a singular object, something that grants him a special power to open forbidden doors as if by magic.

And Barrie discovers – half astonished and half annoyed – that *The Little White Bird* has become one of the popular topics of conversation in the park, almost an urban legend: more and more strangers come up to him to ask him exactly where Peter Pan lives; more and more mothers introduce their children to him hoping he'll immortalize them in a bestseller. Barrie says little in return and keeps walking. Alone. Porthos has been dead for a year. Mary – deprived of babies; Sylvia is expecting her fifth child around this time – gives Barrie a new dog: a black and white Newfoundland that they name Luath. The dog is sickly, but Mary manages to nurse it back to health and restore the power of its barks. Mary is a good mother; Mary could be the best of mothers; and later she'll write bittersweetly about her canine loves, her passion for decoration, and her matrimonial frustrations in three books of memoirs titled *Men and Dogs*, *The Happy Garden* and *Happy Houses*.

On 23 November 1903, Barrie begins work on the play that will eventually be called *Peter Pan*; the first draft is titled *Anon*. The first scene takes place in the Darling children's bedroom.

Nearby, a few hours later, Sylvia gives birth again. Another son. Sylvia wants to call him Timothy, after Captain W–'s invisible son in *The Little White Bird*, but Arthur refuses with resolute elegance to fall into the easy bad taste of metafiction. Nicholas – like Peter and Michael – isn't christened then, but he'll ask to be christened when he's fourteen, choosing Barrie as his godfather.

Arthur also decides it's time to move. The house at 23 Campden Hill Square in Kensington Park Gardens has become cramped for a couple with five children and four servants. After years of hard work, Arthur is beginning to reap the rewards at court, and at last he can permit himself the luxury of a more comfortable home. The houses in the centre of London, however, are still beyond his reach; so Arthur goes looking for something in the suburbs, discovering the Tudor-style Egerton House on Berkhamsted High Street. The biographer Andrew Birkin notes in *J. M. Barrie & the Lost Boys: The Love Story that Gave Birth to Peter Pan* that 'Egerton House . . . seemed to solve all problems. It was close to the station, which would allow Arthur to commute every day to London; it was large enough to accommodate an ever-expanding household; it had an excellent day school (Berkhamsted School, headed by the respected Reverend T. C. Fry) within walking distance of the house; it would provide the growing boys with clean country air; and it was twenty-five miles from J. M. Barrie's doorstep.'

Barrie works so enthusiastically on what he's now titled *Peter and Wendy* that the opening of another of his plays – *Little Mary*, on 24 September 1903; two hundred performances, and, according to *The Times*, 'a rather silly tale' – goes unremarked.

In *Peter and Wendy*, Barrie calls upon all the memories of his own childhood and the childhood of the Llewelyn Davies brothers, as well as the immortal ghost of his mother Margaret Ogilvy. At the indestructible heart of his story beats the promise of eternal youth and the dream come true of being a boy forever, like his brother David, inhabiting a world outside this world. A world that in the beginning is called Never Never Never Land (in a first draft of the play), then Never Never Land (a name Barrie borrows from a region of Australia: Never Never Land, an endless desert), then Never Land (in the performances of the play and the script published in book form) and finally Neverland in the novel *Peter and Wendy*.

Barrie finishes a first version on 1 March 1904. Barrie writes to Charles Frohman that he'll have a new work ready in which Maude Adams can star. Barrie trusts that the actress will play the part of Wendy and that a boy will be Peter Pan. But there are problems: the English laws prohibit the use of minors on stage after 9 o'clock at night. Charles Frohman – without even having read the script; his faith in Barrie is absolute – then suggests that Maude Adams could be Peter Pan in the American production and that they could also find a young Englishwoman; an idea with great commercial potential but which has since led to the bizarre and dubious belief that Peter Pan must by rights be a coveted role for women.

With this matter solved, there are other details left to be settled. The play will require five different and elaborate sets, many mechanical devices, and a cast of almost fifty actors. It's a super-production like few ever seen in England, or anywhere else. And the first opinions about what begins to be known as 'Barrie's Folly' – an extravaganza with pirates, redskins, crocodiles, fairies, flying children and children lost in magic lands – aren't favourable. To begin with, it isn't clear whether it's a play just for children, or a play for adults who want to revisit their childhood. The plot is full of adventures, true, but the dialogue is complex: there are many private jokes comprehensible only to Barrie and the Llewelyn Davieses, and sometimes the whole thing seems to founder on the shoals of egocentric, narcissistic whim.

One night Barrie reads the play to the actor and impresario Beerbohm Tree, specialist in sumptuous stage sets at His Majesty's Theatre. Barrie shouts, climbs on the furniture, plays all the parts. Tree – who has become famous for being willing to try anything and not skimping on production costs – can't believe what he's seeing and hearing; he turns pale and immediately writes to Charles Frohman: 'Barrie has gone out of his mind . . . I'm sorry to say it, but you ought to know. He's just read me a play. He is going to read it to you, so you can take this as a warning from someone who's a good friend of yours, and of Barrie's, too. I know I have not gone woozy in my mind, because I have tested myself since hearing the play; but Barrie must be mad.'

When Charles Frohman arrives in London from New York, at the end of April, Barrie dines with him and proposes a deal: *Peter and Wendy* (which he's renamed, acknowledging its origin and its debt to *The Little White Bird*, as *The Great White Father*, and which, he confesses, he's sure won't be a success but is his 'pet project') and another play, *Alice Sit-by-the-Fire*, a typical Barrie product. Charles Frohman isn't very impressed by *Alice Sit-by-the-Fire*, but he loves *The Great White Father*. He's never read anything like it. Not a line of it should be changed, except the title. 'It has to be called *Peter Pan*, nothing else will do,' he commands, and Charles Frohman smiles, and the play will have to be ready for its West End debut the following Christmas. And Charles Frohman keeps smiling.

Peter Pan in large type, and below it, in smaller type, *or The Boy Who Wouldn't Grow Up*. And then type and more type: the first *Peter Pan* poster is a short-sighted person's nightmare, and reading it all would take as much time as reading a whole newspaper. It doesn't matter; it's better that way. Everything having to do with *Peter Pan* must be like this: different, exaggerated, unprecedented.

Charles Frohman has at last discovered – just as the law of gravity was discovered and not invented; just as the sun was suddenly seen to sit at the centre of the universe with everything spinning around it – the thing that will make him remembered forever, the thing that will make him immortal, the thing that will make him responsible for having brought into the world the most indestructible toy ever.

In *The Story of J. M. B.*, the biographer Denis Mackail says: 'There was no limit on spending. The risks didn't matter. Never had Charles Frohman's megalomania risen to greater heights. Never had this inspired little Jew been happier. And never had any writer for the stage been luckier in being able to count on a producer like Charles Frohman.'

There's no time to lose: Charles Frohman selects Dion Boucicault – son of a famous Victorian playwright – as director and producer. His sister, Nina Boucicault, is the perfect choice for Peter Pan. Nina asks Barrie how she should play her character; all Barrie says is: 'Peter Pan is a bird . . . And he's one day old.' Hilda Trevelyan will be Wendy, and Gerald du Maurier is responsible for the double role of beastly Captain Hook and dull, cautious Mr Darling, married to Dorothea Baird as Mrs Darling. Jane Wren is Tinkerbell. Joan Burnett is Tootles. Christine Silver is Nibs. A.W. Baskcomb is Slightly. Arthur Lupino will be Nana the dog, and he spends hours at Leinster Corner studying Luath's movements. A studio of makeup professionals on Drury Lane take samples of the dog's fur and create an amazingly lifelike costume. The little lost boys are personally chosen by Barrie, who tells them stories at break during the rehearsals. William Nicholson – a fashionable portrait painter – is charged with designing the costumes and the scenery. John Crook will write the songs and the music. I can't remember – there are so many names – who's the first Tiger-Lily, daughter of Chief Great Big Little Panther. So many names – yes, now I remember: Miriam Nesbitt is Tiger-Lily and Great Big Little Panther is Philip Darwin.

Each and every one of them is given a looseleaf copy of the script, and each must solemnly swear not to reveal a single detail of the play to family or friends, let alone the newspapermen who are beginning to smell a scoop; the owner of the Duke of York Theatre is made to hire a small army of security guards who march up and down St Martin's Lane and prevent the infiltration of snoops and undesirables. Which of course doesn't prevent an increasingly elated Charles Frohman from stopping acquaintances in the street to act out selected scenes from *Peter Pan*.

Hilda Trevelyan receives the notice announcing her first

rehearsal, reading, with slight panic: '10:30 – Flying.' Dion Boucicault is waiting for her at the door; he asks whether she has life insurance and tells her that if she doesn't, she should get some as soon as possible. Inside, George Kirby is waiting, founder and director since 1889 of George Kirby's Flying Ballet Company. George Kirby and his troupe soar on the stages of Europe thanks to a 'flying apparatus', a kind of complicated, heavy harness. Barrie challenges George Kirby to design a lighter, more practical model, one that won't – with its many wires and pulleys – be so obvious to the audience. Barrie doesn't want a flying machine; Barrie wants the actors to fly. George Kirby accepts the challenge – the pay is very good – and makes a light rig that can be hooked and unhooked from the stage machinery in a matter of seconds.

Wendy flies, Peter flies, Barrie loses steam.

At the end of October the exhausting six weeks of rehearsals begin, but the Llewelyn Davieses – Barrie realizes all at once – are no longer nearby. Where is little George – his looking glass and sounding box – when he needs him most? What good does it do to hold the key to Kensington Gardens if his playmates aren't there any more? Barrie and Mary have been married for a decade and – as is his habit, fictionalizing reality to make it more bearable – the writer jots down ideas for a novel about a marriage petrified by years of unhappiness:

> – *He says can't we pick up the pieces* (of our love) *& she says no – love not a broken jar but fine wine – contents spilt – can't pick that up.*
>
> – *She on the agonies of years of forgiveness, self-deceptions, clinging to straws, &c, & how all these have gone. Like stick in fire, flaming, red, with sparks, now black & cold.*

Barrie looks for any excuse to leave the house. The arduous and increasingly involved rehearsals – the author rewrites and adds bits at the foot of the stage and the page – are the perfect excuse to escape from Leinster Corner, from the abode of his cheerless marriage, devoid of laughter or applause. When everyone goes home, Barrie stays amid the scenery of *Peter Pan*: his home, his native land, his refuge, his own world, his Neverland.

The character is the theatre.

If all the world is but a stage – as Shakespeare wrote and Barrie read – then I like to think London is the curtain that rises and falls as history wills it and that every so often – during the 1960s, for example – it proves to be more interesting than any play unfolding behind it.

When this happens – when London is *so* – the whole world agrees that there can be no better drama or comedy than the enormous, heavy canvas of the city, so much grander and more entertaining than a blank cinema screen. And no one realizes when all of a sudden it refuses to go up, because there's nothing more thrilling than staring unblinkingly at that curtain frozen in place by all the things happening in the network of its patterns and designs.

When this happens, no one asks whether London is or is not, because it's wrong to talk in the theatre even if the play hasn't begun or isn't about to begin and we're all focused – in a perpetual intermission – on the picture of a city on that vertical flag, hardly stirring in the almost imperceptible wind of millennia.

What is it that we see in a curtain? The dust of all the plays performed behind it? The echo of the actors' monologues and the spectators' coughs? The creak of the timbers under boots? The secret murmurs of the stagehands? The curtain as a permeable membrane warning us that things on the other side aren't like those on this side, much as they may seem to be?

My impossible dream and my unfulfillable desire has always been a life unfolding at the exact point – that wavy line following the folds of the velvet – that separates what's recited from what's said, what's lived from what's acted.

Maybe, Keiko Kai, that's why I claim for myself, on this last night and in this last act, my only chance to be the curtain between my parents' life and Barrie's story. Or between Barrie's life and my parents' story, it amounts to the same thing. I hope to be a good curtain. A curtain that, when everyone has left the theatre, remains barely illuminated by the ghost-lamp, that venerable and poetic tradition: the lamp that a worker lights at the end of each performance and leaves on all night in the middle of the stage to scare away the ghosts of dead actors and live characters. And who knows, maybe a spark will leap onto me – theatres are such in flammable places and they burn so quickly – and that spark will set me blazing, and my whole world will burn with me, until there's nothing left but ashes of everything I once was and will never be again.

I went to see *Peter Pan* for the first time on a cold Christmas in 1966. Snow and the sound of bells. Marcus Merlin takes us. Me and Baco. My father refuses to come.

'Too psychedelic for my taste. I don't understand those children. Living their childhoods at the happiest moment the Empire and this city have known, and they'd rather go somewhere else, to an island with . . . *Indians*,' says my father.

What Marcus Merlin takes us to see is a revival of the Walt Disney movie. Disney's *Peter Pan* commits the most mortal of sins, the most unforgivable blasphemy: at the end it reveals that everything in it – Peter Pan included – was just something Wendy dreamed. And there are those horrible songs and Peter Pan's irritating voice courtesy of Bobby Driscoll – child star of the Disney Studios – who would end up, like so many other more-or-less child prodigies, addicted to drugs and dead of an overdose. Don't worry, Keiko Kai: your end will be very different, more glorious and quicker.

The Disney film isn't magical like the play, of course; but even so, I'm infected by the story, by the myth. I already was: I'd already read the book. The book that someone left in the summer house of the garden at Neverland. But the film strengthens the virus and makes it even more incurable.

And – I see it this way now, Keiko Kai – those two child-manipulators are strangely similar: Barrie is to Walt Disney what the Neanderthal was to the Cro-Magnon man. Something like that. Although maybe the comparison is unfair, wrong, inexact: I like to think Barrie was a more sophisticated being and much higher up the evolutionary ladder than Walt Disney ever could've been. It's clear that Barrie came first; Barrie is the god who makes light and myth and along the way creates a whole new children's universe, a new way of understanding the cosmogony of children. Disney – a hard-working pupil – erects the temples of his theme parks in memory of Barrie. Sacred cities where, after paying admission, you can visit Peter Pan's house, descend to its depths, contemplate the fictional suddenly made real for the sole pleasure and perversion of blurring the bounds between truth and lies and life and fantasy.

In any case, the movie has bright colours and a good story and – I have to admit – the sexiest Tinker Bell who ever existed and will probably ever exist: by the standards of the Disney Studios cartoonists, Tinker Bell is practically a Las Vegas chorus girl or a Playboy Club waitress.

I leave the theatre and go read the book again. I read it until I learn it by heart, until I know the page number where each thing happens. And I begin to find out everything I can about Barrie and Peter Pan.

Baco likes the film, but it doesn't thrill him the way it thrills me. He's very little. He's still at the age when nothing is as good as the recently discovered power of his imagination, nothing can compete: a child's logic may come too close to fantasy, but his dreams are always disturbingly real.

I, on the other hand, like to dream I'm one of the lucky ones who attend the opening night of *Peter Pan* at the Duke of York's Theatre. A play dreamed up by the most grown up of children. Something disturbingly real. The best of both worlds: product of a child's imagination and the resources of an adult. I like to imagine myself there, and it's no coincidence that Jim Yang has never visited that golden moment on any of his adventures. Why him and not me? It doesn't seem fair that my most cherished fantasies – and therefore the truest – should be ceded to my character in the end. And that it should be him and not me who's given the chance to be anywhere in space or time.

Jim Yang doesn't go.

I go.

I go and I'm an egg in Sylvia Llewelyn Davies's uterus, an egg that's just been fertilized. I'm the secret fission of love. I'm the anatomical reaction and the physical radiation of something that until yesterday was just a sperm – an odd-numbered and left-hand-programmed sperm – belonging to Arthur Llewelyn Davies. I'm a son – or, as Arthur would dearly like, a daughter – who will live inside Sylvia just long enough to attend the opening night and then disappear without anyone, even Sylvia, being aware of my presence. I'll be gone in her next menstrual flow – the red bloom of a single night, the most lost of lost boys – swimming in the sewers of London that empty into the river and then into the sea, never to return.

Sylvia travels to London with her sons. It's the beginning of December; classes have ended and won't begin again until after the holidays, and the final, critical rehearsals have begun. Barrie teaches the little Llewelyn Davieses how to use the flying apparatus. They fly. Barrie introduces them to the cast as 'the true authors of the play' and at the last minute he changes the names of a few of the characters so that his best friends are represented in some way on stage. Barrie also makes it clear that the idea for the character of Peter Pan occurred to Sylvia Llewelyn Davies and that in *The Little White Bird* he simply put in writing everything its 'true owner' never felt the urge to write herself.

Opening night is supposed to be the 21st, but it has to be postponed till the 27th. Multiple complications. On the night of 21 December, the stage collapses: too much weight on the floorboards. The machinery that will control many of the special effects is still being installed. Whole scenes must be dropped: the ending in Kensington Gardens, for example. And the scene in the mermaid pool. It doesn't matter. There'll be time to add them later, all the time in the world, Barrie consoles himself. And the stagehands refuse to work over Christmas. The idea that the actress playing Tinker Bell should always perform behind an enormous magnifying glass reversed so she looks smaller has proved to be impracticable, as well as mad. The company – the actors collapse with exhaustion in hallways and seats and dressing rooms; flying is so *tiring* – are convinced that everything will end in a disaster of catastrophic dimensions. A stagehand – at one of the breaks, while a backdrop is being lowered so another backdrop can be raised – comes up to Barrie and says: 'The gallery boys won't stand it.' Barrie thinks that he's a ghost or a sprite. A theatre imp. Barrie ignores him. Barrie never stops smiling. Barrie pays no attention to the torment of his migraines; he barely allows himself a moment to eat something light and drink innumerable cups of tea. Barrie asks over and over again whether Sylvia Llewlyn Davies has arrived with her children. Barrie seems to shine with the brightness that only saints shine with at the instant they first become conscious of their sainthood.

Sylvia, George, Jack and Peter (Nico is still too young to go out at night) arrive at the Duke of York's Theatre in one of those small buses that some companies rent to family groups for excursions to Dover or Canterbury or Stonehenge. The brothers enter the theatre feeling themselves to be the lords of the night and part of the show, and they're seated in the best box in the hall and from there they watch, like small holy emperors, the rest of the mere mortals about to be initiated into the mysteries they know so well.

The version of *Peter Pan* in three acts that goes up at eight-thirty at night on 27 December 1904 is shorter than it was supposed to be. Two or three scenes that were written are missing, and others are missing that there was no time to write, or that Barrie keeps coming up with and jotting down on napkins, in the margins of books, on the wallpaper of some bathroom at some friend's house. But the audience – which hasn't stopped saying 'oh!' and 'ah!' since the curtain rose – doesn't notice, isn't aware. They're adults suddenly returned to the zeniths of their childhood. They're happy.

Queer things happen from the beginning: a little girl comes onstage to direct the orchestra, children fly in and out of the window of a house in London, and to a treehouse in a strange place called Neverland where the actors dance with Indians, do battle with pirates, descend to the depths of the earth . . .

But beyond all these marvels, the most stunning takes place in the third scene of the second act. There, in order to save Peter Pan, Tinker Bell drinks the poison intended for him and is about to die. Then Peter Pan goes to the edge of the stage and addresses the audience as urgently as a hero in an Elizabethan drama:

> *Her light is growing faint, and if it goes out that means she is dead! Her voice is so low I can scarcely tell what she is saying. She says – she says she thinks she could get well again if children believed in fairies! Do you believe in fairies? Say quick that you believe! If you believe, clap your hands! Don't let Tink die.*

The theatre is perfectly silent. Barrie has arranged with the musicians to applaud if the audience doesn't react, to rescue the situation. It isn't necessary: a thunder of handclaps rises from the stalls and descends from the boxes. Has Barrie invented the theatrical device of audience participation? The device that from then on will mark all children's plays, with – to the horror of the parents – the actor transgressing the natural boundaries of the stage to torment those who are seated, suddenly making them feel an urgent desire to get up and go running out?

Nothing of the sort happens that night at the Duke of York's Theatre. The actress Nina Boucicault can't contain her tears. Everyone believes in fairies, and so does she, because could anyone be foolish enough not to believe on this magical, perfect night? It's the beginning of a new era. Men embrace, women cry, theatre critics wave their programmes and their notes as if celebrating a great victory on the field of the happiest of battles. I like to imagine that then someone faints, that someone regains his senses, that someone's hair turns white in a matter of seconds, that someone is converted to a strange religion, and that someone – at the next family funeral, after the customary moment of silence – is inspired by the memory of that moment and begins the odd tradition of applauding the coffin as it retreats: applauding just in case, applauding because perhaps a spark leaping from the friction of hands clapping will cause the blaze of a miracle and the resurrection of the dead.

The whole theatre is standing; the applause goes on for several minutes. Barrie smiles – Barrie is still smiling – and on the stage Peter Pan exclaims:

Oh, thank you, thank you, thank you!

The cast comes out to take its bows over and over again, for long minutes that become a kind of triumphant epilogue, a small play in and of itself, in which Nina Boucicault and the actors watch, dazed, as an audience of grown-ups who seem to have gone mad throw their hats in the air and leap up on their seats as if the spell of a sorceror's apprentice suddenly elevated to Grand Wizard has sent them back in time.

Charles Frohman is in New York. It's nearly five in the afternoon there, and the city is enduring one of the biggest snowstorms in memory. Charles Frohman is waiting for a cable from London that will tell him how everything went; but the storm has cut off telegraph service, so Charles Frohman whiles away the time by acting out the whole show for his friend Paul Potter, scene by scene. Charles Frohman gets down on all fours to be the dog and the crocodile. Charles Frohman barks, Charles Frohman snaps his jaws; but

Charles Frohman tells the story as if he were Wendy, his favourite character. Close to midnight, the telephone rings, and Paul Potter answers and takes down the cablegram, reading the magic words to Charles Frohman:

PETER PAN PERFECT. LOOKS LIKE GREAT SUCCESS.

'Oh, thank you, thank you, thank you!' exclaims Charles Frohman.

The press joins the party and is almost unanimous in its praise of the new show. 'To our taste, *Peter Pan* is from beginning to end a thing of pure delight,' smiles *The Times*. 'The mixture of conflicting elements ultimately yields a product of such originality, warmth, and daring that there's no room for even a shadow of a doubt as to its inevitable and overwhelming success,' predicts the *Daily Telegraph*. 'In *Peter Pan*, Mr Barrie once again relies not on true dramatic appeal but on his marvellous power to keep one entertained at the theatre. Mr Barrie is the only living writer, with the possible exception of Mr Bernard Shaw, capable of erecting pleasure palaces on the most insubstantial of foundations,' enthuses *The Morning Post*. '*Peter Pan* is the best thing Mr Barrie has done – the thing most directly from within himself. Here, at last, we see his talent in his full maturity; for here he has stripped off from himself the last flimsy remnants of a pretence to maturity . . . Mr Barrie is not that rare creature, a man of genius. He is something even more rare – a child who, by some divine grace, has found in the theatre the artistic medium through which to express the childishness that is in him. Mr Barrie has never grown up; Mr Barrie is still a child,' is Max Beerbohm's accurate diagnosis.

Discordant voices can also be heard, some rather horrified by the side effects caused by this new-fledged, victorious monster. Bernard Shaw growls: 'From the dramaturgical point of view, *Peter Pan* is an artificial freak that misses the mark.' The theatre impresario George Edwards shrugs his shoulders and sighs: 'Well, if that's the sort of thing the public likes, I suppose we'll have to give it 'em.' Anthony Hope, friend of Barrie and author of *The Prisoner of Zenda*, can't bear the 'touching' new ending – added four nights after the opening – in which the Beautiful Mothers, a kind of female chorus, appear in the Darlings' nursery to take back their lost boys, who vanished so many years ago. Anthony Hope runs out of the theatre for air, taking deep breaths of the London cold as if it's the antidote to a cloying poison, saying: 'Ah, what I'd give for an hour of Herod!'

Once the excitement of opening night is over, Barrie returns to Leinster Corner, where the wife he hardly speaks to is waiting, and the Llewelyn Davies tribe returns to Egerton House, their home in the London suburbs.

Barrie is finishing the many revisions and too many rewrites of *Peter Pan*, and he oversees the upcoming debut of *Alice-Sit-by-the-Fire* on 5 April, again at the Duke of York's Theatre. The play – once offered as a guarantee against the sure failure of *Peter Pan* – is almost an anticlimax. A light entertainment in which no one flies isn't particularly memorable after such a resounding success, even though the protagonist is played by the divine Ellen Terry.

In the country, the Llewelyn Davieses are happier than they've ever been. Many are the friends and family members who remember the great harmony between parents and children, and to set the record straight, they correct the picture of Arthur Llewelyn Davies, distinguishing him over and over again from the clumsy and obtuse caricature that – consciously or unconsciously – Barrie sketched as the typical Edwardian paterfamilias Mr Darling in *Peter Pan*.

Arthur adores his children and respects them, almost never resorting to harsh discipline, and is patient to a fault. Sylvia, on the other hand, loves them as if they're an inevitable and natural extension of her own beauty. Sylvia doesn't worry much if they hurt themselves, or if they have problems at school, or if they're ill: that's what the servants and Arthur are for. If anyone contradicts her or refuses her a favour,

Sylvia has a disturbing tendency towards easy tears and sulking. And Sylvia is blessed and cursed by a fascination with the good life and easy, boundless luxury. So Barrie is her perfect counterpart, someone who adores her and ministers to her desires and has more than enough money to make them reality. Barrie invites her to Paris many times and to the seaside resort of Dives on the Normandy coast. Barrie is – according to biographer Denis Mackail – 'a rich man and at the same time innocent to a ridiculous degree; someone to use – as Sylvia did – as a kind of extra nursemaid, a more than generous fairy godmother, and sometimes even an errand boy. It became impossible for Sylvia Llewelyn Davies to resist the temptation to use Barrie. She had no sense of limits.'

So time and again Sylvia goes travelling with Barrie and Mary, bringing Jack and Michael (who suffers and will suffer for years from terrible nightmares in which strangers come in through his bedroom window; Michael believes in Peter Pan as passionately as he doesn't believe in Father Christmas); while Arthur goes to visit his parents in Kirby with George and Peter. Little Nico stays at Egerton House in the care of Mary Hodgson.

Comings and goings; and *Peter Pan* has its debut in the United States, where it's even more successful than it was in London. Barrie's made some changes to the script so it may be exported more effectively: Hook's 'Down with King Edward!' becomes 'Down with the Stars and Stripes!' and when Peter Pan defeats the pirate captain, he passionately invokes the patriotic names of Abraham Lincoln, George Washington and John Paul Jones, though this doesn't prevent him from appearing victorious, as usual, dressed as Napoleon on the deck of the *Jolly Roger* – because, explains the little hero, 'Napoleon was short too.'

The critics are won over again, and offer new interpretations in which Neverland is a symbol of the power of the New World, while the figure of Peter Pan can be nothing but the triumph of a youthful New Order over old and outmoded systems. And there's something amusing, something logical, about the idea of Peter Pan as the perfect incarnation of the New Man, of a man who's always new because he's a man who never grows up. Today Neverland, and tomorrow the universe.

Maude Adams – who designs what from then on will be considered the character's classic costume: a green tunic with tights and a hat, too indebted to the Robin Hood look, in my opinion – plays the leading role. Beginning the first night – November 6, 1905, Empire Theater of New York, property of Charles Frohman – it's impossible to get tickets for the play, and after the longest and most successful run in the history of the Empire Theater, the impresario organizes an unprecedented tour across the length and breadth of the continent. Charles Frohman is a convert: Charles Frohman will preach the gospel according to Peter Pan. The play is performed in the metropolises of the East Coast as well as the saloons of the Far West. The San Francisco earthquake doesn't prevent its arrival barely six days after the catastrophe to a city eager to believe in the possibility of happy endings. Real redskins applaud Tiger Lily's dance on the stages of Indian reservations. And Maude Adams suspects – correctly – that there'll be nothing else like this in her career. For the next two decades it'll scarcely matter at all that she tackles other roles and even some plays by Barrie written exclusively for her. Two million people will come to watch her fly through the air and clap enthusiastically each time Peter Pan asks for their help to bring Tinker Bell back to life.

Mark Twain sends Barrie a letter of congratulations: 'I think Peter Pan is a huge and sophisticated and optimistic contribution to the landscape of this sordid, money-obsessed era.' It's Peter Pan mania: boy children begin to be named Peter en masse, toys and costumes and colouring books and postcards are created. Barrie is delighted: Maude has been one of his favourite 'girls' since she vaulted into the top ranks of actresses with his play *The Little Minister* in the American version produced by the Frohman Stock Company.

Maude Adams in the United States and Nina Boucicault in England; when they're rubbed together, sparks fly that feed the flame of Peter Pans yet to come. Like reincarnations of each other, like efficient machines off a production line, like the scream that follows the echo. One after the other – and female after female, because Peter Pan will almost always be a role for which adult women dress as immature men, to amuse themselves and maybe have their revenge. Or perhaps it's a kind of revenge on the former actors of the Globe Theatre: if the first Juliet and the first Ophelia were played by men, then it's only right that Peter Pan should have female parts under his green tights. Here they come:

Vivian Martin (who is offered the leading role in the United States for a season by Charles Frohman); Cecelia Loftus (who replaces Nina Boucicault in England); Pauline Chase (Barrie's favourite, an American who will triumph in London and fall into a pond in Liverpool's Sefton Park during the unveiling of a replica of the statue of Peter Pan in 1928); Madge Titheradge (who doesn't last long; she asks so vehemently for the children to clap to save Tinker Bell that the audience wails in terror); Gladys Cooper (who complains that it's 1923 and Peter Pan's costume – 'that old rag' – has never been updated, and suggests to Barrie that the wooden swords used by Peter Pan and Hook in the duel scene be exchanged for 'real' swords, because in her opinion they look 'silly'); Jean Forbes-Robertson (with huge eyes, almost crazed by the power of the character she's playing, recording the first phonographic version of *Peter Pan*); Marilyn Miller (famous Ziegfeld Girl); Betty Bronson (the first silent film Peter Pan); Eva Le Galliene (the proletarian Peter Pan in the Civic Repertory Theatre production intended to enlighten the workers of the New American Empire and their children, who, well indoctrinated, don't hesitate to storm the stage at each performance to fight for their hero's freedom and dignity and overthrow the pirates of capitalism); Elsa Lanchester (who's Peter Pan for a few performances alongside her husband, Charles Laughton, in costume as Captain Hook); Anna Neagle (who may have been – I'm not quite sure – Peter Pan during the Blitz, when all the scenery was destroyed by Nazi bombs); Sarah Churchill (daughter of Winston); Jean Arthur (with Boris Karloff as Captain Hook); Mia Farrow (who doesn't need to cut her hair for the NBC television version; Danny Kaye is her Captain Hook); Sandy Duncan (Broadway version); Cathy Rigby (once a gymnast famous for her appearances in the 1968 and 1972 Olympics); and all those other little English girls passing through (Anne Heywood, Millicent Martin, Hayley Mills, Maggie Smith, Lulu, Susannah York), until at last we come to the Royal Shakespeare Company's male Peter Pans in 1982 (best of all, I suppose; most interesting) and Steven Spielberg's terrible Peter Pan, played by terrible Robin Williams (an adult, amnesiac Peter Pan), and finally Peter Pan as a boy savage in the film directed by the Australian P. J. Hogan.

Keiko Kai: I won't lower myself here to list the crude gay and lesbian versions, the easy psychoanalytic adaptations, the self-help books and feminist manuals for understanding machismo, the blundering steps of stupid comedy. None of them is Peter Pan, no matter how they usurp his name and likeness.

At one point, Jim Yang asks himself how it can be that no actor who donned the green suit – despite the unmistakable resemblance of the first Peter Pans in all the old photographs to those vacant-faced figures with halos that ornament the ceilings and walls of churches – ever went mad the way the ardent players of Tarzan, Dracula, Superman, or Jesus Christ knew how to go nobly mad. The answer is that – unlike the apeman, the vampire, the superhero, or the messiah – Peter Pan is already mad, happily mad.

All the Peter Pans are remembered in the small commemorative volume I was asked to put together to celebrate the centenary of the character: *Jim Yang and the Peter Pan Clan*. In it, Jim Yang fights a gang of child thieves who are ransacking the museums of the world in search of a hypothetical map that tells precisely how to find the lost Neverland, giving the exact route. Of course, they don't find it, and all of them – while Jim Yang looks on in horror – end up killing themselves as members of a suicide cult, thinking that finally they'll be able to return to the Lost Paradise, the Promised Land from which they were unjustly expelled. Once again, my editors at Bedtime Story Press were a little uncomfortable with the ending. I decided not to insist on the darkness lurking inside all children just beneath the skin, or to explain that children, lost or found, are always much stronger and more dangerous creatures than they seem to be and want us to believe. So I wrote a new last chapter in which Jim Yang catches the little delinquents and takes them back in time on his bicycle and leaves them in Kensington Gardens, where on a victorious Victorian morning Barrie discovers them running wild, munching flowers from the flowerbeds and yanking wool off the sheep to protect themselves from the cold. He decides to make them part of an idea he's working on; Barrie decides that these children gone astray will be the perfect companions for Peter Pan in Neverland.

The character is Neverland.

Ways of getting there: falling out of your carriage when you're a baby, or glimpsing it from the abyss of the deepest dream; or Peter Pan chooses you and no one but you, and comes to get you.

Neverland as a place whose atmosphere keeps you in a state of perpetual childhood. Even better than Shangri-La, where eternal youth is the result of a sort of moral pledge, or a certain Zen, New Age consciousness. In Neverland there's no responsibility at all except to be irresponsible.

And I do have a map of Neverland.

From above, Neverland is vaguely the shape of Australia. Key sights: Crocodile Island, Marooners' Rock, Captain Hook's Cove, the Wild Woods, the Mermaids' Lagoon, the

Lost Boys' house. Many places to visit and of which to take photographs that'll be the envy of friends and family.

The den where Peter Pan and the lost boys live is underground. You get in through the hollow trunks of seven trees that lead to a single, immense room, like the place the Beatles live in the film *Help!* In the middle of the room there's a sizeable tree that must be cut down to the ground each morning regularly and without fail, and that by tea-time has already grown tall enough to be used as a table where the cups can be set. There's a huge bed for everyone to sleep in 'like sardines in a tin', it tilts up and is let down when the sun sets, as Peter Pan tells the lost boys the stories he finds at night on the bedroom floors of the children of London. In a corner of the room, behind a curtain, in a hole in the wall 'no larger than a birdcage', are the private quarters of Tinker Bell: 'No woman, however large, could have had a more exquisite boudoir and bedchamber combined', we're told, as if someone were trying to sell us the property. The lost boys' diet is varied: dishes that are sometimes pure fruit of their fertile imagination, and the bounty of the forest, and things they find lying about. Their clothes are stitched from bear skins that give them a sturdy, almost round look: falling down means rolling who knows where; it's better to walk carefully, to walk without hurrying. There's no rush.

The character is the past.

The character is the way you relate to the past, how you ignore it and how you obey it.

The way, for example, my father thought about yesterday and the way I think about it.

Two paragraphs from the same book. Two paragraphs underlined in my father's favourite novel that I always thought perfectly illustrated the two systems – complementary systems – of looking backwards.

Here they are:

'You may ask why I write. And yet my reasons are quite

many. For it is not unusual in human beings who have witnessed the sack of a city or the falling to pieces of a people to desire to set down what they have witnessed for the benefit of unknown heirs or of generations infinitely remote; or, if you please, just to get the sight out of their heads.

'Someone has said that the death of a mouse from cancer is the whole sack of Rome by the Goths, and I swear to you that the breaking up of our little four-square coterie was such another unthinkable event.'

And then:

'I have, I am aware, told this story in a very rambling way so that it may be difficult for anyone to find his path through what may be a sort of maze. I cannot help it. I have stuck to my idea of being in a country cottage with a silent listener, hearing between the gusts of wind and amidst the noises of the distant sea the story as it comes. And, when one discusses an affair – a long, sad affair – one goes back, one goes forward. One remembers points that one has forgotten and one explains them all the more minutely since one recognizes that one has forgotten to mention them in their proper places and that one may have given, by omitting them, a false impression. I console myself with thinking that this is a real story and that, after all, real stories are probably told best in the way a person telling a story would tell them. They will then seem most real.'

That's why I write.

That's how I write.

Falling to pieces, rambling, going backward and going forward, the real breaking up of our little twelve-numeral, two-handed circle.

The character is time.

Time that gives you structure and limits.

Time and its arrows – dates like darts that always hit their mark, the red and black grid of calendars; dates I use to order Barrie's life. His opening nights, his books, his speeches, his moves; dates that I have too, that I could apply to the course of my own existence, but that do me little good. There isn't much I remember. I remember much about very little. I remember, now, the most important thing of all: my childhood; the memory of my childhood growing like a tree chopped down each morning, a tree that by evening is tall and leafy again and has a powerful shadow sewn tightly to its roots.

For the first years of your childhood, time doesn't exist. Time is measured in birthdays, in summers, and in Christmases, and that's all. The passage of time is slow, a stroll. It's the kind of time there is in Neverland, time that doesn't exist in Neverland because – Barrie tells us – the only watch in Neverland ticks in the stomach of a hungry crocodile and to know what time it is in Neverland, you have to get as close to the crocodile as possible and stay there as long as you can until you hear the sound of the alarm, until time opens its jaws and sinks its teeth into you and you can't escape its bite and you understand that now, at last, after so long, time is going to swallow you up.

Time is going to eat you alive.

The character is age.

One day you're given your first watch. It's the end of obligation-free childhood. The watch is a toy, yes, but it's a delicate toy, a serious toy. A toy you aren't sure what to do with, but all of a sudden, there it is: biting your left wrist like a crocodile and infecting your blood with the virus of hours and minutes and seconds. That first watch means you're old enough and responsible enough now for a first watch. It's the first of the several watches you'll have over the course of your life. A watch for each age. Four or five watches. Enough watches until you wind down and die, your watch stopping when you go to bed forever and you leave it to someone else, the machine that tracked the age of your body and your mind and the way your life assembled itself until it became a little story, one of the infinite bricks out of which the immense mansion of eternity is built.

Along these lines, a paragraph of the dedication that Barrie wrote for the first edition of *Peter Pan* – the play became available in book form in 1928 – always seemed to me defining and definitive:

> *Some say that we are different people at different periods of our lives, changing not through effort of will, which is a brave affair, but in the easy course of nature every ten years or so. I suppose this theory might explain my present trouble, but I don't hold with it; I think one remains the same person throughout, merely passing, as it were, in these lapses of time from one room to another, but all in the same house. If we unlock the rooms of the far past we can peer in and see ourselves, busily occupied in beginning to become you and me.*

Something similar appears in one of his notebooks:

> – CHARACTER: *who fails to develop normally, his spirit still young inside his aging body, constantly troubled by the painful astonishment we all experience at one time or another when we're struck by some external evidence that shakes our faith in eternal youth.*

A last wish: if my cursed bones are used to build an addition to this House of Time, please use them to make a new window. An open window that I can close forever and thus pay, with English alacrity, for so many sins after so much time.

The character is the era.

The sudden consciousness of the era we live in. Or the eras. There are hinge-moments, door-years, threshold-periods when we have the distinct sense and uncertain privilege of living on several temporal planes at once.

Years when History becomes even more historic.

The Victorian era and the Swinging Sixties, for example. They have curious similarities and points in common – and please, it's not because of my father that I say so. The two are golden ages – though the reign of Victoria is an era of genius while the reign of Sgt Pepper is simply ingenious – and unlike other eras of splendour, each is conscious of itself as it unfolds and has no need to wait for the posthumous medals of the chroniclers of things past.

The two ages manage to create new forms of childhood: the New Children and the New Rockers, different versions of epic, happy irresponsibility. One group enjoys a whole new world created for it and the other gambles on founding a new establishment. The former finally understands the terrible truth in the trenches of the First World War and in the rear guard of the Empire's decline. The latter pays for its audacity much sooner, perishing buried under the weight of its own utopia. Two sides of the same illusion, of the failure to consider small, pertinent details: the inevitable passage of time, for example (which erodes everything and brings bad music and crude imitations like *Dr Dolittle* and *Mr Chips*), and, above all, the relentless parade of fashions through the streets of London.

The character is the city.

The character is London, lit by that light so peculiar to London, a glow that's impossible to imitate and that doesn't bathe the city but seems to be radiated by it. A prismatic brilliance. White light recovering its true rainbow state by passing through the drops of a rain that never completely vanishes: in London it's always raining, or about to rain, or about to stop raining.

An island floating inside an island. Maybe this explains the almost reflexive need – like the jerk of the knee at the tap of that little hammer – to travel all over the world in search of answers to the universe's questions. Thus, the swarms of Victorian explorers ready to carry their queen's likeness to the most distant and inhospitable corners of the map: enormous icebergs like palaces, sourceless rivers crossing entire continents, strange flowers with a deadly scent, paintings of swimmers on the walls of caves surrounded by sand and sun. Nothing seems insignificant to these men in motion. And there are so many rooms in the British Museum to fill, and everything is worthy of being recorded in the registers of the Royal Geographical Society in the name of Victoria: a queen and a kingdom expanding like a gas over everything solid and even going back in time with the help of Charles Darwin to find explanations of where we come from, what we used to be like, what London used to be like.

London like one of those cabinets of curiosities where a whole history is displayed in the most logical disarray. The many pieces of different puzzles that still manage to fit together. Inside it: the sandal of a Roman legionnaire who comes to what will one day be Kent in the year 55 BC; a spear point from the army of powerful Boadicea; a Viking helmet; the crowns of Alfred the Great and Olaf; a page from the first *Domesday Book*; a fragment of a paving stone from the first London Bridge; the echo of a prayer recited during the first service at Westminster; the mocking voice of Geoffrey Chaucer reciting one of the *Canterbury Tales*; the dying breath of someone with the black plague; the headless bodies of Thomas More and Anne Boleyn; a curl from one of Elizabeth I's wigs; the feathers of a parrot imported by Francis Drake or Walter Raleigh; the makeup box that an actor at the Globe Theatre used to turn himself into Juliet and Ophelia and Desdemona; a pinch of the powder with which Guy Fawkes tried to blow up Parliament; a brush that might or might not have belonged to Rubens; the rope used to hang the corpse of Cromwell in Tyburn; Newton's telescope looking out over the city burning with fire and plague; a key from Handel's clavichord; a little bag holding some of the seeds left over when Kew Gardens was sown; a new fruit that Captain Cook never dared to taste; a stamp commemorating Victoria's coronation; a scented handkerchief to mask the terrible stench of the Thames; one of the transparent panels from Hyde Park's Crystal Palace in the Great Exposition of 1851 (rescued from the fire of 1936); a copy of the magazine *Master*

Humphrey's Clock in which the story of Little Nell's death is told; a Wedgwood tea cup; one of Holmes's 'elementary's; a railway ticket; a fan commemorating the Boer War; an underground ticket; a ticket to see a Chaplin film; the lost first manuscript of T. E. Lawrence's *The Seven Pillars of Wisdom*, revealing to me alone that 'all men dream, but not in the same way. Those who dream at night in the dusty recesses of their minds wake up the next day to find that their dreams were nothing but pure vainglory; whereas those who dream by day are dangerous men, because they can live their dreams with eyes open and thus make them come true'; a radio that only receives the BBC; the propeller of a V-2 that didn't explode back then but could explode at any time; a can of corned beef from the days of rationing; a happy tear of Beatlemania; a sad tear of Dianamania; and soon a tear of JimYangmania, shed part in outrage and part in surprise, because who ever would've thought that what happened would happen, that what's happening would happen, that what'll happen would happen, Keiko Kai.

A Literary Guide to London, by Ed Glinert, devotes eight entries to Barrie, to the places Barrie immortalized simply by living in them or visiting them, or even just by thinking about them. Barrie's name is one of the most frequently cited in the guide. Dickens gets more mentions; but Dickens always has more of everything. The shrines to Barrie that appear marked on the map are the Great Ormond Street Hospital for Sick Children (to which, as I've already mentioned, Barrie donated the rights to *Peter Pan*; it's the hospital I was taken to after I was captured in Brighton); 1 Robert Street (where Barrie lived from 1911 until his death in 1937); the Savoy Hotel (Barrie was invited there for H. G. Wells's seventieth birthday party); the Travellers Club at 106 Pall Mall (founded to serve those who went on the Grand Tour and anyone who'd travelled at least a thousand miles from London; it's there that Barrie asks African explorer Joseph Thompson what the most dangerous part of his last trip was; Thompson answers: 'Crossing Piccadilly Circus'); the Athenaeum Club at 107 Pall Mall (one evening, Barrie asks an old man sitting in the smoking room if the food is good enough to make it worth staying for dinner; the old man bursts into tears, overcome: 'This is the first time anyone's said a word to me since I became a member here,' and excuses himself to go off in search of a handkerchief and some dignity); 133 Gloucester Road (Barrie's home while he was writing *Sentimental Tommy* and *Margaret Ogilvy* and where he went to live with Mary Ansell after they were married; Glinert rather rashly and irresponsibly notes that 'the marriage failed because Barrie was gay' and had a weak 'sex drive'); 100 Bayswater Road (where Barrie wrote *Peter Pan*); Campden Hill Square in Kensington Park Gardens (the neighbourhood that would inspire T. S. Eliot's *Four Quartets* – originally called *Kensington Quartets* – and where Arthur and Sylvia Llewelyn Davies lived with their children and where later the pacifist poet Siegfried Sassoon would move), and, of course, that appendage of Hyde Park, that smaller Siamese twin called Kensington Gardens.

The character is Kensington Gardens.

Kensington Gardens as the Siamese twin of Hyde Park; born in 1698, growing and flourishing through the eighteenth century under William and Mary. William moved to Nottingham House, next to the gardens, because he said the air of Whitehall Palace aggravated his asthma. William commissioned the design of the gardens to Charles Bridgeman. And he ordered Sir Christopher Wren – the architect who rebuilt the churches of London after the Great Fire of 1666 – to remodel Nottingham House and turn the austere mansion into a palace. Then Queen Caroline – wife of George II – made the Round Pond and the Serpentine flow from a branch of the Westbourne River. And it was from then on that city dwellers were allowed – 'so long as they are respectably attired' – to walk in the gardens and listen from the paths to the laughter of little Victoria, who was born beside Kensington Gardens, or the weeping of Diana of Wales, who lived her last days as a fast, divorced princess there. They've all left now, they're all gone. Kensington Gardens still remains.

Kensington Gardens as a black hole, a devourer of galaxies, of light, of what was and what will be. Kensington Gardens as the password that opens the door to the secret cave. Kensington Gardens as the X on the treasure map and the white outline marking the exact spot where until recently a dead body flowered. Kensington Gardens as the mastermind of all crimes.

Kensington Gardens as a magnet for poets, as a point of attraction for those – as they're described in *The Little White Bird* – 'who aren't exactly adults, who scorn money and only care about having what they need to make it through the day.' In *The Little White Bird*, Barrie describes how the young Percy Bysshe Shelley makes a paper boat with a banknote and, like an offering, sets it afloat on the Serpentine, where it's spurned by the crow Solomon Caw and ends up in the hands of Peter Pan, who makes it his favourite toy, his means of transport for reaching land.

Kensington Gardens and me.

Kensington Gardens, of course, appears in my hypothetical London. A key entry in *A Literary Guide* that follows in my footsteps around the city. But I don't think there'll ever be such a thing, Keiko Kai. I'll be wiped from all records, the despicable sound of my voice will be banned everywhere, guidebooks will disavow me and my works will be forgotten and declared unfit for children. It doesn't make me sad; it's as it should be. That's the idea, after all, the goal of this night full of memories and names and years. Names from the distant past onto which I try to shift the burden of the names of yesterday. A near lunatic recitation, because the only point of all this accumulation of data and stories in my memory is to toss prisoners overboard. I like to think that each date I cite, each name I spell out, disappears as soon as it's spoken.

As if I were crossing them out one by one. As if I were a mad computer at the end of the universe welcoming the reward of amnesia after knowing everything for so long.

But unfortunately it doesn't work that way, Keiko Kai. The process is the reverse: each occasion I call up is a new step in the direction of remembering everything, of not being able to flee as I've been fleeing all these years, refusing to commit my life to memory and therefore to live it. The 70s, the 80s, the 90s, were nothing to me but a breeze altering the marks in the sand on the beach: years that didn't leave deep tracks, that didn't change the landscape. For three decades I spent all my time reading and writing children's books to forget my childhood. I almost succeeded. One Jim Yang adventure per year, more or less, and the rest is an impenetrable fog; I lived in my books so as not to live outside of them. The method worked – Jim Yang as the last brick in the wall of my oblivion. All my memories rising to the difficult task of obliterating my memory. And I did burn millions of calories.

Now, however, I feel the past returning to me. I see how it gathers on the horizon in a snarl of clouds brimming with fury and thunder and lightning. The charge doesn't come from all those years when I mostly just read and then wrote – the 90s, the 80s, the 70s – but rather from what happened before and what seems to be happening all over again, after having been forgotten for so long.

Now the air smells of that crisp perfume, the scent of thirsty soil announcing the arrival of rain. The storm will burst, and I'll burst with it. And nothing will be able to save me from the electric rage of its thunderbolts.

Not even Jim Yang.

The character is Jim Yang.

There isn't much I can tell you that isn't in the books, Keiko Kai.

Not much I feel like telling.

And after all, you're Jim Yang.

Or – so sorry, not sorry at all – you were going to be Jim Yang.

What can I tell you? What can I explain?

It isn't necessary to know much about a hero of children's literature. A quick sketch of his past is more than enough. The rest is a frenzied and constant now. And some pertinent details, some questions worth answering:

Why a bicycle, for example?

I've always liked bicycles. The strange way they have of being simple and yet at the same time sophisticated inventions. The bicycle is a machine of metal and flesh: blood-and-sweat traction and chrome speed. Bicycle and man constitute one of the most just and democratic societies never formed. I won't say anything about its degenerate subspecies except that motorcycles are de facto bicycles and exercise bikes are frigid bicycles and tricycles are dwarf bicycles and unicycles – well, is there anything more idiotic than a unicycle?

Was there a sketch of a bicycle in Leonardo's notes? I think I saw one there: a bicycle crossed with a helicopter or a parachute. And why is it that in *2001: A Space Odyssey*, the computer HAL 9000 bids farewell to his perfect memory by singing a song about the joys of a ride on a bicycle built for two?

All right: the first bicycle was designed by the Scottish genius Kirkpatrick Macmillan in 1839 and its tyres were invented by J. B. Dunlop in 1888; but even so, bicycles seem ageless, atemporal in a way that lets us situate them in almost any era. Or enjoy them anywhere: because the bicycles of Amsterdam and the bicycles of Shanghai speak exactly the same language, a language whose forthright and muscular intonation never changes.

My first bicycle was a present from Marcus Merlin. A new silver Schwinn, made in the USA. I have no idea where he got it. An aerodynamic machine that seemed designed by Mercury himself, and yes, Jim Yang's bicycle is a Schwinn retrofitted to reach the speed of time.

Marcus Merlin brought it to me before my parents set sail

for death and madness. He couldn't believe it when I told him I didn't know how to ride a bike. I didn't know how to swim, either. Or box. Indignant, Marcus Merlin taught me how to keep my balance and float. 'Two essential skills needed to live a worthwhile life,' said Marcus Merlin. He couldn't do much when it came to left hooks and foot work. Said Marcus Merlin: 'Other than swimming and riding a bike, the best way to use your arms and legs – the fourth best way – I can't teach you myself, but we'll find you a willing girl.'

Said Marcus Merlin, giving up in the final round when I still couldn't get the concept of a cross to the chin: 'Some people are born with the gift and some aren't. Anyway, don't worry; I doubt you'll ever have to fight. You have too much money in the bank, and you have every right to pay someone to use his fists for you.'

The text that reveals the most about Jim Yang isn't the story of any of his adventures: it's a short piece I wrote once for the magazine *Uncut*. The publication – a monthly featuring the birth pangs and autopsies of pop culture – published a special issue in which it brought together a number of novelists to write about their favourite song from the perspective of their characters.

I – forgive me, father – chose the Beatles' 'A Day in the Life'.

My short piece – 'A Day in the Life of Jim Yang' – tells the story of a trip Jim Yang takes to the Abbey Road studios in January and February of 1967. The Beatles are making *Sgt. Pepper's Lonely Hearts Club Band* there, and they're getting ready to record what will rightly be considered their magnum opus: 'A Day in the Life'.

More has been written about the many ways of interpreting the meaning of this song than about almost anything else in the world in search of a meaning. That's fine with me. It deserves it. My preferred hypothesis – my chosen hypothesis – is the one that claims the song is a kind of small but exhaustive instruction manual for the perception of reality. A reality altered by the use of a hallucinogenic substance in the case of John Lennon and Paul McCartney, but one that – in Jim Yang's case – I attribute to the miles accumulated as a result of his frequent and ever more obsessive time-travelling habit. 'A Day in the Life' is the impossible wish to make all of history fit into a day: a resounding antidote to our disappointment with the limitations of the mundane, making ordinary life bearable by elevating each part of it to a place in a perfect cycle. 'A Day in the Life' – recorded in a total of thirty-four studio hours – makes the everyday sound different and unique, makes a day like any other special and transcendent. It wakes us up forever with the sound of that alarm clock in the song's bridge, a sound that seems to burst from the belly of a crocodile.

Jim Yang – who would love to be able to stop, choose an era, establish a normal life there, keep his bicycle locked up – covets that day. While the 'day in the life' of the song is 17 January 1967, commemorated by the embellished reading of the *Daily Mail*, in Jim Yang's life it's the moment he'd like to inhabit forever. Get there, stay, never leave.

In 'A Day in the Life of Jim Yang', the young time traveller arrives at the Abbey Road studios for the session at which the symphonic segment of the song will be recorded. Paul McCartney wanted ninety musicians, but in the end there are only forty. The producer George Martin chose them from among the members of the Royal Philharmonic Orchestra and the London Symphony Orchestra. The Beatles hand out masks, false noses, false moustaches, party hats for the musicians to put on as they play. There's something cruel about the way their names are missing from the album credits. I imagine them today, desperately trying to convince their incredulous grandchildren that they were there.

Someone films it all with a handheld camera.

There are famous guests. My parents haven't been invited.

There's Jim Yang: on his bicycle, not knowing what to do or where his own story will go. There's nothing left for him to seek now, and suddenly he feels lost, with no reason to keep existing. Could this be the end of childhood? Has the moment come to grow up? he asks himself.

Jim Yang thinks he feels a strange tension in his bones, the white yawn of a skeleton waking up after a long sleep. A sound like the sound we hear as we approach the sea and the pavement turns to sand and we take off our shoes and walk through the dunes, and at last our eyes are flooded with all that moving blue. Though no, it's a different sound, similar but the reverse: Jim Yang feels it's the sea approaching him and – pardon me again, father, you who were drowned and never buried – the sound reminds me of the orchestral din that's heard for the first time in 'A Day in the Life' and that, in its way, anticipates the beginning of the end of everything.

John Lennon described the sound as 'the sound of the end of the world . . . a bit *2001*', and nothing was ever the same for the Beatles after that song, the way nothing's the same once you've reached the highest peak and discovered that the only thing left to do is to throw yourself from it.

'A Day in the Life' was Jim Yang's mother's favourite song.

The character is Baco.

Baco's favourite song was also 'A Day in the Life'. Although Baco only heard it once. Baco died the night *Sgt. Pepper's Lonely Hearts Club Band* was released. My father came back to Neverland with the album. He put it on to play. We listened to it. My father – I could feel it – liked it despite himself. There were sparks of Victoriana in it that he couldn't ignore or help appreciating: that brass section, 'She's Leaving Home', the description of the different acts in an old circus, 'When I'm Sixty-Four', even the Indian pastiche had something interesting and colonial about it . . . And when 'A Day in the Life' began, I saw in his eyes – more ears than eyes just then – that not only was he conscious of the enormity of John Lennon and Paul McCartney's triumph, but also of the smallness of his own failure.

Baco stood up and started to spin as the orchestra soared up to hell or swooped down to heaven. Baco sang along with Lennon and McCartney, hearing the song for the first time, guessing how it went, as if it were his and only his.

Would Baco have been worthy of appearing among the many sacred faces on the cover of a *Son of Sgt. Pepper* or a *Sgt. Pepper Strikes Back*? Was Baco a prodigy? There's no way to know. Baco died before his genius could be properly certified.

True: at the age of two, Baco had already taken the step of christening his toes because he thought it was 'not very nice' that they didn't have their own names 'like our fingers do'.

True: Baco had a disturbing ability to enthral adults and make slaves of his little friends.

True: Baco occasionally alluded – not in so many words, but what he said meant exactly the same thing – to the cosmic, expansive explosion that thousands of years ago gave birth to millions of stars. Stars suddenly anxious to move apart, stars wary of being seen together. And Baco predicted that at some point all these stars would lose momentum, that having reached the farthest edge of the wave of expansion, they would reconsider their attitude and begin the slow journey home, retreating to that first, blazing point of pure energy. And our sky would fill with stars coming closer and closer together, stars ever more eager to be reunited. And then there wouldn't be night or cold and everything would be light and heat and luckily we wouldn't be here any more to see it, because our match's brief flame would've been blown out and extinguished long ago, smiled Baco.

There's no doubt about it: Baco shone.

But as everyone knows, childhood genius is often a flower that lives only for a day, an ephemeral manifestation, a gift that becomes a stigma and later results in the disfigured face of an adult closer to stupidity than enlightenment.

Maybe Baco wasn't a genius.

Maybe Baco, conscious in some way of how short his life would be, tried to concentrate as much brilliance as possible in the smallest space.

Maybe Baco didn't want to be someone special and unique.

Maybe Baco just wanted the people he knew never to forget him.

The character is family.

My parents and my brother weren't designed to grow old. To say that they died young is therefore inexact. My parents and my brother died – the way dinosaurs die – when the great meteorite of a future that didn't include them crashed into their planet's present.

So it was better for them to be extinguished in a flash than to live in a time when all they'd be was detritus, watches running slow, animals feeding on the empty and toxic and cheerless substance of memory.

The character is memory.

Memory that's constructed out of what we remember, and also out of what we've decided to forget.

It's so hard to remember *well*, even the most important things that've happened to you in your life. All you know is that they've happened, and then, conscious of that, you *invent* the memory of them, and instantly those vague dispatches become something much more transcendent than anything that really and truly could have happened. Thus, our reality is sustained by pillars of unreality sunk in foundations as shaky as those of a dream told the next morning. Thus, our past is nothing but scattered fragments lacking a before and after. Scattered pieces of a watch that we don't know how to put together. That's the comfort of being a child: there's so little to remember that we remember everything. And we remember it well.

Barrie knows this. Barrie's chosen to build his life and work out of the limited but effective combination of these basic materials. Barrie remembers everything and promises himself not to give in to the tendency to forgetfulness that catches up with you as the years go by: there's increasingly more past and less free space in the seventy-five cubic inches of the brain. The real tragedy isn't death, thinks Barrie, but forgetting everything you've remembered over the course of your life. So Barrie won't stop taking notes. Ever. Barrie will sum up everything in sentences in his notebooks, in practical theories, in stories ripped from his life story.

That's what fiction's for.

That's what those books whose style and plot we can conjure up imperfectly but whole are for, those books that connect us automatically, reflexively, to our own experience. Reading is a comparative exercise; literature – the act of writing and reading – is the physical manifestation closest to and most like memory that humans have achieved. Therefore, all novels are inevitably autobiographical for those who write them and shut them; but also for all those who open them and read them.

With the theatre it's different: we remember moments, scenes, exchanges, an actor we like, an actress we hate. There we're simply witnesses or prisoners. We aren't responsible for anything.

With film – there are days Barrie wishes his life were a movie directed by someone else and not a book written by him – it's even easier. We just float. In silence and with all the lights turned out, if possible: the glow from the screen illuminates us.

And at first, film tried as hard as it could to imitate life. It wasn't easy, of course: movies were silent, black and white, too short.

When was the terrible moment that life began to imitate film and forget itself?

In the end, memory is simply the script of the film of our life. Based on a true story, yes, but full of changes that improve the pace and the appeal and the dramatic possibilities of the story and our always deficient and inadequate acting skills. Memory is the tool we use to forget.

Film is amnesia.

The character is film.

The movies.

Jim Yang: The Movie.

I'd always refused to allow *Jim Yang* to be adapted for the screen. It wasn't necessary. There were already enough young writers who claimed to write because their real interest was making movies, telling movie stories, filming their books, writing in the dark.

But all of a sudden, I gave in almost without a fight. A possible explanation for this – which seemed much more normal to everyone than my resistance – has to do, I suppose, with my debt to Marcus Merlin, my gratitude to Marcus Merlin.

Marcus Merlin convinces me. He tells me that I owe it to him. He explains that I can't deny him this happiness, that it would be very cruel of me – he's laughing, joking, serious, as he tells me this – after all he's done for me: Marcus Merlin in the marvellous world of film at last.

But it's not just that. There has to be some other reason. A secret strategy. It doesn't take me long to find it, to understand it, now that it's impossible to turn back: my need, at first unconscious and now perfectly well thought out, to destroy Jim Yang, to end his despotic reign in the minds of the boys and girls of the planet. The film is the first step in his degradation, and although it's perfectly logical, it's always amazing how fast you can destroy something that took so long to build. The swastika, for example: for thousands of years it symbolized peace, prosperity, long life and good luck, and in just a few years Adolf Hitler turned it into the most effective isotope of the unforgivable and the infamous.

The Jim Yang movie will be the first step, the first wave of bombs hitting the target, but – maybe I'm naive to think there'll be a film after what I've already done and what I plan to do – it won't be enough: there's always the more than likely possibility that a terrible film will be loved by millions of people with enthusiastically terrible taste. It doesn't take much to win the adoration of the faithful: a landslide of publicity, an avalanche of special effects, a handful of excellent bad actors – and no, don't take it personally, Keiko Kai.

The truth is I'm not fighting to preserve the integrity of my work but to make it disappear as rapidly as possible from the face of the earth and from children's faces.

Keiko Kai: Jim Yang scares me. I'm terrified by the effect he's had on the behaviour of young readers, of those fans who wait for each book as if it's their salvation. And I'm even more terrified by the way Jim Yang has gradually devoured my life and past. Now I understand, now I think I understand: Jim Yang has been the sedative that makes my pain bearable, the music that puts me to sleep, my way of hiding and denying certain parts of the unauthorized story of my life, which is really literally that: an unauthorized biography; not because it's written by an investigator of my indiscretions, but because it reveals a period of my life whose existence has been disauthorized by me, eliminated from history as if it never existed, in the same way the hieroglyphic figures of some of the pharaohs were erased from the temples and turned into legends or curses by later dynasties.

And so, Keiko Kai, I travelled to legendary, cursed Hollywood. By plane. In first class.

Said Marcus Merlin, who promised to follow me in a few days: 'If you're going to die falling from up there, at least die in comfort . . . And the moment when they make you board early so that the plebs see you and realize you're one of the demigods of the skies is priceless.'

I've never shared Marcus Merlin's fascination with aeroplanes, much less aeroplane luxury, which is nothing but a slightly more glamorous and more comfortable way to hide the same egalitarian terror of entrusting yourself to a machine whose ability to fly you don't quite understand. It's not that

I'm scared to fly: I'm not afraid of sudden jolts, abrupt changes in altitude, lightning flashing outside the little window; I don't feel the anguish of smokers painfully aware that there are still thousands of seconds before they can fill their lungs with smoke. Absolute stillness does bother me: the way the subtle and almost secret changes in the machine's breathing patterns become even more noticeable on perfect flights, and all of a sudden it's as if the plane has stopped breathing, as if suddenly it too has begun to think that after all it never really understood very well when people explained to it how you stay up in the sky. Flying is something that always struck me as overrated. It's a childhood fantasy that may be important to the Peter Pan and Jim Yang stories and to all those children dreaming of midnights in which they drift over cities or fall from the clouds. But it's also a symptom and a compulsion that man should already have overcome: wings of feathers and wood and wax, aerostatic balloons, aeroplanes and rockets and space shuttles and magic flying dust. Anything goes so long as we reach the place inhabited by the gods, who watch us from above because from up there we look even smaller than we always are and always will be. That need to aim high and skyward. Enough. No more. That immature need to drift and climb, maybe because we feel we must in order to distract ourselves from the paradox of growing up and thinking we're getting closer to the sky, when in reality, as our body stretches, we shrink farther from space and closer to the earth. Closer and closer to six feet under, farther and farther from the brilliance of the stars.

I got to Hollywood (for some strange reason I can't call it Los Angeles) and they welcomed me like a king in exile, like a prodigal son. I inhaled the pure oxygen of limousines and felt the way the rhythm of the day changed, the way there were no longer paragraphs, the way everything seemed just barely separated by almost nonexistent full stops. I attended meetings where I said nothing at all. They made me sign papers that I didn't read. They showed me the most recent issue of *Variety*, with a picture of me on the first page under an enormous headline that read 'NEW BARRIE HITS TOWN'. They stared at me without trying to hide that they were staring at me, with that strange mixture of admiration and ridicule and envy with which Americans tend to look at the English. They showed me a picture of you, Keiko Kai. It was then I first heard of you and I can't tell you anything about your face that you don't already know, or at least guess: that implacable and almost hermaphroditic beauty of the best Orientals. And now that I think about it, isn't Keiko a female name? Could it be a stage name, intended to increase your attractiveness to adolescents of both sexes? Or could it be Barrie winking at me from beyond the grave: if Peter Pan was always devoured by actresses, then why shouldn't Jim Yang be the prisoner of a boy who has a girl's name because marketing has ordered it to be so? What does it matter? Who cares? Not the Hollywood magnates, that's clear. They told me you were the star of a popular television series, *Karaoke Kid*; they assured me you were the 'perfect Jim Yang', and that I'd meet you in a few days, at the press conference in London. They showed me models of the sets that were already being built in the studios of Borehamwood and Elstree. Or Pinewood and Shepperton? Or at Twickenham, where the Beatles filmed *Let It Be*? It didn't matter: 'Very close to home, as you stipulated in the contract,' they said, smiling. They gave me a copy of the eighteenth draft of the script of *Jim Yang: The Movie* authored by seven writers and they explained, 'it isn't based on any of your books in particular, there's a little bit of everything; but the most important thing is the way we've reworked the character so that . . .' They gave me a list of Jim Yang toys and franchises, among them a hamburger whose roll had the toasted picture of a bicycle wheel on its face. They slapped me on the back and sent me to my hotel suite where a 'recreational actress' – that's what she called herself – was waiting for me dressed as Tinker Bell in a complex scaffolding of garters and lace and high-heeled shoes. 'Courtesy of Millennium Pictures,' she said, smiling. I thought about clapping for her. Her beauty was almost an insult; her skin seemed airbrushed onto her bones. She opened a little box full of 'fairy dust' – that's what she called it – that the studio executives had given her to offer me. She sat on the bed, spread her legs and parted her lips, and laid out two lines of cocaine on a little mirror. She snorted one and looked at me, raising an eyebrow. I looked at her, raising another eyebrow, as if she were a masterpiece. Something in some museum that you couldn't touch. I explained that I had no need of her company or her services, that she could keep the fairy dust; I signed the Jim Yang books that she'd brought in a bag for her son, I wished her good luck, I hung the magic cardboard talisman inscribed with the magic words Please Do Not Disturb from the doorknob, and I asked that no calls be forwarded to me. It occurred to me that almost without realizing it I'd taken all the steps to set the scene for an efficient suicide. I asked myself whether there was something in the otherworldly air of Hollywood, something in the air or the soil, that makes you want to kill yourself, whether the majority of celluloid suicide victims might not be obeying a secret command, acting reflexively, following the bracketed stage directions in the draft of an INT. NIGHT scene. I opened the door and went out onto the balcony. The dusk seemed almost metallic, saturated with particles of electricity and secrets, with a sound like the breathing of dragons as they sleep. I lifted my hand to my left ear and caressed the nonexistent lobe that my mother had torn off with her last bite. It's a habit of mine: I reach for something I don't have each time I start to think about death. On the balcony there was a high-powered telescope mounted on a tripod. It's impossible to resist the temptation of telescopes and microscopes and keyholes, to look through them with the keyhole of our body, our eyes. It was the time of day when everyone got into their convertibles and went in and out of tunnels and said the same thing on their cell phones: 'I'm losing you . . .

losing you . . . I'm los . . .' In the distance a forest was burning. You could see how the traffic on the highways was being redirected, and how the animals, unlike the humans and headed in the opposite direction, were running towards the fire and crossing it in search of refuge on land that had already been burned. In some houses in the hills, people were getting into their pools to watch the blaze, fully dressed and holding martinis, while below, in the street, people took their blaring televisions out for a stroll in shopping carts, like babies. A small army of sunburned surfers were parading down one of the highways with their surfboards on their shoulders; they were singing something that sounded like a hymn, something about a last wave and an ocean covering everything, the ghost of an ocean reappearing when the moon was full, on nights in the desert where once, many thousands of years ago, whales and dolphins and sharks swam. This was the New World, the Modern Age, the Future that my father had foreseen from the desperation of his Victorian delusions. 'The horror! The horror!' repeated over and over again every two hours without commercial breaks, on the cable channels where movies are shown that you don't see anywhere else, that are never shown. I closed the curtains and turned on the television. Some kind of science fiction. Everything was happening in an intergalactic space ship, or something. A young android warrior in a silver suit – why is it that sci-fi always gets costumes so wrong? – was looking at the camera with a mixture of melancholy and solemnity, and saying: 'To reprogram or not to reprogram.' Someone called him 'Hamlex'. I realized immediately that it was yet another of the many relocations of Shakespeare in time and space. I never understood that urge to adapt it to fit every place and every age. Shakespeare in Manhattan in the 80s, Nazi Germany, the Japan of the last samurais. After all, no one's ever set *Death of a Salesman* in the Middle Ages, or *Who's Afraid of Virginia Woolf?* during the decline of the Roman Empire. Could that be the difference between old classics and modern classics? That the former can be projected forward while the latter are fixed in time? I changed the channel to a news station and turned the volume down. I watched the fire that I could see from the window on television. I sat on the bed, trying to read the script. I couldn't. Barrie could. Barrie had even gone so far as to write a silent film script for *Peter Pan*. He'd resisted for many years, had rejected many offers and many sums with many zeros, but when Jesse L. Lasky – director of Paramount – took over Charles Frohman's affairs, Barrie gave in. Barrie's script was twenty thousand words long, words that described in great detail too many ways of flying. Flying was at the time, and until quite recently, one of film's great challenges: making someone fly without seeing the wires, the false backdrops, the artificial wind blowing hair and capes. Barrie's script was soon discarded by the producers. It's obvious why when you read the fervent pages the author wrote. It's enough to cast a glance at a scene in which Peter Pan and Wendy and her brothers decide to stop on the way to Neverland and rest on the Statue of Liberty, which, when it feels them land on its shoulder, comes to life and cradles them until dawn. Barrie's initial suggestion that Charlie Chaplin would make a wonderful Peter Pan was also ignored. The chosen actor – upholding the tradition that the character be female – was Betty Bronson. The movie began filming in September 1924, was ready for Christmas, and had its opening night at the Rivoli Theatre in New York; the critics called it the event of the season and the *New York Times* judge it one of the ten best films of 1924. It wasn't that good. Actually, movies in general aren't that good. Or rather, the tyrannical bond between film and spectator will never match the democratic nexus of book and reader; someone else wrote the book, true, but it's you who read the story and set the pace and the mood as you turn the pages. That's why almost all good novels are almost always inevitably superior to the good films they inspire: by defending the book, we're really defending our right to choose the way we like to be told a story. And of course Marcus Merlin would say I'm talking nonsense. So I'll hasten to add, Keiko Kai, that the first film version of *Peter Pan*, directed by Herbert Brenon from a script by Willis Goldbeck, has its interesting moments, but it doesn't manage to shake the static quality of a lot of movies back then, with the camera motionless like another spectator in its seat. Barrie, I think, liked it well enough. More than the film, he liked the idea of his creation making the leap to another medium, advancing in its conquest of the world. I watched it just a little while ago. On DVD. I watched it on the small screen of my computer with the disbelief – somewhere between funny and terrifying – that we're made to feel by things that are old but not so far from modern technology when they're suddenly inserted into a new-model machine. As I watched it I was thinking that the next stage in human evolution wouldn't come in the form of a subtle or drastic modification of the skeleton but that it was already occurring – over and over again – and that it was happening outside of us: in the dizzyingly fast mutation of machines; in the brief distance between analogue and digital, between light and laser. I wondered whether at the beginning of the twentieth century, in dark, stuffy movie theatres like opium dens, it was considered appropriate to talk during the projection of silent films. Or whether silence was demanded, as it is in brightly lit libraries. I was thinking about this, I was thinking about the kind of things you can't even think about when you're near the magnetic interference of Marcus Merlin, when the telephone rang. Is there anything more terrible than the sound of a telephone that to your knowledge shouldn't be ringing? I was told it was urgent, a long-distance call from London, from Mr Marcus Merlin. I took the call.

And – new paragraph, at last – they gave me the news.

The character is information.

All the information I've been gathering and organizing over the years. Places, dates, photographs, last names, theatre programmes, books, records.

Alien information – information about Barrie, about other people – as a form of anaesthesia. Searching for and finding out everything about someone who isn't yourself as a perfect system for not having to deal with your own truths.

Information injected straight into the vein. Information that reaches the brain and heart in no time at all.

Information as a drug to which I've been addicted since I can remember, ever since I intoxicated my memory with so much of it.

Information on the sadistic and masochistic aeroplane screen map that tells you how many miles you've gone, how many miles are left, how many feet there are between the surface of the sky and the surface of the sea, how many negative degrees it is outside, how much time is left, how much time has passed.

Information from near or far that suddenly seems to be hiding a secret story, the story told in a manuscript with its pages out of order, a story that's maybe missing just one or two essential events before it can be properly understood and yet . . .

On the return trip to London, in the sky, flying, I read the following things in an issue of an airline magazine. I like airline magazines because they seem to be about someplace else, somewhere in the sky.

I read that an American, in his fifties, likes to dress up as Peter Pan (look, Disney, there he is on his own website) and says he's looking for 'a pretty, loving Tinker Bell' to help him find happiness. There's a picture of the man. He's flying in front of a typical suburban house. He's smiling. His teeth are perfect: they're American teeth, not English teeth. Peter Pan – who, Barrie tells us, never lost his baby teeth – couldn't possibly have such a bright smile, I think.

I read that the palace on Brighton Pier burned for a full day and night just as I once burned in the palace of Brighton Pier for several nights and their respective days.

I read that a team of British psychologists – after having

interviewed more than a thousand people – claims to have discovered the formula for happiness and that it's *P* + *5E* + *3A*. According to the researchers, *P* stands for Personal (your outlook on life), *E* for Existence (health, friendships, economic stability) and *A* for Aspiration (self-esteem, expectations and ambitions). I don't understand. As I've said already, I was never good at maths.

I read that there are more and more men and women who don't want to grow up; who'd rather live with their parents for as long as they can. Who spend hours watching those television stations that only show cartoons. Who spend small fortunes, with no shame or guilt, on toys designed especially for adults, and who buy three of each: one to play with, one to keep intact in its original packaging, and the third as an investment, which they'll sell in a few years for the price of an antique or a work of art. And who dress up every weekend in their old school uniforms – grey skirts and blue blazers – to go dancing as if nothing's happened. Thus marriages and children and divorces are reduced to hallucinations or apparitions from a recent past that's plunging head-first into a brand-new childhood: a virus-like and precocious new form of nostalgia – the grand mal that until recently only struck grandparents – in which you don't miss the good old days but instead strive desperately to transplant those good old days to these bad new days of inevitable and early adulthood, the first nights of creeping darkness.

I read that at New York's New Square Fish Market, a fish that was about to be cut into slices began to scream, in perfect Hebrew, 'Tzaruch schemirah, Hasof bah', or something like that. A fairy tale. I've copied the words exactly as they appear in the magazine. Words that can more or less be translated as saying that we must prepare because the end of the world is coming. Zalman Rosenthal, owner of the fish market and a Hasidic Jew, translated the prophecy for terrified, hysterical Ecuadorian Luis Portales, who almost had a heart attack when the fish – a tuna, to be precise – began to wail. Rosen approached the fish, confirmed that it had been possessed by the spirit of a Jew who died a year ago, and upon trying to kill it, cut off his own finger and had to be hospitalized. The fish, dead now, was sold hours later. The stewardess comes up and asks me whether I want chicken or fish. Chicken.

I read that a Victorian house known as Moat Brae, in Dumfries County in the south of Scotland – where little James Matthew Barrie, author of *Peter Pan*, once played pirates with his good friend Stuart Gordon – was attacked by a few 'young hoodlums' who knocked down the door and moved in for several weeks, later burning some of the furniture and pulling the wallpaper off the walls, on which they painted things like *Jim Yang Is Coming*. The article ended by noting that the Jim Yang books – written by 'that even stranger character, Peter Hook' – seemed increasingly responsible for 'extreme acts by children who proceed from stealing bicycles to vandalism to suicide, and refuse to wear watches or to change from size small to size medium when their parents buy them new clothes'.

I read an interview with a student of ancient religions who explains that certain Indian gods can't rise up to heaven by themselves; that these gods need the help of inferior but essential divinities, a kind of bird that's pure form, or something like that. 'If the gods reached heaven by means of form, men will have even greater need of form to reach the gods,' explains the academic. I don't understand it very well, but I like the words.

I read that the singer and songwriter of Warmgame – a popular rock bank that describes itself as belonging to the 'neoagonist' genre – is anguished by living in a world that worships youth but prevents youth from playing a leading role, and by 'how fast I'm losing my hair; it doesn't seem right'. Warmgame's frontman adds that the B side of their next single will be a cover of a song by the Victorians, 'Small Expectations.' 'Compton-Lowe was a genius,' says the Warmgame singer. And he adds: 'We've been living the end of the world for so long: we're living in the shadow of the spreading wave of the 60s, the moment when the world ended and we didn't notice. All fashion now is like an echo of the 60s. Everything seems to indicate that we'll never get out of this bloody loop with no doors or windows.' I look at the picture of the anguished boy. He must have been born in the mid-70s at the earliest. It occurs to me that the 60s are like UFOS: everybody says they've seen them, but no one has the evidence to prove it. The 60s – for many people, for too many people – were nothing but an uninterrupted series of lies accepted as truths. Automatic truths that no one ever took the trouble to verify, but that had to be true because we'd heard them so many times. The systematic repetition of a fallacy until it comes true is a clear sign of our times, or maybe an enduring human trait. For example, there's the frequently repeated idea that Hamlet recites his 'To be or not to be' speech with a skull in his hand (it isn't even spoken in the graveyard scene); or that Sherlock Holmes wears a deerstalker (which he never does in anything written by Arthur Conan Doyle; illustrator Sidney Paget came up with the idea); or that Rick Blaine in *Casablanca* says 'Play it again, Sam' (he doesn't; all he says is 'Play it'). And then there are the blessed the blessed and cursed 60s; the Swinging Sixties. Just as fairy tales are stories for children, the 60s are a fairy story for adults; for adults who were young during the 60s, and as a result have become the best, most reckless liars in all of history.

I read that an American anti-smoking group has decided to erase the cigarette in Paul McCartney's right hand on the cover of the Beatles' album *Abbey Road*. Yet another way of altering the truth, distorting it, denying it, lying about it. And that's what the 60s are, always: a tomb to desecrate until you're sick of it, something dead that won't rest, a corpse in the constant state of being autopsied, a ghost conjured up over and over again at the least excuse, simply so it can be asked silly, impertinent questions.

I read that it's believed the scientists Isaac Newton and Albert Einstein suffered a mild form of autism; and that the impressionists Monet, Degas, Cézanne, Pisarro, Matisse, Rodin and Renoir were short-sighted. And I ask myself where this odd and increasingly common tendency to diagnose the maladies of genius comes from; who decided to find an explanation for the singular in certain common afflictions. I think that it won't be long before someone claims that Barrie was simply an idiot savant.

I read that the administrators of the Great Ormond Street Hospital in London have summoned the most important authors of children's literature. The idea is that one of them will write a second part to *Peter Pan*; the idea is that the hospital will retain 50 per cent of the rights to this second part. The Great Ormond Street Hospital executives are nervous: the terrible date at which they'll once again lose the rights to Barrie's book is approaching (rights that represent 'a considerable but confidential sum', is all one official will say), and who knows whether they'll be saved by a parliamentary decree; better to take precautions than to bemoan their fate. 'Just as much pleasure could be had from a sequel as from the original,' comments the director of the children's hospital, caught between ecstasy and hysteria. I see the photograph of her. She looks desperate, lost, living the end of a dream, the terrible moment at which you realize fairies don't exist. The article notes that several writers have already expressed their lack of interest. My name is mentioned too, as that of the 'ideal candidate'. Peter Hook, of course, 'has made no comment yet'. 'But let's not give up hope,' adds the director.

I read that it's been proved that after the death of the body the brain continues to live for six to twelve minutes; that you can *think* after you've died; and that to the dead person those twelve or six minutes can come to seem an eternity – like the elastic, horizontal time of dreams – or at least a whole other fantastic life, ideal or terrible. Maybe that's what heaven or hell is: the way we spend those few infinite minutes. I also read that the brain is incapable of feeling any pain; that nothing hurts the brain; that the brain doesn't hurt. And yet, the brain is solely responsible for processing – for *inventing*, for *writing* – the theory and practice of pain. I wonder what the brain must be thinking when it reads things like that about itself. Is it interested in man's advances? Or does it laugh, amused that everything we think we've discovered about it is simply what it wants us to think, what the brain allows us to think about the brain?

I read that an inventor has developed a process for making diamonds from the ashes of dead bodies; that massive pressure on the remains gives them access to immortality, envy, the pleasure of being held up to the light. Goodbye to cemeteries, then. No more of this scattering of ashes in the air, on the water, over the earth. In the same article it says that the custom of burying the dead has become increasingly less practical and less practised: lack of space, lack of money; even the idea that the body must be kept inviolate in anticipation of the great day of the great resurrection is being revised by Vatican specialists, who've already commissioned an inflammatory prayer to be read during the rite of cremation. I like the idea that the dead can return and be resurrected as diamonds; that the dead have no value any more except metaphorically, though their worth is always rising. It remains to be seen, of course, whether good people will make better diamonds, whether certain spiritual principles will reap a material reward, in purities or impurities. Karma as a synonym for carat.

I read the thing I already mentioned to you, Keiko Kai. The thing about the way the death of a child increases the likelihood of the untimely death of the child's parents. And the survival of the child's brother, I add.

Having read all this – flying, the impending end of the world, children as destroyers, floating gods, men gone mad, sick geniuses, my sick father's genius, flames in Brighton, and fairy tales about talking fish in which someone is always in search of the philosopher's diamond of perfect happiness – I feel an urgent desire to vomit. Sitting next to me is an old man who must not have much life left in him: a nearly empty bottle, the last leaves of a tree, the last measures of a symphony, the last flight; so many last things. The man's holding a book but he isn't reading it. Maybe it's the book that's holding the man. I glance at the title out of the corner of my eye: *She*, by Sir Henry Rider Haggard, and, oh, another Victorian aristocrat setting off on a fruitless quest for eternal youth. The man looks at me enviously, maybe with hatred. He studies me with the fury of someone who knows he isn't interesting any more, that little or nothing will happen to him, that his days and nights are numbered and that the fingers of one hand, or at most of two gnarled claws, are enough to count them. And I always ask myself why there are so many inexplicable-seeming juvenile delinquents and so few logical-seeming geriatric delinquents: dangerous old men and women, drugged out of their minds, hooting toothless or cackling false-toothed, dragging themselves down the street or speeding along in their aerodynamic wheelchairs and attacking the spectators of fashion shows full of twelve-year-old top models, knowing they're beyond the reach of the law or any punishment, so invulnerable and so fragile, so deadly to others and to themselves. And now, more nausea for me. I go into the aeroplane toilet, as cramped as a coffin or a confessional, and I get down on my knees and ohgodohgodohgodohgod we're all perfect believers and martyrs when we're vomiting, when our body turns inside out like a glove and the contents of our guts fall like foul manna from the heavens. I stay there inside, sitting on the floor, repeating '*P* + 5*E* + 3*A*' until the aeroplane begins its descent with a sigh of resignation. I have the suspicion that aeroplanes don't like to let down their wheels and lower their flaps, and that they envy the vertical skills of helicopters. I also have the suspicion that someone who starts theorizing seriously about the likes and dislikes of aeroplanes can't be very balanced, can't be very happy.

It's nighttime. It's raining a rain that hardly makes you wet.

Heathrow, sweet Heathrow. Silence. Airports are so much like hospitals. I read it somewhere. Both are no man's lands, neverlands. Places you land in order to take off, places you go in order to leave. Arrivals and departures, hellos and goodbyes, and the continuum of climate control and arrows and signs that deny you the pleasure of losing your way but grant you the torment of losing yourself, of not being able to get to the place where they're waiting for you, and you're called by absentminded loudspeakers or the unforgettable whisper of last words.

I arrive and I go in and I ask a nurse or a stewardess to tell me which is Marcus Merlin's room. They call a doctor who's too young to be a doctor.

He asks me whether I'm a family member of the patient.

I tell him that I'm his and he's mine.

He says then you'd better sit down.

I tell them that even better, I'll faint; I faint for real, I'm not kidding.

The character is lies.

Lies, which are nothing but the original storytelling impulse.

Lies that narrate.

The lies of those first stories our parents tell us: lies we need to believe more than any truth so that right away we can start telling our own lies, our own stories.

Lies we continue to believe, much as we deny it.

Lies that never completely grow up; because the fine art of telling lies somehow keeps us children forever, helps us be more innocent and trusting so we can lie even better when we're adults.

Lies that lengthen behind our backs as we grow up, clinging to us like shadows.

The character is shadows.

Peter Pan's shadow.

In *Peter and Wendy*, Mrs Darling hears Peter Pan's name for the first time 'when she's tidying up her children's minds'. Barrie explains that at night, once their little ones have gone to sleep, mothers tiptoe into their children's rooms to spy on the inside of their heads and straighten them a little so next morning those heads don't wake up in complete disarray, with everything strewn on the floor. Barrie explains that this activity is 'quite like tidying up drawers' and the goal is that when the children open their eyes 'the naughtiness and evil passions with which you went to bed have been folded up small and placed at the bottom of your mind; and on the top, beautifully aired, are spread out your prettier thoughts, ready for you to put on'.

Busy at this, Mrs Darling discovers the name of Peter Pan, and it's a name like an echo, sounding in the untidy head of the girl she once was. Wendy explains to her mother who Peter Pan is, and tells her he visits often, coming in through the window.

One night, when she goes to kiss them good night, Mrs Darling discovers Peter Pan. Nana the dog barks and Peter Pan flies away, but Nana catches his shadow when the window closes on it. Nana brings Mrs Darling Peter Pan's shadow in her mouth. Mrs Darling, worried, thinks about hanging it from the windowsill so Peter Pan can come back and get it, but her sense of propriety stops her: 'it looked so like the washing and lowered the whole tone of the house.' So she decides to roll up the shadow and put it carefully in a drawer. Peter Pan comes back for it the next night. He can't find it, and Tinker Bell shows him where it's kept. Peter Pan takes it out of the drawer and unrolls it, but he can't stick it back to his heels. Peter Pan sobs, waking up Wendy, and Wendy sews on his shadow.

To lose your shadow is to lose your balance.

Our shadow – the thing that walks ahead of us or behind us – is memory.

I lost my shadow during my childhood, too. It wasn't a dog

that guillotined it with a window sash. It wasn't my mother who came in one night to fold it gently and put it under my pillow. It was I myself who cut off my shadow. I cut it off like those animals that gnaw off the paw they've caught in a trap. I cut it off when I was a boy. The black shadow of an accidental Hamlet, of a prince destroying his own line. First I cut it off and then I rolled it into a slender ribbon, knotting it around one of my arms as a mute expression of mourning at the funerals of Baco and Sebastian 'Darjeeling' Compton-Lowe and Alexandra Swinton-Menzies. My shadow is a practical and malleable shadow. Easy to turn into a tie or a handkerchief.

Here it is still, Keiko Kai.

Let me show it to you.

Let me use it to bind your eyes.

The character is secrets.

Things you can't see, though they're there.

Secrets as a strange illness. No cure's been discovered for secrets, for keeping secrets at bay.

Secrets that function as their own best friend and chosen enemy: the paradox of the secret that doesn't come to life – that's in an excited state of suspended animation – until it's killed first and then resurrected and set working. Secrets that don't infect you until they're not secrets any more, until they're shared, disseminated, transmitted.

Secrets are one of the sublimest forms of narrative. Secrets tell stories like nothing else. Secrets know everyone relies on them to tell stories.

Said Marcus Merlin: 'I'm going to tell you a story now . . .'

But what Marcus Merlin's going to tell me isn't a story. It's a secret. A secret that as soon as it's let go, speeds happily – secrets fly faster than rumours – to merge with my guilt.

It's my fault. I'm guilty.

The character is guilt.

My guilt.

'Guilt is magical,' a poet once wrote. And I don't think he was referring to the illusive and illusionist guilt of a man cutting a woman in half or a man humiliating a spectator who offers himself as a volunteer for the next trick; but to the guilt of someone who decides to disappear knowing he's responsible for having made many things appear that shouldn't have appeared.

I'm guilty.

All-powerful guilt. Guilt as the engine of the machinery that drives most of our actions.

The guilt felt by the survivors of concentration camps; guilt that one day, many years later, makes them throw themselves down flights of stairs.

It's guilt and not love – love moves nothing; love paralyses, petrifies – *che muove il sole e l'altre stelle.*

Barrie's brotherly guilt, which is simply one of the possible versions of the guilt I share. Barrie's guilt – the guilt of all survivors – linked to my guilt because it survived as an epilogue and coda to my dead family's final act.

The character is death.

Man is the only animal who knows he has to die. Some researchers of thanatological behaviour say that pigs know it too, that they feel it: the inevitable day, the 'That's all folks.' I'm not sure. Maybe it has to do with the constant looming presence of a wolf with powerful lungs.

Maybe.

One thing is certain: men *must* have more imagination than pigs in order to convince themselves that they'll never die.

Death as the great universal experience, after that other great universal experience at the opposite end of the tunnel, the act of being born. But the consciousness of our birth is really our parents' consciousness. The consciousness of our death is solely our own. It's an intimate and untransferable sentiment, and when we seem to be mourning the death of others – I'm sorry, I don't believe it – all we see in those alien deaths is an increasingly clear and imposing sketch of what our own portrait will look like, the painting that'll be unveiled some day or some night, before a few people or many. A group of people we won't be part of, so that they can tell us about ourselves, saying, upon seeing the portrait – seeing us in a frame, inside the wooden frame all coffins become, as sudden still lives – things like 'It's as if he's sleeping.'

The character is sleep.

The third of our lives that we spend elsewhere without going anywhere. We sleep in order to wake up somewhere else. We sleep in two stages: first comes the physical disconnect and then the mental disconnect. The return trip is the reverse: it's our brain that wakes up first and immediately afterward – a few seconds later – our body. When our brain disconnects, sometimes we experience a sudden muscle spasm; we kick, as if we're fighting against the sleep overtaking us. The phenomenon – I'm told it's called myoclonus, a name that suggests a bad-tempered Greek god – can wake us up and force us to start over again, like when we read a page we don't quite understand and we have to go back a few lines in the story.

Many people resist sleep. They think that to sleep is to waste time, to squander life. It's a childish objection. A taste of their past. They're wrong: night is the factory of tomorrow and the museum of yesterday. It's while we're asleep that we fix our memories in place and sketch our future, and we sink into sleep as if we're descending the concentric sweep of a spiral staircase over and over again, until we reach – if we're lucky – the last step, the step into the deepest and steepest of dreams.

The sleep of children isn't necessarily deep. Light sleep is the kind that lets you glimpse Neverland, says Barrie; the shallow and childish slumber that's easily disturbed by desperate, inexperienced parents who, upon trying to get a child to sleep when he won't stop crying, do exactly the opposite of what they should: they jostle him, sing to him, feed him, and take him for a walk, so that he finally wakes up altogether, terrified, in a place he doesn't know, far from home and his bed and his usual night's sleep.

The recurring dream.

My other recurring dream. The recurring dream I dream with my eyes open.

My other recurring dream isn't a dream, but rather a dreamed-for correction to a nightmarish reality. In my other recurring dream I don't do something I once did. That's all. A small action wiped out in the act. And that small amendment is enough – the changing of one word for another, like a deletion in one of my Jim Yang manuscripts – to make my whole universe, all the way to its last and farthest unexplored corner, regain its sanity, and, after so many years, permanently lose its eternal desire for madness.

The character is madness.

Madness is the Black Wind, Keiko Kai.

No, that's not quite it: the Black Wind is the voice that wakes up the madness. It's a wind you can see, not just the transparent hand that only acquires substance when it knocks into things and pushes them, stealing their shapes.

The Black Wind has shape and colour (never trust those who say black isn't a colour but rather the incontestable proof of the absence of all colour) and even a distinctive smell similar to the chromized scent aeroplanes give off at the moment they leave the earth: a smell of hot metal that makes you cough and tear up and smile a little.

The Black Wind doesn't wail but instead murmurs in your ear. The Black Wind doesn't say 'You've gone mad' but 'You're mad again.' Because madness is our true and original state, Keiko Kai. We're born crazy. After nine months floating inside our mothers with our eyes and fists clenched, the shock of leaving *there* to enter *here* is tremendous, unbearable. Suddenly we forget everything, we speak a strange language, we cry for any reason, our sleep is as erratic as our first love – for our one-and-only mother – is unshakeable, and we don't have any control over our simplest bodily functions.

Yes, it's madness that gets us through our childhood. Madness is the freshly painted white wall on which paintings of sanity hang.

I like to think that they're portraits. That there's a portrait for each of us. An automatic portrait, a self-portrait with a little label to one side that tells our name, the year of our birth, where we're from, our measurements, and the artist's style.

And if we're unlucky, if a window is opened and the Black Wind comes in, then a painting falls to the floor and sanity is lost. The portrait always ends up face down. And the little label with our information on it has no meaning any more and all that's left is the ghostly bright spot on the wall that marks the exact place where something used to be, and where now, if we're lucky, there's just the memory of what once hung there.

All we're left with is the horror of that endless naked wall, that white wall (never trust those who claim white isn't a colour but the ghost of sunlight that hasn't been broken down into the different colours of the spectrum); and there's nothing more terrible than the Black Wind blowing on the surface of a white wall, Keiko Kai.

So it is: the painting falls and the frame is broken and the wall remains.

And we go mad, we go mad again. And waiting for us beyond the madness is the consolation prize of our rediscovery of our former state, a kind of perfect, irrepressible happiness. When we go back to being crazy the way we used to be, we recover our capacity to believe in everything: in fairies; in our ability to fly; in the idea that dying will be an awfully big adventure, and at the same time, easily exorcised with nothing but applause.

Now that we're mad again, children reborn, it doesn't frighten us so much to think about death; because death is the thing that's always happening to other people so that we have the chance to think about death.

The dead are the inheritance we never want to receive, the inheritance we always receive; the eternal diamonds that hang around our necks, that sit on our fingers, that pierce our ears, and that nestle in our navels.

The dead are simply what ghosts become for a few hours when they go to sleep, after they've played all night at frightening the living.

The Dead

There's a moment when life begins to fill up with the dead.

At first we don't see them coming, although we sense them, ever closer, in the same way we sometimes know what the next song on the radio will be, or the next voice on the telephone, or the suspiciously exact ending of a crime novel.

Death – the most plural singular of all – is an apprenticeship.

Death – like childhood – is a commonplace we all make the trip to sooner or later, and it's a journey we think about a lot. We think a lot about death at the beginning of our lives (in an abstract way), and we think a lot about death at the end of our lives (in an utterly figurative way). We understand death as something that in principle is only conjugated in the second and third persons of the singular and the plural. And without haste or delay, death gradually ascends – becoming increasingly verbal and eloquent – until it reaches the last rung of the first person singular, the mode that includes only us, and is just us. Such is the ebb and flow of death: one day we're barely wetting our feet on the shore, and the next day, almost without warning, the water is up to our necks and the beach is very far away.

Barrie and I became familiarized with the principles of death – the unyielding principles of death – almost from the start of our lives, with David and Baco as the initiatory first casualties that immediately defined the territory of our existences. When the death of someone strikes so close (in my case, the death of Baco opening the window to the deaths of my parents; in Barrie's case the death of David opening the door to all those other deaths that stopped by to pay a visit) you have no choice but to feel it as something nearby and constant. Death as the answer to all riddles. Death as a playmate, death as a game in itself.

The opening night of *Peter Pan*, and the play's success, is a clear and dazzling sign for Barrie, unequivocal evidence that there'll be nothing better beyond the grave. It's a kind of death in life: *Peter Pan* as ultimate, unsurpassable milestone. *Peter Pan* is also the public broadcasting of the hitherto private faith of a capricious god. Barrie writes in his notebook:

> *– There is a small and ironic God who smiles on us. And he's on our side until he pulls the rope and then we all fall and go rolling down the hill.*

It doesn't surprise me that what Barrie thought he'd really done with the revelation of *Peter Pan* was to betray a secret oath and awaken the mortal and vengeful fury of the gods.

In any case, it's impossible to turn back now. The hidden temple has been profaned by the multitudes who clamour for more and more, and Barrie throws himself into the preparations for the first of the many revivals of *Peter Pan* – November 1905, the Duke of York's Theatre again. There are new scenes that require the fabrication of new and more complex mechanical devices; and now the play has five acts and is almost four hours long.

It isn't clear why Nina Boucicault is replaced in the leading role by the very inferior Cecilia Loftus, who's won certain fame as a music hall impersonator. Nor is any clarification necessary: Barrie wants it this way and Barrie is the lord and master of *Peter Pan*. Barrie and Dion Boucicault summon her at almost the last minute. Cecilia Loftus lacks the acting talent of Nina Boucicault, but – small, agile and girlish – she gives Peter Pan a rather more infantile and naughty air, like an androgynous dwarf. Gerald du Maurier begins to feel the strain of dressing up as Hook night after night and facing the shrieks of over-excited children, although he consoles himself with the thought that it's better than 'sweeping the floors of a mortuary for a shilling'.

The audience members – mostly return visitors – are delighted by the new scene and welcome it gratefully, as a gift; it includes the postponed mermaids and the instant when Wendy escapes through the air with the help of Michael's kite, while Peter Pan – abandoned to his fate on Marooners' Rock, surrounded by the sea as the tide rises, and lacking the strength to fly after an exhausting fight with the pirates – speaks his immortal line: 'Dying will be an awfully big adventure!'

Peter Pan doesn't die, of course. Peter Pan uses the nest of the Never bird and his own shirt to make a small craft and reach land. Some critics are uncomfortable with the scene and point out the bad example Peter Pan sets for children by tossing out the bird's eggs to make his escape. Barrie takes note of the reproaches of these first ecologists and adds the detail of Peter Pan carefully placing the eggs in the hat a pirate has let fall in the heat of battle.

Michael – manufacturer of increasingly perfect and concrete nightmares – falls ill with that rare mix of happiness and panic with which children fall into illnesses to see what'll happen and to find out what the difference is between the fever of health and the fever of fever. His perfect flu, which keeps him from going out to play until spring, prevents him from attending the opening. Barrie and Charles Frohman decide to take action: they bring a whole convoy of scenery and actors to his bedroom at Egerton House to stage an exclusive performance. Barrie has a special commemorative programme printed, the cover of which reads: *Peter Pan in Michael's Nursery/February 20, 1906.* And its first page: 'By Command of Michael, Mr Charles Frohman Presents Scenes from *Peter Pan* to be played in Michael's Nursery at Egerton House, Berkhamsted, February 20, 1906, by the Growing Up Company of the Duke of York's Theatre, London.'

The next morning, Michael's better, and in 1975, Nico Llewelyn Davies – who will die in 1980 – writes a letter to the biographer Andrew Birkin reminiscing about that therapeutic theatre performance and explaining that 'there was never the remotest feeling that Uncle Jim liked A better than B, though in due course we all knew that George and Michael were The Ones – George, because he had started it all, and Michael . . . because he was the cleverest of us, the potential genius . . .'

In another letter, in reply to the question whether any of them sensed in Barrie the stirrings of a forbidden love, Nico Llewelyn Davies explains: 'I'm 200 per cent certain there was never a desire to kiss (other than the cheek) . . . All I can say is that I never heard one word or saw one glimmer of anything suggesting homosexuality or paedophilia: he had neither of these leanings. Barrie was an innocent, which is why he could write *Peter Pan*.'

Andrew Birkin also notes that it would be wrong to think that all of Barrie's energies were concentrated on the Llewelyn Davies children. This is a time of great activity for him.

Barrie holds banquets. Barrie always has brussels sprouts served as a first course, but he never eats them. He doesn't even touch them with his fork. Whenever anyone asks him about this strange practice, Barrie responds: 'I love to say the words: brussels sprouts . . . brussels sprouts . . . brussels sprouts . . . the letters of those words in my mouth, biting them, swallowing them.'

Barrie plays with the Allahakbarries.

Barrie becomes friends with Captain Robert Falcon Scott, recently returned from his Antarctic expedition. Scott envies the intellectual life; Barrie praises the life of adventure, and takes notes for a play – a play he'll never write – in which a man dying on the immortal ice is 'visited' by different 'moments' from his past.

In vain, Barrie tries to defend his agent and friend Arthur Addison Bright, who's been charged with embezzling his clients' royalties. Sixteen thousand of the twenty-eight thousand pounds that are being claimed belong to Barrie, who, with his indifference to money, hasn't even noticed what was missing and feels a little responsible for having sparked this criminal temptation in Bright. It's a strange kind of embezzlement, an unusual crime: Bright hasn't touched almost any of the money that doesn't belong to him; he's just deposited it in his own account, maybe for the satisfaction of reading the sum entered in his bankbook.

Barrie is named godfather of Pauline Chase, one of the girls who plays one of the twins and lost boys in the first staging of the play and who by 1906 will have become Peter Pan, Barrie's favourite Peter Pan.

Barrie organizes various charitable works.

Barrie accompanies his wife to her mother's funeral.

Barrie writes a couple of light one-act entertainments. One of them – *Mirror Mirror On the Wall* – is never performed; but for once in a Barrie play there are interesting details regarding the Jamesian 'madness of art'. In the play, a successful writer is kidnapped by a man who claims to be one of his characters. The kidnapper accuses the writer of having stolen – consciously or unconsciously – his existence for one of his books, and demands that the 'author of my days and nights' tell him how the story continues after the novel ends. To save himself, the writer tells the madman that in the end he kills himself. The play ends with the suicide of the kidnapper at the moment the police arrive and break down the door. The curtain falls as the police take the body away and the terrified author reads aloud a manuscript belonging to the suicide victim, a story that begins with a writer tied to a chair, a smoking gun on the floor, a warm body, the police coming up the stairs.

Barrie travels to Lucerne to identify the body of his agent, who's committed suicide, and writes his obituary, in which – with perhaps inadvertent irony – he describes Bright, who had been the Bear in *The Greedy Dwarf*, as 'a man who never had much time to be interested in himself he was so interested in his friends'. Golding Bright, brother of Arthur Addison Bright, will be his new agent.

And Barrie begins to frequent the London aristocracy. The Duchess of Sutherland is his favourite. The nobility adopts

Barrie with the intense yet superficial fascination they reserve for artists: those lords without titles, those toys especially designed to amuse the nobility until they wear out or they're broken or they get sick or they die.

I suppose Barrie is happy then.

I suppose, too, that his dramatist's reflexes are already warning him that happiness is fragile and that with the second act will come the difficulties, the tragedy, everything that really makes a play memorable and classic and eternal.

As the curtain rises, we see Arthur Llewelyn Davies in the centre of the stage, looking in the mirror. He's alone in one of the sitting rooms at Egerton House, and at first we're surprised by this streak of secret narcissism in a man who never seemed to place much importance on his good looks. Immediately we discover that he isn't interested in his classical profile but in a slight discolouration that's appeared on one of his cheeks. He touches it carefully and curiously. He feels his slightly swollen jaw. Arthur has just returned from the dentist, who told him that all this could be due to the infected root of a dead tooth, a forgotten fragment of a molar pulled years ago. Just in case, the dentist recommends that he visit a doctor, who, in turn, decides to run more tests. The diagnosis isn't good: it's not an abscess but a sarcoma. There must be an operation at once and – as Arthur tells his sister Margaret in a letter – 'I am afraid it means removing half the upper jaw and palate . . . Poor Sylvia! I have told her everything except the name of the disease . . . After the operation I shall be incapacitated for about 6 weeks, and unable to speak properly for 3 or 4 months . . . My 43 years, and especially the last 14, leaves me no ground of complaint as to my life. But this needs fortitude.'

It isn't long before Barrie discovers what's happening, and he drops everything to come to the rescue: he seeks out the best specialists, assumes the cost of the enormously expensive medicines, and instals himself in the hospital room, at the foot of the bed of his best friends' father.

In his *Morgue*, Peter Llewelyn Davies writes:

If this were a real book instead of just a brief compilation of events, a clear division should be drawn here signalling the end of one of its sections or 'parts'. Because the next entry will mark the start of the material that I like to call the 'morgue sort,' and that, besides being my principal motive for undertaking this task, is also what most makes me doubt whether my effort will have any meaning or value. So the best thing for me will be to continue without asking myself too many questions . . . J.M.B. stepped in to play the leading role; and played it in the grand manner . . . I can sympathize in a way with the point of view that it was the last straw for Arthur that he should have had to accept charity from the strange little genius who had become such an increasing irritation to him in recent years. But on the whole, I must disagree. We don't really know how deep the irritation went; and even if it went deep, I am convinced that the kindness of which J.M.B. gave such overwhelming proof from now on, far more than outweighted all that, and that the money and promise of future financial responsibility, as well as the great tact with which he offered his help, finally overcame my father's resistance.

Between the end of May and the middle of June 1906, Arthur undergoes three operations. Each is more difficult and complicated than the last. Arthur comes out of the operating room with his head wrapped in bandages, floating on the sad bliss of a sea of morphine. Barrie keeps him company for long stretches, reading him the paper and of course taking real-life, on-the-spot notes for his possible next fictions:

–The 1,000 Nightingales. *A hero who is dying. 'Poor devil, he'll be dead in six months' . . . He in his rooms awaiting end – schemes abandoned – still he's a man, dying a man . . . Everything going splendidly for him (love & work) when audience hears of his doom.*

When they remove her husband's bandages, Sylvia – more realistic and practical – howls a perfect, histrionic 'They've ruined my darling's face!' The malignancy seems to have been eradicated, but this doesn't mean that a young lawyer who's lost his looks and his power of speech will have any kind of professional future. Arthur returns to Egerton House. The children have been sent to Ramsgate, to their grandmother Emma du Maurier. Arthur doesn't want them to see him like this and he writes to them every day. Letters that might have been written by the healthiest and happiest and most vigorous man in the world.

Keiko Kai: I envy the strength of Arthur's love for his children, the potency of the medicines he's given, his stoic bravery. Arthur knows he's finished, and that everything from here on will depend on Barrie, who now – in the messages he sends by telegram – he finally calls *Jimmy*.

'Give me your hand, Jimmy,' 'Do write more things other than plays, Jimmy,' 'Vague fancies . . . that I was going to have, or perhaps had had, an infant. All this was vaguely connected with thirst and pain in my face, Jimmy,' 'I'm very happy. This last six months of convalescence have been the happiest of my life. I've received so much kindness. Bless my bones,' 'I don't think anyone has ever done so much for me,' 'I put all the burdens on you because you can help better than anyone,' 'I love to watch you while you write,' 'DEAR Jimmy,' Arthur writes to Barrie on a note pad with many pages. Barrie asks himself what Arthur means by his suggestion that Barrie write 'more things other than plays'. Can he be referring to fat realist novels? To the unreal form of preaching reality by composing perfectly tidy lives and loves and deaths, always at the same narrative tempo? Barrie isn't interested in art imitating reality. It's reality that should imitate art, thinks Barrie.

Arthur recovers enough to take walks with Sylvia, and, from a distance – his face hidden behind a black veil – he watches his children play with Barrie in Kensington Gardens.

Barrie is dressed up as Hook, with Michael as Peter Pan. Barrie has asked William Nicholson – *Peter Pan*'s wardrobe manager – to design a costume for Michael. It's a gift with an ulterior motive: Barrie is already amusing himself with the idea of commissioning a statue of Peter Pan and Michael, he thinks, is the indisputably perfect model. Michael – his legs apart, a stick on his left shoulder, his gaze defiant, his smile bold – *is* Peter Pan. And Barrie photographs him from every possible angle – and why is it harder to describe a photograph than a movie, Keiko Kai?

This is one of those photographs that – *Well I just had to laugh ha ha, I saw the photograph ah ah . . .* – have to be seen to be believed. One of those photographs that says more than a thousand paintings. One of those photographs that should be taken of all children as an essential part of their upbringing, to provide them with useful and incontrovertible evidence so that – years later, looking at it with tired eyes and holding it in trembling hands – they can say: 'Here it is. Here I am. Look. Look at me. You see, I wasn't lying. I was like this. Many years ago, on another planet, in another dimension, I was immortal and brave and happy and perfect like this.' A photograph to keep in a drawer or an album and never hang on the wall like one of those portraits with the ability to absorb sins and wrinkles; because a photograph like this is a fist, a fist striking over and over again, a blow for every minute and hour and day and month and year that passes after the day the photograph that stole our soul was taken; because that photograph *is* our soul. A photograph like this is paradise; a paradise that, by definition, is always a paradise lost: only once we've been expelled do we realize that we lived in a paradise, and that paradise lived in us.

Barrie asks Michael to stand this way and that, and for an instant he's excited by the idea of a sequel to *Peter Pan*: *Michael Pan*, the story of Peter's younger brother. Barrie takes notes, writes down things the boy says and does. Barrie worships and loves him.

Arthur – impossible not to imagine him as one of those Prince Charmings with a pall suddenly cast over him by a hideous spell – cries as he watches them from behind the bushes. Arthur hasn't stopped crying for months: during the last operation it became necessary to remove his tear ducts, and now it's impossible for him to control the flow of his tears. Arthur cries because he can't stop crying.

Barrie hears about a new electric treatment, about a prosthetic metal jaw that makes too much noise yet might improve Arthur's speech and appearance; but nothing seems to work. I like to imagine Arthur as one of those gothic monsters: an automaton half man and half steel, and captive of a jaw that starts to possess him, to grow, to overtake the rest of his body like ivy.

Barrie spares no expense; money is what he has more than enough of. Barrie has made forty-four thousand pounds this year so far, without counting another five hundred thousand just for *Peter Pan*. To the royalties for *Peter Pan* – ready for a third triumphant season – are now added those of *Peter Pan in Kensington Gardens*. Barrie's publishers at Hodder and Stoughton have convinced him to publish the chapters from *The Little White Bird* separately in a special edition with fifty illustrations by Arthur Rackham. The book sells well, and its first page reads: 'FOR SYLVIA AND ARTHUR LLEWELYN DAVIES AND THEIR BOYS (MY BOYS).'

Arthur cries as he reads the book. He cries for real; he cries because he wants to cry, because it seems dignified and appropriate. It's as if now, reading it, Arthur understands Barrie at last. Everything Barrie feels, everything he always felt, is almost exactly what Arthur never felt and what he's beginning to feel now: an exquisite loneliness, so much like the company of death as it creeps closer, like a boundless love for the world that surrounds him and of which he is beginning to take his leave.

The pain increases along with the doses of morphine and soon it's discovered that the cancer has spread to the other side of Arthur's face and that more operations are no longer possible or helpful. The mechanical jaw grinds in desperation. On 18 September 1906, Arthur writes to his sister Margaret: he has six months to a year left, he tells her. The days pass and there's something terrible and at the same time privileged about knowing the coordinates of the end. The proximity of death, thinks Arthur, makes everything seem more alive.

Barrie scarcely moves from his side. Barrie takes a house in London, at 23 Campden Hill Square – very close to where the Llewelyn Davieses used to live and very close to Leinster Corner – so Sylvia can move there with the children. Barrie puts up a good part of the money to buy it. Barrie pulls strings so that George is accepted into Eton (Captain 'Jas' Hook was there; his last words, before being devoured by the crocodile, are 'Floreat Etona') and writes to Captain Robert Falcon Scott to ask for his help in getting Jack admitted to the Naval College. Barrie reports these new developments one by one to Arthur, who, perhaps convinced of the good fortune of his loved ones, no longer has any reason to keep fighting.

Arthur Llewelyn Davies dies on 19 April 1907, at the age of forty-four. The children's grandmother assembles them that night and gives them the news. Peter will never forget that Emma du Maurier is wearing a sleeping cap at the moment she tells them their father is gone. The next morning the brothers go to the seashore to dig holes and build castles. It's a cloudy, windy day on Ramsgate Beach. Nothing is different from the day before, but everything has changed. And how does that lying poem by Edna St Vincent Millay go, Keiko Kai? Oh yes: 'Childhood is the kingdom where nobody dies.' It isn't true, of course. Childhood is a place inhabited by beings short in stature but with a high death rate, and the little Llewelyn Davieses have just discovered this. And it's only the beginning.

Arthur didn't leave much. His brother takes up a collection among the family members, but Sylvia refuses to accept what's gathered and asks that the money be returned to those who contributed. No one quite understands why she wants it that way; but everyone knows Barrie won't hesitate to take charge of the widow and her children. Someone says: 'When Barrie has decided to give, he gives in the full sense of the word, and no one, not even a superman, can escape the force of his generosity.'

Barrie rents a house in Scotland – Dhivach Lodge, perched on the edge of a gorge with views of Loch Ness – and takes everyone on holiday. It's hot; the sun seems to refuse to set each evening; the days are too long; and there isn't much talking. The silence is more than palpable. The silence is almost a colour. Silence comes out of people's mouths when they're talking to one another – in almost telegraphic conversations – and they all seem like actors in a silent film to which someone's forgotten to add the occasional explanatory card. There are no words, there's just the oppressive sound of a sad spring: bells, birds, oars in the water, someone singing a happy song in the distance – you hear his voice but you can't see the singer and it's better that way: few things are more terrible than the sight of others' happiness so close to one's own sadness.

Michael's afraid of going in the water. Michael has nightmares that are increasingly elaborate and powerful. At the end of the holidays, George begins his first year at Eton, Peter enters Mr Wilkinson's famous institute, Michael and Nico begin school at Norland Place, and Jack hates each and every one of his days at the Naval College in Osborne and – politely and cautiously – begins to hate the Barrie who's always ready to save them, to decide and write what has to be done, and to structure the lives of others as if they were characters in his plays.

Sylvia tentatively begins to smile again, Barrie goes back to working on the new revival of *Peter Pan*, this time starring Pauline Chase. There's always something to revise or add. At the request of the London Ambulance Service, the author adds a line of warning about 'no one being able to fly unless they have fairy dust', since he's been told by hospital emergency room doctors that 'many children, after returning from the theatre, try to fly by jumping off their beds, and hurt their little heads and legs and arms'.

At the last show in *Peter Pan*'s third season something unexpected and unprecedented happens.

On the night of 22 February 1908, at the end of the fifth act, the curtain falls and – despite the usual thunderous applause – the actors don't come out to take their bows and the hall remains in darkness for almost fifteen minutes. The audience begins to grow uneasy, a child bursts into tears, and the pieces of that broken weeping spread to the other children in the hall. They're all crying and even their parents are asking themselves whether they shouldn't cry too: the darkness reminds them of the darkness of their childhood, the darkness of those nights when you don't fear what lives in the shadows but the possibility that the light will never return, that the light is gone forever.

Everything is part of a surprise Barrie has prepared for Charles Frohman, who's come specially from Paris and is sitting in the front row. It's a surprise that will never be repeated in their lives: Barrie has written a short sixth act for *Peter Pan*. A coda that he's titled 'When Wendy Grew Up: An Afterthought', and that reveals what will happen many years later in the lives of Peter and Wendy.

Then Tessie Parke – the actress who played the youngest mermaid – appears. Followed by a spotlight beamed from the hall's rafters, she comes up almost to the edge of the orchestra pit and says:

> *My friends, I am the Baby Mermaid. We are now going to do a new act for the first and only time on any stage. Mr Barrie told us a story one day about what happened to Wendy when she grew up and we made it into an act, and it will never be done again. So open your eyes wide.*

The curtain goes up and there's Wendy with the same body and the same face as the actress Hilda Trevelyan; but now her dress is formal and her hairstyle is that of an adult woman and her voice has lost the sharp gleam of childhood. Now Wendy is a woman and she's married and she has a daughter. Wendy is in the children's room. In one of the beds lies an old, tired, nearly immobile version of the dog Nana, as if the actor had left the empty costume there. In the other bed smiles little Jane, Wendy's daughter. Jane asks her mother to tell her a story about Peter Pan.

The audience holds its breath as it watches the scene. It's a strange, disquieting moment. Barrie has written a metafictional appendix in which he makes clear what everyone senses, though they can't explain how it happened: Peter Pan is no longer part of legend; he's transcended his theatre existence to become a legend, a commonplace, part of their lives. *Peter Pan* is now one of the classic fairytales, and the audience has been granted the privilege of living in the era when everything began and when people began to believe in Peter Pan the same way they believe in so many other things.

Wendy explains to Jane that she doesn't remember how to fly any more, because grown-ups forget about flying, and the only thing that flies for grownups is time. Wendy tells Jane about the short life of fairies:

> *You see, dear: a fairy lives as long as a feather stays aloft on a windy day. But fairies are so small that a very short time is a whole life for them. While the feather flutters, they enjoy the happiest of existences . . . with enough time to be decently born, explore the world, dance once and cry once and bring up their children . . . just as it's possible to travel a long distance very fast in an automobile. Automobiles are very useful when it comes to explaining fairies . . . You know everyone grows old and dies. Except Peter Pan, who never had any sense of time. He thought that the whole of the past fit into yesterday . . .*

And then Wendy says how sorry she is that – because of his heedlessness of time, his very un-British lack of punctuality – Peter Pan didn't keep his promise and never came back for her. Then, as if he's heard her, Peter Pan comes flying in the open window. Peter Pan believes only a day has gone by since their adventures together. Peter Pan insists that Wendy accompany him. Wendy refuses. She's too old now, she explains; but – as if in tribute – she'll allow Jane to go with him to Neverland. For a week. Wendy waves goodbye from the bedroom window and muses aloud about the day Peter Pan will come in search of Jane's son or daughter. And so on for centuries upon centuries and child after child, yes: let the little children, 'gay and innocent and heartless', come unto me, amen.

The curtain falls and a few seconds pass before the audience begins to applaud. They're moved. They're not sure they've seen what they've seen. They ask themselves whether anyone will believe them, and they know that years from now so many people will swear to have been there and so many will lie about having been there that to hold them the Duke of York's Theatre would have had to be as big as all of London.

Charles Frohman is transfigured. He cries and laughs and embraces Barrie, who has directed the whole surprise – there was hardly time to rehearse it – from the wings and who, for once, comes out to acknowledge the audience, which is ecstatic with gratitude: Barrie almost hidden in his famous black coat, wrapped in a scarf, hat in one hand. People clap even harder: Barrie playing Barrie is unsurpassable.

Charles Frohman informs Barrie that the suitcases must be readied and the scenery and the actors packed off. Charles Frohman has arranged the Paris debut of *Peter Pan, ou le petit garçon qui ne voulait pas grandir*. Two weeks at the very fashionable Théâtre du Vaudeville. They'll scarely make enough to cover the staggering costs, but Charles Frohman couldn't care less. The important thing is that *Peter Pan* travel, fly, conquer the world.

The work is performed in English but a twelve-page synopsis of the script is distributed – *L'Histoire de Peter Pan*; I bought a copy in almost perfect condition at an auction, Keiko Kai – to help the Parisians understand the already universal mystery of the plot. The show sells out to the very last seat and *Le Figaro* devotes three columns to it, placing special emphasis, of course, on the symbolic and philosophical qualities of the play and venturing rather strange, very French interpretations.

Back in England, Barrie shuts himself up to write *What Every Woman Knows*. It's his first work in three years, and – maybe as an antidote to the influence of *Peter Pan* – it's a play for adults, with adult characters who don't believe in fairies and don't know how to fly, only how to crash. It's another big hit: Barrie's name on the playbills is more than enough to fill a hall for weeks. There are laughs, but they're the kind of laughs that issue from a bitter crook of the mouth. There's lots of talk on stage. Nationalism, politics, and feminism are discussed. All of this is projected on the backdrop of one of Barrie's favourite subjects: marriage as a battlefield and a constantly simmering process of negotiation.

Like his own marriage.

Mary Barrie has given up all hope and flirts shamelessly with Gilbert Cannan, who's seeking solace after Captain Robert Falcon Scott – his romance with the actress Pauline Chase ended – steals the affections of the young sculptor Kathleen Bruce.

Barrie watches this sentimental minuet as if it were another of his plays, unable to see what's happening or pretending to be ignorant of the twists and turns of the plot. What's more, to make things more *interesting* he hires Gilbert Cannan as his secretary on the theatre anti-censorship committee – a cause to which he devotes energy and indignation when the work of a friend is banned – and then invites him to Caux on a three-week Swiss skiing holiday. Sylvia and the boys are included in the party.

Away they all go, and Sylvia encourages Gilbert Cannan to take things even further with Mary. She arranges for them to meet, and at the same time she goes off with Barrie to keep him occupied. Uncharitable minds think Sylvia is dreaming of marriage to Barrie. All that money, all that prestige. There are moments when the tension at Caux resembles that of the most grotesque vaudeville act.

One afternoon, Peter finds Barrie sobbing in the hotel library. He's alone and in the dark. Peter asks him what's wrong, why he's so sad. Barrie lifts his head from his hands, looks at him with his eyes bathed in tears, and replies 'Peter, something dreadful has happened to my feet,' and pulls a lamp close. Barrie's feet are gigantic; they've grown to four or five times their normal size. Peter lets out a yell and goes running. Barrie's laugh – he had the false feet made at Hamley's – follows him down the stairs.

When that night Sylvia puts her hand to her breast and faints, the Llewelyn Davies brothers can't help but think it's another bad joke scripted and directed by Barrie. Because recently, ever since Barrie has become an increasingly powerful presence in their lives, the boys have the unmentionable suspicion – all five think the same thing, but none of them dares say it aloud to the others – that they're inhabiting a play; that reality takes place outside the theatre of their existences, that ever since their father's death everything is written and produced and directed by James Matthew Barrie, and that they are nothing but puppets, puppets without strings, but also without a will of their own. Yes, it must be: their mother's faint was fake, an act. She's played it very well. A great actress. A diva. It takes Sylvia a while to come to her senses. They call a doctor who happens to be there, and who refuses to give a diagnosis with the excuse that he's on vacation. Upon their return to London, Sylvia seems weak and tired and stops seeing Arthur's relatives and the old friends she knew as part of a couple.

Barrie helps produce a play written by Guy du Maurier, Sylvia's brother. The play – a fairly obvious but effective propaganda vehicle – is called *An Englishman's Home* and in it there's a warning about the German threat; it's enormously successful.

And Barrie goes ahead with his plans to erect the statue of Peter Pan. He commissions the job to Sir George Frampton, showing him the pictures he took of Michael in Kensington Gardens. He explains that *this* is what Peter Pan is like.

On 28 July 1909, Barrie goes out for a walk in the garden at Black Lake, and the caretaker, a Mr Hunt, tells him that the cottage is often used by Mary Barrie and Gilbert Cannan when its owner is away. Mr Hunt isn't betraying the couple because he disapproves of their behaviour but because – he'll explain later under oath – 'the lady criticized the way I tend the roses.'

Barrie offers his wife the chance to go on as if nothing has happened so long as she stops seeing Gilbert Cannan. She refuses. Mary believes that it's in her marriage to Barrie that nothing's happened for all these years, and now she's tired of nothing happening.

Three months later, the divorce is official and – to Mary's horror – Barrie seems more in love with her than ever and completely indifferent to the scandal. Mary – who loves Cannan like a man and Barrie like a son – accepts full blame and doesn't even lodge a complaint about Barrie's constant flirtations with his actresses and his strange relationship with Sylvia Llewelyn Davies.

Barrie takes refuge in his imagination as a way of seeking justice and wastes little time writing *The Twelve-Pound Lock*, a pathetic melodrama in one act that revolves around adultery and divorce. The protagonist – a successful Englishman by the name of Harry Sims, soon to receive a knighthood – is too obviously an idealized version of Barrie: he's tall, handsome. At the end of the play, Sims discovers that his wife was never unfaithful to him, that she only wanted to make him jealous because she felt eclipsed by her husband's fame; she reappears onstage as a professional typist and emancipated woman. It's all fairly ridiculous. And there's something so sad about the way Barrie goes back to fantasizing about his own life, rewriting it, fitting it into three acts. The almost pathological need to bury reality alive under the floorboards of a stage in order to be able to bear it: if his matrimonial debacle becomes a succesful play, Barrie thinks, maybe that way it will be less painful. For Barrie, art's supreme mission – and Barrie understands his own existence as a play in progress – has more to do with fantasy than sincerity. Why does life have a single unhappy ending and not several happy endings, one after the other, as they're needed? God is good at creating characters but a bad playwright when it comes to structuring the script he makes us read. The critics treat the play with the irritable mercy only elicited by the embarrassment of others. No one speaks of *The Twelve-Pound Lock*; everyone is too busy talking about the real divorce of the real couple. Rumours abound about Barrie's hypothetical and never confirmed sexual impotence. 'The boy who couldn't go up' is the joke circulating around the London clubs. To everyone who asks her about Barrie's amatory capabilities, Mary insists that 'in the beginning everything was fine'. A group of writers – among them Henry James and H. G. Wells – sign an open letter and send it to all the Fleet Street papers asking for 'respect and gratitude to a man of genius'.

Fortunately, the trial is short. The evidence presented by the gardener with a grudge is more than enough, and when he explains that 'it was normal to find two empty cups of tea in Mrs Mary Barrie's room', the judge orders him to be silent, considering his comments vulgar. Barrie signs everything that must be signed and leaves Mary the Black Lake cottage. He doesn't want to go back there. Nor does he want to continue living at Leinster Corner.

Barrie finds a flat in Adelphi Terrace House, between the Strand and the Thames, across from Bernard Shaw's house. Barrie hires a butler, who soon comes to be known as the Inimitable Harry Brown. I've never seen a photograph of Brown, so I don't hesitate to give him the face of my beloved and also inimitable Dermott, may he rest in peace.

Barrie writes to Sylvia and the boys to inform them of his

new address, and – two days after the trial's verdict – Sylvia faints in the house on Campden Hill Square. A doctor is called who isn't on vacation. Another categorical verdict: 'It's serious. Say nothing to the family.' Cancer. According to Dr Rendel, it's 'too close to the heart to operate'. Mary Hodgson, faithful housekeeper, promises to keep the secret of her mistress's health. She doesn't even tell Sylvia, who questions her as soon as the doctor's gone. Sylvia lies back on her pillows and pronounces herself 'almost disappointed' when Mary Hodgson tells her that the diagnosis is exhaustion due to her recent sorrows.

Her children suspect nothing. It's impossible that anything could be wrong, because it would make no dramatic sense after their father's death. So they spend their days exploring Kensington Gardens with Barrie and their new friend, Captain Robert Falcon Scott – Barrie has agreed to be godfather to his firstborn son, Peter, too, named after Peter Pan – who's preparing to embark on his second expedition to Antarctica.

By July of 1910, Sylvia is convinced that her condition is serious. It doesn't matter what the doctors say. She hardly has the strength to move. Smiling is an effort; but even so she insists on a holiday in Devon. Barrie finds – as usual – the perfect place: Ashton Farm, in the Oare River valley.

There, Sylvia scarcely goes out for a breath of fresh air and lies all day on the sofa, in a black robe. Her mother keeps her company. At some point, Sylvia writes a will. It isn't the first. Since her husband's death, Sylvia has taken to composing morbid funerary texts. In her spare time she writes in an exercise book what she's come to call 'Notes for a Will,' in elegant script. They're observations and scattered ideas in which she imagines a life without her. She writes:

> *I could die at any moment, but I don't think it will happen very soon, since today I feel strong. In case it does happen (God forbid, I think of my beautiful children) I'd like to leave some clear instructions: I think that all my sons will be good and brave*

men (considering that they're Arthur's sons and that they understand how much they were loved by him and by Sylvia, his faithful and loving wife). I hope that they marry & have children & live long & happily & are content to be poor if such happens to be their lot . . . Of one thing I'm certain: J. M. Barrie (the best friend in the whole world) will always be ready to give them loving counsel . . .

In Sylvia's will – which won't be found until several months later – she asks to be cremated and buried next to 'my Arthur' in Hampstead. Sylvia says she doesn't want her children to see her dead or to attend her funeral ('It seems a great mistake; I want them to remember me as I was when I could look at them'); and entrusts her mother with the task of going through her letters (except those Arthur sent her and those she sent him) and, if nothing essential for the future is found among them, 'I would like *everything* burnt.' Her jewellery 'will be put away and shared out among the wives of my five sons when that day comes'.

Barrie never leaves her side as he revises the manuscript of *Peter and Wendy*, the inevitable novelization of his great success that his publishers have been demanding for some time.

A few notes in the margins:

– Peter Pan. Revise. *What time of year, summer, winter, fall? Peter doesn't understand – 'There's only spring.'*
– *The dying. Friends around talk of other things. Wonder about dying, when silent really making preparations for dying – for the journey.*
– Death. *One thinks of the dead as a bird taking lonely flight.*
– The Second Chance: *'Beware, or you may get what you want.'*

Sylvia's children – Barrie's boys – come for a visit. George (seventeen) is one of the most popular pupils at Macnaghten's House at Eton and it's already assumed that in his last year he'll be one of the twenty chosen ones who make up the

Etonian society known as Pop, to which anyone 'would give their right arm to be admitted'. Michael (ten) and Nico (six) have done well at Wilkinson's School. Peter (thirteen) isn't doing badly at his school, while Jack (sixteen) still isn't sure what he's doing at Osborne, and why Barrie has separated him from his brothers.

Sylvia marvels at the elegance of their school uniforms, at how handsome her sons are, how happy they seem. Sylvia stares, fixing them with the gaze of someone who wants to take them with her to the other side, imprinting them forever on the retina of darkening eyes. The boys feel uncomfortable before those lidless pupils that try to learn them by heart. They're disturbed by the all-powerful intensity of the dying that makes the living feel that they're wasting time, that they aren't enjoying life as they should, that they don't deserve the health they're squandering. So they prefer to see her at breakfast and then immediately escape to fish, play golf, lose themselves in the woods, pedal to Lyton, stuff themselves with masses of raspberry jam and Devonshire cream, and explore the lake where Nico swears he saw a monster.

When they return, at night, Sylvia is already asleep and Barrie reads them bits from *Peter and Wendy* in a tremulous voice, beside the fire, gesturing frequently, casting shadows on the walls.

Some underlined sentences in my copy of *Peter and Wendy*. A few words that explain so much more about me than anything I could argue in making my hypothetical defence in front of a hypothetical jury. This, I think, is always the function of our favourite books, our bedside books, the books we read to help us sleep, the books we pick up again as soon as we awake: discovering in them that someone's written us much better than we could ever write ourselves. And knowing that this book – a book that many might've read but that was intended for just one person – is waiting for us somewhere, that all we have to do is go in search of it and find it.

A few sentences, a few words that keep appearing in my head at the most unexpected moments, without permission, as if triggered by a hidden spring that opens a secret door, and here they are all at once, maybe because they sense that this will be the last chance they'll have to pounce on me.

All these words and sentences that once worked as keys to so many doors for me, fitting into a final lock: all these words and sentences at last reaching the almost final instant in which past and present and future are the same room in the same house, here, in Neverland.

Here, Keiko Kai.

And now.

All these sentences, all these words, now:

> *Odd things happen to all of us on our way through life without our noticing for a time that they have happened. Thus, to take an instance, we suddenly discover that we have been deaf in one ear for we don't know how long, but, say, half an hour.*

Now.

> *Children have the strangest adventures without being troubled by them. For instance, they may remember to mention, a week after the event happened, that when they were in the wood they met their dead father and had a game with him.*

Now.

> *Off we skip from home like the most heartless things in the world, which is what children are, but so attractive; and we have an entirely selfish time, and then when we have need of special attention we nobly return for it.*

Now.

> *Peter had seen many tragedies but he had forgotten them all . . . 'I forget them after I kill them.'*

Now.

Tink was not all bad: or rather, she was all bad just now, but, on the other hand, sometimes she was all good. Fairies have to be one thing or the other, because being so small they unfortunately have room for one feeling only at a time. They are, however, allowed to change, only it must be a complete change.

Now.

Sometimes, though not often, he had dreams, and they were more painful than the dreams of other boys. For hours he could not be separated from these dreams, though he wailed piteously in them. They had to do, I think, with the riddle of his existence.

Now.

Peter was not quite like other boys; but he was afraid at last. A tremor ran through him, like a shudder passing over the sea; but on the sea one shudder follows another till there are hundreds of them, and Peter felt just the one. Next moment he was standing erect on the rock again, with that smile on his face and a drum beating within him. It was saying, 'To die will be an awfully big adventure.'

Now.

Stars are beautiful, but they may not take an active part in anything, they must just look on for ever. It is a punishment for something they did so long ago that no star now knows what it was. So the older ones have become glassy-eyed and seldom speak (winking is the star language), but the little ones still wonder.

Now.

We have now reached the evening that was to be known among them as the Night of Nights.

And – now – my favourite of all, the best possible advice, Keiko Kai:

The more quickly this horror is disposed of the better.

Now.

One evening, on their way back from one of their adventures, George and Jack and Peter and Michael and Nico sense that something bad has happened in their absence. That morning, Nurse Loosemore told them that their mother had had a bad night and that she was too tired to see them in her room; that she was resting; that it would be better if they came to her at the end of the day. It wasn't true: Sylvia was awake, she could hear them laughing and playing and running up and down the stairs and leaving the house. Sylvia asked for a mirror. Sylvia looked at herself in it and said: 'Don't let the boys see me again.'

Now all the blinds of Ashton Farm have been closed and the boys come slowly up the path, with the wariness of wild animals approaching a fire. They sense what's happened, but they don't want to know it. One of the doors opens and Barrie comes out. He looks like the desperate little bird that's always trying to escape the jaws of the cuckoo clock and never succeeds. The neck of his shirt is open, his hair is dishevelled, and his eyes are wide, as if he's just fought something terrible, as if he's lost the fight. From inside the house come the screams of Mary Hodgson: 'Cruel God! Cruel God!' George and Jack and Peter and Michael and Nico go up the stairs and come to the half-open door of Sylvia's room and – years later – they'll never be completely sure whether they saw their mother's dead body or not.

'I am almost sure . . . that I saw it . . . All I retain . . . is a dream-like, cloudy sense of looking down from above for a few seconds, confused, unhappy, frightened, looking and yet not looking at the pale, lifeless features and then of escaping to some lost limbo in some remote corner of the house,' writes Peter Llewelyn Davies in his *Morgue*. And he adds, with some guilt: 'It's grotesque: I remember very little of the day my mother died or the day of her funeral, and yet the morning after her death is perfectly vivid: we went with Barrie to Little, a store in Haymarket to buy nets and fishing rods to divert ourselves with during the remainder of the holidays!'

Jack, bitter, will never be able to forget that Barrie took him aside to tell him that his mother had decided to marry him, that she was already wearing his ring – a diamond and sapphire ring that years later Barrie would present to Nico to give to his fiancée. 'If this was true, it's clear she only agreed because she knew she was going to die,' Jack wrote to Peter in 1952, still angry. Peter never believed that his mother might have married Barrie: 'If the idea was intolerable to Jack, I must confess that for me just thinking about it seems repugnant . . . A marriage between Sylvia, widow of the splendid Arthur and still so lovely, and that strange creature who adored her and dreamed, as he surely must have dreamed, of stepping into my father's shoes, would have been an affront to any reasonable person's sense of the fitness of things. And I don't believe Sylvia ever contemplated such a possibility . . . I hope that upon reading this no one considers me an ungrateful person, since on more than one occasion I've written about the innumerable kindnesses and advantages received from the hands of the aforesaid strange creature whose connection with my family ultimately brought much more sorrow than happiness.'

The next morning, the brothers – in mourning again, scarcely three years after their father's death – go walking to the village to send telegrams relaying the bad news to friends and family.

'Despite all the tragedy, today we got up and washed and we could knot our ties and lace our shoes and breakfast wasn't bad at all . . . It isn't the end of the world, men, life goes on,' George consoles them from the lofty perch of his seventeen years, out ahead, first in line, setting the pace.

'Sylvia leaves us with an image of such extraordinary loveliness, nobleness, and charm – ever unforgettable and touching,' writes Henry James, the great critic of death and funerals, to Emma du Maurier upon learning of her daughter's death.

Barrie decides that Michael, Nico and Mary Hodgson will stay at Ashton Farm for the three weeks of vacation that remain. George, Jack, Peter and Barrie will accompany Sylvia's body back to London. It's a five-hour trip. Barrie sits with his back to the locomotive. He always does. Or truthfully, Keiko Kai, I'm the one who does. And Barrie gets it from me, or copies me, or I make him imitate me. There's a barely veiled declaration of principles and aesthetics in this innocent habit: Barrie would rather watch the countryside he's leaving behind than the countryside that stretches out before him. The past rather than the future. An elusive yesterday that seems increasingly happy and perfect when compared to the blind sorrows still to come. My reasons are probably different: I turn my back on the future because the future doesn't include me any more; I look towards the past because my past keeps getting bigger. After so many years kept captive in a small box, my past grows and won't stop growing. Now, after being starved for so long, it escapes its prison, and, loose and slippery like Peter Pan, threatens to devour everything and fulfils the threat. The train stops at every station, and at each one – to the irritation of irritable Jack – Barrie gets out, walks to the baggage car that's carrying Sylvia's coffin – draped in purple silk – and takes his hat off and bows his head. 'As if he were a bloody sentry,' Jack mocks.

The funeral is small – as the dead woman would have wanted it – and takes place in the church in the parish of Hampstead.

Sylvia Jocelyn de Busson du Maurier, widow of Arthur Llewelyn Davies, mother of George, Jack, Peter, Michael and Nicholas Llewelyn Davies, died on 26 August 1910 at the age of forty-three.

Her death and her husband's death once again set in motion the machine that makes the dead. It's a powerful, hungry machine. The dead are needed to manufacture ghosts.

Barrie can feel his new ghosts fluttering, like a curtain in the window, like flags in a parade in the afternoon breeze.

Barrie smiles at them and waves to them.

Since the beginning, since his brother David's death, Barrie's always known: until you have ghosts you can't consider yourself a truly rich man.

If you have ghosts, you have everything.

The Ghost

Life is brief, death is lasting.

And death shouldn't be confused with that last sterile second of our existences, the instant when the lights are turned off and the doors are closed and the keys are returned to our pockets.

Death is fertile.

Sow the dead and you'll harvest ghosts.

The living are the field where the dead are sown. We're the rich soil waiting patiently for the rain of tears, for the time to gather the fruits, to pull up the ripe ghosts by their branches and stalks, ghosts that aren't the dead come back to life but the living dead.

So the dead aren't with us, but neither have they left us. The power of the memory of them settles in our present and the dead appear before us at the least expected moments. Ghosts that have nothing to do with those moaning voids covered by sheets, but that do look something like furniture covered with other sheets. Furniture that makes us realize that the fact that no one has sat in that chair for years doesn't necessarily mean that no one will sit in it again one of these days. The same is true of the dead: we cover them up until – suddenly and almost without warning – we use them, we remember them. The electricity of that memory is the food with which ghosts are nourished.

And maybe ghosts lose all memory of what they were in the very instant they're born. And maybe that's why they return: not to frighten us, but to remember who they were by absorbing the energy generated by our fear, the fear of those of us who recognize them and honour their memory. They return so they won't be forgotten, to prevent their second and definitive death, the death that's longer than any life.

Sylvia's death makes Barrie think of ghosts. Every night. About ghosts of mothers who return in search of their children; about ghosts different from those typical Victorian ghosts of English literature, those immaterial materialist spectres always concerned about the fate of bloody inheritances.

Barrie had already written about this years ago, in *The Little White Bird*, when Captain W— says:

> *Life and death, the child and the mother, are ever meeting as the one draws into the harbour and the other sets sail . . . The only ghosts, I believe, who creep into this world, are dead young mothers, returned to see how their children fare. There is no other inducement great enough to bring the departed back . . . What is saddest about ghosts is that they may not know their child. They expect him to be just as he was when they left him, and they are easily bewildered, and search for him from room to room to room, and hate the unknown boy he has become. Poor, passionate souls, they may even do him an injury. These are the ghosts that go wailing about old houses, and foolish wild stories are invented to explain what is all so pathetic and simple . . . All our notions about ghosts are wrong. It is nothing so petty as lost wills or deeds of violence that brings them back, and we are not nearly so afraid of them as they are of us.*

Now he notes:

> *No one should return, no matter how much they're loved.*

Barrie is thinking about a new play starring a Mother Ghost, and as he takes notes (he doesn't dare work on it yet, it doesn't seem appropriate at this time of sadness and mourning), he finds Sylvia's will. They've been looking for it for months, and at last it appears like a ghost in the drawer of a piece of ghost furniture – furniture covered with a sheet – at 23 Campden Hill Square.

Barrie reads it and – when he copies it to send it to Emma du Maurier, Sylvia's mother – he makes a mistake. Or not. A psychoanalyst, I suppose, would call it a Freudian slip; but I prefer to think of it as something inevitable, something that helps the story along. And that Barrie, as he transcribes the original, starts with his right hand and ends with his left.

Accustomed for years to revising manuscripts, to adding new sentences to *Peter Pan*, Barrie alters Sylvia Llewelyn Davies's will. I like to think he does it for love of the boys and also for love of art and love of a life that imitates art – and could anything be more gratifying for an artist than seeing how the latitudes of others' reality suddenly adjust to fit the longitudes of his own work?

So where in Sylvia's original it reads 'What I would like would be if Jenny would come to Mary, and that the two together would be looking after the boys and the house . . . It would be so nice for Mary' (Jenny is Mary Hodgson's sister), in Barrie's copy 'Jenny' becomes 'Jimmy'. Yes, it's hard to believe Sylvia could think the constant presence of 'Jimmy' at Campden Hill Square would be 'so nice' for Mary. In any case – even if Sylvia hadn't expressed her last wishes – it's almost certain that the result of the negotiations would've been the same, regardless of any 'Jenny' or 'Jimmy'. Sylvia had made it clear that she didn't want the brothers to be separated and sent to different relatives; and who in the Du Maurier family could take responsibility for the needs and expenses of five children? The 'Jimmy' in place of 'Jenny' came as a relief to everyone, and a September 1910 letter from Emma du Maurier to Henry James reads: 'I and Arthur's brother Llewelyn Crompton Davies & Barrie will be the children's guardians, & it's absolutely certain that it will be Barrie who lives with them. I am too old to be of any use to them. Barrie is unattached just now & his one wish is to care for them in the way Sylvia would have wished. His devotion to Arthur during his illness & his friendship & affection ever since to all the family makes us all feel that right & reason are on his side.'

Everyone seems happy with the agreement: Mary Hodgson caring for the boys and Barrie staying with them. As far as George is concerned, Barrie is his best friend. Jack, despite some resentment, prefers to keep living at Campden Hill Square rather than being sent to one of his uncles or aunts. Peter doesn't know whether he trusts Barrie or not; but he admires George and George admires Barrie and in the end that makes up his mind for him. As far as Michael is concerned, Barrie is a god who, in his turn, considers Michael a god. And Nico is too little, has been the least affected by the death of his parents, and doesn't think of Barrie as a father or a brother but as 'the person I like best of everyone who comes to visit me.'

Barrie loves all of them equally and now there will be no more visits. Now Barrie will always be there, leaving Adelphi Terrace House for Campden Hill, opening the door with his own key; with them for ever and ever.

Now, at last, Barrie is the master of his lost boys.

Now Barrie has inherited them.

And Marcus Merlin inherited me.

I was Marcus Merlin's lost boy.

And now Marcus Merlin is lost and he'll never be able to find the way back home, to Neverland.

Marcus Merlin collapsed suddenly, without warning, his illness all end and no beginning, like one of those one-act plays Barrie writes effortlessly in a weekend.

Marcus Merlin is connected to machines that make strange noises that surely mean nothing, that have no reason for existing.

Marcus Merlin watches me through half-closed eyes, as if he were very far away, and with a smile mingling equal parts love and pain.

With difficulty, Marcus Merlin lifts a hand. A gesture that might equally be a blessing or a magic trick, a simple trick but no less impressive for that.

Marcus Merlin speaks in a surprisingly powerful voice.

Says Marcus Merlin: 'A last question, boy . . . Your answer

will help me explain something you never knew and that might not do you any good to know. It'll help you kill me . . . more willingly . . . Maybe you'll actually like it; because it will bring you even closer to those Dickens novels which – sorry – have always seemed hugely overrated to me: unnecessarily long, swarming with dozens of picturesque characters who're impossible to follow, all of them alike and equally dull . . . And all those absurd coincidences. The only thing that justifies Dickens's immortality, if you ask me, is that great accomplishment of his: 'Lonely as an oyster.' Incomparable. Perfect. But let's not stray from the Dickensian matter that concerns us, and from this question: what were your mother's last words?'

I reply that my mother died singing. 'You're not mine . . . You're not mine,' she sang. It was the chorus of her song, her one more or less great hit. I don't remember how high it rose in the charts, but I do remember that it was used as part of the soundtrack of one of those go-go films back then, and in a recent commercial. 'You're Not Mine (I'm Not Yours)', it was called; the song that Bob Dylan might or might not have written for her. 'You aren't mine, you aren't mine,' she – my mother – died singing, biting me, beside the suicide pool at Neverland in the starlight.

Marcus Merlin tries to laugh. A strange laugh that only reflects the state – the bad state – of things inside his body. A laugh whose parts have gotten mixed up and are now very difficult to sort out again. A laugh that ends in a catalogue of coughs that, with great effort and difficulty, finally turn into words.

Says Marcus Merlin: 'Your mother wasn't singing . . . What your mother was trying to tell you was that you weren't hers. You weren't her son. You weren't your father's son either. You were a gift. Mine. Your parents thought they couldn't have children. Then one night I stole you. Well . . . it wasn't *exactly* stealing. It was at Heathrow. There was no one in sight. I don't think there were any planes left to land or take off. You know, the time of night when airports close, like a flower . . . ugh, the morphine makes me so disgustingly sappy . . . Back to our story . . . You were a mystery. And an opportunity. You had fallen out of your carriage. There I was and there you were. The wheels still turning in the air; you were crying as if you would never stop manufacturing tears. Your parents, your real parents . . . were nowhere to be seen. Maybe they'd abandoned you, who knows. It struck them as more convenient to leave you in an airport than at the door of an orphanage, thinking that plane travellers would take better care of you than those who might come to you by car or train. I didn't read the paper or watch the news in those days. I preferred not to know anything. Alexandra and Sebastian didn't ask me any questions. They just accepted you the way the gods accept offerings from their worshippers. They received you the way they received all the other things I'd gotten for them once upon a time, whether they asked me for them or not: a little taken aback, but ultimately grateful, and I loved your parents very much, seriously. Your parents were two angels . . . Fallen angels, but angels nevertheless. A little later, as often happens when couples adopt a child, your mother got pregnant with Baco. And then Baco died. And they died. And I inherited you, as your parents had stipulated. I like that about the rich: they make their first wills at the age of five, don't they? So they can practise the fine art of bestowing rewards and punishments and vengeance. In any case, you came back to me in the end. And I don't think we had such a bad time, after all. It had its moments, it was fun . . . And now, please, I'm asking you to kill me. It's the least you can do for someone who's given you a whole life. A strange life, true, but better than many normal lives . . . Yes, yes, yes: an interesting life . . . Good night, sweet prince . . . Fade to black, please.'

Marcus Merlin closes his eyes and I cover them with a pillow. And I press hard. It doesn't take much.

There's something I'd like to make perfectly clear: it isn't hatred generated by the revelation of my origins that allows me to kill him. It's love that swells from the truth, and happiness that my invertebrate life should at last finally begin to acquire the outline of a skeleton, something that brings it close to the neatness of a precise ending, to the moral order of good and bad, to the tidy structure that lives used to have in other times.

Are you asking yourself whether I felt like an idiot, Keiko Kai? The answer is no. Why should I be ashamed of my ignorance? Didn't many of the inhabitants of Hiroshima and Nagasaki only realize months later that what had struck their cities was a bomb made by men and not divine wrath in one of its myriad forms? I can imagine their radioactive relief when it was explained to them that they hadn't been cursed by the wisdom of the immortals but simply destroyed by the stupidity of man.

That's how I felt then, Keiko Kai. Happy possessor of a certainty that explained so many things that were unclear. A truth, at last. A truth that – like all truths – is a double-edged sword. One of those truths that cuts through the armour of lies and makes you remember so many things, Keiko Kai.

Then came the past, descending like a storm on the desert of the present. And since then, Keiko Kai – since barely a few hours ago – I remember everything that was and little of what is. *Now* has become something very distant and insubstantial. I only remember a few things about my trip to Hollywood (in particular a phone call and my return flight); and that I came out of Marcus Merlin's room; and that in the hallway I passed several doctors and nurses running in the opposite direction. I remember that I went to the press conference at the studio outside of London where the filming of *Jim Yang: The Movie* was being announced; I remember that you were there, Keiko Kai, and that in the middle of the chaos and the crowds and the flashbulbs, I put you in my car and brought you to Neverland and here we are and I have to hurry: I'm sure they're looking for us, and there's too little time left before night's curtain falls and the lights of dawn come on. There isn't much time left, and there's still plenty to tell. So I warn you, Keiko Kai, that from now on until the end of this story – Barrie's story – I'll make few appearances. The minimum necessary, the unavoidable. A Night in the Life: the minutes become seconds and the seconds no longer exist and – an effect of the pills – it becomes complicated to continue in this format, so literarily Victorian and Edwardian and British and so often criticized as impossible and artificial. You know what I mean, Keiko Kai, or rather you surely don't have the slightest idea, but even so: someone telling absolutely *everything* in a single night in a voice that never changes, that doesn't tire, that doesn't hurry to reach the end. That's not my case. I have no problem admitting artificiality, my metabolism processing artificial dictions. Chemistry as a chronocycle melting in my stomach and then immediately following the almost invisible centrifugal ant trail that goes from the heart to the brain and back to the heart and then the brain again and back to the heart and . . . You know, Keiko Kai: the stimulating and spasmodic effect of certain drugs that increase the speed at which blood and feelings and ideas circulate and make your style change. My voice – everything that lives in my voice – changes. I cite photographs, I look at biographies. Rectangular, more sharply delineated landscapes. Shorter sentences, economy of verbs and adjectives, fewer details, faster, faster yet. The wind in your face. The roar of the wind makes you deaf and mute and almost blind, because the wind makes you close your eyes so they don't fill up with wind. It keeps getting harder and harder to think in the first person; it's so much easier to hide behind the third person, as if it were a pillar to peer around and see without being seen. I look at Barrie. And Barrie looks at me. Barrie's so exacting, Barrie always demands and receives so much. I'm, yes, abducted by Barrie, and the end of the century I traversed becomes the end of the century Barrie traversed. Ancient history. *Barrie, James Matthew,* as if it were an encyclopedia entry, and for a moment, I thought about telling you what's left to tell in sweet tones, a silly voice, diminutives; as if Barrie were a puppet or a marionette or a doll or a children's book character entering the shadow of a forest drawn in dark inks; the way people once spoke and told stories to children: *that* voice. But no. Barrie never talked to his boys like that. So I let myself be invaded and conquered by Barrie, I dissolve myself in his words and acts, and – in the words of Peter Llewelyn Davies – I'm one with the 'deep, strange, complex, and growing love' that Barrie feels for his boys. I merge with the passion that at times makes Barrie wish, as he wrote to Michael, that 'you had been a girl of twenty-one instead of a young man so that I could confide what I've always carried in my heart.' A force that moves worlds. A feeling more central than any thing or living being. Impossible to compete and win, especially when – as in my case – I never learned to play cricket, and yes, perhaps in Barrie's eyes I'm an involuntary anti-Peter Pan: a boy who grew up too soon and too fast.

Which doesn't prevent me – every once in a while, when Barrie's distracted, when nobody's looking – from managing to leave an ephemeral footprint, the slight mark of my teeth in his landscape. But as I've told you, from now on I'll content myself with a minimal presence, with fleeting bursts of myself – aurora borealises, poltergeist-style ectoplasmic gleams – in Barrie's firmament. 'Cameos,' Marcus Merlin would've said, cinematographically. Or *blinks,* I'd say: somewhere I read that when we read a book, we blink approximately eighteen times a minute, per page; and that we almost always unconsciously synchronize our blinks with periods, commas, and the ends of sentences. I claim for myself the inhabitance of those blinks; I claim for myself an intermittent and almost secret existence. Keiko Kai: from now on you'll see me, if you see me at all, in fleeting shadows and almost blending into the backdrops of an era that isn't mine but that I, like Jim Yang, claim as mine so as not to have to think about my own times. Disengaging myself from my past, which establishes itself in my present, and, famished, sits down to eat the little future I have left. I'll appear just often enough so you don't forget that I'm the one telling this story, though it isn't mine; I'm the one who's been possessed by it, and as a result, I exercise some rights over its course and destination.

Keiko Kai, make an effort; look hard and find me:

I'm the wardrobe manager of a libidinous music-hall star (I especially like the odalisque gauziness of the Mata-Hari style outfits); I'm a cameraman, astonished to film four illustrious citizens of the Empire dressed up as cowboys (I don't understand what I'm doing here, nor do I understand what Chesterton and Shaw and Wells are doing here, nor how Barrie's managed to get them to obey him without protest, with the docility of tame beasts); I'm a German soldier who presses the trigger of his rifle in the trenches of Voormezeele (I don't even take off my gas mask to sleep and they call me the Hideous Anteater; there's no way for me to know it, but in different battles, I've already wounded Guillaume Apollinaire and killed Alain-Fournier and Hector Hugh 'Saki' Munro, and it's clear that I've got great aim when it comes to knocking off romanticist soldiers); I'm a comrade of Captain Robert Falcon Scott, who never stops singing and whistling as outside the icy winds of death blow (I whistle 'The Mist-Covered Mountains', my favourite song); I'm a student who laughs when Barrie begins one of his speeches (Barrie, nervous, fiddles with a letter-opener, and I shout at him to be careful not to cut his head off by mistake, and Barrie doesn't understand what I've said but everyone else laughs, and later the dean calls me into his office and tells me that I'm suspended until further notice); I'm a passenger on both the *Lusitania* and the *Titanic* (I survive the first and go down with the second, or maybe it's the other way around; it doesn't matter); I'm a young reporter who gives Barrie the worst of news (no one dares to go and ask him a few terrible questions; I'm the newest on the staff and they send me, of course; but I swear I never would've imagined Barrie had no idea what had happened); I'm one of the butlers interviewed to replace the Inimitable Harry Brown (Barrie rejects me, considering me too young to be a good butler; I'd make a good lost boy but never an inimitable and efficient and admirable servant, thinks Barrie); I'm a friend of Michael Llewelyn Davies (when no one is looking I cut a damp curl from his head and treasure it until the day I die in one of those lockets that open like a pocketwatch); I'm the mentally disturbed spectator at one of Barrie's last triumphs (an open-ended thriller in which it's never clear who's guilty; I leave the theatre in the grips of a cold fever and I decide to become a killer who the police will never catch); I'm a bank employee who exchanges a few pound notes for pennies so that Barrie can take them as an offering to a little princess (later, at home, I'll read a letter in which my wife informs me that she's gone and is never coming back; the next morning I'll steal most of what's in the safe and flee to Moscow, to the Revolution . . .); I'm a doctor who prescribes a heroic drug for a hero near defeat (I also use heroin; I'm also a pursuer of visions; I wanted to be a writer, but my father forced me to follow in his footsteps and my grandfather's footsteps to hospitals and surgeries and battlefields); I'm a Scotch gravedigger in the Kirriemuir cemetery (you can call me Mac) who looks up at the sky and asks himself whether it will rain tonight and answers himself that yes, it will rain, it'll rain until the sun comes up; and he promises himself a cup of hot coffee when he's done covering today's grave, which luckily is a very small grave.

Every morning at breakfast the Llewelyn Davies brothers find new surprises: Barrie won't stop giving them presents, spoiling them, Barrie like a genie without a bottle who makes all their wishes come true.

Newspapers are history's echo. The news has a morbid appeal, and it triggers the excitement we feel whenever reality imitates fiction and suddenly we don't know whether it's we who're reading or whether we're being read by someone else. Stop the presses: the man who never grew up has found his lost boys.

Peter's friends at Eton make fun of him and envy him at the same time. Peter starts to hate his name and Peter Pan, and he'll hate both resignedly and determinedly until the evening when he jumps from the platform of an underground station. Peter says nothing to Barrie, who claims not to be so interested in the theatre and literature any more. It's clear that Barrie is beginning to live a ghost life. A postlife. Nothing is the same after *Peter Pan*: Barrie understands, correctly, that the first part of his existence has been the slow configuration of the ideal conditions to reach the point of the Big Bang, and that now, at the age of fifty-one, and for the years he has left to live, he'll inhabit the many ripples of its powerful expanding wave.

The publication of *Peter and Wendy* makes it even more obvious: the critics aren't very enthusiastic and they scold Barrie for the omnipresence of his narrative voice, which inserts itself into the action as if needing to proclaim its ownership of something that belongs to everyone by now. *Peter Pan* was already a children's classic before it became a children's book. Barrie is disappearing, devoured by its shadow. The same thing happens to those who are imitated and immediately vanquished by their imitator; no one remembers them, preferring to admire the meticulous falsification rather than the unadorned original. Peter Pan seems to have existed forever. Peter Pan is immortal and never grows up, and Barrie is suddenly beginning to show signs of the passage of time. He hasn't lost his eternal childish air, but the deep wrinkles on his face seem to have been etched furiously in a single night.

Barrie is happy, but it's a terrifying happiness, the happiness of someone who knows that he's paying an enormous price to get what he's always wanted. George and Jack and Peter and Michael and Nico live with him, yes, but for that to have happened Arthur and Sylvia had to die, and suddenly the sun over Kensington Gardens doesn't seem as warm; the grass isn't as green. At last, Barrie understands that even if you decide not to grow up, time does grow and expand and drag everyone else along, and very soon his boys will be men.

Barrie's silences when he's with his friends are increasingly long and deep, and anything to do with the outside world irritates him. The hysteria over the *Titanic* tragedy; or the shouts of the women who want the vote, as if voting meant anything; or the affair of the Peter Pan statue, for example.

It thrills me to imagine Peter Pan being transported secretly, in the dark of night; his bearers conspiring to drag him through the streets of London, as once it's said Michelangelo dragged the secret marble statue of his David through the streets of Florence – another young king, another giant-killer – to reveal it to the world in the middle of the morning in another square in another Renaissance. I know, I know, I know, Keiko Kai; I told you this already. The story of Barrie and his statue. A small statue from the adult point of view, but the right size for children: a child's-scale statue, a statue that will always be remembered as bigger than it really is, because it's a statue especially conceived and designed to stir the huge imagination of little ones. A much humbler statue than the magnificent sculptural ensemble of the Albert Memorial at one of the entrances to the park, but more powerful, even so. A statue whose story I've told so many times, that I've told maybe a thousand and one times. The story of a statue that I already wrote for you. But I can't help telling it once more. There's something about the idea – so innocent and childish, but also diabolical and brilliant – of erecting a monument to an imaginary character. Exhibiting its trauma to the world so it'll spread everywhere – and meantime making plain the clumsy fiction of all those statues of kings and admirals and real but false gods – Barrie's public monument to a private divinity draws me back over and over again. To see it from every possible angle. To study it. And yes, the Peter Pan statue – despite its failure to live up to Barrie's ideal

– is one of the few statues that doesn't lie, that doesn't know how to lie.

It's set in place the night of 30 April 1912. Barrie doesn't like it: Sir George Frampton, his sculptor, didn't base it on the photographs Barrie took of Michael, preferring to use another boy as his model; one James W. Shaw, who seems too delicate to Barrie, with none of Peter Pan's energetic savagery. The House of Commons debates whether a writer – important as he might be – should be allowed to grant himself the right to erect a statue of one of his characters wherever he wants, whenever he wants. Does Barrie think Kensington Gardens is part of his property? The parliamentary polemic ceases when someone hints that Edward VII is amused by the idea. Barrie doesn't respond; let them do what they want; let them caricature it in the pages of *Punch*; let them set it in rhyme, as Humbert Wolfe does in a short, playful poem in his book *Kensington Gardens* (in which Peter Pan is linked to the Piper of Hamelin); let them melt it down to make bullets. Whatever suits them, whatever they like.

Barrie only talks to the Llewelyn Davies brothers.

Nico leaves Norland Place and joins Michael at Wilkinson's. George continues to triumph at Eton, and Michael and Nico are at the top of their classes. Barrie decides to reward everyone with a holiday at Amhuinnsuidh Castle, in the Hebrides. Jack can't or doesn't want to go along.

There are long fishing expeditions on which Michael develops the maddening habit of disappearing in the blink of an eye – now you see him, now you don't – and Michael-hunting parties are organized. From Scotland, Barrie writes his annual letter to Sylvia, the dead mother, 'telling her how things were now with her children.' Winter comes, and at the beginning of 1913 there's another death, someone else is dead: Captain Robert Falcon Scott perishes on the immortal ice. Barrie takes the news of his end as a fresh personal blow. Of late he had distanced himself from Scott, but that hadn't prevented him from continuing to admire him, or from helping to collect funds for his expedition; now he organizes a public drive to honour his memory and secure the future of his widow and son. Barrie is even more distressed when he learns that with the last of his strength Scott wrote him a fervent farewell letter: 'I never met a man in my life whom I admired and loved more than you, but I never could show you how much your friendship meant to me, for you had much to give and I nothing,' concluded Scott, in wavering script.

Barrie folds the letter and carries it with him always. In his jacket pocket, over his heart. He won't allow the newspapers to publish it, but at any gathering and without apparent motive, it isn't unusual for him to tap his glass with his knife to request a reverent silence and volunteer to read it aloud to those assembled. Barrie likes to culminate his reading with a reflection in which he likens Scott to Peter Pan: 'His body lost, trapped among the glaciers, forever young while the rest of us grow older every second, as if we're melting before a merciless fire . . . Some day, when we're very old, Scott and his comrades will emerge out of those white immensities as if no time had passed for them.'

Why this sudden obsession of mine with Captain Robert Falcon Scott, who is, after all, no more to me than a showy and status-enhancing footnote at Barrie's small feet? Good question, Keiko Kai. A good question that demands a good answer; and the truth is that I have little if any interest in his hero's life. I am, however, interested in his hero's death. Robert Falcon Scott writing a letter to Barrie in shaky pencil on the pages ripped from his binnacle notebook. A letter that becomes warmer as the cold sinks into Robert Falcon Scott's bones and heart and brain. In toasts and at memorial services, Barrie never reads the whole letter in public. Barrie kept the most personal paragraphs for himself, and therefore no one knew why he and Robert Falcon Scott had become estranged. Someone theorized that Barrie had heard chilly rumours about himself. Calumnies that the famous explorer might have uttered or insinuated to second or third parties who ultimately formed the ice floe of slander. Or maybe not. Maybe Robert Falcon Scott didn't say anything and everything was due to a misunderstanding fostered by those out to spite them. Or possibly everything was the result of the unstable nature of Barrie's enthusiasms, Barrie being one of those bipolar personalities who one day loves you forever and the next day doesn't recognize you when he passes you on the street. In any case, some friendships simply grow cold – bad joke, Keiko Kai. What does matter – what I like to return to again and again – is the end of the *Terra Nova* expedition members. The first to die were Wilson and Bowers. Peerless men of the snow who – as Scott tells it in his letter, I think – died singing the recipes for complicated and expensive and delicious dishes. The last thing Robert Falcon Scott wrote was 'It seems a pity, but I do not think that I can write more', and I ask myself whether there could possibly be better words for bidding farewell to writing. I doubt it. Then Robert Falcon Scott delicately laid out the bodies, wrapping them in their sleeping bags. Afterwards, he sat up against the central tent pole and took off his coat and shirt and waited for the cold eternal sleep and the crying of the petrels to overcome him and lull him like the most slumberous of lullabies. A sleep of open eyes and sad smile. And that was how they were found eight months later. And I can't help thinking about my own cold, and my own private, unexplored Antarctica: my Antarctica at thirty years below zero. A truth frozen in time is so much more dangerous than a blazing lie. Like the frozen, uniform, boring landscape that now, as it begins to melt – hole in the ozone layer, global warming, disintegration of elements – reveals me to myself, showing me to be the most broken of missing links, thawing at last and roaring in pain and surprise like a newborn baby.

It isn't long before Barrie offers to take charge of his godson Peter. Scott's widow, Kathleen, thanks him, but replies that it isn't necessary. Kathleen doesn't want to become a second

Sylvia Llewelyn Davies, devoured by the voracity of the little man who consumes little men.

Nico is now the only permanent resident at Campden Hill Square. Michael is beginning his studies at Macnaghten's House at Eton, but unlike George, he can't stand the place. He cries himself to sleep every night. He misses Mary Hodgson, Barrie and – he's afraid to tell anyone – his mother. During the day he writes sonnets and at night he contrives exquisite nightmares: he wakes up howling like a wolf. Michael's troubles inspire Barrie's story 'Neil and Tintinnabulum', the tale of a boy tormented by his inner demons: 'Terror had been after him since he was a child . . . There are moments in life when a boy can be as lonely as God,' Barrie writes in it.

On 13 June 1913, Barrie is made a baronet. He's Sir James Matthew Barrie from now on. But there's a problem, because the new nobleman was always known to the English public as J. M. Barrie. 'Sir J. M. Barrie' sounds odd. Barrie had refused a knighthood in 1909, but how to resist a baronetcy? He's only sorry – since it's a hereditary title – that none of the Five can assume it when he dies.

Michael and Nico start to call him 'Sir Jazz Band Barrie' or 'Sir Jazz'. Jack, rather maliciously, refers to Barrie as 'the Bart' or 'the Little Baronet'. George doesn't invent any nicknames. George is so very big now; he's turned twenty, and – with taste and savoir faire – begins to frequent the company of ladies of good breeding. He goes to dances with Jack, and at a party thrown by one of their aunts they meet the Mitchell-Innes sisters. The three girls are enthralled by the young men, but it's the oldest, Josephine, who manages to captivate George, and early on he gives her a copy of *The Little White Bird*, maybe as if to explain all the many things he doesn't know how to explain.

The date of the ninth revival of *Peter Pan* is approaching, and the children who acted in the play the previous year are subjected to the most terrible of rituals. The lost boys are lined up before Barrie, who reviews them like a general, proceeding to measure how tall they are one by one. He studies them, staring as if his gaze could bore into the young actors' eyes, and, once inside, size up their souls and the potency of their childish glee and their scarcely concealed wish to remain as they are forever, acting in a play, living and giving themselves up to an awfully big adventure. Some of them are about to receive the worst news of their lives, that suddenly and without warning they've reached the end of their first – and best and unrepeatable – act. If you're over a certain height, you're out, and you're rapidly replaced by a new, smaller actor. Afterwards, Barrie opens his script and announces the new speeches to be added, the lines he's come up with over the course of the year. Michael presides as secretary and creative consultant.

Another of Barrie's end-of-the-year occupations borders on the scandalous: he's insisted on writing a show for Gaby Deslys, French sex symbol and chorus girl famous for her scantily clad performances. It's not just Barrie who's succumbed to her charms, but also his boys, inflamed by the fevers of adolescence. Barrie's boys dream of Gaby Deslys. Barrie dreams of his boys dreaming of Gaby Deslys. That's the crucial difference, the dividing line, the impassable and definitive barrier. For Barrie's boys, despite what Peter Pan thinks, a kiss will never be a thimble and a thimble will never be a kiss. For Barrie's boys, despite what Peter Pan thinks, a kiss will never be a thimble and a thimble will never be a kiss. For Barrie's boys, kisses are like needles: kisses sting your lips until they draw blood. As the news spreads, some think Barrie's gone mad; those who know him best realize that it's just another of his theatre passions, as intense as they are fleeting.

This adoration of Gaby Deslys – for whom the newly minted baronet soon promises to write a whole revue – is simply one of his latest platonic obsessions, another actress for his collection of actresses. Anyway, Barrie is consumed by a new hobby. Barrie has discovered cinematography. It's something miraculous, Barrie explains: the actors in his plays grow older as time and performances go by; film actors, however, are young forever. Barrie buys himself a movie camera. He shoots thousands of feet of celluloid at the slightest excuse. He makes a charity film to be shown at benefits and raise money for the Y.M.C.A., though any cause would serve as well: a hilarious version of *Macbeth* retitled *The Real Thing at Last*. 'Pure action and no blah blah blah', the program announces. And Barrie is fascinated by everything that moves, because now he has the power to trap it with his camera and release it at will and set it moving again, like a glowing fairy, like an electric Tinker Bell, on the walls of his flat at Adelphi Terrace House. For Barrie, film is the closest thing to daydreaming, to glimpsing that other world where time repeats itself over and over again.

Barrie films everything so that nothing will grow up. And I ask myself what Barrie might have thought of the biopic that Hollywood will devote to him at the beginning of the new century and the brand-new millennium, at a time when the self-styled 'dream factory' is committed to compulsively reinventing real lives. Surely he would've been flattered at some lunatic Hollywood producer's decision to choose Johnny Depp – 'one of the sexiest men on the planet', according to the magazines – to embody his spirit and image. Tall at last, handsome at last. The magic of the cinema is so much more potent than the magic of the theatre, he'd think. To me, however, the whole business seemed repugnant and almost blasphemous, and I don't know how or why it was that I made my way into a cinema at Piccadilly Circus and saw *Finding Neverland*.

I remember that it was raining and that every taxi seemed to have disappeared from London as if by magic, and that I sought refuge in a cinema – to pass the time and wait for the rain to pass – and that I had scarcely settled into my seat when I began to feel extremely uncomfortable, on the verge of fury or horror. I'm sure that Barrie – once he'd gotten over the pleasure of seeing Depp answering to his name – would have felt the same way upon watching all those falsehoods and distortions pile up until they formed a tower of absurdities intended to acquire the shape of an innocuous entertainment, supposedly moving to the point of tears. Up on the screen, Nico doesn't exist (there's no need for another child) and Arthur Llewelyn Davies is dead long before Barrie discovers his boys (there's no need for a father to interfere with the saintliness of Kate Winslet, modest and long-suffering widow) and grandmother Du Maurier (Julie Christie! my Julie Christie!) bitterly hates the meddling playwright (it's she who contributes involuntarily to the creation of the pirate and archenemy) and Charles Frohman doesn't believe in the *Peter Pan* project and Sylvia dies after the staging of the work at her house. And much worse, intolerable outrages: Peter never resists Barrie's charms and wasn't the direct inspiration for Peter Pan, and Michael (is that really Michael in the film?) was never hurt when a worker holding the rope of the flying apparatus got distracted. And can someone explain to me whose stupid idea it was to have Barrie reserve twenty-five seats on opening night to be occupied by exaggeratedly clean children from an orphanage near the Duke of York's Theatre? And worst of all: the manipulation of reality for the purposes of the production may be understandable; but this version of Barrie – a tall and handsome version – is so much more opaque and predictible and less interesting than the original. I saw in the credits that the whole misconceived affair was based on *The Man Who Was Peter Pan*, a play by someone called Allan Knee. I'm glad it was the first I'd heard of his existence .

I went running out of the cinema and I ran in the rain and, yes, it seems as if all I ever do is run down streets and through parks and airports, Keiko Kai. But really, I swear: anything, even thunder and lightning, would have been better than remaining there, in that lying darkness. And I couldn't help imagining how horrible it would be when someone, in time, would make a loathsome movie life of me, one of those biopics that are increasingly fashionable, it seems. You, Keiko-Kai, would have a role in it – yes, the mirror-image paradox of a young actor playing another young actor – and I don't remember who it was that Marcus Merlin once told me would be perfect to enact my tragic tale. Anyway, what does it matter; maybe I should have signed a special document prohibiting any tinkering with my life. Does such a thing exist? A legal ban on making one's story into a movie? A clause that prevents Hollywood from transforming the forest of one's life into the garden Hollywood thinks one's life should be? In any case, I doubt that the traffickers in celluloid will be too sorry that they can't prune me and blaze trails through the years and graft on some commemorative fountain. They have more than enough lives; and in the last few years they've been calling up the ghosts of the living dead and the phantasmagoric living: Adolf Hitler, Howard Hughes, Alejandro Magno, Sylvia Plath, Ray Charles, Margaret Thatcher, Johnny Cash, Nora and Lucia Joyce, Alfred Kinsey, Jackson Pollock, Che Guevara, Marcel Proust, Diane Arbus, Bob Dylan (I'm not in it), Walter Winchell, Cole Porter, Osama Bin Laden, Glenn Gould, Virginia Woolf, Stanley Kubrick, John Lennon (I'm not in this one either), Peter Sellers (don't expect to find me here), Brian Epstein (or here), Cassius Clay, Andy Warhol (in the future, will there be mini-biopics for everyone that function as each person's inevitable fifteen minutes of fame?), and that enduring classic, always useful when it comes to testing new special effects: Jesus Christ. And, oh, now I remember that in a B-movie thriller about the deaths of Brian Jones, Jim Morrisey, Janis Joplin, and Jimi Hendrix at the hands of a female serial killer who calls herself Jackie the Groupie there actually is a fleeting mention of my parents – made by a Scotland Yard detective – as other possible victims of the monster.

In all these films – except the last, of course – with the leading roles played by stars who make up what's known as the

'A list', it doesn't matter so much that the actor or actress look like the person they're playing but that they themselves be recognized beneath the almost transparent mask. People don't go to the movies to see Virginia Woolf; they go to see Nicole Kidman. Hence, I read recently, the studios' interest in developing a technology that would bring people like Humphrey Bogart and Marilyn Monroe and James Dean back from the Great Beyond. Loading all the available data – processing all their gestures and utterances contained on film – into the brain of a late-model medium/computer that would turn them into slaves, docile, and, most important of all, cheap. A bit of cash to the actors' descendents or more or less distant relatives to get them to hand over the rights to the likenesses of the dead would complete the miracle: immortal stars, never fading. Next, I suppose, will come the digging up of the DNA of celebrities and its chemical manipulation and then – with the fabrication of real-life ghosts we'll come full circle and there'll be no need to preface any film with the line This is a True Story or Based on Real Events. Hollywood as a haunted house. And so it will be Barrie who plays Barrie in a future life of Barrie. And, of course, he'll be a supremely wretched actor in the role of himself.

Meanwhile and until then, Barrie explores the possibilities of a young medium, a technology that has yet to grow up, an art in its infancy. Barrie has a naughty, childish idea: something he calls the 'Cinema Supper' and that involves inviting one hundred and fifty distinguished friends to the Savoy Theatre for the presentation of a series of innocent routines written by him especially for the occasion. He plans to film their reactions, and then, after the show, take them to dinner at the Savoy Hotel and film them again secretly. Later, he'll mix and match their faces – transposing them into scenes of one of Gaby Deslys's erotic numbers, for example. Barrie bounces around the room as he explains his plans to his comrade and producer. Charles Frohman listens to Barrie's machinations with a certain weary resignation. Charles Frohman smiles reluctantly: business hasn't been very good recently. Barrie's new play – *The Adored One*, which debuted at the Duke of York's Theatre on 4 September 1913, after multiple rewrites – hasn't been as successful as expected, and the *Globe* titled its review 'Baronet Booed'.

Charles Frohman's health has deteriorated, but even so he can't forget that this is the same little man who came to him so many years ago with the idea for a play with actors who fly and children who never grow up. Maybe what he needs to lift his spirits is a new and rejuvenating adventure with Barrie, Charles Frohman tells himself. So the invitations are sent out summoning the chosen ones for the night of 3 July 1914, five days after the assassination of the archduke in Sarajevo. The guests are in the mood to enjoy themselves, but they also wonder whether enjoying themselves is appropriate.

One of the guests at the 'Cinema Supper' is the prime minister, who, upon learning of Barrie's prank, sends an urgent letter from Number 10 Downing Street warning Barrie that he prohibits the use of his likeness in any of the writer's wild schemes.

Barrie won't give up, and he invites G. K. Chesterton (who tells Barrie that 'fairytales are superior to reality not because they assure us that dragons exist but because they promise us that dragons can be conquered'), George Bernard Shaw (who's just had a great success with *Pygmalion*) and H. G. Wells (who gives Barrie an abundantly detailed account of his latest romantic adventures) to Hertfordshire, and makes them dress up as cowboys so he can film them playing with hobbyhorses and toy pistols.

The writers feel uncomfortable at first, but almost at once they seem to lose all inhibitions. Something they hardly know, something called 'fresh air' – a thing they almost never experience, always shut up in the comfortable, cerebral prisons of their studies – intoxicates them now. It inspires them to gallop fast and empty the chambers of their fake guns and suddenly realize that it was this that they didn't remember and yet still missed so much. And yes, unlike Barrie, Chesterton and Shaw and Wells – who suggests that they play Elois versus Morlocks and is booed by his companions – are very different now than they used to be. Their faces and bodies don't look anything like their bodies and faces in the yellowing photographs of their green youth. Once upon a time, in their prehistories, life was as nimble and as light as this, they think. Or maybe what's happening is that it's like *this*, abruptly and without previous drafts, that they're remembering it now. And it's like *this* that they rewrite it, the childhood that Lewis Carroll wanted to recapture almost mathematically as if it were an exact science; the childhood that Barrie refuses to give up or lose, caring nothing for any kind of science. An anarchic kind of childhood that exists in all times simultaneously – remembering the whole of the very brief and recent past, living in the elastic fullness of the present, feeling the enormous and extremely distant future as a place where anything could happen – and is very much like writing a book. A book that, while it's being created, is also taking place in every tense, like childhood – in then and now and maybe – but that doesn't have to be characterized by the adult discipline of order or good sense or coherence. This is how people write; this is why they write: to keep being children, to not grow up. Childhood as a story, a *Once upon a time* . . . And at least for an afternoon, it's a pleasure for Chesterton and Shaw and Wells – in the eyes of whom Barrie suddenly seems much more important and wiser than they ever thought – to relive it without having to worry about the right words or tenses or rhythms or tones or genres, and they aim their pistols and yank the reins of their mounts.

The writers seem to be having a good time – I have a copy of the film, Keiko Kai – but Shaw isn't at all amused when Barrie tells him, rubbing his little hands together, his eyes spinning in their sockets like tops, that he plans to 'screen our little western in public with four actors mimicking us in front of the screen'. Shaw confiscates the film and locks it up. Barrie doesn't understand how someone can have such a poor sense of humour and at the same time be capable of writing such funny plays.

At the end of the month, Barrie takes George, Michael and Nico on holiday to Scotland. Jack – sub-lieutenant in the Royal Navy – is at sea. Peter will join them a few days later, when he returns from a camping trip with his Eton friends. Barrie's rented a house surrounded by plenty of land and has gotten permits to hunt and fish in the Orchy and Kinglass rivers. At Auch Lodge, Argyllshire, they're completely isolated from the rest of the world and they aren't even aware that England has declared war on Germany and that all young men of combat age are asked to report to offer their services to king and country.

Peter and George – now officially engaged to Josephine Mitchell-Innes – ask where they must sign, and sign. Barrie, at fifty-four, feels perfectly useless in a landscape that suddenly seems to overflow with young men in uniform. It's a new war, a war for boys who don't know what war is, and who therefore feel an urgent desire to march in it as if it were one of the synchronized waltzes at a Friday night dance. Barrie was never a good dancer.

The prime minister Herbert Asquith writes to Barrie to ask him to give up his frivolous plans to write a revue for a half-naked foreign actress and suggests – almost commands – that he put pen to paper and produce a work of profound patriotic content to inspire the men and women of England. Thomas Hardy and H. G. Wells have already committed themselves, Asquith tells him. Barrie accepts the assignment, but he wants to think it over a little. Meanwhile, it occurs to him to travel to the United States to 'prick the American conscience'.

Barrie sets sail without much further thought, travelling in strict incognito on the *Lusitania*. When he disembarks in New York, the consul general is waiting for him on the dock, with a letter from the British ambassador in Washington forbidding him to make any kind of public political display. It's feared that Barrie's strange ideas might disturb American neutrality and offend the British crown. Barrie doesn't really understand what the letter means, but he obeys. It's been seventeen years since he visited New York and he takes advantage of the trip to see old friends, go to plays, and watch films 'because in them I can see cowboys, and I always wanted to be a cowboy'.

Reporters besiege him, and Barrie entrenches himself in his room at the Plaza Hotel. Brown, his inimitable butler, receives them and distracts them as Barrie escapes down the back stairs. If asked, Brown answers questions in his master's name. He's authorized to do so, he says.

Barrie returns to London on 22 October 1914. Peter and George are already with their regiments, in training, and waiting for the orders that will send them as reinforcements to the frontlines along the Marne and the Aisne, where numerous losses have been suffered.

Barrie writes in his notebook:

> –The Last Cricket Match. *One or two days before war declared – boys gaily playing cricket at Auch, seen from my window. I know they're to suffer – I see them dropping out one by one, fewer and fewer.*

Barrie disbands the Allahakbarries – it isn't right for adults to play while boys are dying, he thinks – and arms himself with the patience to spend his days completing the patriotic commission. It isn't a pleasant assignment. Work isn't amusing, and being required to write a play about the war isn't the same as playing toy soldiers.

Barrie titles the play *Der Tag* and writes it as a dialogue between the German Emperor and the Spirit of Culture. The audience – seeking stronger emotions and simpler messages – finds the whole thing too complex and dark and allegorical. *Peter Pan* has better luck – not that it needs it – in its tenth season, now with Madge Titheradge in the leading role.

In the luckless trenches of France, George discovers that the war is a bad play in which one always plays a supporting role; that it's made up of equal parts terror and boredom with no logical rhythm; that nothing happens, and suddenly everything happens; that victories don't have the epic sweep of medieval sagas but mean winning a few feet of land, conquering a hill, destroying villages that've already been destroyed by the enemy, and getting drunk and shouting out dirty songs about the Kaiser.

George rereads *The Little White Bird* and writes to Barrie that 'the fear of death doesn't enter so much as I expected into this show'. I imagine George reading *The Little White Bird* once again amid shouts and explosions, as immersed in the silence of its pages as if he were trying to decipher the Rosetta Stone, the secret language of his own existence. But he can't. It's impossible. The problem is that George can't read the book in his mind's secret voice – the same voice in which he'd read any other book; instead, he reads it in Barrie's voice and cadences and accent. That's the problem with knowing the writer of a book that we know very well: the book will never be ours, no matter how much of it is about us; it'll always belong to them, to their voice, to the owner of our stories. Away at war, George is now a character lost in a novel without an author. George misses the feeling that someone is writing his story and protecting him and keeping him from harm. Away at war, George grows up. Barrie sends him tins from Fortnum & Mason (fruit preserved in syrup imported from the farthest corners of the Empire; sweets that take exactly as long to dissolve in your mouth as it takes a battle to be born and grow and die, tins of green tea that can only be opened at five on the dot, thanks to a complex and British bit of clockwork; sweet and bitter marmalades that George passes out to his comrades in arms, who use them to paint their faces like Indians and then go running and shouting out of the trenches to plunge into the Peter Pan-making machine of war, into an awfully big Neverland of fire and mud and fury); he tells him that he's gone with unhappy Michael and always cheerful Nico to see a stage adaptation of

David Copperfield ('Too treacly'); and he tells him that now he's writing *The New Word*, a one-act play about the discomfort of two men who love each other but can't express the love they feel. One of the men is a father; the other's a son who's preparing to go off to the front. At a certain moment in the play, the mother remembers the death of another son at the age of seven, a son who 'would be twenty-one now, but I've never been able to see him as anything but seven'.

Barrie's idea is to use *The New Word* as an opening act for what he's writing for Gaby Deslys. Barrie keeps adding and filming scenes for the music hall show that he promised the French diva. Work as a kind of battle, a calling that brooks no pleas for truce or mercy.

George goes into combat. Again and again. He doesn't know how many times. The war has its own time, very different from peace time. George thinks that he'd rather die than be crippled or seriously wounded so that tetanus gets into his blood and – rumour has it – finishes him off slowly and painfully, the infection rising from his feet to his eyes and killing him in the end. They say that tetanus makes your heels almost touch your head and that you die with your body curved and tense as a bow without an arrow and that they bury you in a round coffin. That's what they say, among many other things. George walks through the ruins seeing dead bodies lying in the strange positions only dead bodies can assume. Death – not tetanus – makes all men contortionists.

George looks at them and compares them to fallen warriors in age-old battles. His letters are tinged with a tragic romanticism in which he describes himself as an ancient emperor roaming a devastated world, suddenly moved by the sight of an unscathed altar of a church that no longer exists. But it isn't long before the style of George's letters changes, and he writes 'I've seen the head blown off one of my friends in the trenches.' There's no possibility of poetry in that. Each letter is less romantic than the last.

Barrie tries to entertain him by passing on the gossip of the great city and news of his brothers, but immediately the war invades his letters too. Barrie writes to George to tell him that his uncle, the lieutenant colonel Guy du Maurier – a professional soldier, a sensitive man whose hair turned completely grey after seeing a friend die in the Boer War – has fallen on the battlefield. It's the last letter George Llewelyn Davies will receive, and in it, at the end, Barrie writes: 'It's terrible what you tell me about the man who died beside you; but don't be afraid to write me these things. It's at night when I'm most afraid and I imagine the worst in painfully real detail. I've lost all trace of the notion I once had that war could be the birthplace of glory. Now it just seems to me something unspeakably monstrous. With love, J.M.B.'

George Llewelyn Davies dies at some moment early in the morning of 15 March 1915. His batallion is trying to drive the Germans from St Eloi. George is resting with some friends and says that if he falls in combat, he'd liked to be buried in the place he fought for the last time, beside his trench. He hasn't finished saying it when a bullet pierces his helmet. He dies instantly. His colonel doesn't heed his request – suddenly elevated to last wish – and his comrades dig a grave alongside the road, on the outskirts of Voormezeele. George is an officer much beloved by his soldiers, and everyone goes to great pains to offer him the best they have. They decorate the improvised burial spot with violets and bottles of whisky. I don't know the names of the soldiers in the squad commanded by George Llewelyn Davies, so I've given them names that I do know and that I now recite from memory: Lionel Bentley, D. Bradley, Raymond Brown, Jack Brymer, Alan Civil, Alan Dalziel, Henry Datyner, Bernard Davis, Gwynne Edwards, N. Fawcett, Tristan Fry, Francisco Gabarro, Hans Geiger, Erich Grunberg, Jurgen Hess, Harold Jackson, Granville Jones, Roger Lord, Cyril McArthur, David McCallum, David Mason, John Marston, John Meek, Bill Monro, Monty Montgomery, Michael Moore, T. Moore, Alex Nifosi, Gordon

Pearce, Raymond Premru, David Sandeman, Neil Sanders, Sidney Sax, Clifford Seville, Ernest Scott, Basil Tschaikov, John Underwood, Dennis Vigay, Alfred Waters, Donald Weekes. English names of many nationalities, names impossible then but always appropriate, names that come from the future: the secret names of the lonely hearted musicians lost in the clamour of the crazy orchestra that George Martin assembled for the recording of 'A Day in the Life'.

Keiko Kai: I would've liked to be there, to be one of those lost soldiers honouring the fallen body of their beloved leader with their tears, paying their respects to a Peter Pan annihilated by the fury of a Captain Kaiser.

The next morning, Mary Hodgson hears someone knock wildly on the door of 23 Campden Hill Square. When she opens it she finds a frenzied Barrie – wailing like a banshee, according to Nico – repeating over and over again: 'Ah-h-h! They'll all go, Mary. Jack, Peter, Michael, even little Nico. This dreadful war will get them all, one after the other, until there's not a single one left!'

The king and the queen send a telegram of condolences; and by the weekend the four surviving brothers gather at Campden Hill Square. Jack and Peter are in uniform and they weep silently. This seems odd to Nico: the possibility of crying without making any sound at all. Maybe it's a strange talent that you only acquire when you dress up as a soldier, he thinks. In a trembling voice, Barrie reads them a last letter from George that's just arrived: 'Dear Uncle Jim: I have just got your letter about Uncle Guy. In it, you say that his death hasn't made you think any more than usual about the danger I'm in. But I know it has. Do try not to let it. I assure you I take every care of myself that can be decently taken. And if I am going to stop a bullet, why should it be with a vital place? . . . Dear Uncle Jim, you must carry on with your job of keeping up your courage. I will write every time I come out of action. We go up to the trenches in a few days again. Yours affec., George.'

When he's done reading, and before he folds the letter and puts it away, Barrie makes a note under George's signature, as precise as if he's dating a historic object: 'This is his last letter and was written some hours before he died. I heard the news of his death before receiving it and reading it.'

Peter will write in his *Morgue*: 'This much is certain, that when George died, some essential virtue went out of us as a family. The combination of George, who as eldest brother exercised a sort of constitutional, tacitly accepted authority over us and who was of our blood, with the infinitely generous, fancifully solicitous, hopelessly unauthoritative Barrie, was a good one and would have kept us together as a unit of some worth; as it was, circumstances were too much for Barrie, and very soon we became individuals with little of the invaluable, cohesive strength of the united family.'

A week after George's death – flowers and sympathy cards are still arriving in the mail – the revue Barrie wrote for Gaby Deslys opens at the Duke of York's Theatre. *Rosy Rapture, or The Pride of the Beauty Chorus* is a complete failure. The idea of raising the curtain with *The New Word* as an introductory piece produces the opposite effect desired among the fathers and mothers in the audience. No one wants to go to the theatre to be entertained and then be assaulted without warning by the drama of a son marching off to war. And the appearance of Gaby Deslys – her dresses spun of next to nothing and her famous 'slightly wicked smile' – is spoiled by the elaborate speeches that Barrie has written for her, uttered in very imperfect English. No one laughs; everyone groans. Nico, nevertheless, says 'it's the best thing Uncle Jim's ever done'.

Barrie – who disappeared from the final, crucial rehearsals of the show because of George's death – returns to propose cuts, rewrites, new characters. Barrie sends a telegram to Charles Frohman and demands that he come sooner than he'd planned. He needs him by his side to save what can be saved from the shipwreck of *Rosy Rapture*.

Charles Frohman – as usual – obeys him.

And he's shipwrecked.

Charles Frohman sets sail on 1 May 1915 on the *Lusitania*, despite the dangers of the Atlantic crossing in those days. He shuts himself up in his stateroom and only comes out for dinner. His knee won't leave him in peace and the damp sea air doesn't help much. On 7 May, as the Irish coast comes into sight, a German submarine – 'to the eternal discredit of the human race', as an English newspaper will declare – fires two torpedoes. The *Lusitania* sinks in scarcely twenty minutes. There's no time to launch all the lifeboats, and according to a surviving witness, Charles Frohman gives up his spot and makes his goodbyes, saying: 'Why fear death? It is the greatest adventure in life.' Charles Frohman surrenders to death without the slightest resistance; with suspicious tranquillity, in my opinion. It's as if the theatre impresario were exploiting the epic advantages of the catastrophe to smuggle in a suicidal tourist as stowaway, commiting the perfect suicide; no one can reproach him for it because there's no bullet or rope or poison or final note explaining the inexplicable and asking that no one and nothing be blamed. Maybe, I theorize, Charles Frohman likes the idea of disappearing from his life's performance; from an entertainment produced by him but that has long since stopped being his. Maybe he's tempted by no longer feeling obliged to produce Barrie's follies, and at last being released from acting as his butler-financier. Maybe, Charles Frohman muses – as he watches, smiling, brandy in hand, how the passengers struggle for a place in the boats, for a lifejacket – paradise will be the place where his greatest, most secret wish will at last be granted: to be a matinee idol, to fight a duel on stage, to kiss damsels who are obliged to kiss him because it's in the script. And he'll be applauded. And he'll bow to the audience. Or maybe Charles Frohman imagines that hell will be a constant dress rehearsal, the last and endless day before opening night. None of this matters too much now, as the *Lusitania* sinks like the stage of the Duke of

York's Theatre just before the first performance of *Peter Pan*.

Charles Frohman is one of the one thousand two hundred and twenty-four victims of the catastrophe. His body is recovered from the water the next day. Religious services are held at the biggest synagogue in New York and at St Martin-in-the-Fields in London. Charles Frohman had once remarked that he'd like his epitaph to be 'Charles Frohman: He Gave Peter Pan to the World', and that's how everyone remembers him, as the man who made possible the birth of an immortal creature; as Barrie's faithful theatre blood brother. Someone jokes affectionately: 'If Barrie had asked him to produce a dramatization of the telephone book, Charles Frohman would simply have responded, "Perfect. Who shall we have in the cast?"'

Barrie is sad, but he isn't shattered by the disappearance of – according to Peter – 'the only Non-Llewelyn Davies whom he knew how to love'. Barrie has been shattered for some time. One blow after another to his small body. The abruptly aged face, like the faces of those children with that sickness that turns them into prematurely old men at full speed, their cells dying ahead of time. Barrie's skull, which seems to rise from the depths and now strains against the skin, as if asking to be let out, shouting that it's tired of being in there.

Barrie – just as with the death of Captain Robert Falcon Scott – can't help feeling an almost pathological pride in the relationship between the deaths of the two great men and the even greater figure of Peter Pan. Barrie insists that the survivor *must* have misheard Charles Frohman's last words. Charles Frohman's last words – he's certain – were surely the same ones Peter Pan speaks on Marooners' Rock as the tide rises: 'To die will be an awfully big adventure!'

Living isn't much of an adventure; but Barrie lives: he gives money for a home for war orphans and returns to Scotland for a holiday with Nico and Michael, who he descibes in a letter as 'dark and dour and impenetrable'.

Michael is still suffering at Eton, but – in the fall of 1915 – he's managed to invent a mask of false happiness for himself. To his fellow students he's 'a romantic with a powerful imagination' and 'a cat who always walks alone'. Several of his acquaintances remember him as 'a profound influence'; more than one of them confesses in secret to his diary that he's fallen in love with him in the way English boys at the best schools fall in love: out of admiration, upon discovering that there's someone who isn't like anyone else, someone whom they'd so much like to be like. The nightmares of war, the cities empty of men, the sudden appearance of maimed soldiers on the streets, feed this virile, dramatic passion, the immediate effect of which is the disappearance of thousands of potential fathers and the consequent absence of millions of children; millions of children who will never be conceived or born or reach the exact age at which they'll read *Peter Pan* for the first time, or have it read to them.

Barrie has decided to eliminate the mermaid lagoon and Marooners' Rock from this Christmas's *Peter Pan*: to save on production costs and because the line 'To die will be an awfully big adventure!' seems inappropriate at a time like this, when dying isn't an adventure but simply a part of everyday routine.

Barrie's working on a new play – *A Kiss for Cinderella* – and he records in his notebook nightmares in which he feels a pair of cold hands groping for him under the sheets; when he turns on the light, all he can find is the solidity of his own fear. They're terrible dreams, which he decides to use for a one-act play: *The Fight for Mr Lapraik*, or, better, *The House of Fear*.

Ghosts again. Barrie thinks more and more about ghosts. The ghost of a husband's youth coming back to haunt his elderly wife. The man hasn't died – he's an old man too – but his past is powerful enough to take the form of a ghost. A Jamesian variation on a Stevensonian idea. Barrie's style isn't defined by his writing so much as by his plots, by his obsessive insistence on certain subjects. Maybe now that I think about it, Keiko Kai, a writer's style is more the ghost of his deficiences than the reality of his strengths. Let's see if I can explain: writers end up resigning themselves to doing what they know how to do, leaving by the wayside the things they'll never do well. In the end, what everyone perceives as success is really the reclaimed soil of failure; soil, if the writer's lucky, that's gradually ennobled and purified and perfected. It's what a writer ends up with when he really wanted to do something else, something that in time solidifies into the only thing he can do well, into what he does better than anyone else. A whole phantom oeuvre is left aside, of course. All those books the writer might have wanted to write but couldn't. Thus the writer's style and his work are like antimatter, and maybe – who knows? – in another dimension, on the other side of a black hole, there's a James Matthew Barrie or a Peter Hook writing perfect, realist love stories for adults when they really wanted to write Peter Pan or Jim Yang. Greetings to them from here. Greetings to their ghosts.

Could Barrie ever have attended a séance? There's no record of it, but I like to imagine that he did; that some friend – maybe the credulous Conan Doyle – invites him to participate in an experiment one night, and that there are so many dead voices clamouring to talk to Barrie that it's impossible to understand any part of a noise that's like the sound the audience makes in a theatre minutes before the curtain goes up. Barrie can't bear sitting around those tables in the dark for very long. Barrie gets up and leaves when the session and the trance have hardly begun. None of this amuses him. Barrie doesn't believe in other dimensions or in life after death. And Conan Doyle's childish enthusiasm makes him nervous, too. Conan Doyle believes in the possibility of communicating with the dead because his son died in the war, because he needs to talk to his son and be talked to. Conan Doyle wants to believe, and believes in anything: in ghosts, in fairies. Conan Doyle has turned his suffering into a hobby. Barrie writes about fairies and ghosts, and maybe because of that –

because he's invented them, because he knows how to create them – he realizes that their existence is impossible. And so Barrie hasn't been able to transform the pain of George's death into anything that isn't greater pain. A pain that grows. A real pain that doesn't include any other living being.

Nico leaves Wilkinson's in September 1916 and – to Michael's delight – arrives at Eton, where they'll share a room. Nico and his perpetual smile soon become – according to his tutors – the 'heart and soul of Eton'.

Peter turns nineteen in the worst possible place: on the bloody battlefield of the Somme; and he comes home on leave suffering from shell shock, the concussive neurosis of soldiers. Peter brings back souvenirs from the front that he won't be able to stop seeing over and over again for the rest of his life. Peter has lost his parents, the brother he loved most, and now his own youth among bodies destroyed by shrapnel and lungs rotted by mustard gas.

Mary Hodgson looks after him and drags him from his nightmares as if they're quicksand. It isn't easy. Peter's nightmares – unlike Barrie's – are waking nightmares. Open-eyed nightmares. His nightmares are in colour, most notably a powerful array of reds. Peter's seen things that no one's seen, not even poor George. There were moments when – in the madness of the battlefield, when everyone seemed to be shooting at everyone else, when the mortar fire raised waves of mud in which entire squadrons disappeared – Peter would swear to have seen strange things in the merciless light of the flares: an angel floating over the trenches, a patrol of Roman legionnaires who'd lost their way home, a boy on a flying bicycle. And the screams. Screams that sometimes sound like laughter. Screams that resemble nothing else, and that seem not to emerge from the throat but from the whole body, from all your orifices and the orifices others make in you. And no one knows what a cry is until they've heard those cries, he thinks. Peter wakes up screaming at the sheer surprise of screaming and hearing his own scream. Peter wakes up each morning astonished that he's able to wake up each morning.

That Christmas of 1917, Barrie and the Llewelyn Davies brothers gather in the flat at Adelphi Terrace House. Nico goes party-hopping. Michael reads and edits Barrie's new manuscripts, Peter speaks little but seems happier, Jack reconts his adventures on the North Sea and informs them that he's fallen in love with Geraldine Gibb, the daughter of a Scotch banker he met when the crew of his ship, the *Octavia*, received special leave to go into Edinburgh. Jack has gotten engaged without consulting Barrie, and Barrie – as his guardian – tells him that they'll have to wait a year to marry. Jack hates Barrie a little more than he already did, and now he has a clear and precise reason to stop feeling guilty about hating him.

Barrie tells them that he's writing a new play. It will be called *The Old Lady Shows Her Medals*. The characters are three old women who talk about the war over tea. One of them has invented a son and reads her friends the made-up letters that he sends her from the battlefield.

Barrie tells them that his ex-wife Mary's marriage to Gilbert Cannan is in trouble. Gilbert Cannan keeps romancing other women and – according to reliable sources – he seems to be going mad and is in and out of mental institutions. Mary's never had children; she writes books about dogs and gardens; she's at her wits' end. Barrie has decided to help her, to offer to do anything he can to relieve her suffering. Barrie never spoke ill of Mary. Barrie always knew who was really responsible for the divorce. Barrie knows that the reason he never rose to the circumstances was because the circumstances were too lofty for him. 'She was perfection,' he tells the Llewelyn Davies brothers. Mary, however, misinterprets Barrie's offer. Mary thinks that Barrie wants to try again. Barrie explains that he doesn't believe in second chances – he's writing *Dear Brutus*, a play about the inevitability of repeating old mistakes – and all he does is pay her a yearly allowance and have tea with her just once every twelve months.

Barrie tells them that he plans to move into the top-floor flat in Adelphi Terrace House: more space, a better view (four huge windows from which he'll spend hours watching the city and the seven bridges that cross the Thames; among them Charing Cross Bridge, the one he likes least; the one the trains carrying troops cross on their way to France) and a bigger fireplace (big enough so that Barrie can clean it without having to stoop, since he's so short) beside which to place his sofa, famous for being the most uncomfortable in all of London.

Barrie tells them that he's managed to get the necessary permission to visit George's grave, across the front line, as well as the necessary instructions to find it among so many other graves. Barrie invites Thomas Hardy to travel with him, but Hardy prefers to stay home: 'I have come to the conclusion that old men cannot be young men,' Hardy replies in a letter.

Barrie doesn't tell them about his trip. Barrie arrives at Voormezeele accompanied by a military escort, finds the spot, stays for a few minutes, and then starts back home. There are zeppelins in the sky and fire on the earth, which continually shudders; the air seems something almost tangible, something harsh and full of prickles, something that's hard to force into the lungs, something that refuses to propel the heart and make it march at the redoubled pace set by its sad beats.

Peter returns to the Somme, Michael and Nico return to Eton; Jack sets sail again, but first he invites his brothers and Barrie to Edinburgh to meet his fiancée. They dine at the North British Hotel, near the train station, and they return that same night to London. Barrie doesn't say a word. Geraldine is immediately accepted by the brothers. Barrie admits that his first impression is 'very favourable', and the obligatory year the couple must wait to be married is soon revoked; Jack and Geraldine are married in St Mary's Cathedral in Edinburgh at the beginning of September.

Dear Brutus opens on 17 October 1917, at Wyndham's Theatre and the reviews are the best Barrie's had in a long time, too long. It's a shame Charles Frohman can't be there to enjoy them. Gerald du Maurier directs and plays the leading role in what everyone considers the pinnacle of his acting career. His character, Will Dearth, is an artist who wants a second chance at life and – with the melancholy cheer of Shakespeare's comedies – he's given it. And Barrie – fifty-seven years old, twenty-six of those years spent writing for the theatre – is in vogue again.

Geraldine – 'Gerrie' from now on – moves to Barrie's flat in London when Jack is transferred to Portsmouth. Barrie alternates between extreme loquacity and hermetic silence, and sometimes discusses matters hardly appropriate for conversation with a recently married woman whose husband is away at war. One afternoon, Barrie asks the young bride: 'Gerrie, do you know how Guy du Maurier, the boys' uncle, died?' Eager to please, the girl answers, trying to make her voice tremble as little as possible: 'He was shot, wasn't he?' Barrie fixes her with his gaze, halts his constant striding about the flat, and comes almost close enough to touch her, saying: 'Yes, he was shot. But before Guy died he wandered the battlefield for nearly half an hour with his stomach hanging out of his body, shouting for someone please to shoot him and put him out of his misery . . . Oh, I think that's dinner being served now, dear.'

Gerrie also has to cope with the housekeeper's increasingly gothic behaviour. Mary Hodgson never recovered from the unpleasant surprise of Barrie's being named the boys' guardian, and with the years, she's become a magnified version of what she was in the beginning: a glum, bitter woman who appears as if by magic in the darkest corners, and won't deign to speak a word to the young bride. Mary Hodgson suffers in silence the news that Peter – who has decided not to come home for his next leave – is in Epping Forest, having an affair with a woman called Vera Willoughby, someone twice his age. To

Mary Hodgson it's clear this can only be the consequence of the little baronet's noxious influence. Barrie isn't amused by the matter either, and – for the first time in a quarter century – he and Mary Hodgson are in agreement about something.

Mary Hodgson had already offered Barrie her resignation some time ago. She felt that she had failed and that there was no longer any sense continuing to 'keep the sacred promise I made to Mrs Llewelyn Davies', and anyway, 'her babies', or 'her boys', were men now who didn't need her. At the time, Barrie wouldn't accept her offer. He didn't want to have to look for someone to take her place at Campden Hill Square, and he still hadn't moved to the top floor of Adelphi Terrace House. Now that he has enough space, Barrie hopes that Mary Hodgson will repeat her offer to disappear from their lives; but the woman says nothing. She never speaks. It's clear she won't give him the pleasure of leaving. So Barrie declares a war of nerves and readies a plan to drive her away: he names the increasingly distraught Gerrie mistress of 23 Campden Hill.

'Gerrie, Jack will be returning soon and it would be best if you went to live at his house and prepared everything for his arrival,' he tells her. Gerrie, obedient, heads for the domestic battlefront with no training whatsoever. Mary Hodgson hates her and won't acknowledge her existence, much less recognize her as mistress and lady of the house; she refers to her in the third person even if Gerrie's in the same room. The tension reaches dramatic heights; it's a theatrical tension. Each day Barrie comes by to say hello and sits on the sofa watching the show like a delighted spectator, though he's as serious as ever, resisting the urge to smile. Daphne du Maurier – Gerald du Maurier's daughter – visits every so often for the sole pleasure of observing Mary Hodgson from up close. She likes to study Mary; watching her gives her ideas. She imagines fearsome housekeepers guarding the memory of their mistresses long after their death in dark novels of revenge, full of resentment and fury.

One morning Gerrie finds a note from Mary Hodgson on her breakfast tray: 'Either you leave this house or I do,' she reads. Terrified, Gerrie packs a suitcase and calls her husband, and the two of them check into a Knightsbridge hotel. That same night, Gerrie has a miscarriage; she cries for days, and when she returns from the hospital, Mary Hodgson is gone. She's given up. The guilt the housekeeper feels is enormous, and now she'll never want to meet any of the wives of 'her boys' for fear of causing them some harm with the devastating force of her bitter love.

Barrie recognizes her services by giving her five hundred pounds from the deceased Sylvia, to which he adds another five hundred pounds of his own; he disengages himself from the affair by retreating into the writing of *A Well-Remembered Voice*, another one-act play in which a mother can't be consoled for the death of her son in the war. Her husband watches in despair as the woman goes mad with grief and clings to the false hopes she's offered by mediums and swindlers.

One night, the ghost of the son appears, not to the mother but to the father, and asks them to please stop looking for him.

'I wish you'd understand what a little thing death is . . . It's like passing through a veil. Like a mist. We sometimes mix up those who have gone through it with those who haven't. I don't remember being hit, you know. All I remember is the quietness. When you have been killed it suddenly becomes very quiet; quieter even than you have ever known it at home. That's all. I wish I could remember something funny to tell you, father. I'm not boring you, am I?'

Barrie is bored and tired. In photographs taken at the time, he looks even smaller than ever, beside huge windows through which a terrible light pours, sitting in armchairs that look as if they'll devour him, or standing in rooms where he seems part of the decor instead of their legitimate inhabitant.

Barrie hires a private secretary to help him conduct his affairs. Lady Cynthia Asquith makes her entrance. She's the daughter-in-law of the prime minister who Barrie tricked with his Cinema Supper; she's the possessor of what's known as 'a rare beauty'; and – best of all – she has two little boys, who are the same age as George and Jack were when Barrie 'discovered' them for the first time, playing in Kensington Gardens. Her husband is away at war and she needs money, and once again Barrie comes to the rescue. Cynthia has won the reputation of a modern, liberated woman, and Barrie can't resist her charms. It's a pity she isn't an actress, but nevertheless, she behaves as if she were one of the theatre's great leading ladies. Cynthia Asquith is the last important person to enter Barrie's life. There are too many already. They hardly fit on the stage any more. I don't have the time or desire to follow their movements or study their pronouncements any more. Enough, Keiko Kai.

Michael and Nico feel uncomfortable living with a pair of newlyweds – with Jack and Gerrie – and they move in with Barrie at Adelphi Terrace House. Michael receives his enlistment orders and then – as if the play's backdrop is changed – the war ends; it's over; curtain. Michael proposes that he, Barrie, and his brothers take a trip around the world to celebrate. Or that he go to Paris to live with his uncle George du Maurier and study painting. Or that he become a film actor like you, Keiko Kai. Any cliché of youth will do to celebrate the end of the death of so many young people. 'It's time for death to come after old men again,' says Michael and he claps Barrie on the back, who pretends not to understand the allusion. Barrie smiles exactly a quarter of a smile, and informs Michael that first he must go to Oxford and finish his studies. Michael gives in, and Barrie rewards him with an automobile and a cottage that Michael will hardly ever use.

Peter's discharged and doesn't return home. He stays with Vera Willoughby, helping her manage an antiques shop in Soho. Peter takes rare consolation in sorting through objects from the past and dating them. Peaceful artifacts from before the war whose use never had anything to do with spilled blood, interrupted lives, absurd and violent deaths, faces disfigured by horror and shrapnel. Sometimes a pair of pistols arrive at the shop slumbering in a glossy wooden case, or some heavy sword, or a slender, flexible foil; yes, but these are weapons that were used in secret, romantic duels in which men were killed and died in the name of private love, not global hatred. Peter is a shadow of what he once was and Michael can't stop making plans: he's sworn to learn to swim once and for all. Nico – now that Michael's left Eton – is lonely and has been getting in trouble at school. Barrie receives his letters, reads them carefully, and answers them, offering advice, and, more than once, solutions. But Barrie seems vaguely disconcerted by all this youth orbiting him in ever widening and more distant circles, farther and farther from his light and influence.

Barrie is chosen as rector of St Andrews University and one of his obligations is to give a speech to the students. He doesn't know what to say to them; he knows exactly what to say.

He jots down:

> *–Age & Youth the two great enemies . . . Age (wisdom) failed – Now let us see what youth (audacity) can do.*
> *– Speak scornfully of the Victorian age. Of Edwardian age. Of last year. Of old-fashioned writers like Barrie, who accept old-fangled ideas. Don't be greybeards before your time. Too much advice like this is what makes you so.*

The day of his speech, Barrie trembles, hesitates. Someone shouts something funny from the stands full of men about to venture out into the world. Everyone laughs; Barrie can't hear what they're laughing about. He takes a deep breath. He smiles. He begins. He speaks to them of their youth, their potential, their courage, their chance to be brave and immortal, to defeat their enemies. Barrie speaks to them of the courage they'll need to fight the battles of the fast-approaching future, the 'struggles between young men and their superiors; you being the young men and we your superiors, of course'. Barrie asks them not to be content to leave all decisions in the hands of their foolish elders; because adults tend only to consider their own interests, and their intelligence is bounded by egoism and ignorance. Barrie challenges them to claim what's theirs, what they deserve, what's fair, what they've earned with their own blood. Barrie calls them to arms. Barrie sounds almost like a rock star from outside his own time, like an advance avatar of the counterculture, like a Peter Pan suddenly grown up and turned reflective. Then Barrie reads them a fragment of Captain Robert Falcon Scott's last letter. Sheets that almost disintegrate in his fingers, that seem more like skin than paper, a very fine skin, a skin without bones to stretch it tight and give it shape, a skin handled so often that its prints have worn away. And Barrie ends his speech by reciting a sonnet on the fleeting nature of youth, written, he tells them, 'by a boy who will never grow up and whose name I won't say here.' It's a sonnet Michael wrote during his last holidays, before sinking, going under. A rather bad sonnet, sophomoric. A sonnet that strikes everyone as incredibly beautiful and right for such a momentous occasion, and that, in Barrie's voice, sounds simultaneously like a blessing and a warning, reaching the audience almost from life's farthest limits. At the end of the speech, the applause goes on for minutes and revives Barrie a little, as each Christmas the applause revives Tinker Bell.

Michael is doing many things. Michael is happy at Oxford. He's arrived with several of his friends from Eton, who, remembering him, will call him 'the only one of our generation to be touched by genius'. Lytton Strachey will say that he's 'the only young man at Oxford or Cambridge with real brains'. Some of his friends – like Robert Boothby, future lord – occasionally go with him to visit Barrie and leave nearly scared stiff: 'I always felt uncomfortable in that flat. There was a morbid atmosphere about it. Michael and Barrie's relationship was extraordinary – it was unhealthy. I don't mean homosexual; I mean in a mental sense. If you ask me, I think Michael and his brothers would've been happier living in poverty than amid all the splendour of that odd, gloomy little genius.'

Michael and his friends sit in the drawing room and talk, and it's not until they hear a little cough that they realize that Barrie is watching them from his armchair in the shadows, as if he's a dummy abandoned by its ventriloquist, a dummy that's taken on a life and a will of its own.

Michael and his friends go on an excursion to Paris and when they return, they find Barrie concentrating on the writing of another play. The moment has finally come to tackle an old idea: the ghost mother. *Mary Rose* is the story of a young mother who disappears on a trip to the Hebrides and returns, many years later, without having aged a single day, while in the meantime her son has become a man. Barrie writes slowly. He develops a cramp in his right hand and switches to his left.

Michael isn't around to read the manuscript: he spends his time frequenting the salons of Ottoline Morrell and Dora Carrington and the rest of the Bloomsbury group. He doesn't seem very comfortable among them. He seeks out the spots furthest from conversation. He's shy.

Michael finds the atmosphere of Barrie's flat suffocating and prefers open spaces. When Barrie insists on taking a walk with him, Michael – Barrie's favourite of favourites – walks quickly, striding along, and the little man is rapidly left behind, sad, unsettled, unable to understand what's happened.

Michael spends his time drawing, always carrying a pencil and sketchpad. He uses Barrie as a model and emphasizes his worst features, while never departing from reality; he presents Barrie with the disturbing portraits.

'Michael has been drawing more sketches of me and I begin to feel assaulted. He has a diabolical aptitude for finding my worst attributes, so bad that I indignantly deny them, then I furtively examine myself in the privacy of my chamber, and lo, they are there,' Barrie complains.

Michael has lost all interest in Barrie's work: he no longer asks him about the murder play he begged him to write and he doesn't show the least interest in the great success of *Mary Rose* on its opening night at the Haymarket Theatre, 22 April 1920. Michael explains to Barrie that he's going through a phase in which 'everything makes me think furiously'. He leaves home early and returns late, and he's always meeting his new best friend at the Oxford library: Rupert Buxton.

Think of Rupert Buxton as the classic brooding young Englishman. Pale, and a cultivator of dark, suicidal fantasies. A little Chatterton. A guest at Gormenghast. A typical product of England's upper classes.

Keiko Kai: I like to think of Rupert Buxton as a possible juvenile model for Cagliostro Nostradamus Smith; a boy with an air of exaggerated gloom and a tragic expression and pale skin and dark clothes. A *romantic* in the worst sense of the word, who – transgressive and far from patriotic – likes to open German books to any page and find something interesting to read aloud, simply for the pleasure of being heard, as he walks with Michael under cloudy skies. Rupert Buxton's voice is as cold and deep as a pool in winter, and when he reads something (and he constantly interrupts the things he reads with his own ideas and commentary, so that it's impossible to know what the author wrote and what Rupert Buxton thinks) it acquires the resonance of the overly transcendent, and, as a result, the untrustworthy: 'Death isn't just a consequence of the way we live . . . Death is also what defines our life in the end. It's odd: we can only reach a full understanding of our existence if we look backward, but at the same time we're compelled to project ourselves forward . . . We live by passing from one thought to the next, from one feeling to the next; and yet our thoughts and feelings don't flow smoothly, like a river. Instead they seize us; they drop on us like stones

. . . Look, the leaves have already begun to fall . . . If you observe carefully, you'll see that the soul isn't something that changes colour gradually . . . The colour of the leaves . . . It's a shame, I think, that we can't change colour with the years; that we can't end up a fiery red like a fire that refuses to die, for example . . . What happens is that our thoughts flow upward, like ciphers rising from the bottom of a deep well . . . mathematical . . . Thoughts don't obey the law of gravity . . . That's why one moment you have a thought, and the next moment a feeling, and then another thought, each arising as if from nothing, from emptiness. And if you watch closely, you'll glimpse the precise instant that separates two thoughts, the fraction of a second that, once observed, can only be death; because life is simply the leaving behind of stones to mark our path and the leaping from one to the next each day, over thousands of seconds of death . . . I like that: the idea that death insinuates itself into the cracks of our life and that from time to time it rears its head like some strange, wily creature. A predatory beast that hunts us even as we think we're hunting it, believing that we're the pursuers, not the pursued . . . In a way, our lives are all about balancing, about trying to keep our balance on these shifting footholds . . . Careful, step on that stone and then the next, you wouldn't want to ruin your shoes and . . . Where did you buy them? Did Barrie send them to you? . . . That's the source of our ridiculous fear of a death with no afterlife, because death is the bottomless pit we fall into when there are no more stones to stand on . . . That's what I call the Leaping Malady, the fear that leaps. And the secret, our triumph, is to overcome it, to conquer it. It's our obligation to achieve the certainty that life is sliding calmly by; the moment we succeed, we're at last as close to death as we are to life. We aren't living any more, according to our earthly concept of life; but we can't die, either . . . Oh, the horror of consciousness! Because we've achieved the negation of death as well as the annulment of life. That's our instant of immortality, the instant when the soul, breaking free from the brain, at last enters the gardens of life . . . and now it's time to go back. Let's go back.'

Yes: for Rupert Buxton death is neither the end nor an end; for Rupert Buxton death is a matter of beginnings.

Michael's old friends don't understand this relationship. Robert Boothby, again, always detecting centres of infection in Michael's surroundings, diagnoses: 'Buxton was exceptionally clever, but he also had a melancholic, saturnine side that I don't think was good for Michael. Everything about him seemed to exude gloom and darkness. His very presence produced a feeling of sickness.' And maybe if Rupert Buxton had lived at the dawn of this dusky millennium, he might have become a trash-rock worshipper of Satan & Co. – who knows; he might have. One of those Columbine Kids who comes to class one day dressed in combat fatigues and sprays machine gun fire at his fellow students to teach them a lesson. But back then Robert Boothby was exaggerating, I think: Rupert Buxton wasn't a brutal mass murderer. Rupert Buxton was cultured and independent. Rupert Buxton was, if anything, a rare, highly skilled artist of death.

Barrie never gets to know Buxton. Barrie's too busy trying to know the new Michael. Or maybe it's the same old Michael; except that Michael has grown up, Michael is beginning to be another Michael.

Christmas is coming closer and Barrie seeks and finds refuge in the same place as always. In Neverland. Revisions and additions to the 1920 revival of *Peter Pan*:

– P. Pan. *Child: 'Mother, what hour was I born?' '½ past 2 in the morning.' 'Oh, mother, I hope I didn't wake you.'*
– P. Pan. *'I thought it was only flowers that died.'*
– Play title: *'The Man Who Didn't* Couldn't *Grow Up' or 'The Old Age of Peter Pan.'*

And the next spring Barrie occupies himself with the rehearsals for *Shall We Join the Ladies?*, the crime drama written at Michael's suggestion. Despite all the differences and friction of late, he still writes Michael every day, to the frustration of Cynthia Asquith, who must file his correspondence.

On the night of 19 May 1921, Barrie finishes writing a letter to Michael and leaves the flat to mail it. When he reaches the street, a young reporter is waiting for him, and asks for a comment on the tragedy. Barrie looks at him uncomprehendingly. His next play isn't a tragedy. It's a detective story, yes, but nothing particularly dramatic. The reporter insists, and mentions the word 'drowned'. No one drowns in *Shall We Join the Ladies*?, Barrie's sure of it. Near terror, the reporter realizes that Barrie doesn't know what's happened: two Oxford students, Rupert Buxton and Michael Llewelyn Davies, drowned while they were bathing in the Thames at Sandford Pool, a bend in the river where a small dam forms a natural pool. The bodies haven't been found yet; but the 'terrible incident' was witnessed by 'two men who were working on one of the banks', the young reporter informs him in the language of newspapers.

Barrie says nothing, returns to the lift, goes up to the flat, enters, locks the door. He sits in the dark for almost an hour. Then he makes some telephone calls: he calls Peter, Gerald du Maurier, Cynthia. They all rush from different parts of London to Adelphi Terrace House. Barrie lets them in. He seems to be beyond life and death. Barrie is a ghost. A perfect ghost. One of those ghosts condemned to repeat the horrors of his past existence over and over again, while asking himself how childhood, that other ghost, can possibly be so brief, and old age so eternally long.

Peter goes to get Nico at Eton. Barrie doesn't want to see him; he orders Nico to leave the room. Maybe he fears Nico will be the next to die, right there, and that it will be his fault. A new restaging of the same old death: Arthur, Sylvia, George, Michael . . . The continuous performance – over and over again, the variations of the particular case not altering the same old plot – of the scene in which someone beloved and irreplaceable dies just before the curtain falls. Peter leaves for

Oxford to help with the efforts to recover the bodies. Barrie doesn't sleep all night. Nico runs to Queen Charlotte's Hospital, where Mary Hodgson is working as a midwife. There's no need for him to say anything; Mary Hodgson has only to see his face to burst into tears and run to embrace him.

The next morning, all the papers in the city carry the news on the front page. The *Evening Standard* runs an all-caps headline announcing the catastrophe: 'THE TRAGEDY OF PETER PAN', and adds: 'Mr Michael Llewelyn Davies (20) and Mr Rupert E. V. Buxton (22) were undergraduates at Oxford and inseparable companions . . . The original Peter Pan was George, killed in combat in 1915 . . . Now both boys who are most closely associated with the fashioning of Peter Pan are dead.'

In a sidebar, one of the witnesses says that he saw the two boys in the middle of the pool, with their arms around each other and the water up to their necks, not looking frightened or as if they were in trouble. I like to think that maybe it was mermaids; that Michael and Rupert were seized and dragged down to the depths by women with fishtails and shark smiles and seaweed hair, and that they didn't let them go until it was too late, until they grew tired of playing with them at the bottom of the pool, which I imagine like the theatrical stage setting of some fish bowls: the ruins of a castle, a treasure chest, the remains of a pirate galleon, the ancient phosphorescent bones of drowned youths, romantic and doomed. Since it was public knowledge that Michael didn't know how to swim, his death was ruled an accident, and it was concluded that Rupert drowned trying to save his friend. Sandford Pool was a notoriously dangerous spot: two other students had drowned there in 1843. Which didn't prevent rumours of a suicide pact from circulating around the university.

In his *Morgue*, Peter notes phlegmatically: 'Perfectly possible but entirely unproven.' In private, the brothers think that yes, Michael did commit suicide: his increasingly erratic behaviour, his long periods of depression, a possible homosexual phase that left him troubled, his nightmares and terrors, the hurt he never recovered from after the deaths of Arthur and Sylvia; so many things . . .

The bodies aren't recovered until the afternoon of the next day. I like to think that Michael and Rupert are clinging to each other, that the bones of their arms must be broken to separate them, that they're the damp and marbelized colour of the drowned. And I always thought there was something frustrating and incomplete about the fact that when a person drowns only the lungs fill up with water, not the whole body: wouldn't it be much more beautiful if the water found its way into every last corner of us, if it washed over our muscles and organs and bones and dissolved them, filling us up like a bottle?

Peter waits for the autopsy to be finished. Peter can't help thinking that in Greek *autopsia* means 'seeing with one's own eyes'; and Peter can't help thinking about the perverse behaviour of the human brain at the most terrible moments: it's then it makes you think about everything except the unthinkable.

Peter brings Michael's body back to Adelphi Terrace House. Barrie hasn't slept for two nights. He's a man sunk in a nightmare. Peter recognizes the symptoms; Peter knows those symptoms by heart.

Cynthia Asquith calls a doctor to prescribe a tranquillizer. Barrie takes it without even realizing what he's taking, and travels from a waking nightmare to a sleeping nightmare. The whole world is a nightmare. 'All the world is different to me now . . . Michael was my world,' he sobs.

Michael's death unleashes a kind of mass hysteria among his friends. One embarks on the most licentious and bohemian of existences. Another commits suicide. Another goes to live with Lytton Strachey, who declares: 'If he'd lived, I'm sure Michael would have been one of the most remarkable men of his generation.' His tutor at Oxford writes to Barrie: 'Michael was one of the most important occurrences of my academic career, and what happened in some way marks its end. I'm left with small matters to attend to, all of them trivial.' Simon Templeton-Lux disappears into the thumping black heart of Africa, where it's said that a sect of Michaelites is founded, the members of which are always doomed to drown themselves in a final ecstatic outburst after performing deeds as imprudent as they are indecent. Geoffrey Lyndon never again leaves his Chelsea house and ends up writing an unpublishable novel, thousands of pages long, about 'air and water and earth and fire, and the way they haunt and influence us'. Leander Sanders-Cox sabotages the next Oxford regatta by climbing up to the university bell tower and firing a rifle at the rowers while shouting that the Day of Final Judgement was last week and how is it possible no one's noticed. Conrad 'Conradin' Clovis slits his wrists and lets himself be devoured member by member by Sredni Vashtar, his exotic pet. Spencer Lewis-Kaminski, who will be one of the most exacting and admired brains at Bletchley Park during the Second World War spends whole days trying to 'mathematize' Michael Llewelyn Davies's death, as if it were a precise and comprehensible equation, as if the answer to all mysteries resided in it. John Milford devotes himself to chasing after Harry Houdini on stages around the world, interrupting the magician's performances to explain to the public how he performs his magic tricks. Timmy 'Dixie' Loomis-Cranton flees to the United States where he wins fame as Poker Pan, a player in card games that last several nights and the ensuing days in New Orleans's most dangerous casinos, or as Rule 'Brit' Mattone, ruthless Chicago gangster; it doesn't matter which.

Shall We Join the Ladies? opens on 26 May 1921 – a few days after Michael's death – at the inauguration of the Royal Academy of Dramatic Art. The play is unfinished, open-ended, the identity of the assassin never revealed. The critics and the public love the idea and they talk until dawn proposing possible theories, hypothetical criminals, conclusions at which they're no longer asked to applaud to prevent a death but to identify the author of a corpse. Someone asks Barrie who's guilty. 'I'd like to know myself,' answers Barrie.

On the anniversary of the tragedy, Barrie dreams that Michael comes back to visit him from the Great Beyond. Michael doesn't know that he's drowned and Barrie doesn't say anything. They live like that, in secret and never going out, for almost a year, but as the next 19 May approaches, Michael grows sadder and sadder and asks Barrie to accompany him to Sandford Pool. They travel by night, and when they arrive, Michael hugs Barrie goodbye and sinks down again and disappears into those dark waters.

Barrie wakes up weeping, and makes notes for a story that might be titled 'Water' or 'The Silent Pool' or 'The 19th'. In one of the margins, he writes with his left hand:

– It is as if long after writing Peter Pan its true meaning were clear to me, transparent: the desperation of trying to grow up and never being able to.

Jack and Peter are destroyed by Michael's death. Nico is the one who takes it the hardest: not only has he lost his parents and his brothers, but now he's the only one still living with Barrie – with the shadow of what was once Barrie, a shadow that's lost its owner, a shadow ragged beyond repair – and Nico is convinced that he'll never be able to replace Michael, or any of Barrie's dead. Jack and Peter and Nico exchange glances. They need to embrace but they're afraid to, like Peter Pan, who claimed he couldn't be touched by anything or anyone. Jack and Peter and Nico can't help asking themselves – in silence, each of them, behind the closed door of their thoughts – who will be the next to fall; because it's clear that their family is under a strange, powerful – and yes, awfully big – curse. A curse that never ages (a curse that will never die) and that seems younger and more powerful each day. Arthur, Sylvia, George, Michael . . . One after the other, swept away by the wind, like loose pages, like finished chapters, like dead stories from a sad book.

Nico leaves Adelphi Terrace House in 1926 to marry Mary James and Peter – his romantic bohemian stage over – is engaged to Margaret Ruthven in 1931.

Barrie begins to abandon his life as a hermit and gives dinners again and accepts invitations. He becomes friends with Charlie Chaplin and Mary Pickford. He supports Michael Collins and makes speeches against Adolf Hitler. He exchanges opinions with Winston Churchill. He sees Rudyard Kipling a few times – the creator of Mowgli, that other small and heroic savage of paper and ink, an exotic Peter Pan brought up in the furthest reaches of the Empire – but they aren't pleasant encounters: Kipling has also lost a son in the trenches of war; and unlike Conan Doyle, Kipling doesn't believe in the anaesthesia of ghosts. Kipling's pain is therefore too much like Barrie's pain: it's a pain without magic or mystery or the Great Beyond. T. E. Lawrence comes by for Barrie on his motorcycle and takes him out to tea and shows him the costumes he's brought from Arabia (when he spreads them out like treasure maps, the floor of the sitting room is covered with yellow sand like gold) and, for an instant, Barrie thinks that Lawrence would make a magnificent lost boy; because he's short and he's a hero and his laughter and enthusiasm are like a boy's. And what does all this mean, Keiko Kai? Why now Barrie's puzzling and unexpected concern for troubled reality, for the ravaged times that drag themselves, fall, and who knows whether they'll ever get up? It occurs to me that maybe it's a kind of kabbalistic reasoning, a conjuration: Barrie knows that he's more of a historic character than a normal person, and maybe, he thinks, if he involves himself with History, if he dances a waltz with her, his luck will change and there will be no more misfortunes. Maybe if he grows up and becomes responsible, maybe . . . Hence his shifting personality these days and nights. Barrie's mood changes according to the newspaper headlines printed in his mind, headlines only he can read. Nothing horrifies him more than seeing pictures of himself: what happened? How did he turn into that little man, wrinkled as a gnome? At a meeting yesterday, he was shown a picture that particularly disturbed him: in it he's holding a cup of coffee among brazenly young, hearty men at a stand on the Embankment; he's wearing a hat and a long coat and he's holding his walking stick pressed against his body with one arm. It was cold when the picture was taken; but Barrie feels much colder seeing it at home, beside a blazing fire. Barrie thinks that if someone had told him this was the man who created the splendid Peter Pan, that person would laugh incredulously and mockingly. Barrie thinks that behind his back, behind his small back, maybe everyone is mocking him. Everyone is laughing at the madness that to him seems so reasonable: is there anything more sensible than the desperate desire to play until death parts us from our toys? Barrie alternates between periods of almost compulsive social life and spells of absolute hatred of humanity.

The Inimitable Brown – faithful butler for so long – decides to retire to care for his sick wife on a small farm he's bought with his savings. One butler exits to stage right so another butler can enter from stage left. No matter. It doesn't affect the show's budget. It doesn't change this last act much. Brown is replaced by Frank Thurston, one of my favourite characters, one – I make an effort, thinking the way Marcus Merlin would think – I can't imagine with Dermott's face but I can imagine with Basil Rathbone's. Thurston – he drops his given name immediately, as is fitting – is much more inimitable than Brown. Little or nothing is known about Thurston except that he speaks French, Spanish, Latin and Greek; and that despite this he communicates only in monosyllables, except when, at his master's request, he's capable of perfectly imitating Barrie's voice on the telephone, saying anything, accepting invitations and organizing Pantagruelian dinners for the following night. Cynthia Asquith has nervous attacks:

too much work and responsibility; and, she discovers, she can't separate herself from this all-powerful little man – she's no longer mistress of her will or her actions.

Barrie writes his last hit, a bibically inspired play; but – like everything he's undertaken over the course of his life and work – it's contaminated by his own genesis and apocalypses. Its title closes the circle: *The Boy David*.

Barrie receives an Order of Merit, is made president of the Incorporated Society of Authors, Playwrights and Composers, and is named chancellor of Edinburgh University. He often addresses the students, who look at him with equal parts curiosity and admiration, as if Barrie were an ancient and well-oiled machine.

I have a picture of him, Keiko Kai: a picture from his last days. In it Barrie is being carried on the shoulders of a crowd of smiling youths. Several of them wear old sweaters with Egyptian designs, handed down from their older siblings and made in the days of the great Tutankhamun craze when the archaeologist Howard Carter and Lord Carnavon discovered a lost tomb and lifted the curse from another child king who never grew up. In the picture, Barrie looks uncomfortable; he's pulled his hat down low so he won't lose it along the way and he's looking at the camera as if he isn't sure whether he's being feted or whether they're dragging him to the top of a pyramid where he'll be sacrificed, where they'll rip out his tired and aching heart.

Barrie has a hard time falling asleep. Barrie confesses to Cynthia Asquith that he's afraid of the dark, afraid that in the dark he won't be able to think up any stories, that the dark is like a black page on which it's impossible to write with black ink. A doctor prescribes small doses of heroin that, instead of helping him fall asleep, transport him 'sitting in bed into a state of ecstasy and inspiration'. Barrie thinks he's flying; Barrie thinks that he's so tall now it's as if he were flying. At the height of his delirium, ideas for books come to Barrie that would never come to him if he were in his right mind and his feet were firmly planted on the ground. Books that he might have written and didn't write, maybe because they're adult books, books that someone who hadn't resisted growing up might have written. Books in which a young nobleman becomes a woman and wanders through the centuries; in which two doomed married couples vacation at a German spa; in which a man looks for another man on a dark, dead-end continent; in which a legendary theatre actor and director in the winter of his discontent watches a sea monster from a British beach. Books that're ultimately written by other authors but that are, I think, Barrie's ghost books: because a writer isn't only the books with his name on the cover but the books he might have written, books that escaped like ink through his fingers.

Barrie keeps making little friends: Cynthia Asquith's children, and the young Princess Margaret, who proclaims at the age of three: 'Sir James is my greatest friend and I am *his* greatest friend.' Barrie visits her often, crossing Kensington Gardens, and he even steals a few of her remarks for *The Boy David*. Barrie – as he did for Jack when he used some of his words in *Little Mary* twenty-five years ago, on what now seems to him another planet – promises the little princess a penny for every night the play is performed. In March 1937, Barrie receives an edict from King George VI in which he's informed – in a graciously imperious tone – that the author hasn't paid his debt to his little collaborator, and that he'd better do so if he doesn't want to receive another notice soon from the royal bill collectors and be dragged off to his new quarters in the Tower of London. Barrie sends Thurston to exchange a few bills for coins, fills a bag with pennies, smiles. He'll take them to her personally one of these days. In the meantime – there's no hurry – Barrie starts and finishes a supernatural romance called *Farewell, Miss Julie Logan*, ghost stories being the only kind of story he can come up with; ghosts protect you from the cold and fear that the living provoke in you. It comforts him to feel the weight of the bag full of coins in the palm of his hand crossed with age-lines. It reminds him of the rewards and ransoms that pirates and musketeers and gentlemen of fortune fling into the air; it reminds him of his irretrievable past, the buried treasure of his childhood to which the map has been lost – a map that must surely be in some drawer, in some dark corner of that deserted house like an island where the only survivor of a shipwreck washes up.

There are nights that Barrie goes out walking in London, in a city he thinks he knows by heart; but all he has to do is venture a few streets from Adelphi Terrace House to discover that something's happened, something strange. Barrie loses his way, doesn't know how to get home, has to ask a policeman the way to return safe and sound. The parks and the names on the street signs haven't changed, but the city is a different place. To Barrie, London seems to be made of wax, ready to be displayed in a wax museum as London burning. A London burning and melting into another London. A new London that Barrie doesn't recognize, and in which he isn't recognized. A London more like the space backstage – where the curtains are constantly rising and falling, and nothing is ever quiet – than the familiar and unchanging scenery of a play that opened many years ago. The play that he wrote and that's always up, perpetually running, before the orchestra seats. The same thing's happened to the years, which add up apace: Barrie can't understand how they've sped by so fast, like those magician's rabbits that disappear into a bowler hat that the wind sweeps from your head and carries far away down the street.

One of those nights, in 1934, Barrie turns a corner and runs into a strange boy, a boy with Oriental features holding a bicycle by the handlebars and singing something about a yellow submarine. Barrie looks at him closely and thinks he recognizes him, thinks he remembers something, thinks he remembers everything, thinks he's gone mad or the madness has returned. Barrie gives a little cry and flees. Barrie runs through the streets, runs as fast as his little legs will take him through a new world where his old childhood keeps growing larger and more powerful, yes, but also more zombie-like and mechanical. When he's out of breath and can't go on any more – when everything is pure fear, when energy has been supplanted by terror – Barrie seeks refuge in what looks like a familiar building, a sanctuary. The Duke of York's Theatre. He pushes the doors open, and discovers a performance of *Peter Pan*, revival number 5,347,839, or something like that. On the stage there are four actors, but the seats – there's no one in the seats. Barrie collapses into one of them. All of a sudden, the place is full of girls who scream and cry and seem to have lost their senses. It's the scene, thinks Barrie, in which Peter Pan asks the audience to clap to bring Tink back to life. 'Would those in the cheap seats clap their hands. The rest of you can rattle your jewellery,' instructs a Peter Pan who doesn't look anything like his Peter Pan. What is this? He never wrote lines like that, so disrespectful and vulgar. What's going on here? Barrie applauds feebly, and gets up and makes his way among frenzied adolescents who laugh and cry all at once and Barrie goes running out, still clapping, and he crosses a bridge and the Thames is full of slow, elegant icebergs propelled by the cold current and Barrie seems to see men and women trapped in the ice and suddenly the whole Thames has frozen and where did those skaters come from and Barrie keeps running until he reaches Adelphi Terrace House and gets in the lift without greeting the doorman and luckily, he doesn't need to tell the lift man which is his floor. Barrie doesn't trust his voice not to shake, Barrie fears that he's lost the ability to speak. Finally he manages to get into his flat (is it his hand that's shaking so much, or is it the key, or is it the whole building that's shaking from cold and fear?). Barrie reaches his armchair as if it's the only magic and sacred place where he knows he'll be protected, and he collapses there and asks for the newspaper (the kind that newspaper taxis are made of, he thinks, and what can be making him think such things, he wonders), and he reads on the first page that Sir Gerald du Maurier, the man who will always be Captain Hook, has died at sixty-one of complications after a difficult operation. And oh, all his friends and accomplices suddenly seem to be so busy performing their last acts. Or maybe he reads that Edward VIII has abdicated. Or he reads that the documents and plans have been approved to knock down the buildings around Adelphi Terrace House and make way for a new urban reconstruction project and he's one of the few residents remaining in the building. Or he reads that the experts in horror say that the seeds of a new war have been sown in fertile ground, and that they're sprouting vigorously. Or he reads that nothing will be the same any more and he doesn't even dare look at the horoscope column and Barrie has a fever, or the fever has him and won't let him go all through the long, terrible night. A night that won't sleep, that refuses to sleep, even if it's told all the stories in the world.

Cynthia returns from a trip and finds him looking worse. Barrie tells her he drank too much whisky last night. Barrie's like a child who's lived much longer than expected. Barrie's in a bad mood. The reviews of *The Boy David* haven't been good. He's accused of distorting the Bible, of turning the sacred scriptures to his own ends as he once planted his flag in Kensington Gardens in the form of a statue. He's reproached for changing the sacred story to shape it to his credo.

His health deteriorates – he asks for heroin, he's refused it – and improves, and deteriorates again. Barrie's health is like the London weather. Barrie's mood is like the London weather too. One moment he's the most enchanting of gentlemen, and the next he's exceedingly cruel. Barrie promises Cynthia Asquith that he'll leave her a large sum of money, only to immediately confess that he's ruined and – he can scarcely contain his glee – explain that he likes all this 'playing at being Lear'. His doctor diagnoses neuritis. Few dare to visit him and Cynthia Asquith seriously considers committing suicide or killing him, or both: better to kill him first and then commit suicide. She opts for a compromise solution: Cynthia Asquith flees.

Barrie refuses to acknowledge that she's gone and – as if she's on holiday – he checks into the Manchester Square home for the elderly until Cynthia 'returns from her outing'. He writes a last letter, a letter of thanks to Thurston, in which he also gives instructions regarding whether or not a document enclosed in the envelope should be published after his death; the document is never found.

'I'm very comfortable here, although of course it would be more comfortable to die in one's own home,' he tells Thurston. And he grants Thurston permission to keep the books he likes best from his library: 'Few people who've passed through my flat have treated the books as respectfully as you, Thurston.'

Barrie begins to lose his sense of time and place. He hears strange songs. Sad songs that seem to come from far away, played on instruments making bright new sounds. Barrie asks to see people who're dead. Barrie knows more people who're dead than alive. Barrie has so much to talk about with his dead.

The doctors call Peter at his publishing house, and Peter calls Cynthia: Barrie is dying. Cynthia returns to London. Barrie has fallen into a deep sleep. Maybe it's a coma from which he'll never emerge. He's given an injection and he opens his eyes, signs his will, says a few words, closes his eyes again.

Sir James Matthew Barrie dies on Saturday afternoon, 19 June 1937, at the age of seventy-six, without having recovered consciousness. Beside his bed are Cynthia Asquith, Peter Llewelyn Davies and Nico Llewelyn Davies. I add Thurston so that he can say something in perfect Latin, something no one understands. Barrie dies and someone opens a window so that his last breath can escape, mounted on the back of his soul. From up above, from so high up, his own existence resembles an island – an island he'll never ever see again – surrounded by the ocean of death. So much water surrounding so much earth; earth – Barrie now effortlessly understands – that was never very solid after all, and that isn't so hard to leave behind. Flying is worth it. Flying makes death worthwhile.

Barrie states clearly in his will that he doesn't want a grand funeral, which doesn't prevent memorial services from being held for him at St Paul's Cathedral, Edinburgh University, St Andrews University; the modest last wishes of great men aren't usually honoured.

Barrie doesn't want an ill-lit corner among the poets beneath the stones at Westminster.

Barrie wants the fresh air of the Kirriemuir cemetery.

Barrie wants to be buried beside his mother and his father, next to the two sisters who died and who he doesn't remember, next to his brother David, who he never forgot.

Barrie wants a simple gravestone – his name, his dates; that's all – and an unvarnished oak coffin.

A small coffin, a coffin so light the gravediggers think it seems empty.

Baco's coffin is so light and small, Keiko Kai.

It's as if I'm seeing it again.

My mother and my father and Marcus Merlin and I are at the Kensal Green cemetery. My grandparents have stayed in the car, with Dermott.

Kensal Green is a Victorian cemetery. One of the several private cemeteries that began to grow on the outskirts of London after 1830, to curb the invasion of the dead filling the public ossuaries in the city's centre.

Kensal Green is one of those cemeteries that make you want to die just so you can be buried there. A small, silent city growing downward. Mausoleums like little palaces. Clean, perfect streets. A full-fledged utopia. A triumphant revolution. Everyone lives happily together there. Everyone respects one another. Everyone is remembered. Everyone is peaceful and rests in peace, in peace and love.

I don't remember Baco's burial, but I do remember the cemetery where Baco was buried. I don't remember Baco's grave (one of those small obelisks?) or my parents' (like those regal tombs where fallen monarchs lie in relief, like pudding moulds?), but I do remember Kensal Green and the pleasant feeling of being in a cemetery, of feeling more alive there than anywhere else. I like to think – yes – that my parents, Marcus Merlin, and I walked in a perfect, orderly line, with equal spaces between us, like the Beatles on the cover of *Abbey Road*.

I don't remember whether it was sunny or whether it was cloudy or whether it had just rained and the sun was beginning to show through the clouds. I do remember, however, the statue of the angel on Kensal Rise, in Kensal Green. The classic statue of an angel, the same old angel, the angel that stands in cemeteries everywhere. An angel in a series, but – unlike all its counterparts, renouncing the divine equality of God's intermittent intermediaries – this angel has been divinely impregnated by a tree. At some point, a hermaphroditic seed fell into a fold of her stone robe and set down roots, and a tree – I couldn't tell you what kind of tree, Keiko Kai – grew up around her as the years passed. A decidedly poetic tree, I suppose. A metaphoric but realistic tree: life blooming on the far side of death and all that. Impossible to know now whether the angel came from the tree or the tree sprouted an angel. It doesn't matter. The order doesn't change the result of the miracle, and here we are now, in Neverland, you and I, in the same place I was then.

My room and Baco's room. Perfectly preserved. Like a sacred place or one of those museum chambers separated from the visiting public by velvet ropes that you lean over, craning your neck.

Here – alpha and omega – is where everything began and everything ends, where life ends, ends but never dies; it's the person who inhabited that life for a certain number of years and then stopped living who dies. Life – whatever it is; whoever it belongs to, be it tree or angel; no matter who lived it – always ends up in the same place.

That's where we're going, Keiko Kai.

Take a pill.

A pill for the trip, so nothing hurts, so you don't feel a thing.

Now it's almost dawn, now we don't have much time left, now the Night of Nights is ending.

The sooner we're finished with these horrors, the better.

Time to go, time to return.

Now I'm opening the window.

Now come here.

Now give me your hand.

Now let's go.

Now.

The Dreamer

Welcome to Alwaysland.

Second star to the left and straight on into the neverending night, the interminable day. Alwaysland is mine, and it's unique. None of those multiple Neverlands, one for each child, with their slight variations but always obeying the same geographic laws over and above all aesthetic differences, as Barrie wrote: 'if they stood in a row you could say of them that they have each other's nose, and so forth.' No. Alwaysland is just for me. I'm its creator and discoverer. I got here flying or in a little boat, it doesn't matter which.

Welcome to my afterthought, my surprise revision, my last-minute addition, my alternate, off-programme ending, my new last act to be performed for the first and only and last time.

You all thought the curtain had fallen, that everything was over now. I thought so too, but no: the lights still haven't come on, a few coughs and the nervous murmuring of the audience can be heard in the dark, and suddenly a boy comes on stage, riding a bicycle and holding a lamp in one hand.

That boy isn't Jim Yang.

That boy is me.

The character is me.

'Welcome to Alwaysland,' he says, I say.

Welcome.

Alwaysland is the shape of Kensington Gardens and the size of childhood.

Let me explain: unlike the usual way of things, in Alwaysland everything is bigger than it really was.

Let me explain better. It's inevitable, it's happened to all of us: what we remember as huge and ominous when we were children ends up being smaller and harmless and even disappointing when we see it again; when we return, many years later, hoping to find everything the way we left it and the way it left us.

That's not possible.

The dimensions of the past don't coincide with those of the present.

As we grow up, the past gets bigger and there's less and less space in the present. What was once tall is now short, and the river that swept us away with torrential glee is no more than a stream with the gentle pull of a water nap.

Alwaysland, meanwhile, doesn't lie to us or mislead us or betray our memory: everything is huge in Alwaysland. Everything is even more colossal than in our earliest and most exaggerated perceptions.

Thus, Kensington Gardens – the Kensington Gardens of Alwaysland – stretches away past the horizon, as far as the eye can see and even farther: a green world where mothers stroll in their best dresses, pushing their most baroque carriages; where men play cricket; where children play at losing and finding themselves among the branches of trees full of squirrels; and where the music of orchestras especially designed to harmoniously fill wide open spaces – brasses, strings, uniforms – sounds in the air. A bridge and a fountain and marmalade skies and your head in the clouds and I see it all with kaleidoscope eyes. Sometimes, in the distance, two groups stage what looks like a battle; they struggle to take a small hill, and they all behave properly, and there isn't the slightest disorder, and I watch them from the stairs of Neverland: all those adults playing like children.

And no one knows what time it is, so it's never time to go home. There are no clocks in Alwaysland – no crocodiles with time-keeping bellies, either – and the moon and the stars shine in the morning sky, and in the night sky it's hard to look directly at the sun, which is so happy to finally be able to see and shine on the dark face of everything.

Alwaysland is the best possible place to stay, to never leave, to never grow up.

There, here, I am.

In the exact centre of Alwaysland, Neverland rises. My family's house, my house, now transplanted to the heart of these gardens and growing on the banks of the Serpentine.

I pedal over to it and I look up at the top floor, where my room is. The room I once shared with Baco. The room with the open window.

The window I jumped from with Keiko Kai; when, I can't remember. Yesterday? A century ago? I have a more or less clear picture of the two of us jumping from that window, but that's all. Why did we jump? Were we fleeing someone? I have the disturbing feeling that my memory is beginning to crystallize, to take on the cloudy, fossil-like reflectiveness of amber glass through which light but not the clear image of the light source can pass.

I've said it already: the first thing that changes in Alwaysland is one's sense of the weather; because the weather is always good in Alwaysland. And an hour is as long as a second here. And a minute can contain an entire existence. And I remember having read something about mental time, time in dreams. And I pinch myself to see whether I'm dreaming. And I don't feel anything, but I don't wake up either.

I look at that open window. So near and so far; as if it were another planet, another life, another death.

I look at it until my eyes hurt and I keep looking at it until my eyes stop hurting, until I stop feeling my eyes, until I forget that there's something called eyes and that that something is used to look at the things it hurts most to look at.

I look at that window in that house until it begins to rain; and I look at it a little longer, until I realize that it isn't raining, until I know I'm crying.

*

From outside, the Alwaysland Neverland looks exactly like the Sad Songs Neverland, the Neverland outside of London.

The same size. The same pale-coloured stone walls. The same vines climbing up its sides. The same *vitreaux* with my family's coat of arms over the entrance, so majestic that it makes you a little embarrassed for it; the same discomfort we feel when we see someone we respect making a fool of himself in front of strangers.

Once through the door, though, everything changes: inside, Neverland is huge, off every scale, immense; and its unexpected majesty produces not irritation but the ecstatic stupor felt in certain cathedrals that give us an effortless faith in the incredible, even if only for a few minutes.

Neverland's front hall could swallow all the whales that ever swam in the ocean and swallowed every Jonah; and this hall leads into a long passageway like a highway whose end or destination is impossible to guess.

An impeccable white passageway, with ceilings and floors of tile and glass mosaic, lit from above and below by an almost solid light. A passageway with walls that at moments seem to radiate the echo of conversations, laughter, the sound of glasses clinking in a toast at the least excuse, for any reason. A long, perfect stretch flanked by dozens, hundreds, thousands of doors. The kind of doors that play their own role in vaudeville shows, doors that are an indispensable part of the plot, that end up being the main characters.

Doors I start opening to see what's on the other side, to try to understand the meaning of everything that's happened to me. Doors I open without the least idea what's waiting for me behind them, like in those frenzied television competitions. The difference is that in this Alwaysland Neverland there's no competition for any prize. The only reward seems to be the doors themselves; the actual act of continuing to open them; the knowledge that there are still so many doors to open.

I think I've understood that so long as I keep opening doors, I'll still be here, in Alwaysland. Here I am: opening doors and discovering what the rooms behind them have to show me. Doors that lead everywhere, anywhere. Doors that make me uneasy – again – just like those illustrations interleaved into a novel, a novel I thought I'd finished reading but that – everything seems to indicate, damn it – someone refuses to stop writing.

Today I opened several doors.

Behind one of them I found my father, floating at the bottom of the sea, his eyes vacant, his body wrapped in seaweed. He looked like a creature of the deep; he looked happy and amphibian. He waved at me. I couldn't hear anything he was saying but it was clear he was telling me many things: bubbles issued from his throat in perfectly synchronized bursts, in a clear and precise rhythm. Then I understood that my father wasn't saying anything to me: I realized my father was singing.

Behind another door I saw the summerhouse in the garden of the Neverland of my childhood and I watched someone approach with the stagy movements of a pantomime actor – giving little jumps, looking in all directions, putting a finger to his lips – and leave a copy of *Peter Pan* on one of the marble benches. For a moment I thought I recognized the person, I felt the weight of a name on the tip of my tongue, but immediately it seemed to me to be a man, a woman, a boy, a dog, a shadow . . . and then I had no idea which it might be, and I knew I would never know.

Behind another door I discovered an exact replica of Barrie's study at Adelphi Terrace House. The walls of books. The mouth of the big fireplace like a giant's yawn. A little table where the key to the gates of Kensington Gardens shines like a golden trophy, and beside it, some papers, on the top page of which the handwritten title *Instructions for Understanding Everything* can be read. I realize it's the final document that Barrie entrusted to Thurston before he died. The lost secret. The secret key. The mystery solved and ready to confess down to the last word of its last breath. An uncomfortable empty armchair, and on the floor near its legs, a solitary pair of huge feet, as empty as shoes. I resisted the temptation to go in and sit down to read in the chair, to try on the feet with which Barrie once frightened Peter Llewelyn Davies, to take that key in my hand and open the lock of my misfortunes.

Something tells me I shouldn't go into the rooms; that it would be better, just in case, to study them holding on tight to the doorframe, with all my strength, so that a hurricane of black wind doesn't sweep me away and swallow me up. Who knows; maybe; undoubtedly: if I enter one of these rooms its door will close behind me and I won't be able to leave, ever.

I go and open a door again. There's an old woman sitting at a table. She looks at me without saying a word, with that disquieting mix of love and pity that always gives you the uncontrollable urge to lower your eyes, to look anywhere else. I close the door before I can say for sure whether that would've been my mother if she'd had time to grow up a little, a little bit more. I close the door thinking that if there's anything I regret about all this it's knowing that I'll never be old now, that this suspended animation is no more than the farce of a false eternal youth.

I open another door. It's locked. On the upper part there's a small, illuminated sign with the words RECORDING SESSION IN PROGRESS in blinking red letters. Music and voices can be heard on the other side. I can't understand what's being said, and yet the sound is familiar; something I've heard before, something I'd like to hear again. It's a voice and a piano and an orchestra and the sound of an alarm clock, and now, yes, someone sings 'Woke up, got out of bed.'

I'll go and open one more door. Then I'll take a rest. Then I'll lie down to sleep in front of any of these doors.

I can't open many doors at once. It isn't advisable. Opening doors – opening these doors – makes you as tired as going up too many stairs while holding your breath or as exhausted as travelling through the centuries for too long. I open this door and a blast of damp air hits my face. Unequivocably London air, Victorian air. It's nighttime – night as night used to be, a night impossible to mistake for daytime – and under the cold light of the moon I see the monument to Peter Pan in Kensington Gardens; in the other Kensington Gardens that to me is no longer necessarily the authentic Kensington Gardens.

Barrie was right: it isn't a good statue, it doesn't do justice to the original model or to the real Peter Pan. It's the statue of a boy who could never convince any other child to come and fly away with him, to leap from his window into the sky. It's a door I close quickly, with a furious slam, angry at having wasted my time and energy on it when there are so many other doors to open.

Not long ago I discovered that the doors change places; that the rooms in this Neverland never stay still; that – every once in a while – their inhabitants or their interiors appear before me in the most unexpected spots. I realized it when I tried to keep a map of the doors, a careful record of rooms, an orderly list in my mind. It was hopeless. It was as if the mansion realized my intentions and decided to mutate and confuse me; make me understand that here I'm not lord and master, that my tricks are worth nothing.

Then I – who'd understood my stay in Alwaysland to be like one of those Choose Your Own Adventure books, in which a fake free will is bestowed on little readers, making them believe they can control the plots and falsely suggesting that they're the authors of their adventures, that they're responsible for them – realized it made no sense to continue the search for a sequence that would explain everything. It wasn't worth trying to puzzle out a course that would help me move up and down this passageway saturated with door handles. There was no possible trick or cheating tongue-and-key kiss like the one Houdini received from his wife before the door was closed that locked him in. Too many doors here. A straight and narrow universe; and all those keyholes, which, when you try to look through them – as you strive to discover whether or not it's worth opening a door – only show you the terrible polished face of a mirror, the muffled echo of your own sad gaze.

Sometimes I get depressed. Sometimes I fall apart and I make a great effort and I refuse to keep opening doors and I go running out of Neverland and I run through the trees and hedges and statues of this giant Kensington Gardens and I say to myself and I promise myself that I won't stop running until I reach the borders of Alwaysland, the edge of the map, the last word in the book.

I run through the moonlit days and sunlit nights; and there are moments when I can even convince myself that I'm getting somewhere and that I'm about to leave this place; that I can smell the sea in the distance or hear the rumble of a volcano as it stirs; that I'm expecting something – some jagged, unexpected landmark – to give this place a kind of novelty, something different from what I used to know and is now so new and out of proportion.

Then – when I'm almost sure I'm close to crossing the border – I find that the thing on the horizon I imagined would be an outcrop I could climb, and from it survey a new landscape, is only Neverland again. My house and its doors and its rooms.

I understand that I wasn't even running in circles, but that Alwaysland is a little like those first, primitive theatre backdrops: cylinders at each end of the stage and a cloth painted with houses, clouds and meadows scrolling between them, before which the actors – moving their legs but not going anywhere – simulate walking, running, being out of breath, looking for something and never finding it.

When I'm tired of running, I come to a halt and start to write. I light a fire and I sit in its glow and I play with the scattered pieces of a final Jim Yang adventure.

A book that no one will read except me.

I write it to have something to read, as a means of escape: in Alwaysland there aren't any books except in some of the rooms on the other side of the doors that I've been opening. And as I've said, I'm afraid to go into those rooms.

So I write it.

In fact, I don't write it down. In fact, I *imagine* I'm writing it. In Alwaysland I don't have a computer. I don't have paper or pencil or ink, either. It's a mental book: I learn it by heart, I revise it in the air. Anyway, all books are memory. Instant memory. What we put in writing is simply the immediate recollection of what's just occurred to us somewhere else, far and near, now and then, simultaneously, everywhere, here.

The very last book in the Jim Yang series is called *Jim Yang and the End of All Things* and – in my head – it's already much longer than *Jim Yang and the Imaginary Friend*; it flows with the indolence of something without form or limits, and it takes place during the last days of the universe.

In *Jim Yang and the End of All Things*, Jim Yang is tired of all his adventures and all the odysseys he's embarked on in vain. He can hardly even remember what he's chasing after, what he never reached. The successive and increasingly powerful and addictive doses of so much travel through the centuries weigh on him like the most hideous jet lag; like the time lag that's caused him to transcend the very notion of time. Jim Yang is no longer sure where he left from, what era he's from, how old he is, what time it is, how many decades he's been riding this strange bicycle that's part of his body by now.

Jim Yang pedals at top speed, as hard as legs that've developed an almost grotesque set of muscles can go. Always forward. The past doesn't interest him any more. The past is past. And now there's only one possible direction for Jim Yang: towards the end of all things. A time in which – he thinks – there won't be time any more for anything; a time in which there'll be no time to make up, no time to gain, no time to lose. There'll only be the relief of floating on the perfect and immutable surface of a blank page or a screen void of electricity. And praying that everything ends there, in an ever after without even the slightest possibility of *(to be continued . . .)*.

On the way to nowhere, Jim Yang crosses paths several times with Cagliostro Nostradamus Smith. They don't recognize each other. Or better, they pretend not to recognize each other. Their private war has become a somnambulistic truce. They don't want to see each other, they can't see each other. Their respective hatreds were consumed long ago like so much combustible material, like the last fuel remaining to be tossed into the cauldron of their adventures to keep things moving along.

Cagliostro Nostradamus Smith has also suffered the corrosion of the millennial winds, the acupuncture of the needle-sharp hands of a thousand clocks. The only thing he does now is fondle diamonds that he claims he's made out of the fertile bones of thousands of children who died in great child catastrophes: the children killed by incurable epidemics, the children killed in religious crusades, the children killed by raging adult tsunamis, the children killed by the despair of realizing themselves to be the last children in History, the children who chose to die young rather than live to be old, the children who – now I remember – began to kill and commit suicide under the unhealthy influence of the Jim Yang books, my books.

On his last adventure, as the final days of humankind approach – Jim Yang and Cagliostro Nostradamus Smith were there at the end – no new children are born. The biological water-clock of the race has dried up forever: women don't ovulate; sperm swim against the current, like salmon; and the planet's only inhabitants are all over one hundred and fifty years old. Old people with perfect teeth, more or less enviable looks, faulty memory – because no brain was built to store so much information and so much past – and nothing to do except ask themselves how they've come so far and what the use was of coming so far as they walk slowly through geriatric parks and gardens that were once the battlefields of youth and sit and read children's books peopled by the elderly, by centenarian and long-lived children like Biblical patriarchs; because now, at last, children's literature is about those who can no longer even remember their far distant childhoods.

Cagliostro Nostradamus Smith's fingerprints have rubbed off from so much counting of diamonds, and, almost blinded by the diamonds' transparent brilliance, he doesn't even bother to inform Jim Yang that his mother and little sister were never prisoners; that they simply abandoned him, that they got on a plane and went to live far away with a billionaire who would never have accepted the idea of an Oriental son belonging to someone else. Or something like that. I'm not sure. That's not what interests me most about *Jim Yang and the End of All Things*.

What interests me most about *Jim Yang and the End of All Things* is the end. In the last pages of my memorized book, Jim Yang pedals over a deserted world, over empty cities, over beaches covered with the skeletons of salt-encrusted cars, over oceans that are tired of making waves. The whole landscape has the noble sadness of an inadvertent museum no one visits even though it's free and open all day.

Just when Jim Yang thinks he'll see nothing living on the surface of the earth, he hears someone crying and he heads out to sea, trying to discover where the sobbing is coming from, pedalling until he reaches a rock on which a boy is sitting.

Jim Yang stops his chronocycle and goes up to him, observing him carefully. He isn't exactly a boy. He's a little man of uncertain age, his body and face covered with wrinkles that aren't exactly wrinkles. They're not signs of age but the precise opposite: signs of agelessness. The little man seems to be on the brink of despair, and at the same time, his body radiates a youthful and almost demented vigour.

The little man raises his head and looks at Jim Yang and his voice is nearly inaudible. Jim Yang has to bend down to hear what he says, an insistent sound, that's repeated again and again like the prayer of an astronaut knocked out of orbit:

'To die will be an awfully big adventure!' he says.

And he adds, almost in a sigh:

'Please . . .'

Jim Yang takes the little man's head in his hands. The bones of his neck are as fragile as a bird's and they break almost at his touch. They aren't the kind of bones that make good diamonds, I guess.

Peter Pan dies with the happiest, most grateful, and most idiotic of smiles.

Jim Yang ties the body to his chronocycle and pushes it into the water. He watches it sink and disappear.

Then Jim Yang sits on Marooners' Rock to wait for his murderer and replacement to arrive, some day or some night.

'I hope it doesn't take him too many centuries,' thinks Jim Yang.

Today I returned to Neverland.

Today I opened more doors again.

Opening doors, I've discovered, is as addictive for me as travelling through time is for Jim Yang. The exhaustion of opening doors is better than the anguish of not opening them. It's almost impossible to resist exploring eras and rooms. And when I refuse to open doors, I fall into a heavy torpor in which all I dream of is opening doors. Or I rise up into a shallow insomnia, in which desperation makes me count doors so I can slip into some nightmare in which I walk along a long passageway asking myself whether I was already in this part of the house, answering myself that it doesn't matter: I live in Neverland. Neverland is alive. This Alwaysland Neverland is as alive as the house fairies build for men, 'the house that only those who've slept in it see, because unless you sleep in it you never see it; and this is because there's no house when you go to sleep, but it's there when you open your eyes and discover the fairies have built a whole house around your dreams; and you have to leave it in order to wake up.'

I opened several doors that it didn't help me at all to open: I saw a frozen lake; a man dressed in a shiny suit and dancing (when I saw him I thought of Marcus Merlin, but I'm not sure it was him; rather, it was an idealized version of Marcus Merlin, a Marcus Merlin with the almost supernatural grace of a dancer in a musical); a ship sailing away; another man missing the bottom half of his face; several soldiers singing in a trench; a woman in a stateroom putting on makeup in front of a mirror; a Saint Bernard with a cap in his mouth, ready to leap at me . . .

But the last door today was a useful door. A door that made me remember a number of things and understand certain recent events that explain my stay in Alwaysland.

On the other side of the door was me in what had to be a hospital bed. I didn't see myself from above – as on those astral trips some specialists associate with an exotic form of epilepsy – but as if I were passing by, looking for the room of a sick friend, and I'd stopped to see what was happening in some other room. There was my motionless body, covered by a light blanket and connected to various terminals and monitors of the kind that – we're told and we prefer to believe unquestioningly – track our vital signs, assuring us we're still alive. Beside my bed was a doctor and two men who had to be plain-clothes policemen, Scotland Yard detectives. I knew this because looking like policemen when they think they don't look like policemen is an essential part of their job.

It was a room full of revealing details, so I paid attention, watching carefully and listening to each word that was said.

It was clear that I, in the bed, wasn't saying anything; and that it was more than doubtful that I would ever say anything. On the monitors, my heart rate looked slow and stable; my brain waves were faint and languid. I was breathing; but not only did I not know I was breathing, it was also as if the oxygen, as it entered my lungs, could only think about leaving as soon as possible, wondering what sense there was in wasting so much on so little.

And I've always asked myself why that state I was in, lying in my hospital bed, is called a *coma*, like a truncated comma, and not an *ellipsis*, or, even better, a *parenthesis*. A comma is a brief pause, an almost imperceptible alteration in speech; and not this long, uncomfortable, unpredictable silence. An ellipsis or a parenthesis has many more possibilities: more time, more time out.

My body was giving off that very odd but unmistakable phosphorescence that bodies that are almost corpses give off and seeing myself like this – surprise – allowed me to reconstruct my last acts with perfect clarity.

Yes, I made Keiko Kai stand on the window sill and I stood beside him and we jumped together. And it's clear that Keiko Kai isn't here in Alwaysland; it's obvious he didn't survive the fall. It's understood and I understand that my coma – my comma – was his full stop, and that his death has more than served the purpose I'd assigned it in the logic of my madness.

Inside the room, the detectives were talking to the doctor. They were asking questions about the chances that I would 'recover consciousness or not in order to undergo an exhaustive interrogation to clear up this strange situation'. Two newspapers poked out of the pockets of the detectives' raincoats.

In one of the papers – large type, ink still smelling of ink, headlines telling everything and giving me all the necessary information – it said that I'd succumbed to a murderous and suicidal form of madness; the parents of the world had organized public burnings of the Jim Yang books; and any film adaptations of my work had been aborted. Instead of a children's hero, Jim Yang had become an evil unfit for minors. The author of Jim Yang was no longer a shining hero but the blackest of ogres.

Jim Yang won't corrupt anyone any more as Peter Pan once

corrupted me. Sooner or later – it's certain, inevitable – other false idols will arise to be worshipped: cybernetic creatures, virtual embryos, interactive beings . . . But I won't have anything to do with them, and it's clear that – because of what I did, thanks to what I did – from now on all children's creations will be carefully reviewed, their destructive potential considered, exaggerated precautions taken that'll keep the monster under control for many years and protect children from wolves disguised as sheep.

The other newspaper gives a different version of the same events, and it's from it that I learn that the intelligence that governs and controls Alwaysland's Neverland still hasn't completely made up its mind, and that, like Barrie, it's still weighing the possibility of several endings.

The second paper theorizes that Keiko Kai and I were kidnapped and murdered to prevent the cinematographic bastardization of Jim Yang by one of the many packs of wild children that've been proliferating in recent years. In the newspaper the Pangbourne massacre is recalled, in which all the children of a London suburb kill all their parents and disappear, occasionally reappearing to commit acts of terrorism against the adult world under the banner of their messiah, 'Jim Yang, He Who Will Return With Justice for All and Mercy for None', and in the name of a desperate, unhappy childhood lived in the current state of adult things.

Anyway, it doesn't matter. I understand it now: I was a children's book writer whose only goal was to destroy children's literature; children's literature destroyed me so that I could immediately turn and destroy those around me.

I'm Barrie's remote but exemplary revenge; Barrie, who suffered so much for us, who died for our sins, and whose only and unpardonable crime was having written an infectious creature carrying an incurable disease.

I was infected; and, terminally ill, I consecrated myself to the virus – literature – whose mission, hardly secret at all, is to kill reality and annihilate childhood, supplanting and improving both as thoroughly as possible until they've become immortal stories that will never grow old.

Knowing this helps me to know so many other things, to remember keenly, to at last understand what I'm looking for behind these doors; to be perfectly clear which door I'm looking for, and what prize comes with the room I want to enter and stay in forever.

And something tells me – nothing tells me anything, but I intuit it with that rare sensitivity more typical of characters than people – that the door to that room can't be far away.

In the last few days – or just recently, really; because it's becoming more and more difficult and pointless to associate what happens in Alwaysland with the misleading and comfortable precision of the calendars I knew in my other life – Neverland seems to have taken pity on me. Its rooms no longer open up to impulsively offer me the first thing it occurs to them to show me happening inside. Now I don't see arctic landscapes, complex stage mechanisms, a queen's funeral, cloth that won't stop being woven.

Now, more sharply each time, I feel that Neverland wants to please me, help me, shape itself to the object of my search; as if what it's teaching me is increasingly fine-tuned variations, returning little by little – slowly but coming closer each time – to the aria from which they were spun off.

This room is an almost perfect replica of my childhood room. All the following doors open to the same view. Some seem more finished than others.

In this one, everything appears to be in place except the bunk where we slept – I on the top and Baco on the bottom – and the wallpaper with the psychedelic pattern; these walls are white and clean.

In the next room, the bed and walls are the same as in my past; but I'm there all alone. I'm eight years old and I look at myself and I look at him.

Further along, I see a room reproduced with perfect fidelity; but it's a fidelity of no use to me, an outdated fidelity: I'm in my bed – a single bed that has still to be replaced by the bunks – and I haven't yet been swept away by the invisible hurricane of jealousy. My left ear is intact. In the sweetest of voices, my pregnant mother reads me the book I found that morning in the gardens of Neverland. 'I'm sure Peter himself left it for you as a gift,' says my mother. *All children, except one, grow up,* reads my mother, and I have to make a great effort not to go in there, lie down forever, never leave.

And all the rooms are alike in one way: in all the rooms the window is open, and in all of them a soft, scented breeze blows.

It was I who opened the window of this room and all these rooms. It's I who – when I find the exact room, the scene of my innocent but not therefore less blameworthy crime – will finally be able to rest in peace.

Baco and I are in the room I'm looking for.

Baco's sleepy.

I've already read him my favourite parts of *Peter Pan* again. I'm not really reading them to him. Baco's my excuse for reading them aloud, for hearing how they sound in my voice, which makes them much more mine than when I read them with the silence of my eyes.

Baco always listens to me – I believe – with the goodness that makes him able to respect and even find something appealing in the most extreme behaviour of all those around him. Baco is a benevolent king. Baco closes his eyes and falls asleep.

In that room I open the window because I'm sure that this is the night that Peter Pan will at last come for me to take me far away, to the place I sense is my real home, my true birthplace.

In the last few months I haven't been able to help comparing myself to my father and my mother and my brother, and it's clear I'm nothing like them. Among the three of them there's a subtle repetition of features and gestures: the same piano key, pressed more firmly or more gently, but always playing the same note.

I don't even feel like part of their score.

I sound so different.

So I open the window and I cover myself with blankets and I sit on the floor. It's the coldest and longest night of the year and at some point big snowflakes begin to fall like stars. If my life were a children's book, I'm sure this part would be on an even-numbered page across from its corresponding illustration on an odd-numbered page.

I wake up at dawn, feverish, delirious, talking about a shadow that misses its owner and is hiding under my bed.

My father and mother are alerted to my cries by Dermott, and they come to soothe me, and, puzzled, ask me whether I've seen my brother; they ask me why the window's open. Then I remember that some time during the night – when sleep was beginning to overtake me, to conquer me – I thought, with the crazy logic of children, that if Peter Pan wasn't coming for me maybe he would come for Baco. I remember getting Baco out of bed asleep, being very careful so he wouldn't wake up. I remember lying Baco on the sill of the open window. I remember I left him there like a love offering for my beloved god, and if this part of the book is illustrated, I'll tear out the illustration and rip it into a thousand pieces and throw them out the open window so that they're carried away by the most merciful and compassionate of winds.

I don't tell my parents any of this, not because I don't feel the terrible need to confess it all but because – which is much worse – it seems to me that it isn't necessary, that somehow everything has been said, that there's nothing left to say, and that it's so hard to say anything when everyone is crying and shouting. The dream has ended; we're all awake forever. Now we'll never go back to sleep again.

Now I do feel that I'm coming closer to that room and that night. Behind the doors of Neverland are ever more precise reconstructions, closer to the perfection of my past imperfections.

When I open that door – when I finally gain access to that

impeccable panorama of my childhood; to that terrible last night when everything began, the night that keeps growing nearer and sharper in my memory – I'll go in and close the window and none of what happened will happen. Baco will sleep and wake up in his bed. I'll watch over him as he sleeps. And then I'll enjoy the undeserved happiness and egotistical consolation of having changed a beginning to savour this final instant.

Yes, all the stage lights will go out so the lights over the box seats and orchestra seats can come on. The audience will begin to leave the hall; not in a hurry, but with that pressing need to abandon barren and exhausted territory to continue the search for new and unknown triumphs.

And I'll be left alone like a strayed lost boy; feeling how my glow gradually fades; how my magic weakens; how the spotlights go out one by one until only the ghost lamp is left shining.

And when I've made sure that all the spectators have returned to the reality of their world, knowing there won't be anybody left to hear me and obey me any more; only then – 'Having read the book, I'd love to turn you on' – will I obey, and recite what the script demands, reading it letter by letter, word by word, sentence by sentence, on the crazy screen of a lonely television of literary and nocturnal habits.

And I'll walk to the edge of the stage and I'll ask the deserted theatre – with false passion, with genuine happiness at the impossibility of my plea – to believe in me.

And I'll beg all those mute and empty seats to prove it, to clap with all their might so that at last I – the most awfully big of adventurers – come back to life and live and never grow up and never die, never, never ever, and oh, thank you, thank you, thank you.

For Ever and Ever: A Note of Thanks and Some More or Less Pertinent Explanations

Kensington Gardens – as I hope and wish, and as will, I suppose, have been obvious almost from the first page – neither is nor attempts to be a strict biography of James Matthew Barrie or a precise map of his surroundings.[1]

Which doesn't mean that much of what's recounted about the author of *Peter Pan* in this novel – beyond certain divergences of chronology and plot and liberties taken in the handling of certain texts in order to adapt them to the narrative – isn't strictly true, as incredible as it may seem.

Accordingly, I'd like to acknowledge the help of several books,[2] in addition to those written by J. M. Barrie – novels, stories, plays, collections of letters – about his life or fantasies, that were essential to the book I wrote about him.

They are:

J. M. Barrie & the Lost Boys: The Love Story that Gave Birth to Peter Pan, by Andrew Birkin;[3] *J. M. Barrie: A Study in Fairies*

1 Likewise – another always pertinent clarification – the many 'real' people and personalities who appear and disappear in this novel always do so in a 'fictional' way when they interact with the characters of *Kensington Gardens*. None of what's attributed to them is necessarily true except for their – very useful to the author – first and last names.

2 And, of course, Alibris.com and La Central Bookstore (Marta & Antonio and Joan-Pere), who not only looked for them for me, but found them, too.

3 A fundamental, admirable and indispensable work for me, as much

and Mortals, by Patrick Braybrooke; *Secret Gardens: A Study of the Golden Age of Children's Literature from Alice in Wonderland to Winnie-the-Pooh*, by Humphrey Carpenter; *J. M. Barrie: The Man Behind the Image*, by Janet Dunbar; *Barrie: The Story of a Genius*, by J. A. Hammerton; *The Peter Pan Chronicles*, by Bruce K. Hanson; *The Road to Never Land: A Reassessment of J. M. Barrie's Dramatic Art*, by Ronald D. S. Jack; *Barrie: The Story of J. M. B.*, by Denis Mackail; *The Case of Peter Pan or The Impossibility of Children's Fiction*, by Jacqueline Rose; *Inventing Wonderland*, by Jackie Wullschläger; and *Now or Never Land: Peter Pan and the Myth of Eternal Youth: A Psychological Perspective on a Cultural Icon*, by Ann Yeoman.

Just as useful to me in the portrayal of a city and an era[4] – for a variety of reasons, some obvious and some not – was the plunge into or the contemplation from the shore, the reading or the rereading, of the books *London: The Biography, by Peter*

---

for the clarity of Birkin's text as for the quality of the abundant graphic material. Thank you again. And again. From its pages come many of the photographs and quotes and days that Peter Hook reveals and recites and relates to Keiko Kai all through this night-in-the-life. And the idea of raising the curtain with Peter Llewelyn Davies's suicide was Andrew Birkin's before it was mine, although I hadn't yet read his book when I wrote about my Peter's leap onto the tracks in this book. In any case, I'm delighted by the coincidence.

4 I can't say I know London. I was there for a few days many years ago, during which I hardly left a hotel on the outskirts of the city with a view of the strange building – it may be a factory, I don't know; I think someone once told me it was an electric plant – that appears on the cover of the Pink Floyd album *Animals*. In short: I was never in Kensington Gardens. And yet I know Heathrow very well (an airport that always struck me as the perfect setting for a novel) because I've made connections there on many flights to other European cities. So the idea – in principle – was that I would return to London and even live there for a month to iron out the final details in the writing and revision of *Kensington Gardens*, but in the end, the method used by travel writers everywhere imposed itself: don't go, the better to know it. Or, at least in my case, the

Ackroyd; *The Long Firm*, by Jake Arnott; *An Awfully Big Adventure*, by Beryl Bainbridge; *The Kindness of Women* and *Running Wild*, by J. G. Ballard; *The Beatles Anthology*, by the Beatles; *The Uses of Enchantment: The Meaning and Importance of Fairy Tales*, by Bruno Bettelheim; *Stories and Poems for Extremely Intelligent Children of All Ages*, ed. Harold Bloom; *La letteratura e gli dèi*, by Robert Calasso; *The Oxford Companion to Children's Literature*, eds. Humphrey Carter and Mary Pritchard; *The Portable Sixties Reader*, ed. Ann Charters; *Growing Up in the Sixties*, by Susan Cleeve; *The Penguin Dictionary of Literary Terms and Literary Theory*, by J. A. Cuddon; *X-Ray* and *Waterloo Sunset*, by Ray Davies; *The Deptford Trilogy*, by Robertson Davies; *The Pop Sixties: A Personal and Irreverent Guide*, by Andrew J. Edelstein; *Who's Who in Victorian Britain*, by Roger Ellis; *Duérmete niño* and *Necesito dormir*, by Eduard Estivill; *The Good Soldier*, by Ford Madox Ford;[5] *Krays: The Final Countdown: The Ultimate Biography of Ron, Reg and Charlie Kray*, by

---

better to achieve a city of vague outline matching the elusive character of the narrator. And an odd detail: my books always end up being assembled very far from where they take place. It happened to me with the Mexico City of *Mantra* in Prague and Budapest; it happened again with the London of *Kensington Gardens* in Santiago de Chile and Bogotá and Guadalajara. Maybe there's a need of the European when it comes to the Latin American. And vice versa. Or maybe not. What I am sure of is how grateful I am for the different hosts this novel had during its writing: the Book Fair in Bogotá, the Cervantes Institute of Bucharest, the Casa Encendida in Madrid, *Paula* Magazine of Santiago de Chile, Menéndez Pelayo University in Santander and the Villaseñor Urrea family in Guadalajara, Mexico.

As for the era as planet: I was born in 1963 and I always thought the virological radiation of the golden 60s left a greater mark on those who were children at the time than on those who were its young and enthusiastic and conscious and revolutionary inventors. In other words: Dr Frankenstein creates the monster, but in the end it's the monster everyone knows as Frankenstein. Clear enough?

5 This is where the two paragraphs from Sebastian 'Darjeeling' Compton-Lowe's favourite novel – quoted in the chapter 'The Character' – come

Colin Fry; *Guías visuales Peugeot: London*; *Sad Songs: The Unhappy Life of Peter Hook* and *Ten Parties that Shook the World*, by Max Glass; *A Literary Guide to London*, by Ed Glinert; *The Golden Age* and *Dream Days*, by Kenneth Grahame; *All Dressed Up: The Sixties and the Counter Culture* and *Days in the Life: Voices from the English Underground*, by Jonathan Green; *The Victorian Age: An Anthology of Sources and Documents*, ed. Josephine M. Guy; *The Beatles Encyclopedia*, by Bill Harry; *The Writer's Guide to Everyday Life in Regency and Victorian England*, by Kristine Hughes; *Psychedelic Decadence: Sex, Drugs and Low-Art in Sixties and Seventies Britain*, by Martin Jones; *Ready, Steady, Go! Swinging London and the Invention of Cool*, by Shawn Levy;[6] *Revolution in the Head: The Beatles'*

---

from. *The Good Soldier* is one of my favourite novels too. I've read it many times, never too many; and I read it again – I'd been asked to write a prologue to it – as I was finishing *Kensington Gardens*. Ford Madox Ford's book taught me and is still teaching me the ambiguities of the first person singular as a narrative 'being', the first person as character. It also showed me that certain narrators – despite what most readers usually think, hope or even desire – can lie, or simply not feel the remotest obligation to tell everything. One thing is plain: never trust the insomniac speeches of a man full of pharmaceuticals; or a novel that shifts from a fictional character narrating in the first person to a real hero with a taste for fantasy narrating in the third person; or any novel whose intentions are to tell *everything*. Similarly, the map of Kensington Gardens and the anatomy of Peter Hook are full of black holes, of lost spaces to be lost in. The subtlest of them all – maybe too subtle – concerns whether Marcus Merlin really tells Peter Hook that he found him in the airport; or whether it's simply a lie, an incredibly melodramatic and Dickensian fabrication by Marcus Merlin; or – who knows – whether Peter Hook himself is hallucinating, since after all, just a few pages earlier, he'd described to Marcus Merlin his idea for a book about a boy lost in Heathrow. A disturbing bit of information: in the final Alwaysland Neverland, none of the many doors opens to reveal an airport scene, or to show Peter Hook the faces of other parents who aren't Sebastian 'Darjeeling'Compton-Lowe and Alexandra Swinton-Menzies. So therefore . . .

6 I especially thank this book, too, and its author. Very much.

Records and the Sixties, by Ian MacDonald; *The Dictionary of Imaginary Places*, by Alberto Manguel and Gianni Guadalupi; *The Making of Victorian Sexuality*, by Michael Mason; *The Sixties*, by Arthur Marwick; *Many Years From Now*, by Paul McCartney; *In the Sixties*, by Barry Miles; *Mojo Magazine* (no. 75, February 2000); *The Cornelius Chronicles*, vols 1, 2 and 3, and *Mother London*, by Michael Moorcock; *Die Verwirrungen des Zöglings Torless*, by Robert Musil; *El Eternauta*, by Héctor Germán Oesterheld and Francisco Solano López; *Encyclopedia of Things That Never Were: Creatures, Places, and People*, by Michael Page and Robert Ingpen; *London in the Sixties*, by George Perry; *The Disappearance of Childhood*, by Neil Postman; *Spirits, Fairies, Leprechauns, and Goblins: An Encyclopedia*, by Carol Rose; *I May Be Some Time* and *The Child That Books Built*, by Francis Spufford; *Eminent Victorians*, by Lytton Strachey; *Lights Out for the Territory*, by Ian Sinclair; *The Victorian Underworld*, by Donald Thomas; *Uncut Magazine*; *Kensington Gardens*, by Humbert Wolfe; *The Wordsworth Companion to Literature in English* and the *Wordsworth Encyclopaedia*.

Anyone who wants to see or hear or find certain similarities between the biographies, discographies and artistic credos of Sebastian 'Darjeeling' Compton-Lowe and the Victorians a.k.a. the Beaten Victorians a.k.a. the Beaten, and those of Ray Davies and the Kinks, is, of course, cordially invited to do so. Although – if clarification is needed here, which I doubt – Lowe didn't have a millionth of the talent that Ray Davies had and has and will always have; this book and this author owe him a great deal.

And now that we're on the subject, to bring musical matters and the soundtrack that played in the fields of *Kensington Gardens* during its writing to a close, my thanks also go to Pink Floyd, one of the bands of my mono-stereo, non-digitalized childhood; especially the first three B-side tracks of the album *Atom Heart Mother* and the song 'Comfortably Numb' from *The Wall*: lines from here and there were recorded over childhood memories of Peter Hook. I also thank The Who for *Quadrophenia*, and the never sufficiently praised Kate Bush, who, not in vain, sings something called 'In Search of Peter Pan' on her album *Lionheart*. And as usual, this book – like other books by me – couldn't have been written if the Beatles' 'A Day in the Life' hadn't already existed.

And a brief history of it all: I started to write *Kensington Gardens* before *Mantra*, at the beginning of 2000. The idea occurred to me – or, rather, occurred – one night as I was channel-surfing, and stopped to watch something on one of Spanish Television's Channel 2 'Theme Nights', something that looked like an old domestic film and in which, to my astonishment, G.K. Chesterton and Bernard Shaw could be seen dressed up as cowboys and playing in a garden with a little man whom I had never seen before and about whom I knew nothing and who turned out to be James Matthew Barrie. What was being shown was a French documentary on the life of the author of *Peter Pan*. After it came the first film version of *Peter Pan*, directed by Herbert Brenon. Truth be told, Peter Pan – like the segment of Walt Disney's *Fantasia* called 'The Sorceror's Apprentice', which is also generally believed to be something that figures in the makeup of my DNA – was never one of my childhood or adult fetishes,[7] but what I saw there sparked a certain fascination in me. I'm not entirely sure

7 Exploring the bibliography that I gradually assembled about Barrie and his milieu, I discovered that Andrew Birkin – author of the aforementioned book indispensable to this book – also wrote a 'trilogy' for the BBC on the saga of the Llewelyn Davies brothers. I looked for it but couldn't get my hands on it (although I found some stills on the Internet). And as I write this final note, I read that a film called *Finding Neverland*, starring Johnny Depp, will open soon, in which the story of the genesis and writing of *Peter Pan* will be told in the manner of *Shakespeare In Love*, or so it's said. I've seen photographs in the magazine *Vanity Fair*. Depp – unlike Ian Holm in the same role in the BBC mini-series already mentioned – has little or nothing in common with Barrie. Dustin Hoffman

that the best thing for a writer is to write books about what he feels most passionate about; but it does seem essential to me to become passionate during the writing of the book, whatever it's about. It happened to me with Barrie, and with Barrie's story. A story that, in some way, fits perfectly with my habitual obsessions, and that – as my friend the writer Alan Pauls rightly said about *Mantra* – has once again, and maybe even more so, turned out to be 'a sad, inconsolable novel whose secret place is childhood and whose subjects are time and form: the only two things that childhood never concerns itself with and the only two things that concern themselves with childhood'.

I had just finished a first version of the novel (along with the first part of *Mantra*, 'The Mexican Friend') in October 2000, when my trusty and hardworking Compaq Contura laptop (RIP) decided to bid farewell to this mortal world thanks to a deadly virus that arrived by e-mail, contaminated back-ups, permanently wiped out the DOS (SOS?) locking system, stranded the hard disk on the other side, and, you guessed it, sent everything straight to Neverland on a one-way ticket; my greetings to that first *Kensington Gardens* if you see it around. In any case, I still haven't been able to bring myself to throw my dead computer away because I resist living in an age – the Age of Philip K. Dick? – in which portable computers end up in the same place as chicken bones and old

---

bears even less of a resemblance to Charles Frohman (in the picture I have of him, the Beaming Buddha looks a little like Peter Lorre). And I suppose Kate Winslet's British beauty won't be jarring in her portrayal of Sylvia Llewelyn Davies; but it will never seem right to me that Nico Llewelyn Davies has been wiped from the map – for, I read, 'questions of narrative flow', or some such thing. In any case, it will be a pleasure to go and see *Finding Neverland* after having left *Kensington Gardens* behind and thrown the key over my left shoulder into a ditch – though let's hope no poor devil will decide to take a stroll and let himself into the gardens, at this late hour and with the park overrun.

newspapers. And now that I think about it – in the beginning, in its first incarnation – *Kensington Gardens* was a book that, like Peter Pan, refused to grow up.

There's no such thing as coincidence. Nothing is lost and – with a little bit of luck and good fortune – everything is transformed. And yes, as I finish writing this I decide that now's the moment: the time has come to drop my computer into one of those practical plastic bins on the corner near my house. I go down and adieu and come back up and continue on my Mac PowerBook which – now that we're on the subject – has given me plenty of scares in the slightly less than three years it's been plugged in with me.

And I'd say *Kensington Gardens* is an incredibly lucky book.

The name of the infamous sender of the killer e-mail in question isn't worthy of appearing here; I'm sure that he or she will receive – if he or she hasn't already received – his or her just punishment.

Meanwhile, many other names – and the people those names belong to – contributed in one way or another to the writing of this novel, for which they won't be held responsible if they don't want to be, although *Kensington Gardens* does consider them its great and indispensable friends and benefactors.

Here they are:

Carmen Balcells Literary Agency, Carlos Alberdi, Eduardo Becerra, Juan Ignacio Boido, Lee Brackstone, Javier Calvo, Mónica Carmona, Jordi Costa, Esther Cross, Ignacio Echevarría, Faber and Faber, Farrar, Straus and Giroux, Luz de la Mora, Diego Gándara, Alfredo Garófano, Dolores Graña, Andreu Jaume, Norma Elizabeth Mastrorilli, Editorial Mondadori, Alan Pauls, Ana Romero, Guillermo Saccomanno, Enrique Vila-Matas, Natasha Wimmer . . .

. . . and my usual found men: the Beatles, John Cheever, Philip K. Dick, Bob Dylan, Robyn Hitchcock, Denis Johnson,

Stanley Kubrick, Herman Melville, Marcel Proust and Kurt Vonnegut.

And – once again – a special thanks to Claudio López de Lamadrid, who first believed in this idea and then clapped so it wouldn't die.

And to Robert Bolaño, with us forever.

And to Ana, for existing.